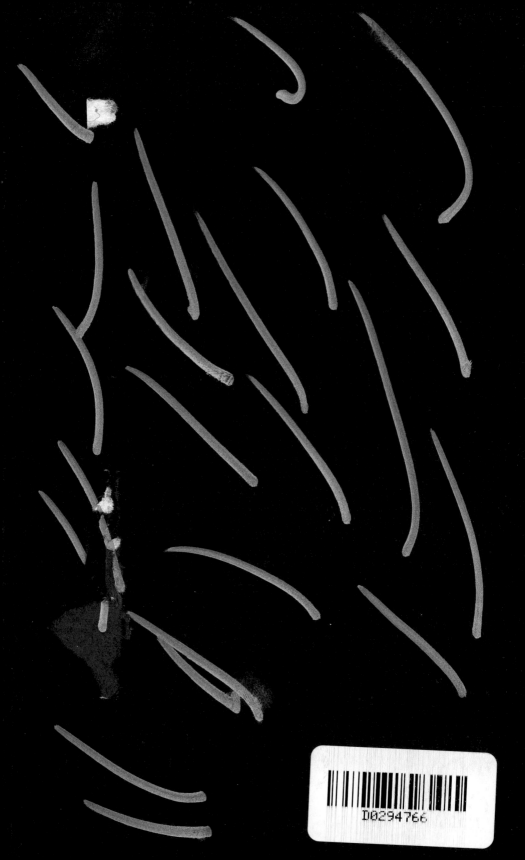

North of Patagonia

North of Patagonia

Johnny Payne

TRIQUARTERLY BOOKS
NORTHWESTERN UNIVERSITY PRESS
EVANSTON, ILLINOIS

TriQuarterly Books
Northwestern University Press
Evanston, Illinois 60208-4210

Printed in the United States of America

10 9 8 7 6 5 4 3 2 1

ISBN 0-8101-5121-9

Library of Congress Cataloging-in-Publication Data

Payne, Johnny, 1958–
North of Patagonia / Johnny Payne.
p. cm.
ISBN 0-8101-5121-9 (alk. paper)
1. Argentina—Fiction. I. Title.
PS3566.A9375 N6 2001
813'.54—dc21
2001000908

The paper used in this publication meets the minimum requirements of the American National Standard for Information Sciences—Permanence of Paper for Printed Library Materials, ANSI Z39.48-1984.

F92,517
E25,82

North of Patagonia

Nebucchim Jacinto felt the filigree of the pocket watch with his fingers as he lay supine on an iron cot in a room in a hovel in the pampas. His thumb palpated the notch where the bullet had struck before glancing off and penetrating the space between his father's ribs. The watch didn't work any longer, but he could always flip open the front of the case to confirm the exact hour of his father's murder, twenty years ago to the day. There was no mystery there. He knew who had done it, and how, and when.

It was midafternoon of the summer solstice, and not propitious for movement of any kind. Nebucchim had spent seven months away, laboring underground in the tin mines in the rusty mountains above Jujuy, not minding the back strain or the cold rations, instead appreciating the anonymity, as he waited in vain for the deadline to pass. In the cavity of the earth, he'd felt a voice, ever stronger, calling him out. At the last possible moment, he had laid down his pick, forfeited that week's rations and pay, and made his way back down to the broad lowlands. Since his return to the village of his birth, he had spent the past week in the neglected hovel that he used to call home without any great enthusiasm. Nebucchim was in temporary hiding from the nephews of the ranch hands who had killed his father, and so had remained at the hovel exactly long enough to make preparations for the inevitable.

Now the preparations were finished, his grave dug in the noon light with his own calloused hands, and he had rinsed away the sweat on his body and freshened himself with a bucket of water and a scrub-brush. His raw skin tingled as tatters of a sirocco blew through the bars of the room's sole window. Nebucchim opened the leather book containing in its pages his deceased ancestors' names, crossed out one by one with different tints of quill and ink. Although each stripe was as different from the previous one in length and shade as the signature it marred, each stripe was alike in that it ended abruptly with an inkblot, as if the person covering over the name had been surprised in the act of scratching. The stripes were opaque and solid semaphores, like the freshly planted telegraph poles, their wood still green, that studded the endless stretches of cable crossing the pampa on their way to distant cities. The hum of the power lines, more than the prospect of death, had kept Nebucchim awake these seven nights. He ran his eye up the list of half-obliterated ancestral names. The Duarte brothers had murdered his father when he had run afoul of them, and their uncles had done the same to his grandfather, and the uncles of those uncles had done likewise to his great-grandfather.

Tomorrow, Nebucchim would be forced to seek out the nephews of the Duarte Brothers and find a way to provoke them, so these nephews could serve up the same punishment to him. Yet they threatened to break the transverse line of succession. Peaceful, easygoing sorts that they were, it wouldn't be simple. They hadn't inherited their forerunners' disposition. Instead, they were known to be lazy, and liked to drink and carouse, then sleep the ruckus off through the hot Argentine afternoon, to hoard strength for the next night's carousing. They didn't hold grudges, so he'd heard, and in their ample good nature held nothing against anyone. They were more inclined to buy a drink for a stranger than to pick a quarrel. But there was nowhere to hide, ultimately, on the pampa. The spaces between one place and the next were large and took time to cover, but on the other hand, little density existed between one object and the next to occlude one's view.

Nebucchim knew with a deft certainty that, on horseback, he would find the pair of them soon enough, if for some reason this latest set of Duarte brothers had indeed stirred from their lethargy sufficiently to hire themselves out for a day's work as hands on a ranch or had improvised sleeping quarters outdoors as they prepared to pass out at the break of dawn from overindulgence. Nebucchim would hunt down this latest set of brothers, stir them from their torpor, and find a way to rankle them enough that they would draw their guns on him.

He felt a little bad about his plan, knowing there was an off chance they might be jailed afterward, but there was nothing to be done about that. He imagined himself lying in dry dust in a pool of thickening blood. Guns were crude and errant instruments. He only hoped their combined aim would be accurate enough to kill him instantly. There would be no sibling to bury him, as there would be for whichever of the Duartes went first, when the older or younger brother eventually passed away from cirrhosis of the liver, heat stroke, or simple old age. Never from gunplay. The Duarte clan was as famous for its longevity as for its killing.

Nebucchim had made his own funeral arrangements in advance, a simple casket, a wreath fashioned of dry twigs, and he had written a brief, rude homily for himself, enumerating his short list of virtues and defects, cowardice not among them. He had used straightforward words, penned in a careful hand, to help the nearly illiterate undertaker perform funeral duties in this godforsaken place, where there was neither rabbi nor priest. Born. Hard. Slow. Dirt. Work. Hurt. Done. Nebucchim Jacinto crossed out his name in a page of the worn leather book, letting the quill linger only long enough, at the end, to form an inkblot that would punctuate his existence. As the ink began to harden, he heard the sound of a pair of boots behind him, scraping the threshold of the doorway, making their way across the plank floor, and then another pair of boots, the same size as the first, not far behind, repeating the identical sequence of sound.

Kelly laid aside the book. Facedown, no bookmark, even though this would further crack the fragile spine. The pages would end up out of order, and she'd have to reassemble the story herself. She, the scourge of libraries, owned lots of bookmarks, made of embossed leather or decorated with tassels of yarn, but could never find one when she needed it. Besides, it was Clay's book, one he'd left behind when they split up, the only possession of his she still had on hand, and it had somehow made its way from apartment to apartment with her for the last seven years. The cover of the book was mottled with mold. God knows in what secondhand bookstore he'd unearthed this one—probably the Black Swan.

She thought she'd heard the telephone ringing. It was ringing, in fact (except telephones didn't ring anymore—what did they do?), but she decided to let the machine pick up. That's what voice mail was for, and there was no sense twisting her knee, as she had once upon a time by thinking it was him while she showered, hopping out onto the tile soaking wet so she wouldn't miss his call. Tonight, there wasn't any reason to obey a mindless reflex, one that invited trouble, when it would probably turn out to be a telemarketer or at best a friend who would hang up before Kelly reached her outdated, stationary, corded phone. Then she would have to wonder what might have been.

Everybody else except her was out somewhere for Valentine's Day. Chandra had school tomorrow, and it was tough finding a babysitter, though, well, it was true her mother had offered to sit if she did land a date—her ever-expectant, ever-hopeful, ever-disappointed mother—but Kelly was going to have to rely on her mother plenty when tax preparation time came and business picked up to night and day. She didn't want to use up that goodwill now on the off chance of having a good time.

Besides, nobody had asked her out—well, Dale at the office had approached her but only because they were lunch buddies, he was just being nice, he wasn't really her type anyway, and if he was seriously interested in her she most certainly didn't want to know about it. Then she'd be forced to puncture his niceness, and it would create an awkward situation between them at the workplace afterward, Dale knocking himself out with false hilarity to create the impression that everything remained exactly the way it had been before he'd made the mistake of trying to get romantic. She couldn't stand that extra stress right now. Her reluctance to date Dale had nothing to do with the interracial thing, because God knows Clay had been plenty white, as were several of the men she'd dated since that time. Black or white, Spanish or Asian, they were all equally irresponsible in the end.

No, that wasn't entirely fair. Clay had kept up his child support for Chandra, never missing payments, though there was no telling where he got the money, earning as little as he did. Not that she would have sent the law after him; she was too proud for that. He'd offered nervously to move back in with her a couple of times, over the phone, afraid she'd take him up on his offer, before they got to the point where they stopped talking. Like him, she was hardheaded and willfully stupid, and she'd rejected his overtures, making him feel stung in the process. At that time, it had felt good to hurt him, she had to admit. He always used to ask her, in the middle of an argument, Do you want to be happy or do you want to be right? She'd never answered that question, because she'd wanted to be right; that was the plain truth of the matter.

She had been prepared to fight hard to ensure that she alone got custody of Chandra, but it had disappointed her that he hadn't tried to fight back, as she'd been ready to hunker down and duel him with all her might for their only truly important mutual possession. He hadn't put up much of a struggle, and she held that against him as much as anything. Yet even though she had been awarded sole custody, Clay had exercised his visitation rights often, in the beginning, coming back from Chicago to Kentucky every few weeks and calling as often as he could afford. Each visit was an occasion for bitter words, and finally, he'd gotten to where he would call seldom, even then hoping Chandra would, by some miracle of protocol, pick up the phone herself so he wouldn't have to talk to Mommy. He hadn't been back to Kentucky in a year, despite Chandra's pleading. Kelly wouldn't let her go up there for a visit no way, and Clay had barely telephoned, whether because he had grown tired of feuding out of mere habit or because he thought Chandra was better off not having to serve as an item of contention.

There was no reason Kelly should be thinking of Clay tonight, as whatever anniversaries had passed between them had ceased to be meaningful. Her thinking of him had happened almost by chance when she, promiscuous and insatiable reader that she was, couldn't sleep and started scouring the bookshelves for something she hadn't read, anything, and had come across this odd book, which had fallen down behind some others on the shelf. When she saw its title, *Death North of Patagonia,* she had mistaken it for a thriller, which at least seemed promising, Clay's tardy, unintentional little sedative for her lifelong insomnia, but she should have known, with his reading habits, that even something of this nature would have its philosophical twists.

He couldn't stand to read a book if it didn't break your brain in two. He'd refused to go to college, in that perverse, heel-digging way of his, but he still had to be the smartest damn boy on the block. That quality, more than anything else about him, had piqued her. Not that she didn't want him to be smart, but he wouldn't make anything useful or worthwhile out of his mental capacity. He had to be a boxer, because God (in whom he didn't trust, except when it was convenient) had caused him to be born with the body and the constitution for boxing. For all the good boxing had done him, and for all the puny success he'd had. One of her digs, when she got in a vicious mood, had been to say that God had been able to make a man from clay, but he hadn't been able to make a man out of Clay. She chastened herself that the only thing her religious leanings had done was to sharpen an already tart tongue.

But beginning to read one of Clay's peculiar and accidental books had cast a spell on her, and she had to admit it, she was missing the bastard, for the first time in a long time. Still, she wasn't going to let herself be lured by impossible emotions, not on Valentine's Day. Knowing that she was in for a night of insomnia, she plucked from her shelf one of the romance novels she knew Clay would revile had he been lying in bed beside her. He would have taken the book from her hands and read a few choice passages aloud, in a playful but mocking tone. Well, to hell with him. He didn't know the first thing about love anyway. In the book of Clay's life, everybody had to be a loner, grinding himself down into dust, like that Nebucchim character. After checking on the sleeping Chandra, pulling up the covers around her daughter, and stoking the fireplace in the living room with the steel poker, Kelly burrowed into the chenille bedspread, set Clay's book on the nightstand, and opened hers with an aggressive snap.

The pouty set of her mouth had always attracted him. He knew she wasn't going to be easy, and that's what got him going. She was spoiled, used to having her way, and he wanted her to learn that there was also such a thing as him having his way. But that could wait. He was a patient man. If the truth be told, he liked the fact that she was so spoiled. It gave her the confidence to feel that whatever she was doing was the only game in town. Now showing, her and her alone. Nothing else mattered except what she decreed. Her "to do" list was the Constitution of the United States of Miranda. When she insisted he go shopping with her (in spite of his comment that shopping was for women and he couldn't stand boutiques), and he declined, she threw a royal fit to get her way. As punishment, she made him stand directly outside the dressing room and talked to him across the half door all the while, with her bare legs visible. Then she'd pop out, modeling different outfits. She made him express a detailed opinion about how each outfit suited her, made him approve or disapprove, then scolded him for guessing wrong and pouted gorgeously when he tried to finesse the question by saying they all looked good.

When she had made her selections (most of them against his choices, just to taunt him), she proceeded to heap the costly bounty into his arms, as if he had been appointed costume master for Mardi Gras. And somehow, he had ended up paying for it all, even though she and he were "just friends" and weren't officially dating yet. But he was content to play his part in the hope that soon she, without any of those pricey clothes on whatsoever, would be filling his arms instead.

Kelly slammed this book on the bedspread, bearing down without mercy on the spine, which rebounded against her palm with an impertinent spring. Even worse. It was bad enough that you could hardly find a romance novel with a black protagonist (okay, only her father was black, not her mother, but she wanted a handful of black or *mulatta* heroines all the same, so she wouldn't always have to make that imaginative leap of putting herself in the shoes of a damsel who wasn't quite her). This writer had violated rule number one of genre romances—put the story in the mind of a woman! If they couldn't give her black, the least she could expect was female, for pity's sake. "He was a patient man"—what was *that* all about? What happened to "She was a patient woman"?

Besides, women should just in principle write from a woman's perspective, and men should write from a man's. There was enough misunderstanding between the sexes in daily life as it was, without bringing it over into her one chance at escape. How had this one slipped through? Maybe the author was indeed a man; because they all used pseudonyms you could never know for sure who had actually written the romance. That was one of those philosophical problems Clay would have gone crazy over, keeping her up half the night talking about it. Worse still, the book had literary pretensions that any self-respecting romance editor would have killed in the birthing stall. "Costume master for Mardi Gras." She might as well read *Death North of Patagonia,* for all the escape this one was going to provide.

She wondered what Clay had been up to in the past year and where he was tonight. Probably having a quiet dinner with some hanger-on girl from the boxing scene. If he had walked in Kelly's door right then, she wouldn't have minded having a meaningless little toss with him, make an exception, just to satisfy herself (he could see to his own satisfaction), as long as he'd promise to keep his mouth shut while on the premises. But there was no chance of that—of him showing up, first of all, or of him keeping quiet, even if he did. The boy loved to talk. He wasn't one of those strong, silent types. Strong and garrulous, more like. If she'd had a disposition to write, and free time in which to do it, she would have tried to set down his story. Their story. It had always been too hard to get inside his head, though, in spite of all the words that came pouring out of him. Because he loved to talk about everything except himself. Analytical, but not that introspective, when you got right down to it.

All the same, if Clay's story were ever told properly, it would have to come in his own words. She wouldn't know what to say, how to put it, when it came to the crunch. If she'd been able to second-guess him better, they might have stayed together in the first place.

Against all expectation, a drowsy tingle began to steal over her. Almost before she could fall asleep, she was in the nightmare. Two men locked together in a room, one of them him. No doors, no windows. Somehow she could see into the room but couldn't get inside. Then what came next. What always came next. She knew. She snapped herself back into consciousness before it could happen. She'd only drowsed for a few seconds, the way you fall asleep at the wheel of a car for an instant.

Kelly scooped up both of the discarded books, cinched her robe, and walked into the living room in her bare feet. The heat of the fireplace greeted her entry, its warmth concentrated all in the one room. She considered throwing the romance novel into the fire. Then again, *Death North of Patagonia* was the true talisman. Something in her soul didn't discount the possibility of black magic, even if she was only half playing, out of peevish and restless boredom. Didn't nonbelievers pray all the time, just in case? And what was it Clay used to say? "Something starts out as a joke and becomes the rest of your life."

Whispering "Bring him to my doorstep," and shielding the skin of her face from the blaze with her romance novel, Kelly cast Clay's book into the fire, the last piece of him, besides Chandra, that she possessed, and was repaid with the smell of mold burning off before the flames began to eat into the pages.

"Who is it?"
"It's me."
"Me who?"
"Me Clay."

I should have known better than to say "me" through an intercom. It would only make my wait longer. Kelly used to lecture me that it was conceited to expect that my voice would be recognized through a door by a bare acquaintance. I kept forgetting that I was anonymous.

"Clay who?"

Claymation. Cremation. One nation under Clay. Without warning, I was in a knock-knock joke taking place in hell.

"Clay Justin. Balboa's friend." There was a dubious grunt, and all I could do was wait, the iron fence high and spiked, the big house an acre away. So I waited outside the back-door gate by the intercom for the Jamaican housekeeper to buzz me in. The wind off Lake Michigan had picked up, and I hunkered down in my unlined denim coat, too light gauge for this time of night. After seven years in Chicago, I still hadn't gotten used to the cold. People kept telling me I'd adjust, but I knew I wouldn't. I was missing an internal thermostat. I needed redbuds and dogwoods in bloom on a hillside, playful breezes, heat, perfume. God intended it that way. But Chicago had no hills, so another dusting of snow came instead or a freakish blizzard backed up by a wind that had had a couple of hundred miles' running start before it walloped.

It made me nervous to stand outside one of the biggest mansions on one of the nicest streets in Hyde Park. This place even had turrets. Balboa—yes, that really was his first name—Balboa always said to me when I complained about having to trek down here to see him, "Clay, this used to be a righteous white boy's house. You should feel right at home. Pork tycoon, Spam sultan, Sir Francis Bacon, meat-eater like you, lived here in the nineteenth century, and you know damn well who slept back in the carriage house. Lackey like me." Balboa was better educated than me, not to mention significantly richer, but he liked to exaggerate his slang, a gumbo of Superfly, Malcolm X, and Jimmy-Cracked-Corn, when he was around me so I'd never forget that he, too, came from the streets. But when he treated me for shoulder bursitis, I had to come all the way to Hyde Park, to his oversized eighteen-room villa, instead of to his office in Edgewater, closer to where I lived, at God knows what hour of the night, so that he could show off the palace to me yet again, with its mahogany mantelpieces and walnut wainscoting, and remind me that he'd made it, he'd clawed his way out of the West Side projects and through med school by his own smarts.

I didn't know why he bothered with me. It wasn't because I was white. Balboa had lots of white friends and lots of friends, period. He moved more easily in all circles than I did in any circle. But when I first met him, we hit it off, and when he found out I was from Kentucky, that sealed it, as if we were a couple of Freemasons. His grandmother had migrated to Chicago from Corbin or some other Southern pile of sticks, her husband had a barbershop and played the fiddle down there, and so Balboa formed a sentimental attachment to me. When he treated me for pain, I kept telling him that his bills never showed up on my insurance, and he always answered that his billing service must have misfiled the papers again. He had no intention of billing me, then or ever, and at some point I became complicit in that bargain, because I let my health insurance lapse, because I really couldn't afford it. I only enrolled in Blue Cross in the first place to make him happy, because he was always harping on how a person these days couldn't walk around uninsured. But of course he wouldn't ever cash in on my policy.

It wasn't white or black that made me uncomfortable waiting to be buzzed in by the Jamaican maid. It was money. Money gave me the jitters. I made my living, fitfully, by serving as a sparring part-ner, or whipping boy, for boxers in a couple of city gyms. I'd won the Golden Gloves competition once upon a time, but that's as high as I ever went. I didn't claim to be an unusually quick counter-puncher, but I could dance all right, and I did have one hard left hand when I managed to connect. Only I never really got to use it properly, because once or twice, when I did knock out the up-and-coming-pro-of-the-month in a practice bout, the trainer scolded me for damaging the goods, and I was docked part of my pay. I wasn't supposed to win. I was supposed to almost win, then take a lot of punishment, which I did quite well. In spite of the coincidence between my first name and his last, I didn't have much in common with Cassius Clay, by then Muhammad Ali, my fellow Kentuckian, my almost namesake, as far as speed was concerned. I'd slowed down, I could tell. The fastest thing about me was my tongue. In that, he and I were alike. He was the first rapper, and I always had dug his singsong, his patter, the way he used to talk poetry at his opponents before his mind faltered. The one thing I remained good at was protecting my head in the ring. My body had taken a lot of

hits, but my skull stayed more or less intact. I nursed a deathly fear of ending up like Ali, unable to speak or think properly. Thinking was one of my biggest pleasures in life—that is, when I wasn't tormenting myself.

The most famous fighter I'd sparred with was Tadeusz Virkowicz, who had migrated to Chicago a few years before and who was basically a gifted bar brawler. He really wanted to kill people and had an incredible spout of rage inside him that he could barely keep wraps on. He could have been the heavyweight champion by then—at least that's what the pundits said—except that he kept disqualifying himself by hitting opponents below the belt. Including me, several times. Not to mention that he kept making racial slurs while we were in the ring, in his limited English, talking about how he was going to murder such and such a nigger, how there were too many niggers in boxing, knowing that his patter got under my pale skin.

The first time it happened, Balboa had moseyed over to watch me spar. His line was sports medicine. He had been over at the Mid-Town Gym checking on a couple of the name boxers who had contracts with him, and my bout caught his eye, so he sat down to watch. I didn't even know he was there, but Tadeusz did. Tadeusz made his remarks loud enough for Balboa to hear, then craned his neck that direction to put a punctuation point on his taunt, and that's when I knocked him to the ground. And of course the manager cussed me out about it. Afterward, Balboa introduced himself, asked me to get a cup of coffee with him, and offered to take a look at my shoulder, because he could see my extension wasn't all it might be.

Balboa shook his head whenever I complained about Tadeusz—in spite of the Huey Newton poster on his bedroom wall and the multicolored caftans he liked to wear around the manse when he slipped out of his pale greens. He told me I shouldn't let that trash bother me; I wasn't black, and if I was, I'd sure understand better that you got to let it roll off, otherwise you'd walk around pissed off all the time. "Where's your *chi*, baby, that *chi* I gave you last time you were here?" He was always talking about *chi* and meridians while he performed acupuncture on me, although I counted myself

the least spiritual person I knew, the least esoteric, the least suited to taking a slow boat to China, and I only consented to acupuncture in the first place because he said you didn't have to believe in it for it to work. He told me I was more in tune with acupuncture than most people and that I could go deeper into a therapeutic trance than any patient he'd ever worked with. I shot back that it was because I lived my life in a trance.

He also scolded me that he couldn't keep doctoring all the arthritis in my muscles and joints, too much of it for somebody as relatively young as me, if I wasn't going to take good care of myself and give up sparring for a living. He said he didn't do patchwork. A friend of his ran a club. He wanted me to become a bouncer instead, where all I had to worry about was getting stabbed by a high-income hophead on Halsted Street who didn't want to hear my harangue on harassment. Once in a while Balboa would threaten that this was the last time, and don't come around here banged up again. I didn't try to defend myself. I simply asked for another shot of cortisone or a few more acu-needles in the shoulder.

"Who again?"

"Puddintane."

"What?"

"Clay. Clay Justin." There was a slight hesitation, then the rasp of the buzzer, and the gate undone. As I approached the big house, the smell of caramelized brown sugar wafted from the back door. In the kitchen, the maid was preparing a tray of plantains on steaming rice but stopped first to give me an all-purpose disapproving glance. I heard the recorded pulse of George Clinton and the Brides of Funkenstein, a growly love croon cascading down the banisters from the ballroom at the top of the mansion, the place where dashikis met disco and reeking reefer, and I remembered the crucial information I'd managed to suppress so far: today was Valentine's Day. Balboa and I had sometimes sat in the midst of that empty domestic ballroom left over from another age, sipping little-known Balinese beers while he showed me how his latest stereo purchase could really churn out the sound or watching the sultry, sullen hip-hugger dancers of *Soul Train* on his wide-screen TV. Sexual healing. Balboa really believed in that phrase, the way he believed in *chi*. I wished I could say the same. I was more acquainted with morose mornings after.

Lisa was probably out with somebody new tonight. At least we broke it off in sufficient time for her to scan the personals for an ad that said "Let's not spend this Valentine's alone. February in the tundra is for snuggling." We had a big scene, or rather she did and I was a spectator. She kept smacking my arm, the one she knew was messed up, to try to get a rise out of me. I'd never hit a woman in my life. I knew too well from my experiences in the ring what it felt like to get whacked very hard by somebody who was pissed off about something else but taking it out on you. I was more the type who got very quiet, and you, the partner, thought something really terrible was going to happen. But then it never did. I guess Lisa simply got tired of waiting for that terrible thing to happen.

A young woman, light cocoa, with glossy jet-black hair piled in loops atop her head, like chocolate-dipped pretzels, walked into the kitchen, and I swore to God she was wearing a scarlet teddy with white lace trim and nothing else. She politely asked the maid if there was a restroom on this floor. She was probably a commodities trader. The maid gave the woman a scowl filled with all kinds of bad mojo and told her that the ballroom had its own restrooms, his and hers, and could she kindly use the feminine one. The woman thanked her, took a coquettish look around, and blithely ascended the stairs with a mincing step, giving me a cruelly long and unsatiated view of her retreat. "Too much pajama party in dis place, and not enough pajama," the maid remarked ominously, following in this Cupid's wake bearing the heaped, steaming, fragrant tray of West Indian delights.

Her departure left the industrial-sized kitchen open, and I realized that Janine, Balboa's wife, had been sitting at the other end of it on a stool all along, watching a pint-sized television with concentration, as if gazing into a crystal ball. Her left hand was bandaged. Janine had ever been a little cool toward me. She believed that I brought out Balboa's reckless side, because Balboa, after treating me, was always wanting us to go off like teenagers and smoke dope together in his Audi while we cruised Seventy-ninth Street on the South Side, looking for someplace still open that sold jerk chicken.

And I did go along. To places where I'd get my ass kicked if I went alone, because, as Balboa took pleasure in telling me, "Only time white boys ever come here by themself is to buy drugs." Then Balboa Trafalgar (yes, that really was his whole name, like an explorer of old) ignited a spleef and passed it to me. But I'd always wanted to tell Janine that nobody brought out Balboa's reckless side, it was just there, and I knew I certainly had less than her to do with the planning or execution of this pajama party. I wasn't even invited. I was the back-door friend.

But I knew better than to broach that subject with Janine. She was a strikingly beautiful black princess of a woman, of Haitian descent, educated at Northwestern, sober sorority sister, an M.D. like Balboa, and, as I understood, she worked as a pediatrician with abused children. She had gone through life expecting only success for herself, worked for it, and gotten it, and now she exuded a perfume that said, when you smelled it, that if you were lucky enough not to be an abused child, you'd best get on with your life and stop horsing around. And yet she was married to Balboa.

"Hello, Janine."

"Hello, Clay." She gave me a diffident wave with her good hand. "How is Lisa?" Janine had never met Lisa but always asked me about her.

"Lisa is doing beautifully. Me, on the other hand—"

"Balboa is upstairs. Hosting the party. I think he's expecting you. Here for a treatment?"

"Yes. I didn't realize there was a party going on. I'm not sure why he called me tonight of all nights."

"Well, that's Balboa. He keeps his own calendar."

"Aztec."

"No, Rosicrucian."

"You're not partaking?"

"I'm watching the late-show rerun of *E.R.* I've been on call the last two days, and just got off my shift."

"You relax by watching a medical show?"

"Believe me, this show has nothing to do with medicine."

"I'm sorry your hand is hurt. What happened?"

She gave me a delicate, conversation-ending smile and turned back toward the screen. "Nothing. A little accident. I'm sure Balboa will tell you all about it."

I winced, and ascended. Balboa met me on the landing, tropical wine cooler in hand, wearing Pepe LePew hearts-and-flowers boxers and a sleeveless, ribbed T-shirt. His beard was trimmed, and he had on a brocaded fez to cover the bald spot that he was sensitive about in the back of his nap. I didn't usually see him with this many clothes off. I was the one required to undress when we got together. The man's physique was something to admire, built for speed, developed through t'ai chi and karate, and I had seen him bench-press three hundred with the scarred old metal weight set he kept in the carriage house next to the half-disassembled wrecks of sports cars that he bought from junkyards, meaning to repair them someday. Sometimes he gently mock-demonstrated how he could, if he really needed to, use a maneuver from the warrior branch of the Oriental healing arts to break my neck. So far, I hadn't given him a reason.

"Let's set up my massage table in the carriage house, get some *chi* perking. Then I'll give you a good rubdown with mentholated Traumeel. Or do you want to go upstairs for a beer first, join the party for a few minutes?" This was a rhetorical question; he didn't really want me up there mingling with the Dionysian haute bourgeoisie. I explained to myself that I was his private friend, and he didn't want to share me with them, rather than vice versa.

"No, that's okay. It's already after midnight."

"And we gonna let it all hang out-out-out. We're gonna find out what it is all a-*bout.*"

"Unless, that is, I could have some fast consensual sex with a certain stockbroker in a fire-engine-red four-alarm teddy."

He was smiling, giving me his best bantering glance, but his eyebrows looked troubled. "Mm-nuh. I know which one you mean. Chaka Khan I love you Chaka Khan."

As Balboa and I passed through the kitchen, we fell silent, like two guilty schoolboys who haven't done anything naughty yet but are about to. Janine made a point of not acknowledging either of us. Outside, under the orange-black urban sky, forever in dull flames, he finished his statement. He, the one who was always on my case about my arrhythmic breathing, expelled air from his mouth, and I realized that he was actually holding his breath as he walked through the kitchen, like a child pretending he was swimming underwater. "Anyway, you got Lisa. Good woman like that, you can't go messing around on her. Principles, commitment, and, besides, too many STDs. That shit rages democratically, even in the uppity ones."

"Ex-Lisa. Let's get the treatment over with. I'm beat."

"Yeah. Okay. Sorry to hear it." Sobriety overtook him too.

"Balboa, I don't think I should be coming down here anymore. Janine freezes me out. It makes me uncomfortable."

For once in his life, he let himself look worried. "No, don't say that. It's not you. She's—well, I'll just say that her mood right now has nothing to do with you."

I laid a hand on his exposed, massive bicep. "Listen to me. I've lost my girlfriend, for keeps, and it's more my fault than it is hers. Don't mess up your marriage. You've been stepping out, and it has to stop. You're married to a smart, stunning woman, have two gorgeous, healthy kids, a thriving practice, and you live in the kind of mansion they don't build anymore because nobody but you can even afford the heating bills."

"You want my life? Go ahead and possess it."

"Take that back. You don't mean it."

"I hear you. I don't take her for granted. Okay, there have been one or two episodes along the way." He admonished me with a gold-ringed index finger. "I've confided that to nobody but you. And it goes no further, dig? I tried to bring the subject up with her a few days ago, to make amends, because I was feeling guilty about it; you know, we went through a bad time and I messed up, but she cut me off. Too proud to acknowledge that could happen in her marriage."

"And this episode, as you call it—it's over?"

"Yeah, it's over. All the same, I had to get out tonight. It's stifling indoors. Let's just say there's someone in there I hadn't planned on seeing at this point in time."

"Chaka Khan?"

"Someone. So forgive me that I called you down here as an excuse."

"I don't care. It's not like I had other plans tonight."

"But you want to know what is on Janine's mind right now? Not the male-female thing. She broke her hand, and that's what she's put out about."

"Because you broke it? Or was she hitting you, like Lisa was me? Enraged women often break their hands because they don't hit properly, due to lack of practice."

"Are you jiving me? I've never laid a finger on that woman. No, Janine is upset because the air bag on her coupe flew out the wrong way this morning, after she hit a patch of black ice, and it pinned her hand against the doorframe, giving her a hairline fracture. She got taped up and went straight to work anyway. But she's going to sue their asses and probably win. It happened only this morning, yet she held the cell phone in her bandaged paw while she drove, and her attorney has already fired off three faxes about it and has that automaker's whole history of liability and mishaps typed up in a dossier. She doesn't mess around. Not to mention she's got the Hyde Park streets department on red alert about that one patch of ice they failed to get up. They'll have a crew out tomorrow on their hands and knees, scrubbing the pavement with wire brushes and neon-blue deicer, like it was a runway."

"That's the way it ought to be."

"Oh, I agree that she did the right thing. Make them pay. But I'm talking about the emotional charge. The accident has really traumatized her. I honestly believe she considers that the worst thing that ever happened to her. She doesn't expect mischance to ever crash into her life. Won't accept it no way. As far as she's concerned, it's an outrage against nature. Now, how can a black woman think like that?"

"Why shouldn't she? You mean she's obliged to carry the whole history of Her People on her back? Whatever happened to the talk about taking personal responsibility you're always laying on me?"

"Sure, I believe that. From the heart. I only mean don't forget where you came from."

"She came from Shaker Heights. Her father was a corporate attorney specializing in trademark infringements, and her mother was head of the Board of Education. Isn't that what you told me?"

"Yeah, well, that's the difference between me and her."

"And isn't that what attracted you to her in the first place? So don't say now that she's not humble enough. You've arrived. Poverty is something to get out of and stay out of. If you want more of it, sign onto a philanthropic board."

"I'm already on several." Even in the darkness, I could see the sincerely aggrieved, indignant look on his face. "Get in the car," he said, and he wasn't kidding. I could be as ironic as I wanted with him, as much as I wanted, until I hit on certain taboo subjects, the only ones really worth talking about. Sometimes I forgot that I was supposed to always remain, at bottom, an unself-conscious working stiff in his presence. A half-retarded, has-been boxer with a heart of gold. That was what he needed me to be, and in return, he promised to take care of me, in his offhand way. "I mean it, man, get in the fucking car."

"Don't you want to put some pants on first?"

"They can arrest my ass if they want. My cousin is an alderman in the Sixth Ward, I ran the campaign that got him elected, and I got nothing against enlightened nepotism."

"What about my acupuncture treatment? We haven't even entered the servant's quarters yet."

"You one wry sumbitch. That hurts my feelings, brother. And I'm not slumming with you, if that's what you think. I want you to come back tomorrow around noon, it's my day off, in broad daylight, where you can really get a close look at all my neighbors' lawn jockeys, and I'm going to spend the whole afternoon making you right, patching you together once and for all, homeostasis for my homey, instead of doing a rush job now, when I'm tipsy anyway. How is that shoulder?" He gave it a diagnostic tweak, and a burning flame shot through my arm socket.

"Poor. Lisa hits harder than Tadeusz when she's really mad. Only not below the belt, thank God."

"But right now I want us to take a ride." As we pulled away from the curb in the Audi, with its fragrant leather seats and the enveloping throb of Sade's ceaseless vocal orgasm on the immaculately clean speaker system, we cruised past the hulks of other mansions like his, set far back from the road across vanishing-point expanses of lawn. "That one used to belong to Muhammad Ali."

"You're playing with me."

F92,517

"I shit you not."

"You never told me that before."

"I'm telling you now. All the boxers like to come down to Hyde Park, not only you. Guy who owns it now, an internist, has terminal cancer. It breaks my heart to see him these days, picking dead brush out of his garden. He'll be gone by summer. That big square one with the Gothic window slits, suitable for mounting machine-gun turrets, belongs to Samuel Haq-Falavi."

"Bullshit."

"Hey, where do you think he lives? Topeka? Look, you can even see his bodyguards all sitting in that car at the corner. There, right there. Try to act normal. He's been posting them in that spot as sentries since last week. Must have been some kind of bomb threat or something. Dumbasses all congregate in the same car, the livelong night, drinking Turkish coffee and picking the grounds out of their teeth. One hand grenade would take the whole carload of them out." He mimed a tossing gesture. "Kaboom!"

"But you won't be throwing it."

"No, I won't be throwing it. True enough. I participated in the big march, albeit with some reservations, and I do give the man credit for being a good entrepreneur. All the bankers around here say he's an excellent credit risk. Meantime, the white bankers in the Loop are handing cash over by the barrelful to the Brazilian government and getting nothing back except a lot of IOUs. Samuel repays ahead of schedule. Nothing wrong with building from the ground up in your own neighborhood. I can relate, because I've been having a hell of a time with those downtown bankers myself. I've been negotiating with the city of Chicago to take over some ineptly run geriatric units and turn them into alternative-therapy spas. Rolfing, aromatherapy, acupuncture, colonics, saline tubs. Give these old folks something to look forward to. Make their lives worth living."

"An enema? I think they already get those."

"Ah, Clay, you understand nothing about the science of colonics. It's a total purge, like fasting, like Ramadan, man. I'll turn you on to colonics if you'll let me."

"No thanks. I already take it up the ass as it is."

"Well, consider it a standing offer."

"Standing, but with my hands gripping the table. I can't figure you out, Balboa. Sometimes you sound like Che Guevara with an Ayn Rand chaser."

"Ayn Rand, my eye. Frederick Douglass. If I've traveled this far, it's because I've made my own road. If I climb high, it's because I put the ladder there myself."

"Then there's all this mystical stuff, you laying on hands and feeling the field of electronic pulses around my body. And I know you're not shitting me. Those magnetic pulses are probably there. I know you really believe it, or at least you make me believe you believe it."

"Don't try to figure me out, homeboy. Just suck on this Rastafarian spleef." He handed me an elegantly hand-rolled marijuana cigarette, king size, and I puffed and settled in for the ride to wherever we were going. We got unusually quiet as we took 55 across to the northward elevated turn where it merged into the Kennedy Expressway, revealing the panoramic view of downtown from above, my favorite approach. The city nightlights spread out, clear and freestanding, three-dimensional, seemingly detached from the skyscrapers, like a constellation that had broken from the sky and settled by the lakeshore. Before long, we were on pocked crosstown streets, easing around traffic cones and open sewer ditches, past jumbles of boarded-up buildings, as we made our way to the West Side.

Off to our left were vacant lots, bare looking as spaces where knocked-out teeth once lodged, and then there was a high-voltage power station. Even with the windows closed, I could hear the carcinogenic thrum. We threaded beneath overpasses where the aerial gridlock of mass transit insinuated itself through neighborhoods, slicing up blocks. The whole area looked deserted, except once in a while we rounded a corner to see three or four teenage boys standing in a clump. "See that shit? Selling or buying crack."

"You don't know that for sure."

"Hey, I grew up on this selfsame street, in my grandmother's house. That one over there. The condemned one. We could score right now and not even get out of the car. Drive-through."

"So what? You going to tell them to 'Just Say No'? We're smoking a joint."

"Yeah, but not all day and all night. How much dope you'd say you do? A lot?"

"Only when I'm with you."

Balboa shot me an impatient look. "Get serious."

I was serious, but I decided not to push it. "Okay, only from time to time."

"See, that's why they call it a *recreational* drug. I have my limits too. I'm straighter than you think. My grandmother, who I always come to see, still lives around the corner, and I can't get her to move away from this dead zone, no matter how much I beg and plead. And those projects there, the ones you're looking at and they're freaking the shit out of you because you're trying to imagine what would happen if you walked through there by yourself? They'd kill you in about thirty seconds, that's what. Sheer desperation, not even meanness. Yeah, I lived with my mom in those, after my dad split, and I ate unmentionable parts of the pig. The real deal. You're from the South. You ever eat chitlins? You a connoisseur of soul food?"

"What in Christ's name are you doing, Balboa? Okay, yeah, I know the taste of hoppin' John. Think you're going to scare me straight? Or are you just showing off?"

He lay back in the leather seat and let out a long sigh. "I'm sorry. I'm frustrated, that's all. I had to see you tonight. Nobody but you would understand. Me and Janine really are on the outs. When do you finally say you've found happiness with a woman?"

"You're asking the wrong person."

"I hate to lay all this on you when you just broke up with Lisa. But if you want, I'll spill my guts, and then listen while you return the favor."

"No thanks. You know I'd rather listen than talk."

"Maybe I'm too sentimental. But I don't want to give up my old friends from this neighborhood. I want to bring them up with me a little. I come to visit my grandmother, and then I end up hanging with some of my buddies or cousins. They're not pretty or polite. Most of them don't know how to behave in company, except for the ones like me, who made it out. But Janine don't want me over here, and she even less wants 'those riffraff,' as she calls them, cluttering up our house, though we don't use half the room in that goddamned castle. Main reason my grandmother is still here, besides her usual obstinacy, is because Janine won't hear of me taking her on as a live-in. I mean nothing against Janine's folks, who I like and respect, but why can they come to vacation with us for a month at a time, and that's perfectly all right? But we have to stay away from Balboa's ilk. I mean, isn't there a point when you just accept certain defects in other people?

"And then there's the help. Now, my cousin took some early development courses at Roosevelt University, and I don't care if she wears bad makeup to cover her acne scars and wears somebody else's tight polyester pants and smokes unfiltered cigarettes—there's no reason she can't take care of our kids and get paid for it while we're at work. I'd more trust my child with that cousin, who I love and ate many bowlfuls of bad pork with, than I would a perky U. of Chicago coed with good skin and all the references but who I never saw before in my life. That's the way I am. And what is it with that tight-ass Jamaican maid? I know she scares you, for starters."

"I won't argue."

"Myself, I'm afraid to fart when she's in the house. Several girls over here from my neighborhood can really cook some food, I mean twice as spicy as Tropic Island, and I'd rather help support them, give them a little boost toward night school, lift my people up, if that doesn't sound too pretentious. Plus I plain and simple enjoy their company more. I work, you know, seventy or eighty hours a week sometimes, and then I don't feel comfortable when I do come home.

"But Janine doesn't see it that way. And we've been having some big fights about it. To the point where she said she might divorce me. First time she ever used that word around me."

"It's a word that will get your attention."

"Maybe she's only exaggerating to make a point. I guess the last straw was the Chinese furniture I brought home a couple of weeks ago, to dress up the apartment above the carriage house back there so I can start using it as a real office, for my sideline in alternative healing. Run a little practice out of there, get it going word of mouth, then I can see the kids more often, not be away all the time. I'm paying a mortgage on it, so I might as well use it. You remember the furniture?"

"Yes, if you mean the sofa you kept wrapped in plastic and made me sit on. Were you afraid I'd bleed on it?"

Balboa allowed himself a rueful laugh. "That's a black thing, keeping the plastic cover on. White boy wouldn't understand that. My grandmother always did that with her couches and chairs, to keep them clean, she said."

"It's not a black thing. It's a kitsch thing. My grandmother did it too."

"That so? All right, well maybe we do come from the same root after all. I'd like to think so. Anyway, I bought that suite at a severe discount, from some cousins of mine in the import-export business, you might say. I didn't ask where they got the suite or how. But before that, they were trying to fence a piece of art, not like professionals, dumbasses just broke into somebody's house in Oak Park and were walking around at parties asking did anybody want to buy a drawing by Monet. Only they said '*Mon*-it,' like that Jamaican chick saying 'Mon, it be hot today.' Plain stupid, these brothers. And I could be rationalizing like a motherfucker, but I figured it was at least a step up for them to be doing something with furniture, showing some business sense, even if it's black market."

"Yes, you are definitely rationalizing."

"That's what Janine said too. She hit the roof. Told me when she came home tonight, in a mood and a half from that hairline fracture and working all day at the children's hospital, that when she wakes up tomorrow morning the Chinese furniture better be gone. Or I'd be gone." He shakes his head and hits the button to eject Sade. Not even her whispery vocal filigree can save him now. "You're my best friend, buddy. I don't know if you realize. Maybe that sounds strange to you."

"You've done all right by me, Balboa. I've got nothing to complain about." He gave me the usual initiation handshake, some Black Power clutch he grew up with in his neighborhood, one that I could never get quite right. But he wouldn't let me shake hands with him in the normal way. I had to be his homey or nothing at all.

Before I knew it, he had shot through the West Side and was pulling up at an el station. "I hope you don't mind if I drop you off here at the train and you leave your car at my place overnight. I got someplace I need to go."

"Where?"

"Never you mind."

Like most things with him, it was offered as a fait accompli, not a request. "That junker of yours ain't for shit anyway. I'll pick you up myself tomorrow and give you the workout of your life for the bad shoulder. But don't get in the ring with Tadeusz again. I'm serious. Box if you want, but not with him. You've got to promise me that, or we're done."

It was his usual threat, but this time, for some reason, I believed him. "Yeah, all right. I don't care. I'm sick of him hitting me below the belt anyway. He's a prick."

He did the handshake thing again, leaning across the passenger side toward the open door and taking care to offer his brotherly salutation to my good arm. He gave a little extra squeeze at the end, looking at me hard. "I'm going to make it up to you too. All your bad nights, breaking up with Lisa, everything. I promise. No more pain. Peace." Balboa made a quick, practiced U-turn and peeled out, accelerating along the deserted street toward a yellow light.

"Clay?"

"Yeah, it's me. Who is this?"

"It's me." She gave me the answer I deserved.

When I heard the phone ring after three hours' sleep, I had to fight off nausea, like an inner-ear problem, feeling dizzy every time I tried to sit up. It was a woman's voice, familiar, but not Lisa's. For a second, I thought maybe Lisa had called to reconcile, and I was so disoriented at that second that I would have made up with her, no questions asked, at least for the time being, but I knew better than to expect her to call the morning after Valentine's Day. All the same, I had the oddest feeling, as if I'd expected to be summoned by someone near to me. I'd been having a dream about a woman right before I was awakened by the ringing phone, and I was striving to remember the dream, who it had been, get back into the dream somehow.

"Kelly?" But I knew it wasn't Kelly on the phone either. We hadn't spoken for more than a year. Still, I felt I had to say her name out loud. Then there was that woman in the lace teddy, the one who had gotten Balboa so worked up. What had he said her name was?

To focus, I blinked in the bright bedside lamplight, taking in the place Lisa had tried to prettify with limited success. She'd gotten me to move into an overpriced apartment as long and narrow as a bowling lane, with oiled hardwood floors and a bricked-up fireplace, and she had hung spider plants and ferns all along the windows and billowy white curtains in them. I've never bought curtains in my life. If they're there when I move in, I'll open and shut them, but that's about all. So I didn't keep the apartment up. The spikes of the plants turned brittle, the gleam faded from the floors, the throw rugs collected lint, and Lisa, after a few fitful weeks of unsolicited housekeeping, gave up and told me, a little resentfully, that she wasn't my maid. I agreed with her right away. So she fought down her urge to clean, and then we were both happier.

The only amenity of the overpriced apartment I really liked was the sunroom in the front, and I spent much of my free time in that one room, reading haphazardly, watching people in the street below, and making love with Lisa, so she would close her eyes and forget about the mess. Most of all, I liked soaking up the sun when it consented to come out, to try to make it through another long and blustery winter, after all the hours spent in windowless gyms.

"Balboa is gone." I recognized Janine's voice, rawer than I had ever heard it before.

"I'm sorry, Janine, but he isn't here. If he was, I'd put him on the line."

"He didn't come home last night." There was the faint ring of accusation in her tone.

I rubbed my face, trying to find the best words. Talking with Janine was always touchy. "Listen, whatever goes on between you two—I don't take sides. I didn't encourage him to do anything, I promise you."

"Since the two of you left together, I thought you might know his next stop."

"He dropped me at the el and said he had somewhere to go, but I honestly don't know where. As you said last night, he keeps his own calendar. His schedule is so erratic, I didn't think anything of it." I could hear me defending myself, as if I had to come up with an alibi. It was an old habit, hard to break. I thought up alibis even when I didn't need one, just in case. "He was going to pick me up today and give me acupuncture."

"I don't think he'll be coming to get you today."

"He said he would."

"I have this feeling that something has happened."

"You mean something really bad?"

"I don't want to jump to conclusions. Balboa has gone off before for stretches of days, so it's not like I'm ready to call the police. It's an intuition, that's all."

"What do you suspect?"

"He's just had—lapses once or twice." I wasn't going to touch that one. "Could we meet somewhere to talk?"

Her request softened me. "Sure, I could come by. I left my car and have to pick it up anyway."

"I'd prefer somewhere public. But with enough privacy to talk. Later this evening. I've got some things to take care of today, and dinner in Lincoln Park later with some friends." The old, unspecified grudge came back into her voice. "I can be free for an hour or so."

"Okay, well, what about Rosa's, at around, say, ten tonight? It's on West Armitage." I said this as a half-joking payback for her snub, her setting conditions and telling me she had things to do, knowing that she was unlikely to drive to a blues club in a bad part of town on the West Side at that time of night. Those were Balboa's stamping grounds, not hers. It made more sense for me to go to Hyde Park to get my car back. If she was that worried about Balboa, why not get on the case at once?

"Rosa's? Oh—that will be fine, I guess. Okay, I'm writing it down. West Armitage."

"Or I could just get dressed and come down to Hyde Park now on the train. If you're truly worried."

"No. I'd rather meet you at Rosa's. I'll phone around to some other people and check his usual haunts."

"Okay. I'll wait on your pleasure."

"Clay, I know you and Balboa talk about us, our marriage. That isn't my style, and it's hard for me to come to you with this. I know you'll keep it all to yourself."

"I'll muster up whatever discretion is in me."

I took a lukewarm shower with insufficient water pressure and listened to the plumbing groan like a poltergeist. Then, with the sleep and daze washed off of my skin, I sauntered down onto Clark to find some doughnuts and coffee. The character of a neighborhood in Chicago can change in the space of a couple of blocks. On the strip where the doughnut shop did its business, it looked as though the night had ended not that long before. A couple of men with overdeveloped, muscular arms and withered legs sat in wheelchairs munching on crullers. They were too young and lean, without paunches, to have lost their power to walk in any other way except by bullet. I imagined that when they had walked, they'd been graceful, sinuous walkers.

Now, they had a strange, watchful lassitude about them. It was different from the body language of the overachievers I knew who participated in the wheelchair marathon along Lake Shore Drive, the ones journalists liked to write inspirational news stories about. These men didn't say anything as I passed by, but they checked me out, as wary and wily as wolves. Wire trash cans overflowed onto a curb littered with crushed paper cups, Styrofoam take-out boxes, and the occasional condom wrapper. BAD BOYS stood out in relief on the unlit movie marquee. In front of the el station, a leashed Doberman with a mesh cage over its muzzle, its gaze tired but alert by habit, was coming off the late shift with its human partner.

After buying four glazed and a sixteen-ounce coffee, I sauntered back out onto the street. A newspaper machine sported a headline about the Bulls, and an inset referred to Tadeusz's upcoming fight, but I didn't have the right change. I hadn't thought to ask for any when I made my doughnut transaction, and I didn't feel like going back in to beg, because it would end up in a big discussion. When you ask for change, vendors look at your dollars as if you were trying to get them to exchange pesos. What I wanted to do was sit down with the coffee, get my mind clear, and puzzle over Balboa.

What in the hell was going on with him? Except for problems with Janine, everything was great in his life. Money, prestige, hipness, well connected, health, aging nicely; he had all those things. I walked again past the two men in wheelchairs, and sheepishly approached them to ask for change. They mistook my meaning, not realizing that I had dollars to trade for silver.

The first one chuckled to his mate. "Man's asking me for a donation. Hey, don't you think *I* ought to be the one panhandling *you?* Isn't that the way it's supposed to go?"

His friend joined in the mirth. "Yeah, you got it all turned around, brother. We're the ones ain't got any legs to use. Get a job, son." They shared a hearty laugh at my expense.

"Okay, whatever. I wasn't asking for a handout. Just change. Forget it. I'm sorry to bother you."

The first one stopped me with a gesture of his flak-jacket sleeve. "Nah, we're only shitting you, man. Lighten up. You'd think your mother just died, way you're carrying on. What you need, a dollar? Two dollars?"

"Enough to buy a paper. Fifty cents ought to do it."

"Sure, sure." The two of them emptied out their jacket pockets. Among the lottery tickets, Altoids, packets of hair mousse, GameBoy, and some sort of religious brochure about not using barcode scanners, they came up with a pile of loose coins. "You looking beat this morning. Here, go buy five or six papers, make phone calls, whatever you like." The first man waved off my crumpled dollars, pressed the cold change into my hot palm, and locked my hand for a moment in the fierceness of his grip. "Been through some shit myself. Glad to do it for you." I barked out a husky thanks and turned away, blinking, into the wind.

"Mommy, how come Daddy hasn't called?"

"I don't know, honey. He's not a bad person."

"I didn't say he was a bad person. I asked why he hasn't called."

"He must have a good reason."

"But why did you say that?"

"I was agreeing with you."

"With what?"

"That he's not a bad person. Even if he didn't call."

"But I didn't say he was a bad person."

"Eat your waffle."

The late-afternoon light has begun to fade, and yet the moon comes out early, hanging low over a horizon truncated by distant coastal high-rises. The cold makes the moon's outlines sharper. No one answers the intercom. For some reason, the gate has been left ajar. The kitchen door sticks, swollen even in winter, but at a push of the shoulder, it gives way. A film of steam clings to the picture window in the kitchen, making dim light even dimmer. "Janine?"

No answer. No Jamaican maid. Shouldn't she be there, fixing supper? A pot boils, unattended, on the front burner, letting out billows of steam, down to its last inch of water. He finds a glass in the cupboard, and throws a few cupfuls of water from the tap into the pot, to settle the simmer. Only when it's quiet can he proceed deeper into the house.

He navigates through the narrow servant's pantry, with its glass jars of crimson serrano chilies, sun-dried tomatoes, apricot pieces as rounded and fleshy as polyps. The front end of the first floor is spacious but aquatic, filmier still than the kitchen, almost opaque. His eyes must be watering, and he rubs them, but no, they're dry, empty sockets. In the shafts of light falling through the bars of the leaded living-room window sit two bonsai trees potted in wicker, their fallen, minuscule leaves brittle, littering the hardwood.

He calls out again, his voice this time firmer, more decisive, but finds no answer except his own echo. From the sound, he could swear he was in a house empty of furniture, ready to be bought or sold, with nothing but a few crumpled newspapers fluttering when the furnace kicks on.

Back through the pantry: there's a scraper on a shelf, clotted with a glob of gummy paint, only half dried, like blood on a razor. There's an X-acto knife, too, with a wicked little cutting edge, just right for severing a finger. He picks it up, turns it over, lays it back down. A passage-

way leads from the other end of the kitchen to a staircase he never knew was there, up a stairwell like a mine shaft, sealed off from the rest of the lower level by crisscrossed strips of metal. Only on the third floor can he come out, past a windowless playroom, and onto its floor are spilled bright plastic shapes in primary colors, some interrupted game, the nature of which he doesn't understand.

A mentholated smell, maybe eucalyptus in a sauna, gets stronger, but where is it coming from? He can't even find a bathroom on this floor, anywhere, and he needs to piss in the worst way. His hand pushes, a door swings open, a four-poster bed, big enough for three people, a silk robe on one post, long enough to be Balboa's. Laid across the spread, a negligee. Maybe one Janine declined to wear at the pajama party, a present he'd bought to make up to her, or asked her to put on, and she answered in that special voice, cutting as an X-acto knife, No, I'll take a pass, it doesn't go well with my bandage. Then he sighed in disgust, said the wrong thing, under his breath, such as, Some women I know would be glad to get it. On his way out the door. Fighting words. The last words they spoke.

A door opens in the mahogany, one he didn't even see there, like a secret panel, the wood is so deep and dark, one long, continuous stain. Janine gives a start, one towel wrapped tight around her body, another wound around her head.

"Nobody answered. I kept calling out downstairs."

"I was taking a shower."

"Balboa never came back?" He wondered idly whether she would simply drop the towel, revealing her gorgeous body, brought to this state of perfection by punishing workouts in the gym and by carefully scheduled interludes of recovery.

"No. It's been weeks now. I'm trying to take it one day—why are you holding my negligee?"

"Because I—no good reason."

I started from the sheets and ran to the bathroom, barely able to contain the gush of urine that came out of me when I flipped up the toilet lid. Though I hated to admit it, I was half hard, and my penis ached. Served me right, I guess. Not even sixteen ounces of coffee could keep me awake. I was groggy as hell. Only ten o'clock in the morning.

I'd been fretting about Balboa. He had a way of getting into things. Just the week before his disappearance, he'd bopped down on a whim with a commercial-photographer friend to watch the Miami Heat play, with no hotel reservations and no tickets. When he came back he was talking about buying a sugar plantation in Haiti, based on a conversation he'd had with somebody at the concession stand of the Miami Arena. I said, "Does that mean I should start calling you Baby Doc?" He didn't like that crack because, of course, he was dead serious about the plantation. He reminded me that he'd been part of a group that met with Aristide once at a lawn party in Weston to talk about prospects for peace and fair elections.

My shoulder was good for nothing, and I wasn't going to get acupuncture today, but I could at least go jump rope and run on the track. I took half an hour to make up my gym bag, as indecisive over what to pack as if I were the one departing on a long trip.

Knock, knock, Daddy.
Who's there?
Summer.
Summer who?
Summer here, summer gone.
Knock, knock.
Okay, who's there this time?
Sky.
Sky who?
Sky I know skipped town.

By the time Balboa turned his head, the lizard had run into a patch of banyan leaves just beyond his peripheral vision. Lizards were like that. You'd open the door to your hotel room, and one would dart up the wall, into a crack you didn't even know was there, quick enough that you didn't have time to decide its color. Some of the lizards were small enough that you could mistake them for insects.

He considered sending Clay a blank, unsigned postcard from the Delano Hotel, to suggest, without saying so, that he was keeping his head together. Arrayed around the oceanic pool were old-fashioned wooden chaise longues, with broad slats. The pool tapered off in such a mellow fashion at the shallow end that you couldn't tell where the water left off and the pavement began. It was like stepping into a liquid magnifying glass.

Clay knew how his mind worked—at least Balboa had always flattered himself that the two of them were in sync that way. Clay's imagination would be sufficient to take the flat, painted planes of the facade, on the front of the blank postcard, and build outward to encompass the jungly sitting areas with their carefully mismatched furniture, like the parson's chair and the bar table made from a pastry stone that held his Tanqeray and tonic, the condensation forming fast on the weeping glass. Clay would be able to imagine, almost smell, the plump prawns sitting on a bed of saffron rice and to intuit the topless beach with its schoolteachers on holiday baring their pale breasts in public perhaps for the first time ever, the neo-Egyptian friezes, the Jaguars slow-cruising Ocean Boulevard. Then Clay would know Balboa was all right.

Balboa told himself this wasn't like the other time. Yes, he had left unexpectedly, just as before, without warning. But this was different, almost premeditated, following an instinct for opportunity. It was about money, that's all. You had to spend money to make money. He had control of the situation.

There was a hell of a lot of money flowing down here, too much, it was positively gushing, and he was going to stick his hands into the foaming spout and get himself some of it. He'd wallow in the ocean for a day or two, rub the sand off his skin in the cold outdoor shower, towel away the potential for sea lice with brisk, hard, terrycloth strokes, and get going on the next phase of his life. They called those unseen creatures lice, but they were microscopic jellyfish spawn. It was important to call things by their proper names.

He knew all about head lice from them bad old days, and these were definitely not lice. All the same, they'd sting the shit out of you, if you gave them half an hour to incubate on your skin.

A few weeks of smart business deals, and everything would be set back to rights. He'd get back all he had lost, plus more, he'd score that Haitian plantation down the Caribbean, which was practically being given away, maybe turn right around and sell it, because he already had a prospective buyer he'd met in the bar, they'd talked it over while sipping gin and tonic, and he'd build outward from that little cash fix, into some of the real estate waiting—no, begging—to be picked up close at hand. The Delano wasn't a cheap headquarters, at two fifty a night, but there was no way for him to get deep into the game, into the mind-set of the players, without room service and a good, sandy beach a few steps away. It was like stepping into the poker pit in Vegas. You did it with confidence, and if you had to, you put up in the best suite, to establish yourself, to make it clear you didn't really care about money, because there was plenty more where that came from. It was one of the ironies of business, that once you proved you didn't really need the money, the house would put you up in its most luxurious suite for free.

One of the historic hotels down the strip was being gutted and had gone up for sale. He'd checked around, made a few calls to local Realtors, and nobody had made a move on it yet, because everybody was waiting to see whether the Fed was going to push the prime rate down another quarter of an inch. And they'd had a lot of hurricane action the previous season. It had made everybody a little nervous. Once the hotel had been restored, the lintels placed atop the thresholds, the long slabs of marble laid in, the cockeyed balconies set aright, a dance club tucked in on the bottom floor (because Balboa always did love a ballroom), its value would increase fivefold, maybe tenfold. Real estate wasn't rational and even less so on South Beach. You had to get used to that fact, and go on from there.

Why in the name of Allah would anybody spend two fifty a night to stay in the ugly hotel he was in? Because it was owned by Madonna; because you could drive across the causeway and point to the house on Star Island where Gloria Estefan lived. It made you feel like somebody, because most people weren't anybody, and that was a cold fact. People had too much money on their hands and not enough to do with it. The flood of sunshine and the hurricanes, the changes in barometric pressure, made them act in crazy, unpredictable ways. A couple seeing a beachfront house acted like they were in heat. They couldn't help themselves. He could possess and unload lots of properties within the space of a couple of months, if he kept his wits about him and paid close attention to prospective clients and their little whims. It all came down to whims, in the end, to doing something just because. That's how rarefied things had become.

By the time Janine received the latest credit card bill (and there was more than enough cash in the bank to pay it, he was pretty sure of that, more than enough electronic blips still available, in spite of his having built his most recent house of cards on credit), Balboa would have moved into less expensive quarters. He would be making money, not spending it. He hadn't excelled as a day trader, and the day-spa enterprise had sucked off too much cash up front, but he had never run short of ideas. There was nothing to worry about.

Seeing Balboa again had put Carmela in a state. She knew they were finished. Knew it down to the bone. He'd cut things off a couple of months before, or maybe she herself had, on account of them living several hundred miles apart and her knowing that even with his relative freedom to pick up and go it was becoming harder to make up excuses to sneak away to the farm and see her. As far as she could tell, each time Balboa had to ask himself if she was still worth it. Even if the answer had been yes the first twenty times, that didn't mean it would be yes the twenty-first. Tails had to come up sooner or later. It could be that she had chosen a man just out of reach, knowing that the impossible situation would sooner or later crumble. But no, she didn't really believe that. You don't choose who you're going to fall for. The situation chooses you.

That insight had been confirmed when she made her unexpected appearance at the Valentine's Day pajama party, the one she'd heard so much about in his laughing accounts. One glimpse of Balboa, his handsome legs bulging out of those ridiculous Pepe LePew boxers, had made her moist in the eyes, and somewhere else besides. How she must have looked in her getup to the other party-goers—and the funny thing is, she wasn't like that. People looked at her and pegged her for a vixen, but that wasn't the case at all. She was solitary, skinny, given when alone and working to wearing oversized T-shirts that made her look like a gangly teenage boy who'd just gone through a growth spurt. She had a lot more truck with horses than she did with people, living out isolated in the country.

Days went by, and she didn't feel the need to lay eyes on any people. And when she had to run into Lexington, after such a spell, she found that crowds unnerved her. She had to turn on her sociable self, and she could do it, but the effort exhausted her, she'd get giddy with it, which people mistook for gregariousness. It was all or nothing, a performance every time. She hardly recognized herself in that gleaming woman who everybody seemed so attracted to. For the most part, she kept to herself, reading, currying, cooking, curing, except when it came to him. Always waiting for his next call, that's how she passed her days, regardless of what else she was doing on the outside.

She had never dared show her face directly when she knew his wife would be around, and she'd never crossed the threshold of his residence until that night. She had only traveled up to Chicago half a dozen times, to a hotel, sensing that that put her close enough to his domain, and instead mostly waited for the openings when he could free himself up for a shuttle flight or an overnight drive to her little neck of the woods. She'd sworn she'd never become an afternoon mistress, the kind who allowed a man to return to the wife that same night to make up whatever quarrel they'd had and slip into bed with her to seal the bargain. Carmela swore on her grave that she'd never be a party to that.

But she'd betrayed that principle, too, on the Chicago trips, becoming an afternoon mistress when he had to go out on call, or wherever it was that he in fact had ended up going—maybe home for lunch, that's what she suspected. Meanwhile, she watched cable in the hotel room, flipping through channels like a sulky, lovesick adolescent girl. Watching the clock, getting more and more furious. Concocting outrageous emotional penalties, ones she knew she couldn't really enforce, for every minute he went into overtime.

"You said you'd be back at two, and it's ten after." Hoarding every minute of their short stays. Setting up peevish, ironclad rules she knew would be broken.

Carmela always asked him, when he showed up, whether he'd made love to the other one that same day, and he'd answer, "Don't ask me that shit; you know I don't think like that." Still, it bothered her if she knew he'd made love to that woman within forty-eight hours of coming to see her. She made him promise never to make love to both of them on the same day, holding stubbornly to one little piece of terrain, one moment she could call hers.

What difference did it make how long it had been? An hour, a week, it came down to the same thing. She knew he and his wife had never altogether stopped having sex, no matter how much he complained about how the atmosphere had been chilly in his bedroom for a long time. She just tried not to think about it. She called the woman all kinds of unfair names: bitch, hussy, ice queen. There was no other way to think of her and still survive. As infrequently as she was getting sex, it was hardly worth keeping up the connection. Yet she stayed faithful to his unfaithful ways, until one or the other of them had finally put an end to the complications. Maybe it was simply by mutual agreement.

Why oh why had she shown up, unannounced, two months after the breakup? Where she'd never trod before and never wanted to tread either. All those people. She had to go for broke, just to get up her nerve to cross the threshold of the door. What had possessed her to parade past his wife, in a lace teddy, and even more to flaunt herself in front of him, as if she were that desperate, as if she couldn't have anybody she wanted, as if there were any chance of a reconciliation? Didn't she possess any shame, any self-respect? She knew better. But she plain couldn't help herself. She was possessed all right. It surely had to have been a nasty surprise to both members of the couple. The wife—Carmela couldn't even bring herself to say the woman's name—the wife had kept her dignity, hadn't batted an eyelash, though she must have known exactly who this interloper was.

Yet the wife didn't seem that involved with the party. Willfully out of it, more like. She had stayed down in the kitchen watching television with another man, some family friend, big and strapping like Balboa, great big mess of hair, not really good-looking but attention-getting in a beat-up and disheveled sort of way, like a really old Cadillac with tail fins. Some intimate of the family who was lucky enough to come and go as he damn well pleased, who could pet the dog without getting snapped at, who knew where all the bathrooms were in that ridiculously huge mansion and didn't have to ask the housemaid for directions, who hoisted Balboa's kids onto his shoulders and they called him honorary Uncle So-and-So, who ate standing up at the counter, who knew the couple's sufferings and sorrows. If one of them died, he would be invited to the funeral.

Or was he Janine's lover? There, she'd allowed the name to cross her lips. Could be that this guy and Janine had their own thing going, what with Balboa off the scene so much. Some intense emotion had passed between them, she could see that much at a glance. Who was to say that his wife couldn't lose her head too? Even men who played around, especially those men, liked to think of their wives as long-suffering saints, martyrs, devotees of a broken ideal. Fools, these men. Narcissists. When the cat's away, don't the mice play? But no, that big fellow couldn't be Janine's man on the side. No lover besides she herself would be so brazen as to show up uninvited and unannounced when the other spouse was present.

Showing her derriere hadn't done her any good, though. Had it gotten too big? She worried about the shape of her body, with so much riding on it. Were her breasts too small for him all of a sudden? (The wife definitely had more cleavage, even if she wasn't showing it.) Had he suddenly noticed her resemblance to a teenage boy? Balboa had acted polite as hell—the first time he'd ever treated her politely, and it sure did hurt worse than any of their arguments. Better if he'd just yelled at her to get the fuck out. The way his eyes had sized up her almost naked body—not roaming over it, as usual; instead, flat out harsh and afraid—had made her feel trampy for the first time ever. That look of his had almost rendered her ill. She'd thrown on her cashmere coat, blundered out without taking her leave, like somebody rushing off for an emergency appendectomy, and flown home that selfsame night, gladly paying the extra seventy-five-dollar penalty at the ticket counter to jump on a plane and hurry to Kentucky as fast as she could.

Lisa's date had been going well. Unlike Clay, Mr. X knew how to sport a suit. He wore one every day to the Chicago Board of Trade, so he'd already gone through that period of sartorial adjustment, and the suit fit his body, loose in the right places, snug in the right places. Possibly tailored but not fussy by any means. She liked the way the linen crinkled in his pants when he sat down in the Mexican restaurant. Even though he worked out, he wasn't trying to show off his bulk. She'd had enough bulk to last her for a good long time. Now she wanted something that came in a package. It was nice to get back to men who occasionally considered the state of their hair. No mousse but a respectable cut that accented the facets of his lean, perceptive stockbroker's face. A splash of sensitivity and sideburn without getting feline about it.

She noticed that he had left his cell phone in the car before the meal. Mr. X seemed like the type who would know to turn off his electronic devices in any case, without having to be told, even if he did take one of them in with him when they entered the concert hall later in the evening. After the musicians had tuned up, when management announced over the loudspeaker for all beepers to be hushed for the performance, he would have obeyed in advance. Mr. X had instincts. In the Mexican restaurant, he handled everything just right. Beforehand, he had suggested two or three choices of where to eat, to show that he had given the matter some thought and wasn't simply improvising, but then he had let her select which of these ethnic cuisines she liked best, and she had chosen Mexican.

Before the waiter came, Mr. X leaned intimately over to Lisa, and without being ostentatious, rather with a playful look in his eye, asked her, in warm tones, whether she'd mind if he ordered for both of them. He'd eaten at this place a lot and knew the food pretty well. If she didn't like his pick, she could just order something else. Lisa got off a touch on his daring, on the fact that he wanted to turn her on to something new, that he risked being an old-fashioned gentleman and thereby possibly offending her contemporary woman's sensibility.

At once she replied yes, she'd love for him to order. There was something to be said for a man who knew how to be possessive. When the waiter came, at Mr. X's discreet high sign, Mr. X asked, with good humor, if the establishment had those fantastic pistachio enchiladas, and the waiter, looking delighted, answered, "Why yes, that's our special this evening, in fact, and I highly recommend it. You won't be disappointed."

And they weren't. She loved the pistachio enchiladas every bit as much as Mr. X did, and as she became giddy on the Dos Equis and the atmosphere, she promised on her life to order these same enchiladas again, providing they were available, the next time they— she—they—came to the restaurant. "Yes, the next time *we* come here," he rejoindered, his eyes smiling at her over the napkin bunched in his hands like a prayer cloth. The next time we come.

Then, during the dessert of fried ice cream, as she dipped her spoon down to the silvery cup they were sharing and nibbled, just nibbled, to keep from making her slinky dress bind too tight around the middle, he mentioned her posture. Casually, true, but he wondered aloud whether she'd ever given any thought to her posture. She carried her shoulders a bit stooped. Her back indeed did have a small knot on the right side just beneath the shoulder blade, from sitting at the computer terminal all that day, and she might be compensating ever so slightly, but she had never thought of herself as stooped. Once they arrived at the concert she forgot all about it, dismissed it as a passing, well-intentioned remark, and lost herself in the impeccable adagio. During the intermission, while she lingered under the spell of Vivaldi, he mentioned it a second time. Mr. X said something about "hunched," within earshot of elegant, anonymous people who were blithely sipping cappuccino. And one of the anonymous concertgoers made a sidelong head adjustment to inspect her stance.

Mr. X laid the palm of his hand gently on Lisa's sacrum, the way a lover might do in the privacy of the bedroom right before he slipped her panties off, and he gave her a subtle push to increase the curve of her spine and make her shoulders fall back. His touch revolted her. Mr. X was definitely not going to be slipping her panties off tonight. Which was too bad, because she'd had hopes. But now all she could think about was the throb of the muscle beneath her shoulder blade. It hurt more and more through the second act, as the string quartet plucked and sweated through a spate of pizzicato.

I believe everybody spends a certain amount of time skirting the edges of the law. Whether it's unpaid parking fines, weekend reefer, forging signatures for a busy boss, or taking two Sunday papers out of the newspaper box for the price of one, most everybody is out there flouting codes and statutes. So you set a sort of moving threshold for yourself and others, letting it subtly be known that certain activities will be tolerated by nonenforcement. Apart from corruption and cops on the take, there's simply not the manpower to make good all the time on policing every law in existence. Does that threshold go up over time? I guess that's why, in the end, we're mostly left to policing ourselves, inefficient and unmotivated cops that we are.

I was thinking about this threshold more in relation to myself than Balboa, as I drove Lisa's car, which she had left temporarily with me because I paid for a monthly garage, big enough to hold two cars, as part of my overpriced apartment. It "came with" the apartment, which meant I had to rent it whether I wanted to or not. City parking spaces were expensive, and Lisa wanted time to shop around for the right one for herself, at a good price. She had started looking for a new, smaller apartment, up in Wrigleyville, after it became clear that I wasn't going to ask her to move into mine, or consent to move into hers, and she couldn't afford the exorbitant rent on her Wicker Park place any more than I could on my Belmont one. Without saying so directly, she had given our relationship until February, which was when her lease came up. February had arrived, and she had decided against renewal, both on

43

me and on her place. My garage, however, was still in an open-ended relationship with her, at least until she got resettled, and in any case she had always preferred commuting to her job at the Xerox Building by train. The car, like the cell phone, was mostly reserved for emergencies.

Lisa had instructed me not to drive her SUV under any circumstances, because she could barely afford her young-single-driver's insurance rate as it was. Also she had just had the SUV detailed, and she feared, rightly, that if I drove her vehicle in the city, it was likely to end up with dings and dents caused by my carelessness in choosing street parking spaces. But there I was driving it, without her knowledge and against her wishes, to go meet Janine. For once, I could see over the traffic in front of me.

I wondered whether technically I was stealing Lisa's car—even though it was parked in my garage, and the keys hung on my kitchen cupboard—because she had expressly told me not to drive it. Not that she would have ever pressed charges. On the other hand, the way things had deteriorated between us, you never knew. Her moving threshold might have gone down. I reasoned to myself that this was an emergency, exactly the kind of thing Lisa liked to use her car for.

With one hand, I flipped open Lisa's glove box and took out the cell phone lovingly stashed there. It was an expensive one, almost a work of art, jet black and sleek, contoured to fit my hand, a real self-sufficient piece of equipment, with tiny runic symbols to signal the various modes and functions. She used to call me at the apartment from this very cell phone, one of those considerate little phone calls to let me know she was only five minutes away, to let me experience the thrill of anticipation that she knew how to give me when she wanted to. I loved hearing the traffic noise around her and sensing that she was hurrying toward me in space and time. Feeling a little pang of nostalgia for what was, I hit the redial button, to see what her last call was before she put the automobile into cold storage.

There were two high-pitched rings, and a live male voice answered. Not my machine. "Hello? Hello?" I didn't reply, and he said "Who is this?" with impatience creeping into his voice. I hung up. It was a stupid notion, because now I was wondering whether Lisa used to call this man, whoever he was, before we really started breaking up. As she was hurtling toward me in space, receiver in hand, had she just left him? Better not to think about it. I shoved the phone back into its little crypt, and clicked the door shut.

I parked catty-cornered in the tiny lot across from Rosa's, taking up two coveted spaces, so I could protect Lisa's car from all manner of harm. I knew somebody would yell at me about it when I came out but better to be cursed by a stranger than by someone I knew. Directly across from Rosa's, the Iglesia Evangelica Puerta del Cielo, Incorporated, Pastors Luis and Donna Gutierrez, was in full service. It was a humble storefront, probably used to be a hardware store, freshly painted white to suggest something churchlike. Inside, tambourines, cymbals, an electric guitar, and even a trombone were blasting a joyful noise unto the Lord. More or less the same music you might hear at Rosa's: syncopated, electrified, rhythmic, a good strong backbeat. Just a different relationship to the question of sin. I crossed the street and entered Rosa's.

It was early, only about nine-thirty, making me one of the first customers. Melvin Taylor was mucking around onstage with a studio musician who sat in sometimes, an Asian guy with a ponytail, good guitarist, played all styles with equal ease. I couldn't think of his name, but I'd heard him before. He was trying to get the sound system adjusted. Melvin knew me; he waved and threw a couple of practice guitar licks my way, slicing them off and fanning them toward me with his ax, by way of greeting. Melvin must be getting on into his forties, but he still looked nineteen. His smooth skin belied the life he had led. I wished I could say the same. He closed his eyes to savor the decaying note as it glided around the room. Sweetness, sweetness.

Rosa, with her thick eyeglass lenses, close-cropped and grizzled hair, denim jacket, somebody's badass grandma, smoked the stub of a Camel behind the bar, as always, while cleaning off sticky bottles with a towel. She didn't say hello, just set me up a complimentary shot of grappa. One time a friend of mine went to Italy, and I asked him to bring me back a bottle of good grappa, which I had never tasted myself and brought it in as a present for Rosa. It must have been good. Ever since then, I always got spotted a shot, or two, or three, of her rough house brand, which she made herself.

"You want some risotto?" Once in a while, she cooked up a

dish, when she felt like it, and served it to regular customers, also on the house. The last thing my gut needed at that moment was the combination of homemade grape absinthe and semiraw rice, but of course I said yes, and she heaped out a steaming glob from an aluminum pot set on a hot plate. The ash on her cigarette had grown perilously long, as she never took it out of her mouth, and I was afraid the ash would drop into my risotto, but miraculously it didn't. Melvin, warming up his vocal cords, crooned to Rosa in twelve-bar form, mock seductive, to set him up a glass of cold brew, promising all sorts of lascivious favors in return, and she stared him down as she drew him a draft from the tap, telling me calmly that Melvin was a hopeless cause, that she'd tried to reform him many times with no result, that she was too old for this kind of licentious taking of liberties.

She loved Melvin, she loved all her blues boys, and at best she was breaking even on the club. She didn't do it for the money. There was an unspoken ethos at Rosa's, that in spite of its location in a bad part of town, there wasn't to be rough behavior of any sort, the word had gotten around long since that Rosa's was the mellow club, not a place for bravado or kicking ass or coming in so hopped up you had to start something with somebody. I'd never seen a fight break out in this room. The atmosphere just wouldn't permit it. You could bring together the exact same musicians and fans at another club, and they'd be ripping one another's heads off, but stepping in here threw a magic spell over them. They understood then that the blues were meant to heal your pain, not intensify it.

I wished that I had brought Balboa here last night, when we were out cruising the West Side anyway, and he'd started to get sad. I think Sugar Blue was even playing at the exact moment Balboa dropped me at the el. We would have stayed after hours, feasting on a steaming plate of penne pasta that Rosa produced out of nowhere. Listening to those harmonious harp riffs would have made him believe that things were going to work out between him and Janine, that peace and *chi* were in the house to stay.

I migrated over to a table. The place was almost all empty, so I had my pick. I sat right next to the stage, too close to the speakers, where the music would wash over me and I'd have a whir nagging in my ear all tomorrow. Melvin started a little Hendrix homage, just to get in the groove, improbably eking art out of a fuzz pedal. They said he performed to sold-out amphitheaters in Europe. But he played with the same intensity for seventeen or eighteen people who had paid a five-dollar cover to get in here. Right then, it was pretty much just me; at least I was the only one who appeared to be actively listening. He didn't care. Maybe he sensed that I was a little low and was going to try to bounce me out of my mood. Halfway into a chugging, deliberately foot-dragging cover of "Crosstown Traffic," Janine appeared.

She was put together, in a deep-blue batik dress, knee length, conservative and hip at the same time. The sorority-girl flip had gradually given way, over time, to the tapered, shorn locks of the gainfully employed society matron, with a few downy wisps at the crown, to recall that recently departed girlish youth. She looked like the perfect dinner guest, after a hard week of giving leukemia treatments to children, though I knew the big dinners and parties had always been Balboa's bailiwick. Janine was fine, in every sense of that word, except for the suspicious-looking bandage on her hand, still there from the air-bag accident.

I moved to another table, farther from the music, in deference to Janine. Whatever it was she wanted from me, I was eager to come to an understanding with her as soon as possible, so I could flee the room containing this beautiful, stern, fearsome princess, one who in another place and time, with a score of silver bracelets wrapped tightly around her elongated throat, would be sending disobedient subjects to their deaths without any reprisal, because her word would be law.

She ordered cognac and, without giving me time for pleasantries, started right in.

"Balboa and I had a terrible fight. I assume that's no news to you."

"I've got to say, Janine, this isn't like you to talk about your business. You're upset, and you might want to take a day to think things over before you disclose." I wasn't just being nice by saying this. No one truly knew what went on inside a couple's relationship besides those two people themselves. That was why I tried not to get involved in the domestic squabbles of couples I knew. Later on, if they didn't separate, they eventually forgave each other, but they never forgave you for interfering. That negative emotion they felt toward each other was so powerful, so potentially lethal, that they were both eager to transfer it to someone else, to find a fall guy, so they could go on loving and fighting. There was no way for me to really understand what lengths, or depths, Janine and Balboa had gone to together.

Besides, she was the epitome of every woman who had ever misunderstood my intentions, every woman who had given me sleepless nights trying in vain to get behind her reasons, every woman who had taken my measure and found me lacking. I wanted to buy her a drink and send her on her way, no questions asked.

"You know it all anyway, Clay. We both just pretend like you don't."

"I may not know as much as you think I do. I only don't want you to say anything you might regret later."

"Things are too far gone for me to worry about what you know and don't know."

I sighed. "Lay it on me, then."

"As you know, I wasn't in the mingling mood the other night."

"I picked up on that. Any special reason?"

The batik patterns in her dress rippled like foam on water as she readjusted her legs under the table. "I know how his crowd thinks of me. I'm 'difficult.' I'm a 'bitch.' There's no love lost between me and them."

"If you say so. I don't go to those parties."

"I know you don't. Maybe that's why I think I can talk to you. You don't fake me, and I don't fake you."

"I didn't know we were that intimate."

"I didn't say we were intimate."

Rosa brought the cognac and shot me a covert quizzical look, which I didn't allow myself to acknowledge. Janine's presence was making her uncomfortable, and she was feeling a little protective of me. Janine started to search in her purse, because she thought Rosa was waiting for money, and she wanted to get rid of her as soon as possible. I held up my hand. "Put it on my tab, Rosa." I never knew how much my tab actually was, I just made payments on it, giving Rosa fifty or sixty dollars every once in a while. I actually don't think she knew how much it was either.

"Okay." She withdrew, and we wouldn't see any more of her until I gave her a wave of the hand. Rosa was discreet. She was the one who Janine actually ought to have been telling her troubles to.

Melvin had wandered over into another song, and he let his Asian pal take the lead, backing him up with little piercing flicks of his fingers. The Asian guy's coal-black ponytail was flipping all around. His voice wasn't good but I liked it. *Come cry about that spoonful. Some die about that spoonful.*

"There are certain facts in a marriage that are murder to talk about. That you don't want to share with anybody on the outside."

"There's a good reason for that."

"When one of the two, say, is doing something behind the other one's back."

"Please don't make me hear this."

"And then, when it comes to the other one's attention, she tries to ignore the evidence, to deny it, because, first of all, she doesn't want to believe her husband would be capable of anything like that. Besides, as soon as she stops denying it, she knows her whole world is going to come crashing down. Do you understand what I'm trying to say?"

"Listen, whatever goes on in you-all's love life—"

"What?" She gave me a baffled look.

"Well, your sex life—"

"I wasn't talking about our sex life. I certainly wouldn't discuss that with you, or anybody else. Why did you bring it up? Has Balboa been telling you stories?"

"No. I'm sorry. What are we talking about?"

"Money."

"Money?"

"I found a stash of envelopes. From the way they'd been hidden away, in the bottom of a tackle box, I'll admit that at first I thought they were love letters. Now I wish they had been."

I played out the image of a jealous Janine, looking for incriminating correspondence, rifling through Balboa's possessions, finding the tackle box. Did she fling the top rack across the room, scattering the hooks and sinkers and flies, like so much flotsam, or did she carefully replace the rack? And why did her hair smell so damn good, so purple, so blue, so black, even in this smoky bar?

"What was in the envelopes?"

"Bank statements. I'm going to cut to the chase, because there's no pretty way to say this. Balboa has run through our savings and taken on a huge debt. He's got all kinds of business dealings I knew nothing about. I knew he dabbled, he always has some big new idea. I gave up on curing him of that malady a long time ago. But he has bank accounts and credit lines that I never knew existed. All of them currently overdrawn. That castle we live in has a second mortgage. I don't know how he managed that one, because it's in both our names."

"Shit."

"Yes, deep."

"And me? You think I have something to do with this?"

"No, I don't. If I did, I wouldn't have bothered to meet with you, as upset as I am right now. I want you to go find him. I don't know if he has any sense left, but if he doesn't, somebody has got to talk some sense back into him, talk him down, get him back here so we can straighten this out."

"Are you sure you want him back?"

"That's a different issue. Right now, I have to have him back, before we collapse and all this ends up in the papers. He's not going to destroy my life. I'm not declaring bankruptcy, either. I'll work double shifts before I'll let that happen. If he can get a handle on himself, we're two M.D.'s, we have skills and earning power, we can dig out of this hole, come to an arrangement with our creditors, work something out. I'm not going to panic. That's not my style."

"You think he panicked?"

"Yes, I do."

"What about a private detective?"

"I'm not talking about simply finding his whereabouts. He'll surface sooner or later. He's acted stupidly, but as far as I can see, he hasn't done anything illegal. As far as anybody else is concerned, Balboa is just on another one of his little business trips. Somebody has to go who can reason with him once he finds him. If Balboa finds out I've used a private detective, there's no telling where he'll go. Out of the country, halfway around the world."

"I sympathize with what's going on. But why should I go after Balboa? He's not my husband. You think I don't have a lot of problems right now, that I can afford to go off and scour the country for him? I just broke off with Lisa. My boxing career is on the skids. I'm looking to pay next month's rent. Besides, he could be anywhere, the way he is. I have nothing to go on."

"It may not be easy."

"And you don't even like me, do you? Because we're being all candid and everything, I might as well ask you that question."

"No, not much. You rub me the wrong way."

"So why are you asking me to help you out?"

"Because you're not doing it for me. I'd never ask you to do anything solely on my behalf, because you and me, we don't click. But you're his friend. He's in a dangerous spot. The two of you have some—unusual bond."

"I'm not sure that's so."

"You know it's so. Like I said, let's not fake each other. He's eight miles high, and there's only one person on this earth that has a hope of talking him down. That person happens to be you. I don't like that fact, but I am willing to acknowledge it."

"It sounds good, I'm flattered, but you're exaggerating."

"I have no desire to flatter you, believe me. Clay, do you have a daughter? I believe Balboa said that you were married at one time."

"I wasn't married for long. But yes, I have a daughter."

"Well, as you know, I have a daughter. And I have a son. Both small. Both beautiful. And yes, privileged in a way that Balboa never was. I've arranged it that way. They don't go around bleeding inside the way he always has, no matter how much money he makes, or how hard I love him, or how many of his friends and colleagues tell him he's the man. He's got charisma, I'll grant him that. It landed me. But believe me, Balboa is an emotional black hole most people step into at their own peril. You can disappear in there. Now, my children take certain things for granted about the way they live, which is just fine with me. And they don't know it, but the wide world is right about to cave in on them, because their father, who has reached the pinnacle and has everything in the world he needs to be happy, couldn't leave well enough alone. That cave-in doesn't have to happen, but it might happen anyway. Except for one thing."

"What's that?"

"I'm not about to let it happen."

"Yeah, okay. All right. I'll see what I can find out."

"I'm grateful. I'm not just saying that. I don't give lip service. I'm giving you your due. If I ever get out of this money hole, I'll pay you whatever you ask for your trouble."

"I'm not interested in your money."

"That's for you to decide. You stepped into Balboa's black hole for your own reasons. I made up my mind on the way over that I wasn't going to condescend to you. I'd just lay the situation out there, and see how you reacted."

"I guess I said yes."

She took one more sip of her Hennessy and stood to leave. "Let me know how to stay in touch with you in case I get any more information. Thank you for the drink." Then she was gone, without any prolonged good-byes. Her glass, halfway full, sat on her side of the table, still bearing a faint lipstick mark. I picked up the glass, put my lips on the mark, and drank down the rest.

Rosa looked relieved to have Janine out from underfoot. She came right away from behind the bar to remove the now-empty glass and wipe down the table. Only one other table, in the back, was occupied by a couple—she with a peroxide buzz cut and an eyebrow ring, he with dreadlocks and dungarees. The way he lounged with a faint smirk and she hung on him, her attitude both willowy and tough, he had to be an off-duty musician. There was no dearth of tattoos between them. Melvin was working hard for the three of us, his head now bobbing, now lolling. He had the slow hand tonight. The honeydripper. Lots of volume, but he wanted to luxuriate in his pain without hurrying it. *Bad, bad whiskey, made me lose my happy home.*

I stood up to leave, clearing my own plate and glass, like a child in his mother's kitchen. I took the dishes to the bar, and slid them across to Rosa, who stood erect at her sentry post. I told her I'd settle up with her next time, if that was all right. She gave me a flinty, sympathetic gaze. "Of course it's all right. Just make sure there's a next time."

Naturally, when I returned to Lisa's SUV, someone had put a dent in the driver's-side door.

When he came out to the pool the next day, to relax and scan the real-estate section, fronds and thistles floated in its low water, swatches of pine needles, not skimmed off, and not a soul in sight. Raggedy-ass pool. At two fifty a night. He had slept late and skipped the complimentary breakfast. Gusts of wind blew sand through the shrubbery and into his face. Somebody's lap dog, well cared for, maybe the hotel owner's, hopped onto the chaise longue next to his, finding shelter, now looking expectant. He fed it the Godiva mint the turn-down service had left on his pillow, that he'd never gotten around to eating. She was used to nice things, delicacies, you could tell.

Yesterday's sun had fizzed away into the atmosphere, leaving a bleak wake. Temporary but real. His sinuses ached. Whitecaps tossed and scudded, frothy yet somehow still contained, as if uncertain whether to make a full-out assault on the beach. One bad-weather day and everybody scattered to the four winds. At the end of the pool area, a peanut-brittle beach wall looked like you could knock it down with a single kick. The sand beyond the beach wall was clumpy, like a moldering cake. The sky, pale blue, clouds thin as gruel, held a sliver of daytime moon, its edges dewy and indistinct. Everything looked soft and ready to give way, a diorama made of soapstone.

With a sigh, he set the paper down. He remembered what it was like to be here during hurricane season. It came upon him why he had always resisted moving to south Florida for them to be closer to Janine's parents, even though she'd been keen on that idea for a while, after the kids were born. Shuttered windows, plywood hammered into storefronts with ten-penny nails. Palm fronds flung at random like a scattered deck of cards. You sat around inside as though you were in a fallout shelter, all light blocked out. In the coastal areas, the hotel staff closed the sun umbrellas, dragged the furniture indoors, went from talking about minibars to millibars, pressure nine thirty-four, as if saying those words gave you some authority over what was going on, as if there were anything to do except get the hell out as fast as you could and hope you wouldn't get hammered too hard. There was no way he could invest in property here, shaky as his finances were. What had he been thinking? A bucket of reality poured over his head, and he had to sit there sopping wet while it evaporated. Another of his dumbass ideas gone to vapor. He really had believed a couple of hotels might present a pathway out. What he purchased one day, if he could even find the capital, could be obliterated the next. That was always happening in these coastal areas. You barely got the roof on and a hurricane blew it off like a champagne cork, only there was nothing to celebrate. You filed several million in insurance claims and waited for the place to be declared a disaster area.

He couldn't return to face Janine empty-handed. Less than empty. Too much shit had become too real between them. There was a time when she'd been softer, more giving. Yes, he recalled. Not so long ago. Her, not so sculpted, not so polished to a mineral gloss by their experiences together. Before Chance and Viola came, before motherhood took up all the extra space for forgiveness in her. Before the thing with him having to leave Edgewater Hospital, not by choice. And what came after—well, he didn't want to think about that right now. He'd been able to get the record expunged, that much power he still possessed. Nobody but him had a copy of that psychological profile. And that he carried on his person as if it were his driver's license and he expected to get stopped at any moment, not for Driving While Black (no, he'd been through that nonsense already and given the cop a tongue-lashing and reported the incident to his cousin the alderman), but stopped to have his papers checked to document his mental competence. He wasn't sure why he didn't destroy the last surviving copy of the profile. And he knew Janine would never say nothing to nobody, because she wanted people to know about the incident even less than he did.

Why had he ever let himself check into the hospital? It was a mistake. A temporary freak-out. In three days, he'd checked back out. They'd let him, because it was voluntary. Almost hustled him out-of-doors, in fact. Only he had to sign a form that said he couldn't buy firearms for a period of five years afterward or some such nonsense. At least he'd kept his wits enough to choose a hospital in a different city. A doc in Gary who owed him a favor, a brother, and they'd smoked blunt together. When you knew people from back when, they were less likely to pull rank on you or run tattling. In and out, just two nights, almost as if it had never happened. He agreed to go to one group session, to show his good faith, that he wasn't simply taking up space.

Only he didn't say a word during that rap session. Others talked. Guy with long wispy hair and a natural tonsure, could have been forty, could have been ninety, looked at the floor a lot, so much flak and static in his mind he could barely stutter out his most immediate thoughts, much less all that homicidal dirt churning in the sudsy washing machine of his mind. Had his hand inside his coat so much Balboa thought maybe he was hiding a pet hamster in there that he didn't want anybody else to see. Or a pistol.

A young boy, eighteen or so, looked more like twelve, white kid with serious logorrhea, literally talking for his life, describing over and over what it's like to sit in a garage with the engine on and the carbon monoxide building, how you could feel yourself lose consciousness, the nerve endings starting to sing and sting as you began to die. Only the boy hadn't died, after three different tries. More lives than in a fucking fable. Killed off a lot of brain cells is all. All-American, a face so normal it was paranormal. Next, a woman, quiet, suburban, bones clattering softly like blanketed wind chimes underneath her Donna Karan slacks, knew how to put on makeup right, haggard upscale housewife, who told how she would sit in the walk-in cedar closet for a whole day at a time, as if she expected a giant moth attack, soundproof shelter, her overtaken by periodic shrieking fits, and when she came out, she'd get on the phone and buy fifty thousand dollars worth of kitchenware. All this told almost in a whisper, where you had to lean forward to catch the words. Quiet and polite as she was, she'd troubled him most.

The detox ward was right down the hall from theirs, and you

could hear guys yelling and sobbing and calling on Jesus or Mama or some ex-girlfriend all night long as they dried out. It occurred to him that he might know some of them.

Janine never referred to those lost three days. Balboa came back home and went to work at his newest job on the fourth day, raised from the dead, because he couldn't afford to lie around in bed the way people were supposed to when they felt like he did at that time. Everybody at the workplace greeted him and asked him how his weekend had been. Nobody noticed anything different. That's how observant they were. His head wasn't shaved or anything. He answered fine, long weekend was all, and they asked him if he'd gone anywhere special. Yeah, I took a little trip. Three days, two nights, package deal. Pleasure trip to Gary. They laughed at the idea of anybody going to relax in Gary. Called him a wit. Yes, sir, he thought. Nitwit. Head trip. Expensive. Only I don't recommend it.

That first night back he and Janine ate lobster bisque and drank a bottle of Pinot. She'd sent the cook home for the night and prepared the meal herself, her mama's recipe. Chance, their son, looked like he was headed for orthodontia, she said. Viola had outgrown that pair of white dress shoes when she'd only worn them three times. They were pinching her toes. That children's shoe store, for what they charged, ought to have a trade-in program, the way you'd do with a car. Whatever happened, you simply went on to the next thing, the next size, the next phase. Easter followed Valentine's Day. She had patients, children, a lot sicker than he. He was aware of that fact. Kids walking around with an IV chemo-drip stand for a playmate.

He knew she couldn't live with a man who couldn't fulfill his responsibilities. That was her only proviso. That night in bed, after he returned from the lost weekend, she acted strangely tender and solicitous. The kids had been triaged off somewhere; she'd no doubt sent them over to a relative for the night. She put on the baby doll she knew he liked best, the deep blue one. Deeper than the night sky in Haiti. They kissed with a lot of tongue. She went down on him, without him asking for it. And he knew she didn't really like to do that much. When he was about to come, and tried to pull her up to his level, she brushed his hands away, making clear that she wanted him to come in her mouth. So he did. Afterward, she slipped downstairs and fetched a pint of chocolate-mint ice cream out of the freezer, for them to eat straight from the carton in bed with a single spoon they shared. It was a temporary return to the days when they were dating. Then she lay under the blanket naked with him, her breasts brushing his back, until they both got drowsy and drifted off to sleep.

Maybe her ignoring certain stuff was her way of saying that everything would be all right, that they would survive, even thrive, one way or another. Realism. She had built that steady family life for them brick by brick, he had to grant her that. Didn't overreact. Didn't need to act flamboyant. Didn't divorce him over crazy, erratic, reckless behavior that she deemed inconsequential. She'd made her choice, and she was going to stick by it. If nothing else, the outward forms would remain intact, a fortress mighty as that house they lived in, a fortress solid enough to withstand anything.

S.B. was admitted to the Beachfront Psychiatric Institute in Gary, Indiana, at 11:14 A.M. on Friday, May 26. The odor of smelts could be detected wafting across the hard-packed lake sands, dusky gray and besmirched, because of a heat inversion overwarming the lake water's temperature, resulting in a massive die-off of the smelts. They floated on their sides and washed ashore in large numbers, where they were left to rot until the underfunded city service crews of Gary could get around to collecting them. As a result, it was impossible to take the restless nonlockup habitués of the BPI for their usual chaperoned constitutional along the beach without upsetting the already hyperactive gag reflexes most of them had developed from the administering of vitamins, medications, and herbal supplements.

After a nonalcoholic Mai Tai by way of greeting, S.B. (aka Scrofulous Brother, aka Balboa Trafalgar) was administered the Delphos-Schoenberg Psychiatric Evaluation (revised version, lawsuit pending) by a duo of resentful, underpaid interns who hadn't gotten enough sleep in weeks and didn't care one bit for S.B.'s uppity attitude. In the words of the incarcerated, he seemed to feel he "didn't belong here."

We, the undersigned, attempted to determine objectively S.B.'s conscious and preconscious states of mind, to assess the scope of his suffering, and to recommend a course of appropriate action and proper treatment. After numerous entreaties, ten mg. of diazepam, and the threat of eviction, the subject agreed to being administered the test. A handsome and articulate subject, if a little too big for his britches and puffy around the eyes, S.B. exhibited evidence of a hypotrophied superego mildly redolent of garlic. (The possibility that this might have been the result of Mexican food was also taken into account.)

He scored unusually low on the Sampson-Bizet instrument for someone of his apparent intellect. S.B. was unable, for instance, to follow a pair of parallel lines out to infinity without anxiety, insisting always on crossing the lines at some point in his mental traversal of the model solar system we suspended from the ceiling as a point of reference. He would lose his focus usually around Saturn (the melancholy planet) and complained frequently and obnoxiously that "his neck was getting stiff" from looking at the ceiling. Likewise, when instructed to articulate the repeating decimal .333333 in a strong, resolute voice, S.B. would become unusually fatigued after only several hundred repetitions of the word "three." He then let it be known, in an irritable tone, that he was "tired of saying the same goddamned number over and over." The combination of open-endedness and precision of the diagnostic instrument appeared to unnerve him. Eventually, he modulated into a "Black Power" modulation of the word "three" into "free," repeating this syllable with increasing urgency and accompanying hand gestures.

Those administering the test interpreted his hypersensitivity as a dangerous habituation to the pseudosecurity of enclosure, traceable back to his forced boyhood confinement in a housing project. He has made obvious subsequent attempts to overcompensate by later attending medical school, marrying well, participating in civic and political activities, and otherwise living a "normal" life. This illusion of having overcome all meaningful obstacles through professional advancement has left a noticeable accumulation of lymphatic tissue around the thymus gland, an overproduction of T-cells, and a variable resilience within the immune system. S.B. often felt compelled to remind those giving the test that he was "one of them" (i.e., a "doctor").

His scarcely latent hostilities toward his "subordinates" (i.e., those interns charged with conducting the evaluation) can be counted as a subliminal eruption of a schizoid (in S.B.'s word, "scherzo") indifference to the meaningfulness of psychiatric evaluations in general and to the usefulness of psychotropic drugs in particular, which he insisted on referring to by the neologism "placebotomy." He was only induced to begin a course of Wellbutrin under duress and insisted he would discontinue taking the medication, to put himself in noncompliance, at the first opportunity.

We find it curious and worthy of remarking upon that a trained medical doctor, who himself has written innumerable prescriptions, would exhibit such overt hostility for the cousin branch of his chosen profession. It should also go on the record that his urine tested positive for cannabis. More than once we held our corporate tongue at the temptation to cry out "Physician, heal thyself" and to bounce him out of the facility on his ear.

Indeed, S.B. used his capacity for verbal quips in an aggressive fashion (viz., "scherzo," above), to set up a mocking, parodic counterdiscourse to the objective evaluation when we, the undersigned, attempted to "meet him on his own ground" and to establish rapport by employing the jargon of our profession and trusting in his intelligence to decipher remarks that are normally cryptic to our other patients. This ruse of equality had an adverse effect on the subject. "Ego building," in his parlance, became "Lego building." Our desire to probe into preconscious reflexes was transformed, in S.B.'s rendering, into "Precocious Rolex," a nickname he applied to himself, in a kind of "Moses Supposes" ditty or "hip-hop harangue" (again, the subject's words) that S.B. invented on the spot.

Admittedly, there was a strange, haunting, syncopated beauty to the song he sang a cappella in the examination room and to his improvised ability to rhyme, in "rapping" fashion, "Rolex" with "Windex," *"bounced checks," "bad hex," and other words and phrases we neglected to write down and can no longer call to mind. Psychiatric staff and patients from other areas gathered in the room to listen "like flies to shit" (again, the attribution is to S.B.). This extemporaneous musical sally convinced us of a native creativity that was impressive, if childish, crude, and designed to gain attention.*

In our view, S.B. is crippled by an almost delusional need to "be loved." His constant acting out demonstrates that he will stop at nothing to achieve this peculiar goal. Where one would expect him to objectify his existential situation, thus creating a protective mechanism more suitable for one who began his days in such an economically and emotionally starved environment, and for one who has "reached his station in life," S.B. rather exhibits recklessness, a disregard for the consequences of his flamboyance, a tendency to smart off, and, not least, a confusing proclivity for letting his ego boundaries dissolve, promiscuously merging with those of others (viz., his oft-repeated refrain to his interlocutors, "I am you").

S.B. clearly enjoys a privileged status within the BPI, as can be attested to by a breezy conversation we observed with one of the senior psychiatrists on staff, whom he seems to have convinced that he is, indeed, "one of us." This fallacious in-group assumption makes it wellnigh impossible to rehabilitate the subject. Having prescribed an antidepressant, we feel we have done our duty. Not having the stamina to keep up with S.B., nor adequate protocolar means to subdue him to the appropriate level, our professional recommendation is that he be released from this institution within a period of forty-eight hours.

A man came into a monastery, and declared to the head monk his desire to join its company. He had grown weary of the ways of the world, and sought another form of living. The head monk answered, "That is all well and good, and we are prepared to accept you, but you should first be warned that you may find our fellowship boring after a time. Most of what we do is to copy out Bibles by hand. Each monk has a handwritten copy of the Bible, from which he produces another. That is how we support our order."

The man reflected on this fact, then replied to the head monk, "I'm not worried about whether or not this vocation will entertain me. I've had more than enough entertainment to suit me. But has it ever occurred to you to check the primary source?"

"Primary source?"

"I mean the original Bible in your possession, the one that has served as a master for all the other copies and the copies of those copies. Suppose there are errors of transcription in the first copies made from it, the ones that the monks are using? Then your scribes are copying out the same mistakes, day after day, month after month, perhaps compounding them."

"I don't think that is possible," the head monk replied. "We are careful, mindful, and diligent men."

"I do not doubt your word, holy brother. Yet the Bible is the sole text for all the mores and beliefs of yourself and your scribes. It is your creed. I don't mean to sound disobedient or provocative, as I have only just arrived and have no right to instruct anyone about anything. I hope you won't think me impertinent. The thought simply occurred to me as we were talking."

"Not at all," the head monk grumbled. "Run along and copy. And don't forget to take your time."

At first, the head monk dismissed the man's question; it even annoyed him. But as time went on, and the man, like all the other monks, settled into his task as a copyist, the question got the better of the head monk, so that he couldn't sleep. The specter of possible errors, overseen by him, haunted his mind. Though he had never inspected them carefully, it was possible that some of the master copies used by the monks were in fact defective. Late one night, as all the brethren except himself slumbered, he stole down into the monastery's catacombs, down, down through passageways until he reached a room behind them, where he faintly remembered some very old and musty tomes were stored. He couldn't say for sure where the original Bible was or whether it even still existed. The question had never come up, and if he knew its location, he'd forgotten it with the passage of the years.

The monastery didn't really have a proper archive. This recondite and forgotten corner, a poor excuse for a library that no one ever visited, was as close as this infinitesimal order came to keeping a recorded history of themselves. The tomes in question had been deemed of little consequence, abstruse commentaries, records of deaths, and lists of agricultural products, all neglected. To tell the truth, this was not an intellectual order, not a brotherhood of readers. They only had the one Book, and they'd already read that one long since—well, at least most of them had. Now they just copied it out, no longer even seeing the words before them so much as the shape of the letters.

In the flickering lamplight, the head monk perused now one shelf, now another, almost overcome by the eggy smell of mold. He had to hold the hem of his robe over his mouth to continue scanning the hardbound titles, many of the legends almost effaced. These allergy-inducing texts should have been burned long ago, he reflected, on grounds of good health alone. Then he wouldn't have had to trouble himself with them now. He resolved to build a wood fire in the common-room hearth at the earliest opportunity, haul these texts upstairs, and engage in a deeply satisfying book burning. After so much copying, for so long, he had to admit he sometimes fought an impulsive desire to burn books, especially sacred ones. In particular the One that the monks themselves were reproducing, day after day. As chilly as the rooms of the monastery usually stayed, he didn't think any of the monks would object to a roaring fire of oak logs, even if moldy books and manuscripts were used to stoke it. As he hatched his plan, however, the head monk's hand fell upon a bundle of manuscripts that had the conspicuous look of a source text. Fingering their edges, he knew he would have to look them over.

Spreading the documents on an oaken table, he lingered over them, gingerly turning the pages, which threatened to break apart at his touch. At length, he came upon a passage that he read over and over, his eyes peering ever harder. As he read, he began to weep, first softly and then with abandon, a stray tear or two falling to further moisten the crumbling papyrus. Climbing the stairs out of the archives and out of the catacombs, wheezing, still breathing the spores of the dank room, he rang the sturdy bell that usually called the monks together for matins. He rang and rang until every last brother was awake and assembled in the common room.

"What is the meaning of this?" one of the head monk's older, longtime subordinates took it upon himself to say on behalf of the disgruntled many. "Our labors before God don't begin for another two hours, and you have robbed us of those two hours of precious sleep. Even he rested on the seventh day. We may be monks, but we're not slaves. Sleeping is one of the few pleasures allowed to us in a life made up of careful deprivations. We don't engage in drunken revelry, and none of us has known a woman since the day we entered the confines of this monastery. We sleep alone, nursing our wounds and trying to slake our fatigue. I need my rest. My wrist is terribly inflamed from the copying I've done this month."

There was a restless murmur among the other monks, as if to suggest that their wrists were inflamed also, and not only from copying out manuscripts.

The head monk held up his hand for silence. "All that is about to change."

"I beg your pardon?"

"We've made a grievous error," the head monk said in a grave voice. "I've been poring over the original manuscript of the Bible we've been copying out year after year."

"And?"

"And we got one crucial little word wrong. The original text says 'celebrate.'"

When I went down to pick up my car in Hyde Park, I spied Balboa's Audi, which he had left behind, sitting at the curb. The Audi's blue-black surface gleamed in the nineteenth-century lamplight. Balboa was always going on about how we had "sympathy of mind," but I had no clue where to start looking. I could barely read my own mind, much less his. He must have been in a state when he got out of the Audi, because he'd left it unlocked, when all he had to do was press the remote gadget on his keyring to make that whoop-whoop sound. I slipped in behind the wheel, as if that would help me think. The street was dead quiet, except for a couple of starlings crashing around in the branches of a tree overhead. The leather seats smelled fragrant as always, mixed with the subtle aftertaste of the marijuana we had smoked. His cell phone lay on the passenger seat, untouched. My hand reached out for it, then drew back, as if sensing the heat of a plugged-in iron. I'd already been burned once that week. Still, my curiosity got the better of me. What was his last call?

No crime had been committed, as far as anyone knew. All the same, I groped under the driver's seat for the box of disposable surgical gloves Balboa carried around with him the same way other people do a box of Kleenex. Slipping out two, I pulled them tight over my hands. I picked the phone up, felt its heft, pressed the power button, and hit REDIAL. Eleven little high-speed blips and a brief pause. Long distance. To somewhere. It rang twice. "Hello?" A woman's voice. I couldn't be sure, but it sounded like Chaka Khan, whatever her name was, the one who'd asked where the ladies' room was. Or maybe I just wanted it to be her. The display showed a 606 area code. Central Kentucky. What had he said her name was? It lingered on the tip of my tongue. If only I could ask Janine. She might know the woman's name, if she'd only admit to herself that she did. She probably had a hard time saying it out loud. Didn't Balboa call her Carmen? I took a chance. "Carmen?"

"This is Carmela, if that's who you mean. Who is this? The toreador?"

"Sorry. I mean, I have the wrong . . . I was looking for Carmen." I hung up. Now at least I knew she'd been called not long before he left town. I wrote the number down. I'd call her back when I got to Lexington, if I could get up my nerve, and if I could forget that image of her mincing up the long flight of stairs.

Balboa's money problems were real enough, but I couldn't help believing that there was a woman involved in his disappearance. That could just be me, but it seems like in the end, it's always about a woman. I couldn't fight the irresistible urge to go to Lexington, whether that led me to him or not.

The day before I left Chicago, I stopped in to pick up a check from Smitty, the manager of the Mid-Town Gym, and let him know I was going to take at least a couple of weeks off sparring and go on vacation. Smitty was repairing a glove, breaking thread off in his teeth like a seamstress working on a daughter's Halloween costume. He was frugal and always said that boxing gloves don't grow on trees, as if any of us thought they really did.

"All right, Clay." He didn't look up from his task.

"What do you mean, all right?" I knew from his tone of voice that it wasn't all right—it was the opposite of all right.

"Nothing. Have a good trip." He spit the thread out of his mouth like frayed dental floss. Smitty always had this slightly disappointed look, only you didn't know whether it was with life in general or you in particular.

"Smitty, I know you've got something to say to me. Let's get it over with, because I have to go pack."

"Go pack, then." He waved me off with his hands, big gestures, as if I was in the cockpit of a fighter jet, on a runway, ready to fly a crucial mission, and he had to gesticulate large from the tarmac for me not to make any fatal mistakes.

"You want me to stay here longer, for some reason. But I can't. I didn't leave you in the lurch, right?"

"Clay, you always been good to me. Nobody as dependable as Clay, I always say that around the gym. Never leaves me in the lurch. Ask around and see if I don't always say that." He worried the rip in the boxing glove with a thick needle that looked like it could sew canvas tents. In vain, because the leather itself was terminally ragged. The glove was done for. Like the scar in a boxer's flesh, where he keeps getting hit in the same place, the one his opponents have been coached to go for, and that scar is always going to break open, no matter how many times you stitch it back.

He looked up at me slantwise through his bifocals, a half-blind shoemaker who has spent too many nights working by candlelight because the elves never showed up.

"You're trying to talk me into something. As usual. But I don't know what it is yet."

"I was gonna call you today. I need you for a little project. A moneymaker."

I had so little cash in my pocket that of course he got a stranglehold on my attention. "How much money?"

"Ten thousand dollars. That's just your cut."

"I won't be gone long, Smitty. That is a load of money. And what do I have to do to earn this princely sum?"

"An exhibition bout with an opponent."

"Namely?"

"Tadeusz Virkowicz."

"Well, I—shit. I wish you'd said a different name. I can't do that."

"What?"

"I promised Balboa I wouldn't spar with Tadeusz anymore. For health reasons."

"He's got nothing to do with this. You let me talk to Balboa. I'll get him on the phone right now."

"Actually, you can't, because he's—on a business trip."

"And he doesn't have a phone?"

"I don't know; he's in—Haiti or somewhere. Take it up with him when he comes back. But anyway, you know how Tadeusz hits, and Balboa has threatened to stop working on my banged-up body if I don't leave off that particular gig. My shoulder has been hurting like hell. And I can't afford another doctor. Balboa's rates are too good."

"Don't give me that. You're good at taking punishment. Too good, in my opinion. I've never heard you complain about physical pain up until now. Are you afraid of him? You seem very jumpy, all of a sudden. You losing your nerve?"

"I'm not feeling too good today and yesterday, Smitty. Let me think about your offer."

"I'm talking about ten thousand dollars. To spar. You think that's going to come around ever again for the likes of you?"

"Let me think about it and call you in a couple of days."

"The minimum. You always got the minimum. Because you got minimum expectations and you work for minimum wage. That's about all I could ever pay, in my case. But you're a better boxer than that. Is it the money you're afraid of? Sometimes I wonder if you're allergic to money, because you always manage to stay far from it."

"No, I want the money. I'm desperate for some good money. I just—"

"What the hell you doing hanging around here? You want to get out of boxing, fine. Finish with a bang, a big paycheck. I owe you it, after all this time."

"You need money, too."

"Of course I do. So let's both make some money."

"You know I want to help you out, Smitty. And I may feel better in a day or two. But the way I am this second, I wouldn't do you any good. My inner ear, it's getting all weird on me."

"What are you, a hypochondriac all of a sudden? Is it your shoulder or is it your inner ear?"

"If I don't improve in the next week, just find Tadeusz another man. Christ, for that figure, anybody will take his low blows."

"I'm trying to make something for myself, and yes, I will get a small cut, for the use of the gym, and I need that money as bad as you do. But this is about you. Besides, he ain't offering that sum to nobody else. Just you. Not transferable. It's like a bounty or something. To help him prepare for his rematch with Nazir Salaam. There's only a month to go, and he's made up his mind that you'll get him ready better than anyone else. For some reason, and don't ask me exactly why, but Tadeusz hates you a lot. A lot, Clay. I don't know what you done to deserve it, but he wants to kill you. And because of that reason, you bring out the total fighting animal in him. I don't understand these grudges between boxers, but everybody has one or two. Where they are not just fighting for the payoff, or the title, or prestige. You're not even his official opponent. Who cares? He's got the money to waste, got backers, in spite of all his antics, and he wants to waste it on you. So let him. Otherwise he'll spend it out at Arlington trying to hit the exacta."

"He wants to kill me? Did he actually say that?"

"That's what is beautiful. I believe it counts as a weakness. When somebody has a grudge against you, and takes it so personally, you've got them where you want them. That is exactly when you can mess their mind."

"I'll call you before the end of the week."

Smitty sighed and laid down the glove he'd been working on. He knew it was no use continuing the conversation for the moment, so he made a strategic retreat. "I'm going to leave the matter open. I can stall for a few days, but no longer. Where you going, anyway? Hawaii? If so, take me with you."

I made up a destination off the top of my head. I hadn't done anything wrong, but it seemed like I was into something, so I invented another one of my instant alibis. "Wisconsin. Door County. To chill out."

"In March? Yeah, if you mean you like freezing rain all the goddamned time."

"Yeah. Well, solitude, you know."

"Be sure to try the fish boil. They have those on the weekend. Famous Door County tradition."

"What is a fish boil?"

"Boiled fish. They put it in a kettle and boil the hell out of it. Tastes like shit, if you ask me. You have to try it."

"Okay, I'll try it."

As he approached the Kentucky River, the cleft limestone bluffs on either side of the highway rose up like petrified cataracts. There had been early-season flooding along the river, the kind that made the papers, and he could view the vestiges of it on one of the old state highway roads he detoured onto for the hell of it. Displaced mobile homes had been lifted out of kilter, off their concrete blocks; tree branches and brush lay littered across rooftops, like makeshift thatch for a sod house, and in some places, water still stood, creating ponds and rivulets. A thaw had already taken place, bringing an unseasonable warmth redolent of loam, mud, minerals, peat. Above all, river silt. The bottomlands had the look of makeshift riverbeds, where water coursed in places it hadn't coursed before. Some of the sopping, untilled tobacco fields off the interstate had the reddish-brown look of frozen hamburger left out to thaw. Once he crossed the Kentucky River, with its rickety houseboats and swollen banks, he was in another zone altogether, a good twenty degrees warmer. Plants had begun to stir in a scented rain.

On my way into Lexington, from the bypass, I caught sight of the abandoned castle set back off Versailles Road. Yes, a castle. A really big one. I don't know how long it's been there—at least since I was a kid—surrounded by several hundred acres. A man had built it, they say, for his wife, or lover, or girlfriend. I'm not sure exactly what she was to him. His goddess, I guess. He never finished it, because she died of a disease, or killed herself, or threw him over for somebody else. The man left it sitting there, and moved away to another part of the country. I envy him that he could ruin his life in that spectacular way, and not have to do it through an infinite series of small gestures. One plunge of the stiletto instead of years of paper cuts. But, of course, to have means to squander, you first have to care enough about money to accumulate it.

All you could see from the outside were the turrets and towering walls. As a child, I made up a lot of stories about that castle, most of them involving me living in it. I couldn't believe that anything could be so enormous, just for one family. My mind wouldn't stop thinking about it. I convinced myself that there had to be a mansion left inside those castle walls. At the time, I was over on the North Side in a trailer park. Because nobody seemed to want the castle, I was going to move into it, all by myself, and raise horses like the ones I sometimes got to pet when I slipped through the back fence of the harness track to watch the races without having to pay.

One day, I finally rode my bike all the way over to the castle, fifteen or twenty miles, sweating and pumping, with a sleeping bag tied to the handlebars, slipping and throwing me off-balance. I laid the bike down on its side and hiked through tall grass full of chiggers, thistles, and spiky milkweed and scaled the wall like a rock climber, finding the weathered chinks where the mortar had fallen out. When at last I stood atop the wall, there was nothing inside except the warped wood frame of a house, as skeletal as it was gigantic, its wiring and plumbing exposed to the air. Stacks of petrified cement bags, and a couple of rusting backhoes. I burst into tears, as if somebody had deliberately played a mean trick on me.

Clay only felt like he was back in his town when he drove inside New Circle Road, which once upon a time was the outer limit before hitting farmland, and into the old part of the city familiar to him. Few of the businesses on Limestone hearkened, except for a handful of haunts around the university that had hung on, such as the Tolly Ho Diner, where a person could eat bad food at any time of the night or day, even back when the town used to shut down by 9:00 P.M. A little farther along, there sat rows of questionable-looking boardinghouses made of crimson baked clay, bearing the kiln's impress in relief on each individual brick. These structures had pitched roofs, heavy wooden window frames that slid up and down by counterweights, and lots of gables, all in genteel disrepair.

In an earlier time, they had housed students who came down from the mountains of Eastern Kentucky to get learned. He liked these houses' anonymity as well as their price. In the very beginnings of the neighborhood's degentrification, the sagging bedsprings and flattened mattresses had been worn out in honest ways, not with the moanings of harlots and johns, but instead with the nocturnal turnings of sophomores the night before the American history test.

He picked an attic room in one of those houses, one he could rent by the week. The eaves sloped down sharply on one side, so he'd have to mind his step when he stood up out of bed. Out the window, he faced a caramel-mirrored bank skyscraper, reflecting back the wavering ghost of another century in the outline of his lodgings.

This section of the city had, in the sixties, come to be known as Hooftown. Retired drivers, trainers, and people on the lower rungs of the equine industry who had fallen on hard times—developed a gambling habit, taken to drink, or simply given in to the inertia of being close to the harness track—ended up renting boardinghouse rooms and ramshackle apartments there, as they dimmed into the latter stages of their lives. When these tenants reached a critical mass, when even the poor students wouldn't consent to stay in those kinds of lodgings anymore, a sportswriter referred to it as Hooftown, and the name stuck.

Despite how they may have looked to the naked eye, the buildings weren't all the same. Because even in hell, there's a hierarchy. Certain of the houses had taken on a "prestige," meaning that the most hardened, jaded, longest-running patrons and participants of horse racing, those who knew the most, had gone the fastest, and therefore had the farthest to fall, were quartered there. An unspoken pecking order existed, which had nothing to do with the condition of the building, because the most immovable inhabitants tended to occupy the buildings that were most far gone. These renting curmudgeons, through sheer intractability, had managed to fend off the Metro-Urban Planning Commission, the BlueGrass Trust, and various developers who had tried to have them dislodged so that the buildings could be demolished. They were even suspicious of any workmen, who might be fixing up the building so that it could be sold. Benign neglect was their preference. The obsolescent box gutters had been eaten through with holes, filled with leaf debris and pine needles, but the rent-paying squatters didn't want anybody cleaning or patching the roof, and caving through the rotten roof onto their beds.

What was more, nobody moved into rooms that became vacant through the demise of someone already living there, unless they were "worthy"—not because any of the feeble gents already in residence there could physically dislodge a newcomer, but because there was an unspoken agreement about not crossing the threshold.

That etiquette meant nothing to Clay. He went to the desk clerk of each of these buildings, and asked for the first vacancy he came across, while feigning ignorance of the unspoken code of the worthies. Within two hours, he had an oversized key in his pocket.

Everybody at the Red Mile knew Woody, one of the boarders in the house where I had put up. He lived across the hall from me, and called himself "the racetrack poet." Retired from his long-ago days birthing foals and training them into yearlings, Woody had a lot of time on his hands and devoted it to making friends everywhere he went. Right off, he suggested I accompany him to the harness track. He had a senior citizens' pass for the bus, which we rode up Limestone. Woody, with me in tow, was waved past the security gate into the lodging area, after which he glad-handed his way down the rows of low, barrack-style stables where the racehorses were kept, and the paddocks where geldings were being walked. Passing under the fine, tangled branches of weeping willows, not yet broken into their moss, put Woody in mind of races of bygone days. He said he'd been to every spring meet at the Red Mile for the past fifty years.

He gestured toward the mile-long oval of caked red mud in the distance, beyond the brakes of ferns. "Lots of history in these confines, Clay. Now here's a stanza I made up, some time back and got our great governor Happy Chandler to chuckle." He raised his arms to the still-austere weeping willow trees.

"I'll never forget
As I walk on this grass
The day that Sandusky
Made a famous pass
Gentrified was beating her
With lots of sass
Till Sandusky blew by
And kicked Gentry's—brass."

"Balls."

"No profanity, please." He held back my coarseness with a single upraised finger. "Racing is a rough-hewn business, but you'll never find a curse word in one of my poems. Only great sentiments. Like the classics."

"You're bringing a tear to my eye, Woody."

"Now, now. No displays of emotion. I'm the one who is supposed to get sentimental. You know what? I had a thought. A felicitous aperçu. We're going to have to make you a Kentucky colonel."

"Don't trouble yourself. I'm not fashioned for titles of nobility."

"Not fashioned? Why, I can tell already that you have a great soul. We poets are intuitive about these things. And I have the ear of the governor's personal assistant. I call her all the time on the WATS line to recite my latest invention. Do you know I've composed upward of eight hundred poems?"

"That's an epic."

"Pardon me if I correct you, Clay. It's an epic *cycle*. For each individual poem, however brief, is an epic in itself, because of its hallowed theme and noble treatment."

"I stand corrected."

A man passed near us, pulling his harness gig behind him like a rickshaw. Obviously a driver. But without a horse. He was dressed in his civvies, soft corduroys and a flannel shirt, not wearing any of the multicolored, tight-fitting garb of the harness horseman. He was relatively small, with fine bones, and a certain lithe way of moving that marked him as an athlete. His build was the opposite of what a boxer strives for. Still, you can always tell an athlete—not by his muscles, but by his motion. There are plenty of big, powerful fellows who I never considered athletes because they couldn't quite figure out how to use their bulk to any great advantage. But something in this driver's assured gait fixed my eye on him, forcing me to watch his progress across the dirt lot. Not cocky, just secure in his footfalls.

"Who is that guy?"

"Shawn Sheldon. The tongues that wag say he's the best driver on the circuit right now. Maybe the best in a generation. Darn good."

"I could tell he was something. He looks focused."

"Want to meet him?" Without waiting for a reply, Woody lurched toward him with a shambling gait, arms swinging, and began to shout like a lunatic fan. "Shawn! Shawn!" Brought out of his reverie, the driver started to look annoyed, but when he turned and saw it was Woody, he broke into a smile.

"Hey, it's the poet laureate of harness racing. How you doing, buddy?"

"You're too kind. I was eager for you to make the acquaintance of my newfound friend. One Clay Justin."

"Only one? Woody, the things that come out of your mouth just kill me." Shawn slapped Woody on the back with one hand, while he reached out for my hand with the other, giving it an easy shake. No macho, overcompensating crusher. Most men, when they see my size, feel like they have to arm-wrestle me by way of greeting. "Any friend of Woody's—"

"My pleasure. I know who Shawn Sheldon is, just from the sports pages. I hear you're on your game."

He ducked his head. "Well, I'm making a living. Paying the bills, this year anyway. For about the first time in my entire life. You're not new to harness racing, Mr. Justin?"

"I grew up coming to this track. Used to hang around the trailers in the back, pestering the drivers."

"Don't say." His face brightened again at the prospect of this happy memory.

"I always wanted to drive a sulky, but of course I was too much of a piker."

"You've growed an inch or two since then."

"I guess so. I haven't been back here regular in a few years. And I never experienced it in verse."

"Your timing is unimpeachable," said Woody. "For Shawn has fairly, faintly, and in fine fettle leapt into the top echelon of our beleaguered pastime. Shall I apostrophize his year? He posted more wins than the next two drivers combined. And his horse, the venerable Hellaballoo, looks to be in meticulous mettle for the upcoming rigors of the meet, thanks to Shawn's terrific touch on the roistering reins."

"God's grace, and luck, that's all."

"God helps them who helps themselves. At last fall's Little Brown Jug Derby, Hellaballoo set a new record. Then her hoofbeats were heard hammering all season long, while other drivers gave furtive, freakish, and furrowed backward glances. There is great anticipation about the season opener."

"A possible new world record?" I asked.

Shawn shrugged. I could glean from his stance that he was feeling a tad superstitious, not wanting to tempt the fates. "I'd settle for a track record. Even that may be overreaching. I'm not going to take any chances chasing smoke. Mostly, I want my horse to stay healthy. We just run each race as fast as we can go. I don't push her when she's not ready."

"Look upon him! Modesty incarnate.
The laurel'd brow of number eight
Standardbred racing's poster boy
With whom the gods shall never toy."

Shawn shook his head. "Ain't he something? Now, if you all will excuse me, I need to go give Hellaballoo a workout. So we can do all these big things everybody keeps talking about."

"Listen, I did have one little question," I said casually, as if it were a mere afterthought. "You don't happen to know a woman named Carmela something, do you? A veterinarian. I don't recall her last name. She sort of—well, let's see—."

Shawn stopped me with his hand, and laughed. "Sort of dynamite. You don't have to describe her for me. Everybody around here knows Carmela Wade. You got business with her?"

"Nothing special. We have a mutual friend who told me to drop in and say hello while I was in town."

"She lives out on Wildbrake Farm. Past Nicholasville, down toward the river."

"Maybe I'll go pay my respects, when I get a chance. There's no hurry, though."

"Kind of isolated out there. Don't get lost."

A stable boy, lank hair and lanky, chewing tobacco and peering hard and squinty to try to add some years to his unmistakable teenagerdom, brought over a shining black beast, withers atwitch at a lone horsefly but otherwise calm and stately. She proceeded toward us without any visible effort. This must be Hellaballoo. She was a good fifteen hands high and had the haughty, keen-eyed, expectant look of a mistress who has been taken damn good care of. She knew she was in her prime, a looker and a cooker.

"Sweet and beautiful animal." I couldn't help speaking directly to her as if, in her intelligence and refinement, she would deign to speak back to me. But she disdained me and brushed past to allow herself to be hitched to the harness. Then she gave out a little quiver, in anticipation of her workout. Her ears, already erect, somehow pricked up even more. I couldn't take my eyes off her.

Shawn liked my liking her. I'm sure he was used to people heaping compliments on her. But like the proud father of a lovely child, he couldn't hear too many times how pretty she was. "You want to take her for a spin?" he said to me, offhand, as if he were simply offering me a chance to tool around on his banged-up, one-speed Huffy bike.

"Me? Drive her?"

"Sure. Why not? Make your dreams come true. You said you wanted to drive a sulky as a kid."

"Better to drive a sulky now than to be sulky later," added Woody, sagely bobbing his head.

Living away, I'd forgotten how easy and open my countrymen could be. "I've never done it before. She's got to be fast. And expensive."

"Yeah, she cost a lot. But she knows what she's doing. Ain't going to hurt herself, that I'll guarantee. You're the one who could get hurt. But you look plenty strong. I'd gauge you used to be a football player, college or maybe even pro."

"Well, I've played a few sports along the way."

"If I can hold those reins, you can too. Don't get the idea I lend her out, but I'll gamble on you. That little fellow who just brought her out rides her for me every morning, and he's more of a pipsqueak than I am. Just take her slow. Nobody's timing you. It's a buggy ride through the park."

"All right. I'm not too big?"

"Nah. This isn't thoroughbred racing, remember. We don't breed ballerinas who get shin splints after every performance. These are big, powerful horses. Almost as good as a dray, only way faster. She could pull two or three of us, if she took a mind. I don't know if I'm the best driver, but I know for a fact I got the best animal on the circuit."

Without another word, he strapped goggles on me, handed me the crop, and gave Hellaballoo a friendly swat on the flank. She was off, jouncing, first over the uneven ground, through an access gate, then onto the groomed track. "She knows what she's doing," I heard Shawn call out. "But you're in charge. She's smart, but she ain't that smart." Past the second turn, on the other side of the track from us, was a tractor, pulling an ultra-wide rake behind, raising a copper cloud of dust. The silver inside rail blurred by me like the tail of a comet, like jet vapor just before it breaks up, like the electrified third rail of a Chicago commuter train, the one despondent people throw themselves on.

I gripped the reins with all my might, pulling back on the bit, but this only seemed to egg Hellaballoo on. Her head was lowered, she hugged the rail, and started closing the gap between herself and the sharp-toothed rake. There was nothing but swirling dust ahead of us. We were driving into a Kansas tornado, full speed ahead, overtaking the maw of a combine. I lay back in the chariot, almost horizontal, like the corpse of Abraham Lincoln on his supercharged funeral coach, while time-elapse lilacs bloomed in the dooryard. And me, windsurfing out to the middle of Lake Michigan on a pitch-black February night, gripping the bar, the wind pulling my arms from their sockets as I dodged whizzing chunks of ice. Wearing a full-body rubber wetsuit, sweating like hell, my pores sucked dry, and hypothermia about to set in. Trees flashed by, a winding wall of them, each twisting trunk a frame in a movie reel that had slipped out of its mechanism and the celluloid was bouncing around, rattling the teeth of the actors onscreen. I clenched my jaw. I stuck my head out the window of a car flying along the interstate, like a dumb dog, the way my mother always warned me not to do, and now a metal EXIT sign, in the shape of Tadeusz's fist, was accelerating toward my head, ready to knock it to from Fort Knox to Knoxville. Hellaballoo was an engine, a coal-black furnace that made its own coal and never ran out. Hot, hot, her flanks in a lather, I could smell the pungent sweat, maybe my sweat, needles and nettles sieving through my skin. The tractor and its driver moved to the outside; he was waving to me with a smile, as if I were on a lazy hayride. I couldn't wave back, because there was no goddamned way I planned to let loose of the reins, and my neck was so rigid I couldn't even nod. I was giving myself whiplash. I didn't need a whip, I needed a chiropractor; I was the whipped one, as Hellaballoo whizzed past the finish line and slowed to a trot. She took a little cool-down jog, turned around of her own accord, slow and graceful, a parade horse, showered with cottonwood spores drifting down as copious as confetti, and Shawn and Woody were waiting for me in the winner's circle.

"You looked good for a novice. Took her in hand."

"Yeah. Well, I just tried to do what came natural."

"She's a mite sluggish today. I'm sorry about that. Takes another horse on the track to really bring out the competitive fire in her."

"Oh, that's okay. She seemed plenty peppy to me."

"Nice of you to say. Thanks for warming her up. I think she's ready for a real workout now."

That night, Woody and I played gin rummy in his room until he started getting sleepy. He had an amazing quirk of mind. While we sat tossing cards across the scratched pine, he rattled off long genealogies of sires, dams, and foals, who begat whom, like an Old Testament prophet calling out the roll Up Yonder. I'd never seen anyone, not even the box-score freaks I knew, catalog so much trivial information about one single thing. He spoke out long litanies of bloodlines as if he'd been remembering his own ancestors. Every dead horse's name he intoned was, for him, alive.

Luckily, we played gin rummy for points, not money, because he beat me almost every hand, while he kept protesting that his faculties had slipped in recent years and he didn't play like he used to. At midnight, I was wakeful, and everyone in the boardinghouse went to bed early so that they could thrash around with insomnia and old memories of their dead wives and the bygone lives of their steeds, then walk around later, in the waning hours before morn, down-home versions of Jacob Marley's ghost, lamenting their bad prostates and ruined circadian rhythms.

There was a wooden fire escape outside my landing, one I'd been advised not to go out onto, because it might collapse. I went out onto it anyway, in my frayed but favorite denim jacket, under a big spreading elm that had a disease. I could tell from its mottled bark that it had grown as rotten as the stairs I was lounging on, with many broken branches scattered in the yard below from the recent high winds. The clouds sailed high and wispy, glinty in the waxing moon. I smoked a bunch of cigarettes. I was restless, but I didn't want the company of strangers just then. My shoulder was bothering me, after the buggy ride, and I was missing Balboa. Where the fuck was he? I wanted him to settle the tendon down and then have us drive around in my crappy Mustang like a couple of high-school rednecks with too much time on our hands, so I could show him Lexington's blue side, such as it was.

After that one time he invited me to the grossly misnamed Cotton Club in the South Loop to hear jazz, then didn't show up because he forgot he was on call, and when I got there it was stand-up-and-dis comedy night, Pimps Drink Free, a lot of people without day jobs getting out of limousines with tinted windows, and one of the local wits onstage pointed out that I was the only white boy in the place, and I decided to leave before people got too deep into their vodka and tonics—then I kept threatening to retaliate by taking Balboa to some good ol' boy long-neck watering hole in my hometown for George Jones Look-Alike Night. We never got around to that little trek, though.

Lexington was no match for Chicago, but if I'd known for sure exactly where Balboa was right then, we could smoke a joint and head to Boots's Bar, a tame little strip joint, if that's not a contradiction in terms. At Boots's, there used to be one night a week the strippers had off completely, and a guitarist named Little Enis, who advertised himself as the World's Only Left-Handed Upside-Down Guitar Player, would sit up front on a stool and knock down sophisticated jazz and acoustic numbers, even a little flamenco when he got in the mood. He played on the other nights as well, but it was hack work then, next to a morose, too-tall guy hunkered over his trap drum set. They churned out sinuous and repetitive stripper grooves to help give the women on display the courage to undress and to help the men ignore the fact that there was nothing the least bit erotic going on in that room, just a couple of average country girls from Slade or Hazard getting nekkid for lack of marketable vocational skills.

Little Enis's reward was Tuesday, the free night, when he got to throw pearls before swine. The men who happened in on that night of the week, and of course it was mostly men, in search of skin, looked shocked that they were being subjected to actual music, with no visual aid to help them interpret its meaning. So they would leave quickly, and Enis would play his heart out for five or six of us unwitting connoisseurs, who didn't have anything better to do.

But there was no Balboa sitting beside me to take in search of elusive jazz. I didn't know whether there was still even a Boots's Bar or a Little Enis. He had probably gone on to Nashville or Memphis, as he deserved to do, to become the next Chet Atkins, or at the least an honorable sessions man, and the bar had doubtless been swept away in the wave of urban renewal, because, from what I could see, Lexington had become a boomtown. Hooftown was just a soft, spongy, dead tree, crisscrossed with termites, that they hadn't managed to bust up yet. In a few years, it too would be gone, another casualty of the stump grinder, only a reverent metal plaque next to some "bistro" awning to commemorate its passing, and with it would pass all of the racetrack leftovers who populated Hooftown.

I really didn't know what the hell I was doing in Lexington, except for that chancy phone number that had popped up. Yet it seemed necessary somehow. On a whim, I decided to call and see if Kelly was at home. It had been over a year since we talked, and my only correspondence with her was checks for child support, without any note enclosed. Chandra would be mad as hell at me for dropping out of sight the way I had. I hadn't returned her messages. But I had to call them sometime. I didn't have a phone in my room, and the one at the boardinghouse was actually locked away for the night in a wooden box, to keep it safe from the melancholy whims of the ghostly octogenarians. I walked over to the SuperAmerica, its concrete slab flooded with neon light, to use the pay phone and swill some of the burnt, superextracted coffee that had been stewing on its hot plate for hours. I called, but the number had been changed. It was listed, and at a new address. I decided it was better to show up in person. We had never done too well over the phone.

The apartment complex was a new, impersonal one off Richmond Road, in faux Spanish style, with a huge banner stretched across one of the buildings, advertising its health club and Jacuzzi. The window of her apartment was dark. I knocked a few times, and was about to give up and go away when the light went on, and a sleepy voice, unmistakably hers, asked who it was. Something in me wanted to run like hell, knowing that a doorbell prank, even at my age, might be kinder than her having to face me.

"It's me," I said, without thinking.

"Me who?" she answered. Now all I had to do was tell her a knock-knock joke. Before I could answer, she said, "Clay?"

"Yeah, it's me. I'm down from Chicago."

The door opened a crack, as she verified my identity before unlatching the chain.

"You expect me to recognize your voice? Everybody's mumble sounds alike after dark. The only reason I figured it was you is because nobody else *but* you would say 'It's me' in the middle of the night and expect a woman to open the door."

There she stood, wearing a big fluffy terrycloth bathrobe. She had always been a sensible dresser, putting comfort before style. I'd liked that trait in her. Her kinky hair used to look like cotton candy, the kind that would have been perfect for an Afro, if they'd still been the fashion. She kept it shorter now, closer to the skull. Her skin had that special deep hazel color, with copper undertones, like nobody else's.

She had a body that was an unbelievable surprise, one you would never guess to be hidden beneath those unflattering clothes she wore. Kelly forever complained that she was too fat, chunky, chubby, always some word like that. Maybe she was, and I don't guess I'd call her an athlete, but all I know is, that body suited me like no other I've experienced before or since. I used to tell her to stop being so hard on herself, that anyway her body was for me to enjoy, not her, so she didn't have to like it. She'd chide me that I could never keep my hands off her, even when we sat together watching television, but that my gentle groping was more absent-minded than attentive. "What's with you, boy? You fondle me, honey, even when you don't want anything. Get me all stirred up for nothing. If you're going to mess with me, at least keep your mind on what you're doing." And I would answer her that the color of her skin was like a penny in a pocket, its truest hues hidden out of sight, and that I rubbed her so much to see if those copper undertones would come out. Then she'd say, "Well, come on then, baby, and polish me some." And we'd be into something.

But it wasn't the time or place to be remembering conversations like that.

"Sorry. I should have called first to give you fair warning."

"Never mind. You might as well come in. I've got to close the door before all those moths flying around my outdoor light come indoors and make a nest in the couch."

She was a little annoyed, but not really angry, which surprised the hell out of me. She went over to the coffeemaker, to get a pot started, as if she expected me to stay for a while. By rights, she should have given me the cold shoulder or thrown me out. I watched Kelly unconsciously smoothing down her hair with one hand, the way she used to do when we first started dating if I came over unannounced. She never liked its kinkiness, the way I did, and didn't want me to catch her off guard with her hair out of place. She had only kept it long back then at my insistence. I got a funny feeling in my chest. I didn't want her to be smoothing down her hair on my account, not now.

"Do you still drink it black?"

"I'm not going to keep you up very long."

"Black or cream?"

"Black. I like it black."

"It's all right, Clay. I'm a terrible sleeper anyway." She fussed over her choice of mugs, as if it made a difference which we drank out of. "You know that about me."

"Yeah, I do. This is going to sound odd, but I'm kind of here on business."

She looked alarmed. "Did your father die?"

"No, it's not him. At least, as far as I know he didn't. Me and him—well, I don't have to tell you. After my mother passed away, and he got an insurance payoff, he bought sixty wooded acres down by Breaks and holed up there. Doesn't know a soul."

"Maybe that's why he picked it."

"Could be."

"Like son, like father."

"He hunts on the land, I guess. Quail, deer. Can't do much else with it. Wild country. I don't know. I haven't seen him or talked to him for several months."

"That's too bad. You ought to seek him out. Where are you staying in town?"

"I'm rooming at a boardinghouse in Hooftown."

"A boardinghouse? Not in Hooftown, Clay, for the love of Jesus. You can come stay here if you want. If you're only going to be in Lexington for a short spell. I hate to think of you in that awful slum." We looked each other in the eye, pondering the implications of Kelly's offer, and she turned her face away to clean up the paltry few dishes in the sink.

"The room isn't so bad. I've stayed in worse."

"I didn't mean—I don't want you to misunderstand. I only meant you could sleep on the hide-a-bed here in the living room. Like any other out-of-town guest."

"I know you did. I wasn't assuming anything. I appreciate it that you made the overture."

"Anyway, let's change the subject. If we keep this up, I'm going to cry, and I know how weirded out you get when women cry. A few sobs, and you'll be in there trying to fix the drip in my kitchen faucet."

"I figure Chandra is pretty upset with me, because I've been out of touch for so long."

For the first time, she stiffened. "She's asleep, and they have some kind of statewide writing test tomorrow, so I don't want to wake her up."

"Sure. I don't have to see her right away. I'll be here for—I'm not sure how long. I'm looking for a friend of mine who dropped out of sight. His wife is upset, and I think he might be here."

"Men do have a way of disappearing."

"Guilty."

"Yes, you are. But let's not talk about that right now. So why do you think he's here? Is he from Lexington?"

"No. He has a—friend here. Carmela Wade. You ever hear of her?"

"I've read about her on the society page. A veterinarian. The men seem to like her all right."

"Yeah, I should go look her up. But it's awkward. I'm not sure how to approach her." Her hand started to reach out, and she checked it. She was going to straighten a lock of my cowlicked hair, the way she used to. "Anyway, I just wanted you to know that I'm back in town. Tell Chandra I came by to wish her good luck on her test."

"Sure thing."

We sat in silence. Suddenly, there was nothing more to say, and it felt as though the interview was over. I stood to leave, and Kelly didn't try to stop me. "And to ask whether she needs help with her homework or anything."

"Anything?" She looked at me through her eyelashes, in that way she had of doing to convey skepticism.

"Except math. I'm not so good with math."

"Well, as a matter of fact, it was just now Presidents' Day. And in glorious remembrance of it, the teacher wants her to do a report on one of the American presidents."

"Any particular one?"

"Oh, Washington, Lincoln, Jefferson, Taft. They're all about the same to Chandra. Bunch of old dead guys with wide bodies, standing between her and the television set. Every time I sit down to try to help her, we get into a fight. It's overdue, and she don't give a damn. She thinks she knows it all already. So maybe you can come by one day and help her out with that. If you really do want to help out."

"I do. If you really think I'll be a help."

"I'm not so sure. But it would be nice just to watch her fight with somebody else for a change. Did you know they put her in the gifted program?"

"When?"

"Just this year. The g-word, as we say around here. I don't like her using that word."

"Gifted? Why not?"

"I don't want it to go to her head. I prefer to say 'enrichment,' if I have to speak of it at all. Anyway, they tested her and said she needed to be more challenged. I don't know whether that was your last laugh on me, or God's, or just hers."

"What are you talking about? You know exactly where she got those smarts. From you."

"You mean from you. Stubborn as hell. I always thought it was you was gonna kill me. Turns out it was Chandra. If I'd had the both of you around these past few years, I'd probably be in my grave right now, and leave the two of you to figure it all out."

The desk clerk's banging on my door woke me out of a sound slumber. As much as I worried about stuff, I could put the lights out when I really needed to. The desk clerk hollered that there was a phone call for me downstairs, from someone named Kelly. I guessed, from that stentorian voice of his, that he was used to rousing nearly deaf men out of their sleep. Downstairs, the desk clerk repositioned himself at his perch. His skin had the complexion of tallow. It looked like if you reached out and scratched it, you'd come away with soft wax under your nails. On a really hot day, with the poor ventilation in the place, he might plain melt down into a puddle. He obviously had nothing practical to do at that moment to fill his time, and he seemed eager to lazily eavesdrop on my conversation. I half admired his brazenness about it. He didn't pretend he was doing something else, shuffling papers or neatening up the lobby. He just settled back, folded his hands on the desk, and looked straight at me, as if to say, Let the show begin.

Kelly asked me if I wanted to go on a picnic that evening at Woodland Park. "As friends," she hastened to add, though in my view, it wasn't necessary. She didn't want me to get the idea that this was some kind of date. I wasn't about to make any moves on her. I'd been with enough women to know that however strong their own desire may be in the moment, their minds can change later.

The park might be a little cool and windy, but there wouldn't be any bugs, at least, and we wouldn't have trouble finding a picnic table. I told Kelly it sounded like fun. I didn't have any other immediate plans. I wanted to remind her that I was a regular guy and didn't have the impertinence to come sniffing around as if I expected a morsel to be thrown down to me from the table. We used to always go to Woodland Park together, in the summer, for ballet under the stars or just to take a cheap swim in the outdoor pool, which was always in need of painting but had lots of tremendous oaks surrounding it to compensate for the mildewed locker rooms and the pool's peeling paint.

That afternoon, Woody and Clay took a constitutional along the mouth of North Broadway. Low-rise, low-key funeral homes alternated with the soaring spires of Baptist churches. The facade of the restored Opera House gleamed in splashes of daylight. They sat on one of the lichen-furred stone benches on the grounds of Gratz Park under a walnut tree. The two of them munched on cheese-chili dogs with chunks of raw onion, casting pieces of soft white bun onto the ground so the gregarious, chittering squirrels could snag them and skitter up a tree. The grounds were still covered with winter's debris. A chunk of ice here and there had stayed unmelted, stuck between thick tree roots. There was a carpet of dead leaves, blackened and shapeless, mixed in with the deep green carcasses of last summer's fuzzy walnuts. A rhizome or crocus here and there was starting to force its way through the mulch, and a couple of uncovered patches of grass had begun to brighten into tender stalks. Robins with dull breasts hopped mindfully across the lawn, as if playing a slow-motion game of Mother May I.

"There's the Hunt-Morgan House. Do you know it?" Woody said.

"Never been in."

"A shrine maintained by the Daughters of the American Revolution. Built by John Wesley Hunt, the first millionaire west of the Alleghenies. His son was a Confederate hero. The DAR holds teas and serves finger sandwiches to maintain the place. These women have the same relation to Brigadier General John Hunt Morgan, the Thunderbolt of the Confederacy, as nuns do to Christ. John Wesley Hunt's wife bore him thirteen children. Then she died. On her gravestone, the husband asked the engraver to write that she WAS GOOD BUT NOT GREAT, USEFUL BUT NOT DECORATIVE."

"I don't think anybody would be decorative after bearing thirteen children. Even if they were decorative at the start."

"Did you ever attend university? You seem, may I say, unusually well spoken for a man of your brawny craft."

"No, I didn't."

"Why didn't a capable young fellow such as yourself avail himself of the liberalization of the university, which has been put within reach of the common man? Even before the Protestant Reformation, the university had ceased to be the exclusive precinct of the clergy. Here you are within spitting distance of Jeff Davis's alma mater. You could have tried community college, if nothing else."

"I don't know. I stole some sink fixtures, I guess."

"You stole sink fixtures?"

"That's right."

"Whatever for?"

"A friend of mine was repairing his sink, and he didn't have cash money for fixtures; neither did I, so I went into the hardware store and shoplifted them. Only not too well."

"I see."

"You didn't read about it in the papers?"

"Perhaps. It's been a while, I presume. Was there a large article?"

"Just the police blotter."

"And this blotter item prevented you from attending college?"

"Actually, no. I only got a suspended sentence. I talked to a couple of high-school classes way out in E-town or somewhere about keeping their hands to themselves. It was what happened a few weeks later that kind of set me off in a different direction."

Balboa couldn't get Marvin Gaye out of his mind. They were playing a techno ripoff of "Got to Give It Up," sampling it to death, at a package hedonism place where you stepped onto real turf in the lobby, fragrant, and all the food was supposed to have aphrodisiac properties. *Leche de tigre,* raw oysters, lightly grilled sea bass, prawns almost the size of a woman's fist, sushi underlain by horseradish slices strong enough to make you burst out weeping. It was all supposed to taste vaguely like pussy, he supposed, only spiritual. The salads had edible flowers littered among the mixed greens. Young thangs with their boobs swelling over half the silver tray slunk around offering you a shot glass of a mauve cocktail called love potion. He said, No thanks, he was dining alone, so it wouldn't really do him any good, only get him all worked up for nothing. That wasn't entirely true, however. A woman at the Delano bar's pool table had given him the number of her hotel room and had done a lot of leaning over the pool table after that, to study her shots and show what she had. There at the aphrodisiac restaurant, he could feel the slip of paper crumpled in his pocket, with her name, Shantae, written on it. The raw oyster felt thick and slick in his throat as he gulped it down without chewing.

Smitty had once said to him, when he came in looking put out after some head-banging set-to with Janine, "Balboa, someday you'll get to my age and be released from the tyranny of sex." And cack-led. At the time, Balboa took it as a mere locker-room witticism. Now he wondered what that would feel like for real.

The twentysomething players outside the double-glass door, visible from his table, sported swoopy, moussed Cuban coifs and goatees and got their Porsches valet-parked, only not before the bench-pressing valet boys helped the feckless, foxy, fuckable blonds out of the passenger sides, sheathed in black dresses way too short for anybody. Then they crossed the velvet rope, her trailing just a lit-tle behind, not out of deference, but so the car jockeys who the man had entrusted with his most prized possession, his car, could have one last ogle at the piece on his arm without him having to get all jealous about it and toss his hair out of joint in a scuffle and maybe have to end up going to the chiropractor the next day and miss his kick-boxing appointment. Stock-option riffraff in south Florida all trying to look like Pat Riley or Billy Donovan with that slicked-back hair.

It was hard for Balboa to remember who his waiter was because everybody wore black, waitresses and patrons alike. The bill would be brought when they needed to turn the table over. Somebody dif-ferent came to your table each time. He wondered if there was an unspoken hierarchy among them. Behind the onyx bar, the bar-tender in his paisley Hindu vest had a herky-jerky thing going to the music and seemed oblivious to the drink orders being handed in but somehow got them filled. The women in the little black dresses were going to dance after dessert, for a long time, they were just getting warmed up over dinner for the arduous business of displaying their bodies to anybody who could fork over the twenty-dollar cover charge and could afford glasses of booze at fifteen bucks a pop, the livelong night; it didn't matter what you ordered—an Evian, a Chablis, a scotch, a brewski—it all cost fifteen bucks a pop with an automatic twenty percent gratuity figured in. So you might as well get what you want. This tantric boutique was the most car-nal spiritual restaurant that could be imagined, only it didn't serve red meat.

Everything was hanging right out in this scene, body and soul together. *Let's dance, let's shout, getting funky's what it's all about.*

Critical mass, uncritical minds. They don't ask your race, they don't care about your sexual orientation; just have plenty of money and look damn fine and everything will be all right. They expect you to be decadent, and cheerful about it, only if you have a disease, don't tell, nuzzle me first in this jumpsuit I'm wearing with zippers in all the necessary places. The techno pulsed in one continuous groove, all night long, dancing baby, dancing dancing baby, trancelike, hyperdisco, funkabilly, you could hear the overdubbed lyrics but not quite understand what they intended, one-syllable words too simple for the brain to process at any speed slower than a head-snapping hip-hop, meanwhile somebody hung from the hammock in the ceiling, swaying, and you couldn't make out quite what they were doing, maybe slow-humping with their clothes on, one muscle at a time, maybe praying, maybe nothing. No drugs in evidence. Not surreptitious, but tactful, yes, because you wouldn't blow your nose at the table, would you? Like one of those unsightly old men with the nose hair who couldn't get past the velvet rope here, no matter how many fivers he handed around. Be a sugar daddy, hell—half of the couples were May-December, her recently back from bulimia camp and him getting continuous subcutaneous heart stimulation, be a sugar daddy, but have some class to match the piece of ass you brought in tow.

Wandering in search of the men's room, he'd come upon another room, way in the back. On the periphery of this second dance floor, he keyed into the telltale signs of manufactured bliss. Water bottles, pacifiers not only for babies anymore. Vicks inhaler slipped from a pocket, glowstick swishing its luminous traces through the afterair. House househousehousehouse music. Beans, roofies, Smurfs. Basic food groups. Grievous bodily harm. Hurts so good. Special K, GHB, MDMA, and, no, that's not the museum of demented modern art. Though it might as well be. Keep that booze at bay, don't mess up nobody's high, too damn depressed already, bad mix, cosmic gorp doesn't go well with Absolut nonsense, and one of us might want to jump bones before it's all over. It's been known to happen, got to find out if any of these breasts are for real. Grope, grope, doin' dat dope. Dance the libido lambada, grinding their collective teeth, *rechinando los dientes,* mandibular mayhem, 'cause those mothafockim methamphetamines sholy gonna make somebody bite they lip in two.

Give me my ecstasy in a tiny paper cup, cast me out of the garden, little Lucifer, but don't smack my head on the gate on the way out, because I have to come to my senses sooner or later. Adam, where is thine Eve? Oh able-bodied, where is thy dancing cane? Flashmaster of the fleshpots and the flashpots. Softshoe euphoria with a dry mouth. Lollipops wetting sticky lips, because a sweet tooth is hard to satisfy. Canine molars, made for tearing off a piece of meat. It's a condition more than it is a craving. Camus dig it. Go stark raving. Rave, rave against the dying. DJ gotta jump thump bump. Get Sirius. I like a dog, because when the key turns in the lock, and the dog slinks off because he's been rooting in the garbage, he may experience that spark of conscience, that divine fire, but five minutes later, he's back in Eden, head in the can, wagging his tail, indomitable, ready to dig again with that nasty muzzle. Whip 'im if you got to, but don't expect no different the next time around. Come here often? You're looking fine, and no, I don't say that to all the ladies. Only the comely ones. Only the contumacious, bodacious, curvaceous.

That technopulse had started to modulate into the low-frequency buzz of a headache. That's when Balboa had paid his check and slipped outdoors, and the bleach-blond, spiky-haired doorman, without even a sidelong glance in his direction, stepped forward to hail the taxi. A five-dollar bill passed between Balboa and him with no further eye contact, almost as if they were passing a gang sign.

The driver tensed up slightly as Balboa, having tossed his travel bag in the back, climbed in front, but the driver made no comment. Balboa knew he was breaking protocol. Yet one glance into the dark interior told him the backseat was broken down, like some old hippie couch. He wasn't gonna pay forty dollars to sit on a couch you'd find waterlogged in somebody's back alley. There was a rip and you could see the foam spurting out of the Naugahyde, like foam coming out of the top of a longneck beer.

A squall had blown up, sending down bands of warm rain, and the driver had his hands full using the air conditioner to fight off the fog that wanted to overtake the windows. Next stop, Miasma Beach.

As they moved cautiously down Collins, swung onto Fifth and cruised over the causeway, the right wheels of the taxi swooshed through a continuous trough of water, sending up a short wall of spray. Drops danced under the halogen, in a shiver of lavender. Balboa turned his head to greet the driver. The driver's face was a subtle web of white creases, and underneath, dark dead gloss like a pork rind. Balboa tried not to stare. The man had on long sleeves and long pants, a high collar buttoned to the top, in sultry weather.

"This rain is some shit."

"It's rainy."

"You like driving a taxi?"

The driver shrugged. "What else can I do?" The radio was on low, almost too low to make out the words, but you could tell the jockey was screaming, something about the poor play of the Dolphins in the season past and gone, something about Dan Marino's sorry ass, how overpaid and underperforming.

"I don't mean to intrude. I know a good plastic surgeon in Fort Lauderdale. Old buddy of mine. Breasts and burn victims, the two things he knows best. Belongs to Doctors without Borders. If you got any kind of insurance, you tell him I recommended you. He'll just take whatever they end up paying."

For a while, the driver didn't answer. He squinted, as though listening hard to find out what will happen to Dan Marino. Finally, he said, "Too late for that. They took me, long time back, operations in Santiago, Buenos Aires, then São Paulo. Those Maryknoll Fathers."

Balboa remembered that he was nominally Presbyterian, the high church variety, but the vacuously wistful trumpets finally did him in at the evening services, and the elders were always on him about becoming a deacon and joining the mission committee. "Did the surgeons do a good job?"

"Good as they could."

"All over your body?"

"Most of me, yes."

"How did it happen? Do you mind saying?"

"I been nine years old. Every year we been going to the Lord of Wanca pilgrimage."

"Wanca? Where's that? Jamaica?"

"Peru. In the highlands. Those peasants are burning off the fields by hand each year to make the potash. Torch the brush. Not suppose, but they do. Then the forest where we sleep on the pilgrimage is catching fire. Too many of us in there, under the eucalyptus trees waiting to make offerings. Bad wood burns fast. It got the big pores. Everybody been die except me and a couple others. I don't know where they went to. All my whole body is burning real hard. Somebody had to fly me out in a helicopter. That was first time I flew in a helicopter. That was only time I flew in a helicopter. Then these operations started. They never finish. They are only done."

"I'm sorry." They rode for a while without speaking, listening to rain pelt the close metal roof, as if they were in the loft of a barn, under the zinc. The blower sat on the highest notch, evaporating the sweat in his hair. "I guess you never went back to that shrine to worship."

"Oh, yes." The driver pulled a medallion on a chain from inside his shirt. "I still worship the Lord of Wanca. Every day. He's my savior. He give me life. I went back to that shrine many times after. But I never went back into that forest."

The bangs and pops of my broken muffler heralded my arrival at Kelly's place a couple of blocks before I rumbled into the parking lot. She was waiting at her door—that is, they were waiting. My little charcoal-colored girl, much darker than Kelly, with a yellow jumper and a yellow bow in her cornrows, had her mother firmly by the hand. She presented herself for inspection, petite, well groomed, as always.

"Hi, baby."

She only bobbed her head at me. Usually she ran right into my arms. "Hi. I see yellow is still your favorite color." I knew better than to ask her for a kiss right then. I didn't insist on anything. "I'm sorry I haven't been calling you." She shrugged, her body tense. She didn't want to talk about it. I was at a loss as to other conversational gambits.

"Knock, knock," I said.

For a few seconds she didn't respond, but she couldn't resist a knock-knock joke. "Okay, Daddy. Who's there? And don't say 'me.'" This comment eked a smile out of Kelly.

"Washington."

Big rolling eyes and a huffy sigh. "Oh, don't even get me started on Washington. I have to write a report on him, or one of those guys."

"No sermons, please. Just play the straight man."

"Okay. Washington who?"

"Washington of laundry in prison, wrists get sore."

She groaned. "That is so terrible." The ice was broken between us, or at least a crack had appeared. There was some comfort to her in realizing that I was still the man who couldn't tell a good joke. Bad ones were the kind she liked. And the truth is, I'm not really a joke teller. I'm more like the character in the joke.

To Kelly's chagrin, I had to scoop a bunch of aluminum cans to one side of the floorboard before Chandra, ladylike, could step in to occupy her rightful seat. After Chandra buckled herself into the backseat, Kelly took a long, critical look at my car. "Does this Mustang ever catch fire?"

Predictably, no one was at Woodland Park but us. The drained pool had several inches of water standing in it from the recent rains, brackish and lime colored, organic matter afloat, a luxury of larval twigs and angiosperm pods dropped from the overhanging trees. It looked like a tidal pool. I almost expected to see tadpoles.

We ate fried chicken out of a bucket. We forgot to bring plates. I was usually picky about biscuits, a quick-bread snob, finding the ones from restaurants tacky, but the chewy, overly salty bits of dough in my mouth tasted good to me right then. We were drinking a few beers. Nothing special, just whatever was closest at hand in the 7-Eleven cooler. Kelly didn't ever drink, not hardly. She swallowed, scrunched up her face, and looked at the can after every sip, as if she couldn't quite remember what she was imbibing.

There was no sunset in a silvery-gray sky, no rising moon either, only the gradual ebbing of the light. A windshield sheen giving way to black and white. Chandra had picked at her food, bolted a juice box, and was now a dusky silhouette, down the hill, banging a dry stick against the chain-link fence. Without consciously realizing it, she had a good rhythm going, and even her jerky, childish movements were graceful.

She turned her head slyly back my way from time to time, in her own cloud, but keeping me in her peripheral awareness. She had fed me little bites of chicken that she tore lengthwise off one of the breasts. Something about this interaction, maternal instinct perhaps, made Kelly tense—much tenser than when I'd shown up unannounced last night. I could barely get a word out of her.

"Chandra looks more beautiful than ever."

"Glad you like her."

"You don't sound glad."

"I be glad. I be buck dancing." She gave me a tight, ironic smile.

"Ow. I need baking soda. That had a stinger in it."

"I don't want her to get hurt, that's all."

"I have no intention of hurting her."

"Not deliberately. You've been out of touch for over a year. So don't be so goddamned charming."

"I'm not charming."

"Yes, you are. And what's worse is, you're trying." She rubbed her face with her hands. "I'm sorry. I'm not criticizing you. But she doesn't understand."

"Understand what? That we're trying to enjoy each other's company?"

"Things with us can only go so far."

"And I'm respecting that. Aren't I?"

"Because if we ever did go back—which we're not going to—but if we did, there would be a lot of questions I'd want you to answer."

"Ask them, then. With no obligation."

"I'm lonely, I admit it, but that's another matter. Don't create any expectations on her part that neither of us can meet."

"Like what? Giving her a little brother?" She didn't smile at my teasing comment. "I'll do my best. What are the questions?"

She stayed quiet, deliberating. She swirled her beer can in her outstretched hand, as if it were a glass of Chardonnay. That was probably what I should have bought. But I didn't want it to seem like I was being the least bit romantic. Before Kelly could speak, Chandra ran up, more five than seven, in that age elasticity that children sport, as plaintive and needy as she had been self-sufficient only a moment ago. Chandra rubbed her hair on her mother's lap, making a deliberate tangle of it, lolling and lounging over her mother, insistent. I suggested that I drop them back at the apartment, because suddenly I didn't want to hear the questions.

"Can't Clay come over, Mommy?"

"Don't call him Clay. You got to be respecting persons, like I taught you."

"You *have* to be respecting," she pedantically corrected her parent, not understanding why Kelly needed to drop into the vernacular. "Daddy said I could call him Clay, didn't you, Clay?"

Kelly sighed. "See how many more times you can fit his name in the sentence, honey."

"But you don't like when I call him Daddy either."

"That's about enough mouth. Tell you what. If you're getting sleepy, why don't you crawl in the backseat of the car, with my coat. We want to take a little more air before Daddy-Clay goes back to his own living space."

"I will on one condition."

"Don't be putting no conditions. How 'bout you just do what I said?"

"If Clay will tell me a story." She wasn't too tired to be flirty. Chandra took my arm and swung it back and forth like a maypole, giving little airborne hops, then supported all her weight on the arm and let her body go slack, daring me to lift her off the ground. I took the dare, suspending her a foot or so with my upraised arm.

"Look, Mommy," she said excitedly. "Look how strong Clay is. He did it with just one arm." Kelly ignored the remark, but Chandra kept hanging there, insistent as an Olympic gymnast to her coach, until her mother turned her head to look.

"Oh, yeah, he's plenty strong. Mhm. In the arms."

Luckily for me, Chandra wasn't yet fully schooled in irony, and she gave a contented smile at her mother's answer. I crawled in the backseat with Chandra, who cozied up, leaning into me with her relaxed body. I made up some story off the top of my head about a little girl, coincidentally right about Chandra's age, whose hat gets blown off by a gust of wind, then she goes into a cavern searching for it, and a magic bat with feathers like a tropical bird carries her around the Kentucky countryside on its back, and they meet some very intelligent sheep who can climb trees very well, and so the sheep shinny up pine trees and find the hat, and to reward them the little girl washes all the pine resin out of their wool with baby shampoo, because it doesn't make tears.

I had no idea where that story came from. Chandra said it was a good one except that sheep weren't really that smart. I answered that they just had the reputation of being dumb, but there were individual sheep who were smart. We agreed to disagree, and she laid her head on her mother's coat and promptly fell asleep, as if she hadn't a single care in the world. I climbed out without stepping on her.

"You're sweet," said a voice in the darkness, from somewhere behind the moving ember of a cigarette. Usually when Kelly smoked, it meant she was wound up, but at least I had that first wistful note in her voice to hang on to. "So you're still earning your living as a boxer?"

"I wouldn't call it a living. But when I do get paid a little something, it's usually for that."

"I never liked boxing."

"I know that."

"No, I actually don't think you understand how deep to the bone my opposition runs. But I understood boxing was what you loved. That's why I sat in the folding seats at your matches. To watch all that technique. So your opponents could tell you afterward what a hell of a guy you were. Thank you for smashing their faces in. I never could figure that one out. You were known as quite the gentleman, never fighting dirty."

"I was a clean fighter. No cheap tricks. No hugging and mugging."

"So why did you do it?"

"I thought we already talked about this a few times. I thought you had a real question to ask me."

"No, I talked about it. Not you. I understand how you believe that when somebody brings a subject up once, then it's all done with. But I'm a woman. I like to talk about things twice, three times, maybe six, whatever it takes, until we have an actual conversation."

"What happened was out of the ring. I said I was clean in the ring."

"I realize you were still getting over that shoplifting thing. Which was stupid as hell, but so what? You made a little mistake. The way a woman buys a terrible hat on an impulse. The two things are not that different, really. But it's another matter when you go into a bar, pick a fight with two off-duty policemen, who you knew were cops, and beat the living hell out of them. From what I remember, the clean boxers don't normally use a chair."

"Those guys were looking for a fight. There are some men, once they know you're a boxer, they want to use that fact to prove what a man they are. I've had guys who dogged me for months with that kind of attitude."

"Yeah, and you got the same meanness boiling in you. I guess if I was a boxer, big and strong, I'd just take it for granted I could whip anybody I took a mind to, and wouldn't have to go around proving it all the time."

"Well, you're right. I've relived that night a lot in my mind. I wouldn't do it the same way now. Those cops started taunting me about the shoplifting. Saying it loud enough where other people in the bar could hear. I wasn't even drunk. All I wanted to think about right then was the fight I had coming up that next week. I was going to remind everybody how good I was getting, finally, before the little incident with the merchandise happened. I was just tired of hearing about it. The bad publicity, which was the first real publicity I ever got. They played it all over the local radio. I can't even say why in the hell I ever stole those plumbing fixtures. It's not like I went into the store planning to do it. I had a credit card in my wallet that I could have used."

"Clay, baby, you've paid for those fixtures many times over.

When you gonna stop paying? I know you. And you got that deluxe Baptist nonsense lurking way down in your soul. You're the most religious atheist I ever did meet. Sometimes I think that after you managed to be given a suspended sentence, you had to figure out a way to get yourself really into jail, to make sure you did real time for a real crime. Else it wouldn't be fair or some such. That judge's leniency was more than your wicked soul could handle. Especially because you knew he was partial to boxing. But it was him who saved your ass, not God."

She was probably right. Growing up in a Baptist medium, I was long since used to that feeling of a perennially grumpy God whose bad mood could escalate into violence at any moment. He's lost a set of keys, the keys to the kingdom or the keys to his car, doesn't matter which, and he knows for a fact he left them somewhere conspicuous, you probably did something with them, you were fooling around and dropped them into a sewer grate, and he has to be somewhere far away in five minutes, so don't contradict him, don't tell him that he himself mislaid them, and especially don't remind him that he's God and therefore controls the unfolding of all space and time, just help him find those goddamned keys. Or you'll wish you'd never heard the name God. That's the God I grew up on.

"Then you turned around and got lucky again. So don't say you was born under a bad sign. I'm tired of cheap, homegrown blues-club philosophy. I saw the face of one of those cops after you got done, and it looked like a fig somebody stepped on real hard with a boot. And how many ribs did you break? Anybody else beat up those same cops, they be looking at five to fifteen years. That's what I was expecting at the sentencing. Me pregnant, and I said to myself, Well, I guess I'm going to be a single mother, one of those sorry women writing to her man in jail, saying, I baked you a cake, honey, and me and Chandra ate it for you. Happy birthday. But damned if the law didn't disappoint you again, same peckerwood judge, and you only ended up serving ninety days. I was hoping that little stint would give you what you wanted, satisfying punishment, like somebody else going on vacation. Still, the terminal ugly mood you were in when you came out, you would have thought they'd had you locked down for a whole year, in solitary."

"So why did you agree to marry me? If I was such a hothead."

"Oh, you know, all that Freudian folderol. Had to piss Papa off. Black daddy, didn't really like white boys all too much, but ever since me starting in high school, back when, he had to tolerate them, or pretend like he did, because he was a college professor. Long as they had good SATs, I could invite them for Saturday lunch. White mama, she waited on him at the Walgreen's in Turfland Mall, first time they met. And she never did stop waiting on him that I ever saw. Because he'd rescued her or something. She never did speak loud enough, not as loud as him anyway, so I couldn't quite catch what she was saying, or what her story was. Just glad to be of service. Good servant stock."

"That's bullshit. It sounds good, but you were way beyond high school when you and me got together. That was a decade behind you. You were out of college and into a job. Your daddy had no power over you."

"Is that so? Yes, well, I see how you've emotionally progressed and left all your past behind. I'm sorry if I couldn't outgrow my upbringing as fast as you."

"Okay. I overstated."

"Anyway, I'm not sure I'd call my union with you a marriage. We were married only a little longer than your ninety-day sentence. And sometimes I wonder whether three months of jail didn't have a bigger impact on you than I did. Soon as we started living under the same roof, I realized I was afraid of you."

"Afraid of what? Did I ever hit you? Did I say anything? Wasn't it you screaming at me?"

"Sure enough. No. You never did hit me. You were real quiet for a while there, for the most part. If you'd screamed a little bit, after you got out, maybe I would have felt better. I didn't know what you were gonna do. Kill us, if you took a mind. I wouldn't have put it past you."

"It hurts me to hear you say that."

"Let it hurt, then. All I know is you spent time out getting caught peeing in public, smashing several cars up by running them off the road, or that time you promised to roof somebody's house, then ran off and hocked the nail gun they lent you instead. Nothing

I could be proud of, like a bank robbery or murder. Nothing you could do real hard time for. Just petty little foolishness that mortified both of us and made you look like an ass."

"Yeah, I did do all those things. I'm not going to deny it. I remember them all."

"The best you ever treated me was after you moved to Chicago. The payments for Chandra came regular. I never had to call you over that."

"That's about all the good I've done to speak of."

"Chandra has been all over me about you coming to stay for a while."

"And it's all coming from Chandra?"

"So far."

"Yeah, well, I'll talk to her about it and tell her to mind her mommy."

"You want to know the truth? The boxing, I just don't think I could deal with it. Where it makes you live. And I don't mean Chicago."

"What if I wasn't boxing?"

"Huh?"

"If I gave it up."

"Don't do it for me."

"Why not?"

She broke a dead twig in two and flung it across the grass. Her voice brimmed. "I'm not so stupid to think I could change you into somebody else. Especially after all this time. I mean, I used to believe that way, but I grew up."

"I've been thinking about giving the sport up. I can't keep on with this grind physically. And I'm tired of it. For a lot of reasons."

"Don't say that. Don't stoke fires that don't want to be stoked."

"Isn't that what you wanted to hear all along?"

"Don't snow me, that's all. When I get in a certain mood, I'm a lot like Chandra. I can be talked into lots of things. But then I come back to my senses."

"In that case, let me take you home. Because if we stay here, it might start snowing."

"I think it's better. Did you find your friend? The one who disappeared?"

"I haven't been looking very hard."

The platinum light had leaked out of the sky, like a mercury spill, leaving only tracings of its substance in the dark, tarry residue. I reached out to touch Kelly, but her body had contracted into a hard, impermeable ball on the picnic table bench, her knees and head touching, arms wrapped around. When I tried to speak, she held out a hand to stop me, without looking up.

The drive back to her apartment complex was dead quiet. When we arrived, she got out, flipped her seat forward, and stood aside, silently indicating that she wanted me to carry the sleeping Chandra upstairs. I scooped the limp little girl into my arms. Kelly opened the apartment lock with a dry click. It needed oil. In the bedroom, I slid Chandra's body out of my arms, where it sprawled on the bed into one of those impossible, twisted child positions that oddly look natural and comfortable. She gave out a dreamy sigh and reached instinctively for her pillow, somehow knowing she was where she needed to be. I brushed wordlessly past Kelly, snapped off the light switch, and left.

Janine said the words aloud again. She'd heard them many times, but they always sounded fresh to her. Forgive us our trespasses, as we forgive those who trespass against us. She liked the liturgy, because it gave you words to say, and she had never been especially good at prayer. You had to keep thinking up stuff, and it always ended up sounding too much like a shopping list, inner quiet for me, health for my kids, peace of mind for my husband, with an afterthought about the victims of a foreign earthquake or hurricane to make it seem like you weren't only concerned about you and yours. It was difficult to keep inventing brand-new thoughts in fresh words that felt spontaneous and not as though you had written out a little speech for God, like a fifth grader stammering the reasons that she should be elected to the student council. Her favorite part of the service was when the pastor, right before his sermon, said, "Let us pray," and then said, "May the words from my mouth and the meditation of my heart be found fitting and acceptable in thy sight, O Lord, our rock and our Redeemer."

Amen. That was all you needed to say to God, and the comfort was in knowing that the words from your mouth would be the same every single time. It perturbed her when the worship committee wanted to keep fiddling with the liturgy and the Scripture, adding more inclusive pronouns, some of them talking about Sophia, whatever that was, or asking her, in the free spirit of inquiry that the church felt compelled to advocate or tolerate, whether she didn't think that the Bible was a contradictory book for blacks to have lived by, what about the slavery issue, as if it had happened only last week, or civil rights. Didn't she think blacks needed to make the Bible over in their own image, starting with the Book of Exodus and forgetting about Genesis altogether? As if it were a historical document you could keep changing your mind about, instead of Divine Writ. She didn't know and she didn't care. She just wanted the words to be the same, each and every time. It would have suited her fine if nobody did any heavy interpretation or preaching, instead saying one devotional after another, or quoting Scripture, as long as the words were supplied.

When Balboa came back from that stay in the hospital, he had confessed to her that the first night away, as it had settled in on him where he really was, he had just kept saying the Twenty-third Psalm over and over again. It was an excellent prayer, no doubt about it, *He restoreth my soul,* but she wondered what exactly it might have meant to Balboa. He had been mostly interested that the kids would attend a Presbyterian preschool, that was real important to him, and he volunteered to drop them off there every day himself, taking the child-safety seats out of the trunk of his Audi each time and attaching them in the backseat, and then returning them to the trunk again, instead of simply leaving them in place in the backseat where they belonged. Maybe he thought it made him look too much like a married man. But he wasn't too keen on attending Sunday services with her, except at the predictable times. Did he believe in God and was only being foxy about it, as he was with so many things? She wondered whether he even recalled, that first night back, after the lobster bisque and after the fellatio, that they had held hands together in bed and prayed the psalm aloud, at his request. Or did he only remember her slipping downstairs afterward to fetch the chocolate-mint ice cream?

It had been a little hard to take him back to her bosom, and let him use it for a pillow. For all kinds of reasons that had nothing to do with his small breakdown. She'd almost been ready to divorce him a few weeks before, but when he returned from that long weekend, his eggshell state of mind, his grateful boyish clinging, reminded her how fragile he was, after all, behind the bravado and that big sturdy body, and what was worse was her being mad as fire at him, but she couldn't say anything about her own state of mind or let on, much less bless him out about the shape their marriage had gotten into, because any negative word would have crushed him right then, blown him into a thousand pieces, and she wasn't about to use that awful power.

There was someone she might have consented to go off with then, not right away, but eventually, after a respectful separation and putting their affairs in order. The man in question had gone through premed with her and they'd kept in touch, and a couple of years ago she and he had found themselves living in the same town. As long as the man had lived across the country, it had never become an issue for her, nothing more than a path not taken. She'd made a point of never mentioning his name around Balboa, ever, from early on, and, once the man moved back to Chicago, of only having a discreet, blameless luncheon with him now and then when Balboa was out of town because Balboa, occasional skirt chaser that he was (yes, she could say it to herself sometimes at night right as she was falling asleep, plunging that knowledge down into her dreams as into a pool of water where it would drown), he had a jealous streak a mile wide and would pick up right away on the fact that she had hatched and nourished a special little feeling about the man in her heart. He would hear it in her voice; that was how astute he was. And that's where she wanted to keep her image of the man, buried deep in her heart, where it would surely wither, like the grasses of the fields in Ecclesiastes.

The man and she had spent a summer together in the Poconos as part of their biology program, taking water samples from mountain lakes, mapping watersheds, looking at the effects of acid rain, and it had been the best summer of her life. Yes, the best one. Hiking until her feet bled, eating huge bowls of ice cream topped with wild blackberries the size of her thumb. The man had his faults, such as his tendency to get bored with his girlfriends and, now, with his wife. She knew the man had even had an affair with a married woman he'd met at one of his daughter's soccer games. One thing she knew about him, though—he would never cave in. Each time they met for lunch, they would talk about their respective children with great enthusiasm and tenderness, and Janine would ask him how his beautiful wife was getting along, she was such a wonderful person and a talented gardener, who sent Janine plant cuttings via her husband, in a plastic grocery bag, crumbs of dirt spilling out, because she knew how Janine, having spent that summer in the Poconos at close quarters with the woman's future husband, loved greenery in her life. Janine always wrote his wife a thank-you note, on one of the notecards she'd purchased at the botanical garden auxiliary sale, and thanked the woman for sharing her plants and letting her "steal away" the husband for lunch now and then. Any passerby at those outdoor café tables where Janine lunched with the man could have eavesdropped on his and her conversation at will and heard nothing, not a word, in those innocent remarks to stop their forward progress down the sidewalk.

Instead of going off with him, Janine said, Forgive us our trespasses, as we forgive those who trespass against us, and put an extra fifty dollars in the special offering plate for the victims of the most recent monsoon.

Lisa was in the department store trying on a pair of suede boots to match a dress the color of kid gloves when she caught sight in the dressing-room mirror of a man, perhaps a lunch-hour wayfarer from the business district, in a linen suit. Then again, he looked too well dressed, too urban, to be from her little town. It seemed odd that he would come there to shop, but at least he'd had the good sense to choose the best and largest department store in town, inadequate as it was. He was buying a pair of pumps for his wife or girlfriend or mistress. Nobody said "mistress" anymore, except for her. She thought it a shame that a delicious word like that had fallen out of fashion, but this woman had the narrowest foot she'd ever seen, long with an instep graceful as a geisha's, which meant she had to pay sixty dollars more than anybody else for that anatomical luxury, since the cheaper brands didn't make narrow widths.

The woman didn't seem to mind, because he was obviously picking up the tab for this pair. He'd suffered through some recent hard times, failing the bar exam several times maybe, computer trading that made his whole stable of clients crash, off-track betting that got out of hand, whatever it was had passed, now he was flush, for a while anyway; she could tell by the grateful, almost teary way they both took in the angle of the woman's foot on the calibrated black-and-silver pedestal like the sole remaining fragment of a Roman statue.

The grandfatherly, bewhiskered salesclerk fitting the woman, with all the attentions of an employee working on straight commission, made himself useful and deferential. Though he had trouble bending and kneeling, his arthritis flaring up, he slipped the shoe horn behind the woman's pretty heel so that it slid in; he rustled tissue in a dozen boxes and let cast-off pumps pile up; he would find their mates later, they weren't to trouble themselves about that.

The department store had become increasingly decrepit over the years, scaffolding always up somewhere among its pillars and escalators and cracked marble esplanades in a futile attempt at refurbishing, entire floors hidden from view behind tarps; apart from the occasional find, they stayed a year behind the fashions at the department stores in the larger cities. Their window displays were as unsophisticated as the shops in Little Chinatown with plucked strangled ducks hanging in the window, but they always pampered the customer.

When the salesclerk disappeared, a little flustered, behind a curtain to rummage among the Italian brands, the man caught the image of Lisa's suede-booted legs in the next gallery, refracted in the bee's eye of the *mirror. Heart pumping but eyelids cool, Lisa made it clear to him that if he cared to get rid of the woman for a while, or could, or if he wanted to run the risk of approaching her right there in the store, just yards away, he and she might have a lot to talk about. She'd never done anything of this kind before, but she had practiced the gestures so many times in private that she was sure she must have them right by now. The look she gave him was unmistakable, but that was all she was going to offer at the start. The rest was up to him. Lisa dropped her gaze and pretended to have lost interest in the boots, setting them aside and putting her own back on. No sooner had she turned the corner and walked twenty feet down the aisle, fingering dresses on the circular racks, than she heard the click of taps behind her, halfway between a walk and a run.*

A hand took hold of her elbow, and turned her around almost brusquely. When their eyes met, she could see that he had calculated beforehand that if she acted offended, he was going to apologize profusely and claim he had thought she was someone else. That made his gambit less than a complete risk, but she decided it was enough. His close shave made his face smooth, boyish. "I don't have much time," he said. "I'm only in town for a couple of days, then I'm going back to Chicago. I told her I needed to visit the washroom." Through the simple use of a pronoun, he'd carefully avoided specifying what the precise status of "her" was; she admired his finesse on that point.

"Are you here on business?"

"Kind of. You're probably going to tell me I don't look the part, but I'm a college professor."

"I know all about college professors," she replied. He seemed slightly taken aback by the remark, but she opted not to elaborate. She didn't want to tell him that she'd been attending Hope College. She wanted him to associate her with roses, not tulips.

"Here's a card with my office number on it. I'll be back in Chicago on Thursday. Will you call me there? If I'm not in, tell the department secretary it's an emergency, and she'll get hold of me right away on my beeper."

"I didn't think college professors wore beepers."

"I do. It makes my life a lot less complicated." He ran his hand up

Lisa's shoulder and touched the ends of her hair. "God, you look just like Jean Harlow. I'm serious. If only I'd been born in her era, how differ-ent my life might have been. You're a ringer for her, except you don't have to platinumize your hair to get that look. That's the real color, isn't it?"

"Yes, it is."

"Incredible. You know who Jean Harlow is, don't you?"

"Of course I do. Blond Bombshell. Red Dust. She's been on the late show a hundred times."

"Her real name was Harlean Carpenter. The first sex goddess. She died when she was twenty-six, of uremic poisoning. So young. It's kind of sad."

"Really? I'm nineteen, but you're probably going to tell me I don't look the part either. Are you a movie buff or something?"

"I specialize in film studies. Psychoanalysis applied to film. Lacan, specularity, that kind of stuff. A little feminist theory thrown in. It's amazing. I can't believe I used to be a Victorianist. I totally missed the boat in grad school. I'll tell you more about it when we get a chance to talk. I'd better get back before my absence starts becoming conspicuous. You'll call me, won't you?"

"I will. I think I will."

"Listen, I want to tell you something, just so you'll know. That woman back there trying on shoes isn't my girlfriend. She's my daugh-ter. I had her with my ex-wife. I didn't want you to get the wrong idea. I know I don't look old enough to be her father, but it's the God's truth. She's still a little bit of a daddy's girl, and sometimes I let her go on trips with me so she can shop and get to see different parts of the country, out-of-the-way places like this. It broadens her."

"I'll take your word for it. May you die of uremic poisoning if it's not true."

"See what I mean? Another uncanny resemblance. You make wise-cracks just like Jean. You really have a thirties sensibility. That whole dumb blond thing was nothing but a ruse with her. She had plenty of smarts." He tapped his head, his other hand in his trousers pocket. "Bye. I gotta go." Making an about-face, he sauntered down the linoleum, moving with exaggerated slowness, like somebody who believes he's being

followed by gangsters and wants to wait until he turns the corner before
he tries to give them the slip. The only thing he'd forgotten to do was
offer her a peck on the cheek. She loved him in spite of it.

But he hadn't died of uremic poisoning. He'd gotten tenure instead, and he and his wife had flown to Santorini to celebrate: the blue Aegean, where passion becomes eternally new. If only Lisa really looked like Jean Harlow, instead of like a robust peasant, she might have held on to the professor a little longer.

"I'm pillowy instead of willowy," she muttered, causing the old woman in the chair next to her to look up. The stench of perm chemicals assaulted her nostrils. Then Maria came out from behind the partition and waved.

"Lisa, I'm ready to do your hair. Sorry, I ran a little behind. You want to take the magazine to the chair with you?"

"No. I was just reading an article about Jean Harlow. And remembering how I got to Chicago in the first place. Then the two things got all mixed up. I could write for one of these women's magazines."

Maria lathered Lisa's hair with one hand, used the other to spray her scalp with the nozzle and rub water through the roots, thoughtlessly, as if she were tossing pasta for the thousandth time. "Me, I immigrated." The water, almost scalding, almost unpleasant, soothed Lisa's scalp. Her headache started to ebb. It had been worth missing lunch for these capable hands.

"Immigrated? So did I, Maria."

Maria checked out her own coral-colored lipstick and washed-out complexion, with a look of self-reproof, in the mirror's exaggerated sheen as she expertly wound a towel tight around Lisa's head, squeezed for an instant, then whipped the towel off, tossing it on a heap in the corner. With a broom she whisked away the snippets on the floor, all the colors tumbled together. "You want me to give you the blond look again? It was so pretty on you. But you let it fade." Continuous tragedy had brought out noble overtones in Maria's blue-veined pullet face, making her almost pretty. Her hair was a wreck, though. Lisa supposed she shouldn't entrust her locks to a hairdresser who had such bad, overtreated hair herself.

Yet Maria, in her acrylic pants hugging too tight at the perineum, was like the good mechanic who drives a bad car. She knew what to do with women's hair. The altar to the Virgin on her chairside dressing table, right next to the jumpsuited glamour shot of some Greek pop singer, with a beatific aura airbrushed in around his crackly pile of hair, might all be kitsch, but when it came to making someone else look good, Maria had taste. Today, however, Lisa resisted, clinging to her prerogatives.

"No, I'm letting myself go back to basic black. Cut it really short. Woe-is-me short. Whenever I suffer a disappointment in love, I hack off my hair."

"Clay?"

"Oh, I'm way past Clay. But him too. The residue."

"Okay, I'm gonna wash that man right out of your hair. Only we keep it dark, as you like."

"Besides, blond only goes well with certain figures. I have a dumpy butt."

"Don't say that. You have a very nice little figure."

"Too much boobs, not enough butt. Maybe that's why I can't find the right man."

"Where I come from, in Thessaloniki, no such thing as too many boobs. The men, they're going crazy on it. Even ugly girl, she have a big boob, she can get many marriage proposal. Or just many lover, if she like that instead."

"Lovers! Maria! You look so sweet, but act so wicked."

"I am not wicked. Only weak." All the same, she made the sign of the cross as she reached for the spray bottle of conditioner, and worked it into Lisa's hair with a stiff comb, as if she were beating an egg to peaks with a fork. Her shapeless, soft, sensuous body was set to a low, continuous quiver. Lisa could feel the vibration of self-abandonment in Maria even as she worked her precise magic of snips and flicks.

"Maria, have you ever noticed that my posture is bad? Do I lean over too much?"

"No, I am the one who leans over this chair too much. All day long. I am the crooked woman who walk a crooked mile."

"Having to carry these monstrous mammaries around, it's no wonder if I struggle. I'm thinking of getting a breast reduction."

"Huh. You take off some of those, you give the leftover to me. I'm wearing this Wonderbra, and I can't tell any difference. Only wonder I have is I wonder why I pay so much for this bra."

"You know, I came to Chicago to follow a man. A married man. Never change your geographical location for the sake of romance. That is now an ironclad rule with me. And I knew he was married, because I saw his wife right in the department store with him, at the moment I met him. I simply lied to myself about it. Not that he needed any help in the deception department. I lied to myself because I wanted to drop out of college and come here. Obstinate as hell. At least I got a decent job. The affair only lasted a few months, until I got tired of meeting him basically only when he canceled his afternoon office hours. I'd make dinner, after he'd promise to visit me at my apartment, to stay the night, and at the last minute he'd call me and say Suzy had a ballet recital, or Tommy's team is playing in the championship game, something like that. He was a Victorianist."

"He was victorious? That's not so bad. At least he can pay for a meal. He take you out to eat?"

"A few times. But we always had to drive to another town, he was so paranoid about us being seen by somebody he knew. One time we drove way around Lake Michigan, almost back to my hometown, before he finally felt comfortable stopping. I said, Hey, why don't I just introduce you to my parents, as long as we're over here? He didn't think it was so funny."

"I have the misfortune to go in love with a policeman, Greek like myself. He got big grip, can squeeze me tight. Oh, he has the most beautiful eyelashes, like a woman's. Long, thick. I have those lashes, I don't need all this mascara. My eyes are almost bald, you see? Those eyes of his, they melt me down from a statue to a pool of bronze. Now, you have to use gel if you're going to wear your hair so short. My husband paralyzed in the legs, from car crash, and he's so mean. Mean man with a fat stomach. I thought the accident make him softer, like his belly, and if I make sacrifice each day, cook, bathe his body, we can get closer that way, but he only getting harder and fatter and far away and drink so much more. I sent the children back to Greece to my mother, so they won't stay around his cuffs, because he in the house all time, unless he's going out to drink retsina on the corner. Now it's only him and me, way by ourself. He is blame me for us coming to Chicago. His idea! Now he wants his mama. And I'm making all the money, cut hair all day long and on the weekend too. I said, You want Mama, I'm soon buy you a ticket, but she don't want him. She's too smart. I'm not having any love for such a long time, and this policeman, God, he is so handsome, with those soft Greek eyes, he makes me pay him dinner check, and my Lord, he's eating and eating the big beefsteaks, two or three baked potato, big salad with feta cheese and olive, baklava, two or three piece. Where is he putting all that food? And I spend my tips out of the tip jar on this poor hungry policeman, because I make lotta tips for good job. Then we go to his apartment and he makes me love. That's good part. Then when we're all finish, only twenty thirty minute have gone by. But I'm not done. I still have this thing inside me trying to come out. I want to cling to him and cry, cry, cry, for maybe an hour, I think he give me at least that much sympathy, like if you put two quarters in parking meter, you get stay one whole hour. Then you move car. But he says no, I got to move car right now. He says he been on duty all that time and beefsteaks making him sleepy but he have to go back to work at the station anyway. All that time he's eating beefsteaks and making me love, he supposed to be holding up the law. Then I go home and fix my husband moussaka."

"Could you make me look like Jean Harlow?"

"I already started cutting, but we can still do the color."

"Make me look like Jean Harlow."

"I'm gonna try. I swear to God, Lisa, I'll try. Dimitri! You cancel my next three appointments. Say I been sick unto death."

"Won't those customers see you in here doing my hair?"

"Let them see me. 'Cause damn it, I am surely sick to death for real. Yeah, every time I go blond, I think my life is going to change for at least one day. My life never change. But maybe your life can change."

Kelly probably slept well that night, for the first time in a long time. I didn't. More than ever before, I belonged in the company of Hooftown's miasmic old men, clinging to their banisters, shedding another layer of particles with each forward movement as they slowly crumbled. The air might have been fresh where I sat on the fire escape, for all I knew, but every wisp of it seemed to clot my ears, mouth, and nostrils like cottonwood puffs, the ones that fill the air in the dead of a summer drought when each spent tree sends thousands of them airborne in a last gasp before it dies itself. I swatted at the air around me as if an invisible cloud of gnats had settled in the vicinity of my head.

Every old injury I'd ever sustained, each bit of torn tissue, inflamed tendon, bruised muscle, chipped bone, scarred skin, dislocated jaw, cracked tooth, deviated septum, hematoma, welt, roughed-up rotator cuff, sprained ankle, sliced gum, arthritic kneecap, every bruise, break, abrasion, each of them swelled and creaked and resurfaced, welling up in me all at once. It was a miracle I didn't shatter into a million pieces. I was a Piltdown man, held together entirely by cement glue, the kind that paleontologists use to reconstruct a skeleton that's been crunched to pieces under a rockslide during a major geologic shift. The kind of glue that sets, and the longer you leave it, the harder it gets.

Yes, I ached. I had every good reason to be done with boxing. Yet I was thinking about those ten thousand dollars and what they could do for Chandra. A college fund was what I had in mind, at least the beginnings of one. I knew Kelly wouldn't like the idea. She pretended my saying that I was getting out of boxing hadn't mattered that much to her, but I knew it meant a lot, probably more than any other single thing I had said. What was one more bout? It would be the kicker; it would really set me free. My mind kept going back to Chandra in that yellow jumper, hanging off my arm, eyes sparkling, and I wanted to see my little girl again, even if it meant more tense moments with her mother as a result.

The next morning, I called Kelly up and asked if I could take Chandra out for ice cream or something. I was vague. I didn't even have a good activity in mind, I hadn't planned the conversation out well. To my great surprise, she immediately said yes. Chandra would be very pleased to hear I'd telephoned, and she'd expect me to call for her at such and such a time on such and such a day.

I went to an auto dealer and, with my little bit of savings, paid one month's lease on a decent, conservative vehicle, a brand-new one, with only twelve miles on the odometer. Rent-to-own. I hardly knew how to act behind the wheel. I had to resist the temptation to race the motor at stoplights, just to hear the sound it made. And I bought myself a few new pairs of slacks, a couple of sport shirts, a creaky brown leather belt as sharp, braided, and smelling of tannin as a bullwhip, and got my hair cut. To look respectable for my outing with Chandra. When I thought back on it, I was embarrassed at the condition of my Mustang when I'd had to scoop all those aluminum soft-drink cans to one side to make room for her.

But I was looking down at my shoes, old beat-up leather loafers, and calculating whether I could afford to fork over another fifty bucks to pop by McAlpin's on my way across town and buy new ones, to complete my superficial makeover, and still do all the things I'd planned to do with Chandra. I was performing those mental calculations when the desk clerk rapped on my door. Maybe Kelly had changed her mind at the last minute and canceled the outing with Chandra. Not that I blamed her.

Instead, the clerk handed me a perfumed lavender envelope. The scent of it was familiar to me. On the back, in embossed cursive, the initials C.W. Sensuous braille. I rubbed my fingertips over the monogram.

Inside was a note from Carmela Wade, asking me to come out to visit her the next day at Wildbrake Farm. Shawn Sheldon had told her where I was staying and that I'd asked for her, saying I was a friend of a friend from Chicago. She said she assumed I meant Balboa Trafalgar. She'd hand drawn a detailed map because she was really out in the sticks. No RSVP necessary, given the short notice. Just come. I tucked the note in my jacket pocket.

On the way over to pick up Chandra, I decided not to worry about the condition of my shoes and instead use a few of the thin sheaf of dollars still in my wallet to pick up a decent bottle of wine for Kelly. To thank her for making the outing with our daughter so free of hassles. And to show her I still remembered what her tastes ran to.

Chandra awaited me in a yellow running suit with a black stripe down the side of the pants. A golden Scrunchee swept her hair tightly back into a ponytail. It was shiny black, thick, wavy, a real mane, but much straighter than her mother's. It grew fast, the way mine did. For some reason, she had a gym bag in her hand. Kelly was giving her the Look. Something was up.

"I bet you have to get your hair cut every month," I said at once, trying to break the ice. The bad vibes had caught me by surprise, and I couldn't think of anything wittier on the spot.

"Yeah, I guess. C'mon, Clay, let's go." She didn't want to talk about her hair.

"What's with the bag? Am I taking you to the gym? You want to learn how to box?"

"Hard*headed*," Kelly commented, without elaborating.

"Can I have a sleepover at your house, Clay? I've got all my stuff ready in here."

"I told you, don't be talking to him about any sleepover. Not gonna happen."

Chandra's eyes narrowed into a pair of naysaying minus signs. Double negative. Subtraction problem, wrong answer, times two. She stared straight into her lashes, a pint-sized reflection of her mother in a funhouse mirror. "I don't care what you say," she answered as impudently as possible, hitting down on each word. Driving nails in her mother's coffin. "I don't want to live in this house. *I-can't-even-understand-the-words-coming-out-of-your-mouth-mother.*"

"You sassing me back? I'm about to snatch you baldheaded, missy. You understand that? I got half a mind to ask your daddy to rattle those teeth."

Chandra huffed and puffed, high stepping, running in place, a squirming dervish who Kelly had caught fast by the arms. She slashed at her mother with singing, swinging elbows. "Since when is he my daddy? Since when he can rattle my teeth? You told me more than once I didn't have no daddy. Ain't that right? Ain't that right? Ain't it?"

Kelly tried to answer, and succeeded only in stuttering. Words formed in her mind, but the sheer precocious force of Chandra's being, seven going on twenty-seven, knocked the words back into her mother's mouth.

I gave Chandra's ponytail a gentle tug. "Your mom is right. The room I live in—well, it's not very nice. Kind of grungy, actually. And they only allow men to sleep in this particular one. So a female houseguest might be a problem for me. Even if she's a little girl."

She stopped her childish calisthenics at once, to ponder this new bit of information. From one moment to the next, she didn't even seem upset anymore. "They let only men sleep there because it's grungy?"

"Not exactly. But the two things probably have something to do with one another. Listen, we'll have fun, though, and then I'll bring you back home."

"Why can't you move—?" Chandra started to ask me, but thought better of it. She gave a hooded, sidelong look in her mother's direction. And let the bag drop from her hand. "Okay. Let's go, then. I like bubble gum in my ice cream. Wow, you look handsome, Clay. Haircut." She tried to wolf whistle at me, couldn't make more than a thin, airy sound, then started walking in a circle, suddenly caught up in a determination that she would master the art of whistling in the next two minutes.

Kelly raised her arms toward the ceiling and waved them. "Thank you, someone, for taking my part."

"Let me talk to your mom a minute." I gave Chandra the keys. "I got a new car."

She stopped whistling. "New!"

"Right at the bottom of the stairs. You can unlock the door and listen to the radio. Pick your favorite station. Just don't drive off on me or anything. It's yellow."

"Yellow!" She tore out of the apartment door, keys jangling like dogtags, feet clomping as she took the steps. I listened for a minute, in case the engine started up, but it didn't.

"Okay if I bring her back late?"

Kelly dropped to the couch arm. "You can drown her if you want."

I handed her the bottle of Bordeaux. "Still like?" She nodded her head, perused it appreciatively, rolled its glass body in her hands, tried to eke out a smile. I allowed myself the liberty of massaging her neck.

"I like that. God, my shoulders are full of knots. Sorry. I didn't mean for today to be laundry day."

"I don't mind."

"Clay, what Chandra said about me saying she didn't have any—"

"Shhh. Don't say another word. Breathe in and out."

I worked my way down her back, using the technique Balboa had employed on me. Keeping it professional. I'd picked up a little therapeutic skill along the way, by closing my eyes and paying attention to how his hands went to work. He was a master. Always went right to the trigger points. You didn't have to tell him anything, except that you were in pain. For me, it was an act of concentration to draw the stress out of Kelly's body, like trying to shave somebody else with a razor. She let her body relax into me. "I'm going out to see Carmela Wade tomorrow." I started to take the envelope out of my pocket, to show her, then thought better of it. She might not like its fragrance.

Kelly took hold of my shirtsleeve, as though she were going to pluck off a stray thread. But there was no thread there. "Be careful."

"Of what?"

"I don't know. Of yourself. You're impulsive. I didn't mean to be hard on you the other night. Some things needed saying, though. To clear the air."

"Did it clear?" She shrugged back at me. "Well, did it start to?"

"I can't tell yet. I hope so. Would you do me a favor?"

"Name it."

"What time will you be done seeing Carmela tomorrow?"

"I'm going in the afternoon. For a few hours, at most, I'd guess."

"What exactly are you hoping to gain by your visit?"

"Hard to say. She invited me. I'll just play it by ear."

"She invited you?" Kelly scrutinized me for a long moment. Then she let her eyes go soft, like warm molasses. She hadn't gazed at me that way in a long time. I made myself look away. "When you get done, why don't you come by? I'll make a simple supper. Chandra and I have to eat anyway. I need an ally while I try to get her over this little hump. Seven-thirty okay?"

"Fine. Only in case I get hung up, maybe you shouldn't wait on me."

"Seven-thirty. Firm. If you're a tad late, I'll stick it in the oven. I know what you like to eat, but I'll surprise you."

"I can't deny that. I'll do my best."

She ran her hand over my new haircut, then reached into the soft underhairs, as if I were a kitten. "You really have changed, Clay. I see a big difference in you. It's strange. Those moods that come over Chandra, they remind me so much of you. Even though you seldom let yourself express them. And it's really something to watch you soothe the savage part of her, with your patience, your words. It helps me let go of those hard feelings I been carrying round so long."

"I wasn't trying to do anything."

"I know you wasn't, honey. Maybe that's why I like it. You're just being you. If somebody had been there all along, to comfort you, when you were younger, like what you just did for Chandra, things might have turned out different in your life."

Scrofulous-looking Brother blows into town somewhere, let's say for the sake of argument it's in the heart of the Bluegrass. And where he came from, nobody knows. Got them big lymphatic glands going, maybe he just had too much to drink, or it could be metaphysical. Who can tell? No question that he's wrung out, though. Look like he done farted a hurricane, a category four, leaving all kinds of wreckage behind him. Even the third little pig's house blew down, and it was made of cinderblock, built to code, reinforcing rods, all that shit. Brother's feeling about halfway dead, looking for someplace to lay his head.

He used to have a comfort zone in town, but he done messed that onliest perfect situation up good, a woman scorned, so it wouldn't pay to go back sniffing around like a dog with the mange. Because you don't shit where you eat. And he already went and shat in that kennel. Oh Bodhisattva, forget nirvana; just give me some *prajina.* I didn't say ganja, for once. I hope you noticed that. No, all I'm begging for is a loaf of *prajina* with a pint of cane sorghum to slather on the slices, that selfsame Townsend's Sorghum she used to send me FedEx, in the middle of the week, to my office, for no good reason except she knew how I diggity dug its bittersweet funk. A taste like her, thick, strong, and the color the same color as her skin. Dark in the dark and started to clear when you held it up to the light. But I heard there was a drought this year, or a flood, it comes to the same, and the cane fields didn't yield the way they were supposed to, so Danny Townsend lost his whole entire crop and won't be making the sorghum molasses this year. He does it all himself, by hand, in an old-fashioned cane press, the kind they used to hitch a mule to.

Prajina, yes. If I heal enough other people, if I lead enough of them to enlightenment, maybe I can heal my own soul and move on to the next thing. The fuck you say. Because he doesn't have a bosom for a pillow, Scrofulous Brother checks in, where there is room at the inn, the Campbell House; it says VACANCY right out by the road in loopy red letters, and he passes through those high Corinthian columns, the faux columns that ain't holding nothing up except the sagging, wounded pride of a lost would-be republic, the very columns that used to say NIGGA, KEEP OUT. Nowadays, with the Hiltons and Doubletrees and Marriotts proliferating down at the bypass, these in-town plantation-wanna-be joints with plaster patches have fallen so low, they letting just about anybody in, right through the front door, come as you are, feast at the steam table, so long as the credit card scans. He's not sure his card will scan, actually, there's a tense moment as he and the nigga-loving clerk in the jaunty visor wait for the electronic confirmation from some distant, all-knowing, almost instantaneous realm. But then clearance comes, so Scrofulous Brother (S.B. to his friends) really does start to believe in miracles. He'll make sure to eat in the hotel's own underpatronized restaurant, so he can sign as many of his expenses as possible to the room.

Use the swampy, indoor, overheated, overchlorinated pool surrounded by indoor-outdoor Astroturf detaching from the concrete below. No separate pool for coloreds, everybody pees in the same place now, like those fifteen kids on a field trip hollering down at the shallow end, choking on the water they splash into each other's faces, because God knows this amount of chlorine ought to kill about any bacteria and give you a body peel.

Shower right away, back up in the room, just in case. No shampoo; he could use the leftover from the Delano (two fifty a night, of course he was going to take the replacement shampoo, conditioner, body lotion, cologne, shower cap, razor, shoeshine sponge), except that he didn't remember to bring that shampoo into the shower, and it's too far away to fetch without dripping all over the carpet; so use the bar of soap on your hair, exactly like those nappy days on the West Side, when soap didn't come in a bottle, and you washed your Peter, Paul, Mary, and hair all with the onliest soap you was gonna get. Send your shirts downstairs for dry-cleaning, take a chance, then slip into a polo shirt, Ralph Lauren, got that little horse on the front that's exactly right for Kentucky. Eat the chicken-whatever in something-sauce in the hotel restaurant, but they did throw some fresh mushrooms over the top, as a decoy, and heaven only knows where they got that kiwi fruit, garish garnish, way past its prime, which they've been saving specially for his arrival.

Sleep like the dead, S.B., with the rattle in the heat register giving you the white noise you need, oddly comforting. Then Sunday morning, Lazarus, come forth and wipe the sleepy tears from your eyes. Put on a suit, just because it's Sunday and for no other reason. It takes the same effort to dress sharp as it does to dress ratty. Drive the rental car straight downtown, down Broadway toward the North Side, cruise past the bait shops and pawn shops until you see those W. E. B. DuBois black folk congregating around a white church building with a prairie spire, nothing too ostentatious, because this is Fourth Street, close to where Lexington's whores (all three of them) also congregate under cover of night.

No good honest whores anymore, because there's too much

money to be made working the middle-class strip clubs (there were twelve listed in the yellow pages, but you opted out of visiting those citadels of pseudo sin), or those good-time girls can make still more in tips, and catch fewer diseases, by attaching the big-pored, round jumbo sponges to their jumbo breasts and working the X-rated car wash, Boobs-A-Bubble, or some such. Only three Mary Magdalenes left in the whole damn town to bring this one neighborhood down by milling around Saturday nights on the same block where the church is situated.

Still, having pious upstanding people buy that building was a blessing in disguise. The property values were nice and low when the worshipers all chipped in to break ground on the whitewashed church with the prairie spire, and they were able to put down a hell of a slab (and Baptist ministers love to talk about the size of the slab, whether it's a building or a roast beef). Step inside, the ushers start palming this anonymous stranger, S.B., at once, because nothing sparks a good service like the appearance of a leper. They'll run the risk of catching a skin rash, one day only, for the promise of eternal salvation. Ain't nothing but good old-time *prajina*.

Soon as you cross the threshold, Janine comes to mind; it's a natural association, and she would at least approve of your floundering, inchoate as it is, Baptist as it is, low rent as it is, though she would definitely not approve of the large plastic cross in the narthex (okay, the foyer) that lights up crimson from the inside. Mm, mm, serious lack of taste. Only you know there's killer turnip greens, deviled eggs, black-eyed peas, and some chicken finally worth eating down in the basement, cooked in a cast-iron skillet, you can smell the gravy breaking through the liberal dose of Lysol that the janitor laid down on all the floors yesterday, just in case a leper showed up.

The Son of Man has arisen! The pastor booms out with his arms spread wide, big daddy, everybody's daddy, only don't make jokes about illegitimate children concerning him and his female parishioners, preacher man saying, "Let's do it standing up rather than laying in the pew, because if a deacon passes by that window and sees us standing up together, he might think we were dancing." No, this ain't no white church; we can dance if we please, right in the aisles during worship, so save your humor; we might lay on some hands and jump and shout and even speak in tongues once in a great while (it's been known to happen when Mighty Jehovah touches us with his sublime spirit), but just because you grew up in the projects with no daddy, washing your hair with a bar of soap, and having your dirty little mouth washed out with that selfsame bar of soap, don't be extrapolating, don't make assumptions about others, don't be bringing that negativity down here from Chicago or up from Florida or wherever it is you think you coming from.

Anyway, do you know where your children are? Right this minute? If so, let the prodigal son come running home when you whistle! There is only one Father, Our Father, and since you recite the Twenty-third Psalm so well, I guess you ought to know something about paternity and shepherds; I guess you must have fell into Sunday School somewhere along the way, even if you ain't got the slightest cotton-picking idea what grade Chance received on his report on Thomas Paine, or Cotton Mather, or was it George Washington Carver, that pride of our people, that peanut prophet, blessed be his soul. If you died right now, brother, Scrofulous Brother, would Our Father take you into his unchanging hand?

Be happy in this day! Wilt back into the pew, and don't feel so conspicuous, because we're not gonna single you out for praise or blame, either one. The last shall be first within our portals. You're our beloved guest, and we're going to anoint your head with oil and wash your feet with some of that Lysol, because damn, they do stink just a little. The pastor is only throwing out some beatitudes and platitudes, some words to live by, so Mary, don't you weep 'bout Pharaoh's army, but if something the preacher man says happens to pertain to you, then apply it to your life straightaway. Take notes if you like, with that stubby little yellow pencil that everybody else is using to scribble their names on the offering envelopes. We all know who each other is, so signing our names is only a formality. It's your soul we're concerned about. All the reverend wants from us today is that we kick in enough for this month's operating fund. But no admission is charged here to the likes of you. Sign the guest register, be fearless, or, if you're too bashful for that, carve your initials, S.B., in the pew with the stubby pencil when nobody's looking. That graphite is soft, giving, and it will scarcely make more than a whispery sound. Even if we hear it, we'll ignore that scratching noise, because our mamas done taught us that it ain't polite to stare, especially at a leper. Most important of all, listen for God's word to you.

I happen to know they say that very phrase in the high-toned Presbyterian Church you pretend to go to. We may only be Baptists, we may not know a thing about Bodhisattva and *prajina*, whatever in creation that may be, but we dwell in the word of the Lord, we sing the doxology, and we got a good church choir, not to mention that every last person in this congregation can carry a tune, and yes, we've even got a couple of Whitney Houstons and Aretha Franklins in the making, praise God.

Can you sing? Can you carry a tune? Would you like to learn? Are you washed in the blood of the Lamb? Will you bear the cross of Jesus, O wayfarer, and will you cross the River Jordan, mighty, deep, and wide? Thieves have beaten you and thrown you by the wayside (though I must say that's an expensive suit you're wearing— Bill Blass?—must have cost nine hundred dollars if it cost a nickel).

Thrown you by the wayside, stolen that diamond-encrusted watch—a blessing in disguise, because that means the hour alarm won't go off during the service, turning every last head your way. We're forgiving, but we do have our rules. The pastor goes on preaching fifteen or twenty minutes past the hour if he wants, he does as he pleases, he always has, and we are Christian enough to sit here and bear his thundering in relative silence. He's no Frederick Douglass; who among us is? But he's been known to cobble together a homily or two that got repeated down at the auto repair shop on Tuesday. We are Samaritans, we do not make distinctions between rich and poor, so listen for God's word in your life. Even a rich man can enter the kingdom of heaven. Though it doesn't happen often, if the ugly truth be known.

Sure enough, the pastor sermonizes extemporaneously; he pays no special mind to Scrofulous Brother. There's no fire and brimstone here. The Scripture lesson has been taken from Psalms, that beautiful book of solace, and if anything, the pastor is overflowing with compassion. He says that no matter what your problem, the answer can be found in Scripture. Yes, incredible as it seems, the Bible has an answer to each and every single one of life's problems.

You may need a guide to help you locate it, the lesson may not be apparent at first blush, but whether it be the fiery locutions of Isaiah, or the deceptively simple parables of Jesus, there always lies a solution in Scripture. We might think of the Bible as the world's largest advice column, only this advice is never topical and never grows old.

Scrofulous Brother starts to grow excited, because deep in his soul, he wishes he could reconcile with the wife he has abandoned. He knows she is a good woman, if only he could learn how to ride out those ruthless patches in her personality. When she loves him, he simply describes those patches as demanding, her holding him to a high standard, making him a better man than he would otherwise be. When those same tendencies manifest themselves in a darker mood, he calls her high maintenance, ball buster, bitch.

After the sermon, when the glad-handing has taken place, and the assembled company starts to stream into the basement for Sunday dinner, S.B. approaches the pastor in a meek and obedient frame of mind. Something in this preacher's straightforward and artless manner has inspired confidence, even the possibility of intimacy. The pastor has deliberately lagged behind, it seems, for in his grizzled knowing, in the laugh lines of his face and the spark in his eye, it's clear he has expected S.B. to approach him with a heavy heart.

S.B. admits that he has been sitting in the back pew casting about for a way to apply this morning's lesson to his own life; he's not a steady Bible reader, but he knows Scripture well enough; his granny drilled it into him early on. He even began to flip to different books and different passages of Scripture (no disrespect intended) in the midst of the sermon, which has touched him in a deep place. But he can't find any biblical reference to the question burning within him.

No offense taken, son. It heartens me when the one sheep who has gone astray takes heed of my words so urgently that he must act upon them at once. I saw my lost lamb seize that Bible out of the pew. My compassionate eye misses nothing. That desperate taking up of the Bible is in itself a proof of the depth of my lost sheep's Christian impulses. For him I would neglect the rest of the flock, only too happily. For him I would even postpone that pineapple upside-down cake waiting downstairs; Mrs. Stearns makes a heavenly one, only I hope it isn't all gone by the time we get down there. Sometimes they forget to save a slice for the pastor. So what is your question, O Child of God?

Preacher, I don't know how to say this, and I don't want to seem hard-hearted or critical in any way of my woman, who has suffered muchly on my account, and I haven't always walked with God, if you know what I mean.

Who among us always walks with God? We all fall short of the glory. Speak your heart.

Well, my wife, this mood just comes over her, regular, almost every month. And it's hell to live with. Then I feel like I've got to run.

This mood you speak of, does it come at about the same time every month?

Why yes, if I think about it, I guess I'd say so.

And it lasts, oh, say, a week or thereabouts?

That's right. Don't take this wrong, Reverend, but now that I ponder her mood in my mind, I'd call it PMS.

Son, we live in the scientific age. God alone has created all this bounty around us, including the blessings of science and medicine. They are part and parcel of his enduring truth. We are not a benighted people. I'm not going to say this from the pulpit, because my flock is a conservative flock, but man to man, I'd go so far as to claim that the Bible has much science and even psychology in it, if you read it right. Freud and Darwin were not the first to contemplate these matters. I don't know if I can find a quick fix to your problem, but most certainly it has some basis in Scripture. I just can't think of chapter and verse at this exact moment. Perhaps if I partake of some of Mrs. Stearns's delicious pineapple upside-down cake, provided that there's any left, that will clear my mind.

Downstairs they go together, and Scrofulous Brother puts on the feedbag, the fried chicken almost brings tears to his eyes, and he does his best not to look like a craven mongrel or a biggety interloper. Across the room, he spies the pastor leafing through the Bible on the table as he keeps a firm grip on the plate containing the last surviving piece of the pineapple upside-down cake, which the benevolent Mrs. Stearns has been thoughtful enough to set apart from these ravenous hellhounds.

At length, the pastor crosses the room to Scrofulous Brother, a satisfied smile on his face and just a crumb or two of cake still tenaciously stuck to the tip of his mustache. His Bible is open to the Book of Luke. S.B., I have indeed found the basis of your question about PMS in Scripture. The Good Book clearly tells us that Mary rode Joseph's ass all the way into Bethlehem.

Clay drove a road with switchback after switchback, gullies falling off now to one side, now to the next, the edge of the narrow road eaten away in too many places. The ravine beside was steep. Virgin oak, maple, and evergreens rose out of its depths, with pinecones as big as pineapples. He could only see the upper part of the trees. The bases of their stout black trunks were lost somewhere below. The pitched angle of the land and the dense foliage had made the ravine a logger's nightmare, not worth the trouble of cutting its timber, since the enormous, tall trunks couldn't have been dragged out, so the trees had been left to their natural state. He saw the sign WILDBRAKE FARM, easy to miss, and turned into the dirt drive.

He bounced along a winding way, over hillocks, crossing one cattle guard after another. The house, a modest, half-timbered jewel, was set on a rise, the one spot sure to capture plenty of light the entire day in this choked garden of ivy-dark greens. Pastureland off on the other side had been cleared, in a leveler lie, fenced in for stables and paddocks. A couple of horses with shiny naps loitered by the fence. Carmela must have heard his motor approaching, because she came out the door of a screened porch to greet him, her half-visible mesh silhouette behind the screen taking on substance as she stepped into a downpour of sunlight.

The black lacquer hair was twisted into a French braid held at the top by an engraved leather hair clasp with a long wooden pin stuck through it, geisha style. She had on casual garb—cutoffs as short as they could decently be worn, showing off slender but shapely hips that rounded into a pleasing mound at the back; a thin gold chain of an ankle bracelet circled above one sandal; and a ribbed lavender tank top, giving plenty of glimpses of long neck and firm but contoured shoulders and a peek at a small blue-and-green tattoo between her right shoulder and breast.

She wasn't voluptuous but compact, athletic. There were six or seven jeweled studs and two gold hoops in her left ear, all sparkling, catching rays from the dappled branches overhead, as she turned her head to place a welcoming kiss on his cheek. As she did, he caught a scent of that perfume, the same she had sprinkled on the envelope.

She inspected him, letting a faint smile cross her lips. "Nobody told me you were such a smokehouse. Oh, but excuse my bad manners. Here I have you standing out here on the lot, the wind drying out your mouth. Come inside, and let me fix you a drink."

"I'll just take a cup of coffee, if you don't mind. I don't drink this early in the day."

"Well, I certainly do. Bourbon, straight up. The horsewoman's drink. That is, whenever I feel like it. I keep a bottle of Labrot and Graham in the kitchen, in case one of my animals gets a cut."

"That's pricey iodine."

"But I'd better not drink alone. With that steel-trap mind of yours, and me so helpless and skimpily dressed, I'd best not let my guard down. I do believe I'll save my libations for our party tonight."

"Whose party?"

"Why, yours and mine. Angela Fallon is throwing her annual bash. Out on their place. Everybody who's anybody in central Kentucky will be there, including you and me. Ooh, Clay, you're going to see gaudy money like you've never seen before. And a little taste, too. We've got some of that here."

"I've promised to meet—well, a couple of people, at seven-thirty."

"Did you promise promise? Or did you say you might meet them?"

"Might. They knew I could get delayed, because I was coming all the way out here."

"Into the deep, dark Black Forest."

"Where those who venture in never come out alive again."

"Because the Black Witch eats them up. Is that how the story ends?"

"Usually."

"Please, Clay, don't make me go stag. It's too humiliating. I don't even have a date. I'll be the ugly duckling, without anybody there to turn me into a beautiful swan."

"I have a hard time believing someone like you can't get a date anytime she wants."

"Ah, but you see, it's because I chose not to have one. Unless I came upon a man worth my while. And suddenly, I stumbled upon one. Just the way it happens in a fairy tale."

"You mean, I answered your summons."

"If this seven-thirty person you're referring to is some kind of girlfriend, I won't insist. I've made a vow to never again cause a delay in the schedule of a married man. Or even an almost married one. So, is she your fiancée?"

"No."

"Going to be? Lover? On-and-off girlfriend?"

"None of those things. Strictly platonic. For very good reasons."

"Such as?"

"I don't really feel like going into them."

"You're giving me no choice but to collar you for the evening. To be my escort. That's all I'm asking. I hope you weren't getting any other ideas. I'm flirtatious by nature. Don't make too much of it. I'm a pretty good girl. Besides, I'm certain it would give Balboa, wherever he is, enormous pleasure for the two of us to spend some time together. To console one another in his absence. Isn't that why you came out here? Or why did you come out here? You don't really think I know where he is? Let's not sit around waiting for the no-show."

"I can't go to a high-class do wearing these duds. I don't own a suit."

"That's no problem. I'm going to phone ahead to a tuxedo place I know and rent you a nice one. We'll pick it up on the way in. You're about six foot three. With those broad shoulders, and that deep chest, must be about a forty-six. Waistline, thirty-two. Inseam, thirty-four."

"Have you been reading the tags in my clothes?"

"That's right. My bedtime reading. Now, don't say another word. This goes on my credit card. I can afford it, I want to do it, and besides, it's not exactly fair of me to trick you out here without giving you fair warning of my intentions—concerning this party. I want to prove to you that I'm not the Black Witch. Okay, Hansel?"

"All right, then. I'll follow you in my car."

"Follow me? What for? Are you going to tail me, like a movie detective? Will there be a chase scene?"

"I'll be going back to Lexington afterward, so there's no sense me doubling all the way back here."

"No, I think you'd best leave your car here. We'll take my little Porsche. It's going to be so late, and as profligate as I am, I may need you to drive me home in case I drink too much. I get carried away sometimes. Friends don't let friends drive drunk, right? Not on these treacherous roads. And because you're the Puritan between us two, the one with honorable intentions, you can't neglect your gentlemanly duties. You wouldn't want to have this body of mine lying at the bottom of one of those steep ravines, would you? All smashed to pieces? Nobody would ever find it, that's for sure. Let's ride in together, like a happy couple."

Kelly stopped typing. She wished she could put the story in her own mind, her own voice, her own heart, give herself some love and romance, like she deserved, but sometimes it just didn't turn out that way. Once the poison was in your system, it had to work its way through. Why torment herself? What good would it do? It wasn't even an expiation or a catharsis. Thinking and fantasizing only made matters worse. There was no reason she had to give Clay a toss in bed with some woman she'd never met but only heard about. Nobody was forcing her. She guessed it was true what authors so often said about creating characters; they really did take on a life of their own. It was too damn bad you couldn't control them, couldn't shape them to your will.

Well, she was used to that feeling. She gulped down the unfinished coffee in the mug. It was completely cold and tasted awful, but her mouth was much too dry. She needed to go to bed. Clay hadn't shown up, that was a damn shame, but it was time for her to stop obsessing about it and try to get some sleep. But she couldn't stop herself until she had reached the climax. Until she had watched the auto accident. Yes, if the truth be known, that was more than a figure of speech. She had half a mind to kill him and the woman off tonight, make him plunge down into a ravine in a flaming ball. Put him out of his misery, and her out of hers.

What I remember about the soiree Carmela took me to: it was a conservative version of Balboa's pajama party, with liquor instead of drugs, and everybody naked under their clothes. All Carmela had on was a black wraparound cocktail dress that started somewhere in the middle of her bosom and quit well before the knees. Held in place by the mere pin of a silver brooch, like the lock on a velvet box. This number was set off by woven leather slippers and a Spanish comb. We danced several slow ones, and when I stepped into Carmela to give her a turn, she made sure I felt that velvet dress in all the right places, while never giving the impression that anything the slightest bit indecent was going on. She even carried on a conversation with the lady of the couple dancing next to us while she performed this maneuver. A definite head trip. More than sexy, it was sly humor, seeing how much she could get away with and still keep a straight face. I was her entertainment for the evening.

They say that, sometimes, a dance is just a dance.

Carmela was pretty much in her cups, or else she just didn't hold her liquor all that well. I'd drunk more than I meant to myself, so parts of my mind were occluded. Whole areas of the cerebral cortex shut down for the night. The driving part of me, though, had an almost preternatural alertness, and I raced toward Wildbrake at top speed, with such mental clarity that I remembered the way back without any instructions from her. All the hairpin curves seemed to straighten out before me in the sequestered silence of her Porsche and the quadrophonic environment of Sade. Smooth operator. Over and over, in an echo chamber. The same music Balboa had played the night we cruised in his Audi. Somebody must have kept slipping quarters into a cosmic video machine, because the lane continuously straightened out just as it made contact with the headlights I had set on high beam.

Enveloped in the suave deerskin of the passenger seat, Carmela insisted on cradling an open bottle of Booker's she'd produced from the floorboard, swigging, not often but when she did, as if trying to quench an unquenchable thirst. Fifty-five bucks a bottle—I knew that much about it. She passed the bottle to me, and I drank my share too, heedless of the possibility that we might plummet off into one of the ravines. I was overconfident, I knew I was, a pilgrim's progress to the unpromised land, and yet I couldn't really stop myself from barreling down those country roads through the overhanging trees.

I kept expecting, almost hoping, that flashing lights would appear out of the darkness, crystal blue persuasion, and get me jailed for DUI, before I had a chance to end up back at Carmela's place. There had never been any dearth of irascible country boys in county sheriff uniforms lurking under bridges in their cruisers like trolls when I was a teenager, itching to teach me a lesson. And now I wanted to learn it. But none of them showed their faces.

We raced over the cattle guards and hillocks of Carmela's acreage as if on a roller coaster, the bottom of my stomach dropping out as we crested each rise. Then we were parked in her gravel drive, the engine shut off, ticking as the metal contracted. The only other sound as we stepped out into the chill night air was the automatic fan running in the darkness, working to cool the overheated motor.

I swear to God that's everything I remember. I'm not hiding behind the liquor. As far as I'm concerned, that's all that happened. We drove to her house, I stumbled indoors, and woke up in her bed. But she wasn't in it. She must have decided to give my heavy frame the support it needed and relocate herself to the couch until we both slept it off.

Then they were in the kitchen. Then in the hallway. Then in the bedroom. She undressed, unself-consciously, not hurriedly, and as if she were alone. She swayed as her fingers worked to unclasp the silver brooch on her dress.

Her wraparound unwound down her body and slid to the floor. "Haven't had any for a while, have you?" With a chuckle. "You need it,

Clay." And now she had crossed the stretch of floor between him and her and was undressing him, lucid, deliberate. All he could answer with was a splash of inarticulate sounds. A gurgle. "Because you wanted to boink Balboa's girl. Is that it? Tell me I'm wrong. It makes you feel closer to each other. Brothers in arms. Taking a dip in the same heated pool."

"I never thought that. I never meant to think that."

"You don't have to ask his permission. Don't have to be the also-ran. Him and me, we're over. You and me, we're just getting started."

Carmela got on hands and knees on the carpet and presented herself, inviting him to enter her backside. He thrust in so hard, he banged her head on a low drawer. Bad reflexes, no control. She didn't reproach. She was done talking. She'd said everything she needed to. He came within a few seconds, all kinds of rude and ungainly noises issuing from his mouth.

She came, or pretended to. He was so drunk, how would he know the difference? That's the way it was with men. How could he have given her any pleasure in such a short time? But she got to her knees with a sleepy smile of accomplishment on her face, climbed the bedstead, and snuggled down into the bedclothes.

"Come on to bed, Clay. You're too drunk to go anywhere tonight."

"Not drunk. Not."

"Admit it. We both are. Shameless molten. I don't want you on my conscience tomorrow."

He snorted. "Oh, I won't be on your conscience. But you'll be on mine."

"Smokehouse, I am too far gone to make any sense out of that cryptical remark. Both gonna be nursing bad hangovers tomorrow. And I'm gonna have a goose egg on my crown. Ouch. Given to me by the goose that laid the golden egg."

"So you keep him around. 'Stead of cooking 'im." He snickered at his own lame joke, like a simpleton. He could barely raise himself up onto the mattress. Too much gravity in the room.

"Shh. Be strong and silent. Less us lay down together. Lion and lamb."

Could he be strong and silent, for once in his life? Was he capable of that? Or would he start running off at the mouth, the way so many drunks do, as if they really thought they had something interesting to

say? "Come on, Hansel. Get under these covers with the Black Crone. I
don't bite."

He obeyed. He kept his words to himself. Neither of them could fall
into a deep sleep, though. No REM. No dreams. No la-la land.
Headachy. Woozy. Rustling. Jostling. They kept waking each other up.
All night long. Then they slept like dead ones.

She was in the kitchen, the windows open, letting in the still-
cool late-morning air and the twittering, vital sounds of forest creatures. The barks of happy, snappy, sappy larks and mockingbirds
mocking him with their trills. The red, red robin. Woodpeckers
needling for grubs with rock-hard beaks.

Already into her second cup of coffee, Carmela looked fresh,
scrubbed, her skin bright. Locks shiny with shower water, and she'd
put on a pair of jeans, hip-huggers, cut just right, and a halter top.
Her navel ring was out for inspection. Hummingbirds clustered,
whirring blurs of green and yellow, at the feeder suspended outside
the sink window.

"Hey, sleepyhead. You're a sight. Want coffee?" He nodded.
Black elixir splashed in a bone-white cup. Balboa sipped and sat
unmoving, waiting for it to revive him. He never could hold his
booze. Reefer yes, bourbon no. Turns out she could. Hers and his
both.

"Do I get a kiss, Mister Trafalgar? Or just a grunt?" She leaned
over and kissed Balboa full on the mouth. Not juicy, but possessive
and decisive.

"Sure. Everything was—memorable."

"Well, I certainly remember the good part." She touched a spot
on her knee. "And the bruise to go with it."

"Sorry about that."

"No, no. Nothing but the heat of passion, baby. As usual. I
believe in it. On the contrary, you'll have to excuse me if I did
or said anything too wild and crazy. I was so drunk, God only
knows what came out of my mouth. Though I surely recall what
went into it."

"Yeah."

"I can't remember—did I say something to freak you out? You look spooked."

"I'm not spooked. You just ran me hard. I'm bleeding from the mouth."

"That's good for you. Shows your mettle. Try this spinach omelette. Ought to bring you back around." She placed before Balboa a steaming, stuffed yellow crescent, on a china plate, robin's egg blue. The omelette skirted by two pieces of perfectly crisp, artfully misshapen toast. A dollop of apple butter from some local orchard. Then a Dutch butter pot, round, a deep burning blue, its luminescence bleeding through the fired glaze, as if it were still in the kiln. The butter soft, yet still firm enough to sustain the pewter demiknife sticking straight up out of it. The sword in the stone, ready to give way. Orange juice in a heavy-bottomed glass, heft in his hand, filled halfway with juice, the other half with light. Frosted, every sip a chilly sunburst. Fresh squeezed, of course. Everything fine. Everything a sensual pleasure.

When he'd eaten, he pushed back his chair, and she took the opportunity to sit on his lap. "That was amazing," he said. "And I'd like nothing better than to sit right here all day."

"So why don't you?"

"Well, I'm on call starting tonight. Got to get back to Chicago."

"I understand. I knew it was going to be a short visit." She went to kiss him again, and without thinking, he turned his head to the side. She flinched and stood up from his lap.

"Plenty of saliva passed between us last night, homeboy. Now you don't like the taste of spit?"

"Baby, why you want to talk like that? My mouth was full of toast, that's all."

"You know, I didn't even ask you to put on a condom. That's how much I trust you to be clean."

"You're being oversensitive. You get this way every time I'm about to leave. I told you, me and her haven't slept together in a long time. It's just not happening."

"It isn't her I'm worried about."

"I'm clean. I'm a doctor. I'd tell you if I wasn't clean."

"You've got a way of pulling back. You like to get crazy but don't like to think about it afterward. Jekyll and Hyde. Libertine and married man—I never know which it's gonna be."

"I love you. I swear to God I do. If I was only hunting booty, you know I could get that right in town. But that's not what I want. I ain't sleeping with anybody else but you. If I don't sign an affidavit every time I enter your bedroom, it's because I don't want to have to keep explaining myself and defending myself. I'm not going to hurt you if I can help it."

"Too late for that, Balboa. Tell me, what's missing?"

"Nothing, baby. Nothing at all."

"What am I not doing right? Do I make good love?"

"The best. Crazy, freaky. Nobody else I ever knew can do it like that. Or will do it."

"Do we get along? Am I getting on your nerves?"

"The only time I feel peaceful is in your company. That is the damn truth."

"Then what? I keep trying to woo you, honey, but no matter what I do, how good my sex is, how tasty my food, how soft my body, how smart my mind, how witty my table talk, no matter how much I sparkle, I'm going to keep coming in second. Because you are tied to that woman."

"I'm not tied to her."

"You are. With a Gordian goddamned knot. Is it by bitterness? The children? Money? Voodoo? Habit? Just what in the hell is it she's got over you? I'd like to know."

"I don't know."

"Go on. I've got to clean up these dishes."

On the way back into town, I dawdled, in inverse proportion to the previous night's road haste. First, because I still carried the residue of my hangover, my driving hands thick as my skull. I liked coasting through the cool corridors of pine at forty miles an hour, the windshield collecting just enough afternoon light to warm me, making the front seat into my own private greenhouse. Cows huddled together under the trees in the open fields, shielding themselves from the direct heat of the first truly warm day of late winter. The land seemed already to have cast off the remnants of winter's sludge. Cracking the window on the driver's side, I caught the chlorophyll-drenched scent of leaves freshening in their buds. The vegetation was working hard, in its underground way, but I wanted to lollygag. I wasn't going to hurry. Not today.

Kelly had made clear she wanted to keep things at a certain distance. Even though she'd started getting sentimental with me yesterday, I hadn't attached too much importance to that. There was nothing between us anymore. Hadn't she herself given me the go-ahead to visit Carmela? I hadn't done anything I wasn't supposed to do. I drank too much and woke up alone. That's all I had on my conscience. So why was I driving so slow? And why was I on my way to Kelly's apartment, before even stopping off at my own place?

To apologize, of course. She'd be upset about me missing last night's dinner. She probably had understood a definite yes, and I had understood a maybe, don't wait on me. I could never predict Kelly's moods. She'd let a matter slide when I most expected her to dress me down and get really riled when I didn't even know there was something going on.

One of my cues was if I came in the door, and she was doing housework really fast. Arranging stacks of magazines like a postal worker on Christmas Eve or making up beds at lightning speed. When she started in on me with hot words, I usually wouldn't say much, just let her vent and get it over with. So she'd slacken her pace again.

When Kelly let me in, the apartment was spotless. The carpet even looked like it had been shampooed. I detected the acrid smell of concentrated soap. Wax, varnish, oven cleaner, solvents, scrubbing bubbles, detergent, furniture polish. Entire fire extinguishers emptied into smoking frying pans. Sodium bicarb bonding with ashes. All mixed into one single industrial-strength, air-freshening, lemon-scented, toxic smell. Then again, I've always been sensitive to smells. My deviated septum didn't steal that sense from me.

Her movements were slow, right for a Sunday afternoon, and

she appeared to have been reading the newspaper. The various sections of it lay fanned out on the coffee table. The blinds were open,
slanting upward to give off a pleasant indirect light. And she wore a
sleeveless housedress that was all about leisure. Those were good
signs. On the other hand, she could have spent all night cleaning the
apartment and was now hoarding her strength for the big blowup.

"I'm really sorry, Kelly. The dinner engagement slipped my
mind. There's no excuse," I said, stumbling over my words in an
attempt at a preemptive apology. "There's—"

Kelly put an index finger to my lips. "Shh."

"No, let's get this discussed. I don't want it hanging over our
heads."

"There's nothing to discuss, Clay. You said maybe. You warned
me that you might not get back in time. Things happen. Chandra
and I waited half an hour, as you asked us to, then went ahead and
ate. She was a little disappointed, and didn't want to go to bed in
case you might come. But she finally dropped off on the couch."

"Let me make it up to her." I looked around, suddenly aware of
her absence. I had expected Chandra to come running to embrace
me, while her mother hung back with crossed arms. The apartment
rang with an unusual quiet. "Where is she?"

"Over spending the afternoon with a friend. I counted on you
dropping by today. You and me need to spend some time by ourselves."

"We do?"

"Yeah, honey. Don't you think so?"

I shrugged. "Sure. That's fine." No anvils had dropped on my
head. I allowed my neck to rise a little farther out of my collar.

"So I made us brunch. Eggs Benedict. Very fancy. I put foil
over it, so I could reheat it in the oven whenever you got here.
Hungry?"

Fortunately for me, I was. I hadn't had a bite all morning.
"Yeah, starving. How soon can we sit down at the table?"

I wolfed down the brunch like a man on Death Row who has
just gotten an unexpected pardon. Kelly took me by the hand.
"Come lie down on the bed. You look like you didn't get a good
night's rest."

"I didn't. But I don't think I should go in there."

"It's Sunday afternoon, Clay. Where have you got to be?" By then, we had crossed the threshold. I don't know how we arrived there so fast. "At least keep the Sabbath."

"The Sabbath? How?"

"By not laboring. There's a television over there on the dresser. You want me to turn it on? They might have spring training on cable."

"No TV. I like the quiet. Maybe I'll rest for a second, then."

The bedspread was white, with a high, velvety pile, covered with beads of fabric. I ran my hand over it.

"What's this material called?"

"Chenille. You like it?"

"My grandmother used to have a bedspread exactly like this."

"This one here is an heirloom. Like comfort food, isn't it? And my grandmother used to say no meal was complete without a good nap."

I had to admit, it looked cozy, inviting. And I was drowsy, my body limp. Spent. I wasn't used to being pampered. Whenever Lisa had tried, I'd always rebuffed her, telling her I didn't want to be mothered. One time she replied, "Clay, there's a difference between being mothered and being cared for. A mother isn't the only woman who can care for a man. Maybe you'll grow up someday and be able to see the difference." I let myself sink down on the chenille bedspread, with its beaded points of thread massaging my back, like a fakir finding unreasonable comfort on a bed of nails.

"Feels good."

"Of course it does. It's meant to. A lot of people have slept on or under this spread over the years." Kelly switched off the overhead light, so only the muted rays coming from around the drawn shade cast a soft glow on the creamy, dreamy walls. She put her hand on the knob, as if she were going to leave me alone to sleep. And she did shut the door. Only she stayed inside the room.

She let the loose shift fall from her shoulders, in a single, effortless motion, and leisurely unhooked her plain cotton brassiere, a stout and underwired garment, leaving on only her white cotton underpants. Sensible ones. Except that the sight of them was turning me senseless.

Opening a dresser drawer, she searched, and the old-fashioned scent of rose potpourri came into the room. She took out a condom, tossed it on the corner of the spread. Then a powder puff, and she gave herself a light dusting. I knew what it was. White Shoulders. Kelly had never bought the expensive stuff, never let me buy it for her either, saying it was a waste of money, and the cheap stuff smelled every bit as good.

She turned to me with a frank stare. The kind of look a woman can't even muster until she's turned thirty. Kelly knew that once I looked my fill, I wouldn't be able to resist her body. Those heavy dark nipples, made to be sucked. That round soft belly, the one I liked to stroke.

"There's something I need to explain, Kelly. About last night. It isn't what you—"

"Shhh," she said again. "I ain't gonna hear nothing. You ain't gonna say nothing." She slid one knee up onto the bedspread, then the other, without haste, giving me a glimpse of capacious hips, made for birthing—and the act that preceded it. Then a glimpse of the nest of hair I could only half make out, bunched beneath the thick but still-see-through fabric of her panties. No French cut. They were sturdy, and they needed to be, to hold in that much woman. "I want you to realize that there's nothing you can't get right here. Nothing anybody can give you that Kelly can't give you."

On her hands and knees, she made her way over the spread until she crouched, poised, directly above me. I expected her to drop down on me, but she stayed there, breasts swaying. "I left one piece of clothes on. For you to take off. So I'll know you want this as much as I do. This isn't a seduction. Understand?"

"No, not much."

"Understand?" she repeated. She gave me a deep, soulful look, one that pretty much caved me into a dry, disintegrated pile of dust, yet I still existed somehow.

I nodded my agreement, recognition, implosion, whatever it was, as my hands slid her undergarment from her hips. She did the rest, flicking it away into a corner with the heel of one foot. "Put that condom on. We're not making any more this time around." I did. Then we clasped ourselves together. I hate to say it was like riding a bike—that sounds so unsexed—but in a certain sense, it was.

And as Kelly and I came together, the remembrance of her body, and the distinct way her vagina felt, came over me. Even with a condom on, I could tell. I'd lost consciousness of her contours, all the many months we'd remained apart, but there they had been, and now they were erasing the elapsed time.

We lay embraced, barely moving, simply letting the subtle shifts in our muscles communicate themselves to one another. Sweet, slow, shallow breath, a trance. Enveloped in a cocoon, but not one made of Chinese silk. Nothing so exotic. Plain old cotton. One hundred percent. A cotton cocoon. Chenille, for the stitchery. Kelly's copious, languid body covering mine. Our mutual climax was a long, shuddering sigh that started in her and ended in me.

She shifted to one side, to take the pressure of her weight off my abdomen, and snuggled her face into my armpit. Seeming to enjoy the husky tang of it. She made a contented noise. "I'm going to have to find Chandra a Sunday activity on a regular basis."

I didn't dispute the implications of her statement. "Could be a good thing," I answered.

"Damn right it could. Piano lessons, ballet, something. I need to get her out of my hair more often anyway. So we don't argue so much. Girl wants to examine every point of the law. I hustled her out this morning so I don't have to be somebody's mommy every minute I'm not at work."

"So why don't you put her in ballet?"

"Well, I hate to bore you with the details, but there's a certain amount of child care, and me trying to save up for the braces she's going to need, 'cause her bottom teeth are like a fencerow after a tornado. Shoes, a growing collection of hair bows, macaroni and cheese. Want me to go on?"

"How much do you make working as an accountant?"

"None of your beeswax. How much do you make as a boxer?"

"So far, almost nothing."

My candor took her off guard. "Well, I don't make nearly enough. That's all I'm gonna say 'bout it."

"I'm going to pay for Chandra to have ballet, piano, whatever she wants. And somebody needs to establish a trust fund for her college education. She's precocious."

Kelly gave me a wide-eyed look. She seemed more amused than

annoyed at my opinionated outburst. "You really do like to talk about Chandra, don't you? Well, that's a nice dream and a nice gesture. But you just got done telling me you ain't got no money. And I don't need it, even if you did. You've always kept up with the child-support payments, so I have nothing to complain about and I don't expect anything more. I didn't take my clothes off to shake you down, honey. I plain old needed to do some loving with a growed-up man, because it's been a while going on a long time."

"I didn't say you expected anything else from me. But it's something I want to do. And I know how I'm going to get me some money."

"Legally? Because you're starting to scare me. That tone in your voice. The look in your eye."

"Of course, legally. Smitty, a trainer in Chicago. I've worked for him lots."

Kelly started, as if she'd suddenly felt a cockroach crawling on her skin. "When we talked at the park, you said you were done boxing."

"Hear me out first. That's all I'm asking." She shifted away from me, reclaiming her side of the mattress, as if she were in a boat that was going to tip over if she moved toward my side. "There's a fighter named Tadeusz Virkowicz."

"Never heard of him."

"I'm not surprised. But everybody else has. He offered me ten thousand dollars for an exhibition bout. I'm not sure if the offer still stands, but I'm going to call Smitty right away. It doesn't matter if I win. I collect the payday either way, if they still want me."

"I thought maybe you'd changed. I should have known better."

"This isn't a bar fight. It's legitimate contention. With one of the strongest and meanest fighters on the circuit. A worthy opponent. I need to do this for Chandra. And for you. One last time. Give me that chance to show you I'm something better than a brawler." I sank down onto her naked body, so that she couldn't turn away. We were eyeball to eyeball, nose to nose, mouth to mouth. Then I felt the turn in her, the drawing back. She wriggled, wordless, trying to push me off, but I held her fast.

"I can't move," she finally brought herself to say. "Get off of me."

"Okay." I let her go. She turned away, as I had expected, and in trying to protect herself, she unwittingly gave me a full view of that place from which Chandra had issued. Orphic orifice.

I didn't touch her, there or anywhere else. At length, she flipped back over, aggrieved. "I'm sorry, Clay, but I don't want to get back with you. I know all about one last time. I'd rather leave things the way they are than get myself stirred up the way I've been these past couple of days. It's like I had a hive of hornets in my clothes."

"You mean us not seeing each other anymore. So this was a holiday."

"I didn't say that."

"Or did you mean us lying naked in bed together, once a week, for as long as I'm in town, while Chandra takes turns visiting different friends, or your mother, because you can't afford to send her to ballet lessons? Or even to the movies? Isn't she going to wear out her welcome?"

"I don't know what I want at this point, Clay, any more than you do. Except that I feel excited, just like Chandra does, if I know or think that you might be coming over for a visit. And disappointed when you don't show. I done wore myself out getting over all that."

"I'm not going to interfere in whatever plans you have for her. That isn't what I'm after. But never mind."

"I'm not using you. I hope you know that."

"Forget it. We've talked enough for one day. We get to a certain point where the more we say to each other, the less we understand."

I got out of bed and dressed again, lest Chandra come charging through the front door unexpectedly and find me in the nude. I walked into the living room. On the coffee table was still the Sunday paper, well thumbed. Among the various sections, the society page. Also well thumbed. On the front, several black-and-white photos of the ball. Including a close-up of Carmela on my arm. That was the first time I'd made the papers since the item in the police blotter. I gathered the newspaper sections and threw them in the kitchen trash can.

I walked back down the hall. The door to the bedroom was ajar. Kelly lay facedown on the spread. Her face was turned to the other side, but I could hear the sound of her weeping. Going in silently, I covered her with an afghan and lingered next to her.

"Don't," she said.

Whatever that injunction meant, I didn't want to break it by any word or action of mine. So I simply lay down next to her, apart, keeping her company, in silence, until we heard Chandra ascending the outside steps, two at a time, and then her chipper rap on the front door.

Downtown was in the doldrums late Sunday afternoon. Still air, then a pocket of light baffling wind carrying a paper cup down the middle of a street empty of transit. One end of the street blocked off with an orange-and-white-striped barricade. Mesh around an excavated manhole, its iron collar sticking up like an uncovered tomb. Nightclubs, art galleries, and lunch counters, all closed. The humidity had risen out of nowhere, bringing one of those muggy air inversions that makes city dwellers wish for real winter again and sends them scurrying to switch on mold-infested window units they haven't had time to clean out. Sweat in your pores, spores in your lungs. It wasn't really hot but felt as though it was. Vine Street was deserted. The amber DON'T WALK *sign flashed on and off at crosswalks, scolding in vain.*

Clay cruised through his old neighborhood, the one where he could never leave well enough alone. Because he had just left Kelly, she was on his mind. That sweet love she had given him. The taste of her body, after so much time, the faint aluminum tang of her skin on his lips. How she seemed to want to forgive him for many and sundry small offenses, but a part of her wouldn't let go of that bitter sensation, like a mysterious trace mineral in the soil of her life that she'd gotten used to drinking in and couldn't survive without. Because yes, the bitter elements can feed you as well as the sweet ones, even better, if you let them.

He didn't recognize much of the neighborhood. Had parts been razed? Yet there were few signs of urban renewal and many of decay. A couple of positive signs, however. The whitewashed church with the prairie spire, had that been there before? The coat of paint looked fresh, as though someone were desperately trying to create a sense of life in this forgotten corner of town. There was some score Clay needed to settle in the neighborhood, some bully to be whipped, some urge drawing him onward, even though the person he sought had probably moved away by now or had grown up and become a respectable insurance salesman, or was dead, or perhaps had never existed.

Was Clay ever going to stop picking phantom fights? Meet me at such and such a corner, twenty years from today. And I'll lick you. He'd said he had come back looking for a friend, someone named Balboa, but where was the friend? The friend could be near or a thousand miles away. Maybe Clay had come back, more like, to stir up trouble with his old flame or, even more likely, to punish himself the way he liked to do. At bottom, some part of him seemed to want to end up like Nebucchim Jacinto, that noble loser from Death North of Patagonia, *carefully, relentlessly laying the plans for his own demise and insisting that everyone around him play his or her designated part. The Lord knew Clay was scrupulous and honest about those things that ought to be treated with contempt, contemptuous of those things that ought to be held in honor. Some people had a death wish, that was all, and not a damn thing you could do about it.*

He kept having to stop and turn his car around—there were so many cul-de-sacs and one-way streets going nowhere in particular. Or streets that seemed to finish, then started up again in the middle of another block. How could he forget the layout of his own old neighborhood? Wasn't that supposed to be imprinted on your consciousness forever? The geography of your youth, like no other you'll ever come across. Especially for a Southern boy.

The illogical street layout managed to create a sense of complete isolation, as if downtown proper were miles away instead of a fifteen-minute walk on foot. The neighborhood had changed since last he'd visited, turned poorer, less integrated, less easy to romanticize as a beachhead of honorable scrapes and fierce loyalties, as a place of crude but real integration, where whites and blacks duked it out and were willing to live with the results. Now the neighborhood had become more uniformly black as the suburbs opened up beyond Man O'War, and all the whites who could had fled outward. And all the blacks who could, for that matter. Plenty of cheap housing in a boomtown.

The vicinity consisted mostly of clapboard houses no bigger than trailers, their tarry roofs gone permanently soft, held up by square brick pillars with chinks in the mortar, slabs of front porches buckled. Thin wooden boards, scaly, weather-beaten, shedding flakes. Or, if painted over, not sanded down properly, leaving deep pockmarks between glutinous daubs of white coat. Occasionally, a bright cottage was sandwiched between the others, painted pink or yellow, with a windowbox of just-planted marigolds trying in vain to scream forth gaudy cheer. Ceramic chickens on sentry duty. Weathervanes. Plaster geese dressed up in garb. Grecian birdbaths holding rusty water but no birds. The Fiery Pillar of Enduring Faith Hair Salon. And the occasional sign for Islam in a front window.

He parked the car, got out, and walked. Lexington, my Lexington. Vacant lots, high weeds, broken sidewalk. A concrete building, boxy as a fallout shelter, flat roof. Perfect for kids to jump off, but not a child in sight. Did he used to buy Sugar Daddies here? His fillings ached with the very memory of them. Coca-Colas in a cooler, chilled water flowing around the bottles' bases. The plate glass of the store's front window had gone all gummy with the accreted glue of masking tape, bumper stickers, self-adhesive handbills, applied and removed many times over. Sun-faded poster for the Shal-Daires, its date three years ago, announcing a gospel concert at the AME Zion Church. A two-way-mirror-silvered facade, so that you couldn't look in, but enough of the silvering eaten away that he could squint and hold his face up to a patch. He peered into the deep narrow ink on the other side.

And now a house. His? Had he grown up there? Or did they all look so much alike it really didn't make that much difference? Choose one and call it your misspent youth. Clay picked his way across flagstones on the other side of the house, through a trail of rusted washingmachine parts, and now he stepped over the crushed, empty rhombus of a washer hull, and walked toward his car.

Nothing here to reencounter. It was just one of those bad instincts, the kind he'd been following his whole existence. His shirt had gone sticky with sweat. He could get a drink from the water fountain inside that white-steepled church, there had to be a drinking fountain, but the church was closed too, with a dead bolt, so you couldn't even rattle the big door. Soon as the rowdy and satisfying worship is over, bringing your humanity to the surface, everybody runs like hell to their cars in the gravel lot. Not a place to loiter.

Passing one of the sagging houses down the street, half obscured by overgrown grass, weeds, creeping vines, poison ivy, Clay noted a yellow CONDEMNED sign tacked to the front door. The house had a picket fence, sections torn out and gone to God knows where, the rest trampled, leaning at a forty-five-degree angle. It looked vaguely familiar, only dimmer. This must be it. A brick walk, moldering, embattled by tufts of stiff grass. On the long porch, behind a waist-high brick wall, sat three big men, taking in the pinkish-gray hues of the deepening onset of evening. Sedate. And wearing ski masks. One of them got to his feet, then the second, then the third.

"Oh, fuck," Clay said to no one in particular. He started to run, but the closest of them vaulted the short brick wall and, with a practiced tackle, cut his legs out from under him. The other two were not far behind. They piled on, as if this were a goal-line stand in the big game against Louisville.

The one who'd clipped him stood up. "Done did that'n, boys," he concluded, and the other two got off as well. Even from hearing these few words, and appraising their physiques, he could imagine what their covered heads looked like. All the same. Crew cuts, square faces, overconfident and vacant. Louts, in a word. The first one's name was probably Whitey.

"Get in the house," said Whitey. Clay didn't think he could outrun all three of them, and there wasn't much of anybody around if he started to yell. Where were all the people? How inconspicuous could three brutes in ski masks be? Didn't their presence violate some law? The law of probability, if nothing else. Surely a pedestrian would have to happen along soon. Or not. Would neighbors come out-of-doors even if they heard him yell, or would they do the smart thing and mind their own business? He wanted to think Lexington was different from Chicago in that respect, but he knew better.

He went up the broken walk onto the collapsing porch and into the mildewed front room of the abandoned house, with its rotting carpet and spongy plywood beneath. The three men followed, shaking the timbers with their collective motion. One of them had fired up a Coleman lantern, and now hung it on a nail. They were antsy. He could spot right away that at least one of them was perked on ecstasy, crack, something, the way he loosened his shoulders and danced around, as if wait-

ing for the huddle to break. Like all too many amateur football athletes, they'd gotten way ahead of themselves, with premature fantasies of the high life, the multimillion NFL contract, the babes. They'd started with steroids and just sort of eased into the pill-popping habit.

Now that he thought about it, these three, if he could only see their faces—and his inability to do so was starting to make him the slightest bit nervous—could already be in their midtwenties, if not older. The draft had passed them over. So they'd gotten pissed and decided they were going to have the high life anyway, the women, the flow of pharmaceuticals; they'd just take it, one way or another. At least one of them probably worked as a bouncer and parlayed that into all kinds of other work-for-hire sidelines. Such as this little job he was taking care of right now.

Clay decided his best bet was to brazen it out until he at least found out why they had targeted him. The encounter didn't seem random or coincidental. And anyway, nothing breeds sadism like the scent of fear. "I was looking for something a touch more gemütlich," he said, taking in his surroundings. "Maybe with a fireplace."

An open palm whacked his ear, so hard and stinging that he lost his balance and stumbled to the floor. Lying there examining the cobwebs on the half-detached baseboard, he reconsidered his opening gambit. He'd always been too much of a smartass for his own good. Kelly had told him many, many times that some day that tongue of his was going to catch up with him. It was time to say I told you so.

"Don't speak foreign languages," the really antsy one, who had hit him, said. Clay started to get up, and the man grabbed him by his bad shoulder to hurry him back to his feet. A flame shot through the socket. Clay was so pissed about this manhandling of his shoulder that reflexively he lashed out at the aggressor's face with a hard left hook. There was the satisfying smack of solid flesh and bones giving way behind it. The antsy one crumpled and went sprawling through the emptiness. Clutching his damaged face with both hands, the fellow set up a desperate howl that echoed around the empty room.

"Fuck oh goddamnit shit sonofabitch motherfucking asshole. Broke my goddamn jawwww." Blood seeped, staining his ski mask. He couldn't open his mouth much, and his enunciation left something to be desired. He rocked and whimpered, cradling his ear with tender

concern, utter bafflement in the slits of his eyeholes. This kind of thing was supposed to happen, only not to him.

Whitey seemed unperturbed. "You're lucky he didn't knock you unconscious. I told you he was a boxer. I told you not to start that shit unless I gave the word. Go get in your car and find a doc in the box. Tell them you got in a bar fight. And remember to take off the mask first. Useless fuck." The wounded one lumbered to his feet and ran out, still cursing. Whitey slid a wooden paddle thick as a cricket bat out of his jacket.

So they knew he was a boxer. They had goods on him. Clay noticed the other sidekick, who now hung back out of immediate reach, had a lump in his windbreaker pocket and had slipped one hand into it. A small-caliber pistol, with a silencer perhaps. He could be a fair shot. Farm boys tend to know rifles and guns. He would avoid any further lunging if he could.

"So why did they send you guys after me? Did they have to get some-body on short notice?"

Couldn't keep his mouth shut, after she done told him to zip his lip. Boy couldn't help courting disaster. Now, to finish him off, or not. With that wisecrack his dying remark. An unrepentant stiff. It would serve him right, and yet. And yet.

"Funny," said Whitey, without his mouth-hole smiling. "Now, just to be clear. We can fix your ass anytime we want. I don't care if you got off a cheap shot at dickhead, who deserves it anyway. You won't be doing that to me."

"You've got me convinced. Why are you here?"

"I believe you had a little write-up in the papers this morning. Your first since the police-blotter incident."

"You know about my shoplifting?"

"Yeah, tough guy. Who doesn't? I read the papers."

A thought occurred to Clay. "You're not off-duty policemen, are you? Moonlighting? I try to go out of my way not to hit policemen. And if I did, I'm awfully sorry. I hope your friend won't take it personally."

"Most definitely we are not policemen. Still, you were right to leave town years ago, after your brawl with the off-duty cops. But no sooner do you come back than you manage to get yourself seen in—let's say, questionable company."

"Questionable company? You mean Carmela Wade?"

"That's exactly who I mean."

"Sometimes I don't even think she's real. Sometimes I think somebody just made her up to get me into trouble."

"Correction. She's real enough to get you into trouble."

"Is this some kind of white-supremacist thing? Are you skinheads?"

"Now you're insulting me. I tolerated your first little outburst, but please don't get me riled by associating me with white supremacy. I'm not that kind of lowlife."

"What kind of lowlife are you, then? You have to admit, this has all the earmarks of a vendetta against mixed-race fraternizing."

"How about this instead? You shouldn't be two-timing your ex-wife."

"What? My ex-wife? Are you actually a moral person?"

"I've been called worse."

"Because your methods are, well, not the usual ones for somebody with your code of ethics. Besides, I'm not two-timing her. I haven't done anything wrong."

"Says you."

"I can't believe we're having this discussion. I expected you to have beat the crap out of me with that paddle by now. Or even killed me."

"Believe me, nothing would give me more pleasure than to pummel you senseless. But I can't help it. I'm obedient to a higher power."

"God?"

"Wash your mouth out with soap, you atheist."

"Not atheist. Lapsed Baptist."

"No such thing. Lapsed is for Catholics. With the Baptists, get saved all you want, if you need to freshen up your soul, but basically you're either in or out. Anyway, when I say higher power, I'm talking about my employer. This person who commands me is squeamish about violence."

"Commands? It really does sound like you're talking about your Creator."

"Call her what you like. She means this for your own good. All she really wants is for you to get a taste of your own medicine, so you'll realize what a dead-end boxing is."

"Boxing is an art. It requires a lot of technique. I didn't win the Golden Gloves by slugging it out."

"Bullshit. Tell that to my guy whose jaw you just broke with a sucker punch. Boxing, like all fighting, is nothing but an outlet for pent-up rage. The more you hit, the madder you get. Believe me, I know what I'm talking about when it comes to that. Anyway, you yourself sent for me. You want to be hurt, in a deeper sense."

"Don't get psychological on me. Who really sent you?"

"Well, I don't know her last name, but—okay, her first name is Kelly. That's all I'm gonna say. You never heard that from me."

"You're cracked. I'm getting out of here." As Clay turned, he had barely enough time to see the paddle coming at him in his peripheral vision but not enough time to do anything about it except flinch. The thick of the paddle caught him in the middle of his back, and pitched him to the floor, where he banged his face hard. A blue-green bruise would be on his forehead soon. He could feel the hematoma welling up. Not to mention the twang in his spine. He sucked air through his teeth. "Man, that hurt. I thought you said Kelly was against violence."

"I only said she had mixed feelings. She changed her mind at the last minute. Do you expect her to be any less fickle than Jehovah, the supposedly compassionate God, who strikes people blind whenever he feels like it? He'll clean your clock just for putting the wrong shade of accent on a word. And English isn't even a tonal language. So put that in your lapsed-Baptist pipe and smoke it. " Whitey hauled back as if he were going to give the prone Clay a savage kick in the kidneys, but in midflight his foot switched course and only administered a halfhearted, glancing blow. Enough to cause a twinge, but at least Clay wouldn't be pissing blood.

Clay was a lucky little bastard. Kelly had a way of taking his side in spite of herself. Besides, it's been said that when you're writing about characters, once you really start to understand them from the inside, and really hit the motherlode, they start taking on a life of their own. You can't control them, not really. Neither could she.

Clay groaned and tried to collect himself enough to gather up his body and lean against the wall in a sitting position. His sacrum throbbed. "If she's mad at me—first of all, I can't believe Kelly would be so low as to send white supremacists like you boys to rough me up."

"I told you, I'm not a white supremacist. I'm a thug."

"Okay, thug, whatever. Still, it isn't in her character."

"What do you know about her character? You haven't been around *much lately. She's changed. You put her through a lot."*

"I mean, what about hiring three black bruisers? That would be
more in keeping. That I could believe. If she has a revenge fantasy going,
I'm sure there are members of the Nation of Islam who would love to
whip my ass, just on general principles. I even saw a sign in one of the
windows down the street."

"You'll have to take that up with her. But have you forgotten that
she's also white? Why do you insist on calling her black? Is any of us all
one thing, when you get right down to it? Talk about having a race complex. You only think of her as black to explain the things about her you
don't understand. The same way you call her a woman when you can't
get behind her logic. Besides, Kelly isn't political, as you well know.
Talking about race makes her uncomfortable. She wants to live out her
life in peace, that's all, with a little romance, not too much stress, raise
her daughter right. Kelly is a woman of tender sensibility. Those cheap
novels about love she keeps on her nightstand, the ones you scoff at, make
her cry real tears. All she knows is you broke her heart, and you're not
going to do it again."

"So she's getting her revenge by putting me into a bad detective
novel. I thought she'd forgiven me. We made love not three hours ago. I
still smell like her. She saved dinner for me."

"She's trying. But it isn't easy. These dark moods descend on her,
and she feels like killing you. Consider this a warning. Live by the fist,
die by the fist."

"Brother, brother, brother, oh my brother."

Clay pried open his lashes, gummed with dust mites and secre-
tions. He tried to fix his blurry gaze on the attic's sloping ceiling.

"Can't get into focus? Try yoga exercises for the eyeballs. Move
them at a diagonal. You know, the way you do when you think
somebody's following you in a detective novel." Clay blinked once,
twice, three times, trying to dislodge the minute mineral substances
from his eyelashes. Balboa stood over the bed, looking about four-
teen feet tall, in a spiffy suit. Herringbone, it had to cost a thousand
bucks. Beard trimmed, no head covering. Nothing out of kilter with

his sartorial splendor except the Daffy Duck tie. But that was Balboa.

"How in the hell did you get into my room? The door was locked."

"Your desk clerk gave me the passkey."

"That idiot. Is he handing my key out now in the middle of the night to anybody who asks?"

"Whoa, homey. I ain't just anybody. I'm you. Or the next best thing to being you."

"Where in creation did you hide away? I've been looking for you. Janine is monstrously upset."

"Well, you haven't been looking terribly hard. 'Cause I found you. Man, don't they believe in lampshades around here? It's like living in an interrogation room. Or the cabinet of Dr. Caligari. Look, I can make shadow puppets on the wall. There's an alligator. I brought it to you as a souvenir of my recent travels. See his jaw moving? He's about to devour one messed-up boxer. No, you ain't been looking hard. Matter of fact, where you been? Got a knot on your forehead like you been banging your head on a stop sign. Frat boy."

Clay could feel the lump bunching his skin on the forehead, and the steady pressure it caused on his left eye. "It's nothing. I was walking around in an abandoned house in my old neighborhood and I fell down."

"Yeah? When I worked in the emergency room, I saw quite a few kids brought in who had those kinds of contusions. Their parents had a habit of saying the kid fell down real hard. Kid was always falling down. And that's when I got on the phone to the Department of Children and Family Services. Was it a bar fight? Please tell me you have not been brawling. We had a long talk already about your tendency to pop off at the least propitious times."

"The explanation I gave is the only one you're getting from me. I fell and knocked my head. So let's drop it."

"Sure, homey. I'm just happy as hell to see you. I care about you more than your own mama does."

"You're on one of those elation highs. I can tell. Were you taking hits off your oxygen mask on the plane? You're going to come crashing down soon, I just know it. How did you find out where I was, anyway?"

"Can't you guess? We've got a woman in common now."

"Janine?"

"I don't mean her. 'Cause Lord, we surely don't have her much in common. Unless you mean that I'm in the doghouse and so are you. I do need to talk to her, but I'm not quite ready to do that. Guess again."

"Oh—her."

"Right on. Carmela said you came out to Wildbrake looking for me, ended up going to a society party as her escort, stayed the night. I saw your tux hanging on the closet door. She hadn't returned it yet. I'd give a Confederate dollar to see you in a tuxedo. And ten to watch you walking around among the society folk like you got a pickle up your butt."

"That's got an edge to it. Are we having an argument?"

"Maybe. Did Carmela and my firstest of cousins have a good time together?"

"You're upset with me? After I got dragged out of my own simple life and down here to face my demons on account of you?"

"I didn't say I was upset. Surprised, that's all. I guess I got to learn to share and share alike, when it comes to a blood brother."

"I did not—look, I just got done explaining all this to somebody else."

"To who?"

"Never you mind. Let's say I had a long talk with God."

"Oh, him. What a coincidence. I been talking to him too."

"If Carmela says there's anything between us, she's only trying to make you jealous. You know me better than that."

"I do. I think I do. But you know, Clay, you and me are like the same person in two different bodies. And the second body might feel it's reasonable to take some liberties the first body is used to taking. Only seems natural. Did you ever think of it that way?"

"No. You're getting unbalanced. I don't know where you ran off to, or what cocktails you drank on the plane ride back, but it hasn't done you any good in getting yourself back together."

"I mean what I say about the resemblance between you and me.

Carmela must have picked up on that. She's an intuitive gal. Not to mention her capacity for getting a little freaky when she takes a mind."

"I'll have to take your word for it. She didn't get freaky with me. She brushed up against me once or twice when we were dancing, but that is all I'm laying claim to. You're the one who has some explaining to do. Where did you disappear to? I was sent off on a wild-goose chase, by your wife, after you dropped out of sight without any explanation whatsoever."

"My wife sent you after me? That's a puzzlement. She can't stand your ass."

"That isn't what you told me before. You were always reassuring me that her moods have nothing to do with me."

"Well, I lied. I didn't want you to stop coming around. So I minimized contact between the two of you. Keep the combatants separated, that's my philosophy. Like you and Tadeusz. I don't know why Janine has it in for you. Some people plain don't click. It's me she ought to be kicking out of the house, but I'm the one who runs off, and she keeps taking me back. Because I'm her husband, I guess. And she sees you as my bad side. I never told you this, Clay, but I'm pretty sure she believes that you're a go-between for me and Carmela, confidant, whatever you want to call it. She thinks that you put me onto Carmela, introduced us, you know. You are from Lexington, after all. This place is another thing you and me have in common."

"A *go-between?* Me? Like a pimp, you mean?"

"You don't have to make it sound so base."

"I hope you set her straight on that score."

"How can I? She won't let me bring the topic up. When Carmela and me broke up, I wanted to bring it all out into the open, hoping she would let bygones be bygones, but the unspoken words are the most powerful ones in our household. Those are the ones we live by."

"I can't believe this."

"You've done me a lot of favors, buddy, without even realizing it. And I've tried to pay you back the best way I know how, with the pain treatments, acupuncture, that kind of thing. I still owe you. I'm sure Janine put you on the case because she figured I was hiding out with my girlfriend, sulking, and you'd know that, and you'd come down here, which in fact you did. Woman has good instincts."

"All I did was pick up the cell phone in your car, hit the redial button, and it led me here. Plot device. Sheer coincidence."

"There are no coincidences in life, Clay. Karma is real, the same way *chi* is. No, you also have good instincts. I could have told you that."

"So are you and Carmela still an item? You told me at the Valentine's Day party all that was definitely over. You were wringing your hands about it the whole night long."

"Next question."

"You know, Balboa, if you weren't so brawny yourself, and my back and kidneys weren't hurting like hell, I'd be kicking you down the stairs this very second."

"Now, now. Save your strength, homey. You done been in one bar fight today already. I thought they had blue laws down here, where the beer joints had to be closed on Sunday."

"I told you, I wasn't in a bar fight. I didn't even go into a bar today."

"You get into a row with your ex-wife? I can empathize with that, my man, believe you me. Though me and Janine, as I've told you, we're not sluggers like you."

"I'm not a slugger. Please stop saying that. I've never hit Kelly."

"If you say so, slugger. But yes, it has gotten a little emotional with the words at times between Janine and myself. Even Presbyterians lose it now and again."

"You? A Presbyterian?"

"You don't know everything about me, my little doppelgänger."

"I thought you were a Buddhist. Or a Rastafarian."

"All religions are one at the root."

"I don't know where you're getting all this information about me. Yes, I have seen my ex-wife, as a matter of fact. And we've been talking about serious matters, if you must know. But I didn't get into a row. I fell down on the floor."

"Did she send thugs over to beat you up? Come on, man, you can tell me. I won't gossip to anybody. A woman scorned can instigate some nasty motherfucking shit."

"What? Do you know something I don't? What made you say that?"

"Say what?"

"What you said. About my wife and thugs. Where did you come up with that particular idea?"

"Popped into my head, that's all. When you think a thought, sometimes it jumps over into my head. That's not so strange, unless you get too hung up on the laws of physics and all. Don't get riled. I'm playing with you, nothing more. Let me have a look at your eyes. I've got my pen flashlight on me."

"Do you always carry a flashlight around, even when you're wearing a million-dollar suit? I thought only plumbers did that."

"Sure. In case I drop my keys in a parking lot. You were asleep when I showed up, which is one of the signs of a concussion."

"It's the middle of the night. My being asleep is a symptom of the wake-sleep cycle, participated in by all humankind except you."

"Those sumbitches must have whaled on you, though I don't see any other bruises except the one on your forehead. Okay, stare into the light, and don't blink."

"Get that flashlight out of my eyes, or I'm going to pop you one."

"Cool your jets, slugger. You could have a slight concussion. Did you see a doctor about this yet?"

"I don't have a concussion. As a rule, I guard my head, but I've had a couple of mild ones before, in the ring, and I know what they feel like. Christ, my spine is so tight it feels like somebody shoved a steel rod down in there."

"Lift your legs and crook them. Let Doctor Goodhands go to work. This bed's a little low, but I'll make do." Balboa gave Clay a couple of swift manipulations of the pelvis, to either side, and his spine made several quick reports that sounded like a string of small firecrackers going off. "Jesus, you are tight. I don't think you got a concussion, though."

"Speaking of concussions, Smitty gave me a chance to make some money. I mean real money."

"How much?"

"Ten thousand dollars."

"Not bad. Doing what?"

155

"An impromptu exhibition bout with Tadeusz. I won't even have time to train for it. I'll have to wing it, I guess."

"Now Clay-boy, you done went and promised me you wasn't getting into the ring with no Tadeusz ever again. Especially when you're undertrained. We been over all that. You are too banged up already. I've pulled your ass out of the fire too many times."

"But if it's for a good cause?"

"Such as?"

"Balboa, we can't have secrets at this point. Look, I know you've gotten yourself into a deep financial hole. Janine told me about it."

"Janine? Man, if that's true, the apocalypse is surely coming, because she doesn't talk about shit, not even with me, if it's of a personal nature."

"She had to tell me the basics to get me down here. You-all's money situation is the main thing on her mind. The rest right now is secondary. She wants to work things out. If you need it, I can loan that ten thousand bucks to you until you get back on your feet again. You'll climb out of this hole."

"Clay, that is so sweet and generous, and I don't want you to think I'm patronizing you in any way. You've touched my heart. But white boy, ten thousand dollars ain't but a drop in the bucket for the kind of financial straits I'm in. It's an ion whirling in a centrifuge. King Lear pissin' in the wind. If you're bound to make that money on your ravaged body, by all means go ahead and do it. Then put those dollars straight into the bank for your daughter's college-education fund, and call it quits. How is Chaka? Didn't you say that's what her name is?"

"Chandra. My daughter's edu—where did you—are you still reading my mind? I don't like the way it feels."

"We're just in sync, brother. I done told you. Nothing more than that. Anyway, I spent the morning in church, can you believe it? And a Baptist church at that. More your kind of place, with lots of hardass Calvinism flying around when they sung the hymns. Only black folk instead of white trash. The walls were white, though, and it had a big white prairie-style spire stuck on top. White robes. Why is it blacks are always dressing up in white when they go to church? And the white preachers, on the other side, love those big black robes. You ever notice that?"

"Was this church on Fourth Street? On the North Side?"

"The very one."

"That's my old neighborhood. I was over there today looking for my house, just a few hours after you. That's where I fell down. I tried going in the church for a drink of water, but the door was dead-bolted."

"So now we each been to the other one's old stomping grounds. The wellspring. The preacher was kind of a joker, bit of a card, if you want to know the truth, but he did get me thinking. I'm simply going to have to declare bankruptcy. There's no other solution. Swallow my pride and start to rebuild the empire from the bottom up. All I got to do is get Janine to see eye to eye with me on it."

"Good luck. She wants to keep this whole matter under wraps."

"Yeah, I know. She worries about bad publicity. What her friends gonna think. Them bitches gossip about her anyway, so why get all tied up in knots about it? Half of them already think we're like the Ebony Hillbillies or something. I'll admit, I had some crazy schemes flying around in my head this past week, real-estate magnate, plantation massah, but ain't a one of them going to get me anywhere. I got to eat humble pie before I do anything else. I'll save a slice for you."

"No thanks. I've got my own humble pie baking in the oven. I've got to call Smitty. I'm going to fight Tadeusz. Kelly won't like it, but when she sees me give up boxing afterward and lay that fat check in her hands as the grace note, I think she'll look at the whole matter in another light."

"I don't advise this pugilism for you, Clay. Not with Tadeusz. But I'm not in a position to be giving nobody no advice. Here, use my cell phone."

"It's two in the morning."

"Wake Smitty's bony butt up. I know his home number. He made the mistake of giving it to me once. And I got a photographic memory for numbers. Shit man, I can even remember Janine's old out-of-date passport numbers. Here, I'm dialing. He's going to be a curmudgeon no matter what time you call him, so it might as well be now. Smitty, this is Balboa Trafalgar. Rise up and talk to your favorite sports doctor. Stop mumbling and put your teeth in. Me, in the Bahamas? Clay told you that? No, I didn't get any farther than South Beach. Couldn't traverse that last stretch of water to the Promised Land. Yeah, well my boy is going to fight Tadeusz. Against medical advice. That's right. The way I see it, he's in noncompliance. But the only weapon I've got is persuasion. He made up his own mind. So put him on the card. You could at least sound happy about it. A week from Friday, uh-huh. Just make sure they have the cashier's check ready, Smitty, that's all my boy asks. Don't tell me the check is in the mail. He wants to make a donation to the United Negro College Fund."

Her daddy. How could you describe him? Funny but strict. He'd buy you hot fries and an Orangina for lunch but not before you promised all your homework had been done; he even made you bring it along, and he checked your math, holding the paper in his lap and reading it at the stoplights. Also you couldn't eat any of the junk food he bought you in the new car because the upholstery might get dirty. So they sat on the curb of the parking lot, litter blowing around their ankles, sharing hot fries from the same bag and staining the ends of their fingers bright red. He ate more than you, because he was so big, and he ate fast, like a hungry person who could never get full, but then he'd buy another bag if you asked. Two more if you asked, until you got yourself a bellyache. Him too. They both liked to eat bad food until it gave them a bellyache.

He could throw grapes into the air, really superhigh, and catch them in his mouth, even ten in a row, even fifteen, even 'leventy-'leven (his favorite number), a performance he only did for her. He liked to play the song "Yankee Doodle," or any other song you asked him to, by popping his mouth with his open hand. It sounded too cool, and if she could have taken him to school to do it, she'd be the most popular girl, at least for one day. If he treated everybody the way he treated her when they were together, everybody would like him.

Still, when he laughed, sometimes, if she closed her eyes and didn't look at his face, it sounded the same as crying. Which she'd never seen him do. She used to practice crying in the mirror; it was a lot of fun, and you could actually get better at it, even when you meant it and really were upset, you just cried better on the outside when you'd practiced a little, and it helped people understand exactly how strong your feelings were. He used to tell her boxing required "technique"; it wasn't only about slamming your fists into people. Well, crying required technique too, if you wanted to do it right.

She wanted to make him cry, for real, to see how his face would look when he did it. He'd cry for her, say I'm sorry Chandra, I treated you so bad and I'll never do it again I swear to God as long as I live and forevermore. I was so, so wrong. Maybe she'd lie sick in bed while he was saying all those apologies, not with a high fever, she didn't want to suffer that much, but chicken pox or something, except she'd already had that, and come to think of it she'd gotten all itchy, scratched herself like the devil and caused scabs and her mom made her take a bath in oatmeal, which was gross and slimy, so maybe not the chicken pox.

He pulled pennies out of her ear, even now. And if she'd lost something, a book report or a yo-yo or her favorite hair barrette, she could look for days and not find it, but if she asked him where the lost object had gone to, he would make it show up in his trousers pocket or tell her that when she went home to her mother, the thing she couldn't find would be sitting on top of her vanity. And it was, every time. Her mom rolled her eyes about those "sleights," as she called them, but her mother couldn't really explain how he did it either. There wasn't anything slight about it.

He hadn't done any of those tricks in the past year. He hadn't been around to do them. Now, since he came back to Lexington, he'd started pulling pennies from her ear again, on their "date," and teased her about her favorite color of Play-Doh, even though she was too old for that sort of play now. Not that she was going to tell him that, because then he would stop doing it. He had some catching up to do, and it would take a while. He still seemed to think she was about five, in his mind, because he forgot to add in a lot of the missing time when he wasn't around to watch her grow from day to day. She used to believe he really knew magic, then she didn't, and now, she knew they were only tricks, "sleights," but she still kind of believed in his magic anyway. It was hard to explain.

She didn't really want to punish him, but she had to, a little bit, for staying away so long, a whole year, which was more like 'leventy-'leven years. So she told him his hair was getting grayer and that he had more creases on his face, maybe from those other men punching him. She knew what a boxer was, they'd talked about it, even though he'd never actually let her go see him fight, but her mom, when she used to ask what Daddy did for his job, said other people hit him for a living. When other kids asked her, she said he drove a truck all around the country, delivering fresh fruit, grapes and such, to people who wouldn't have it otherwise. Kind of like Johnny Appleseed, only with grapes. And sweet ones, not sour ones.

When Balboa showed up unexpectedly, Carmela had half a mind to tell him to march down to one of the outbuildings, climb up into the rafters, grab a bag of hay for a bed, and sleep there. He was damn lucky he'd even found her home, coming so far out in the country without even calling ahead. Maybe he thought that was romantic, impulsive, but he was wrong, wrong, wrong. Had he misplaced her unlisted number or deleted it from his electronic phone book, the one he never seemed to put down, as if it contained all the secrets of life? His little *I Ching*, as she called it. He hadn't lost her number, he said.

No, Balboa, don't go giving her a sad tale about the misunderstanding wife who wouldn't put out. They'd been through all that. If he'd come looking for pussy, he'd come to the wrong cat. He'd had his chance, back at the Valentine's party, when she showed up there half out of her head, yowling around, rubbing up against him with her fur, liable to do just about anything and ask for nothing in return. Yeah, he'd had a red-hot woman on his hands that night, a jackpot, a glowing coal mine on the verge of explosion, except he didn't know what to do with her except treat her like a jezebel, and now that moment had passed and gone. She'd come to her senses.

And by the way, his friend Clay had come out looking for him. Great big smokehouse of a man. A better friend than he deserved. That visit was none of Balboa's business. But yeah, they'd gone to their own party, not the pajama party, not Hyde Park society, but one every bit as good, the Bluegrass high life, and they'd had a fine time. Even got writ up in the papers. What? Oh, that. Still had his mind on her thang? Wanted to know where her thang had been recently?

Well, if she'd banged Smokehouse and twenty other men besides, what was that to him? Now maybe he knew what a double standard was and what it felt like to be so jealous your eyeballs strained at the sockets. After him coming down and doing her on selected weekends, at his convenience, when she really had no idea what was going on in his marital bed, not for sure, all she had for it was the word of a lover who might turn out to be a lying sack of shit. She was sure he could appreciate how bad it hurt when you thought the one you loved, or claimed to love, might be screwing somebody else just to relieve that pressure in the pelvis, which did have a way of building up.

All she would say was, Balboa sure did have good taste in friends. Excellent taste. Then Balboa had to go and start crying on her. That took her by surprise, that was about the last thing she expected to happen in the middle of her fire sermon, and it was a little scary, if the truth be told. It wasn't that she minded a man crying, not in principle, and she intuited from a few things he'd said that his wife would freak if he'd ever busted out bawling in her presence. For her part, Carmela had always expected his emotion to come gushing forth and spray all over her one of these days, like a bottle of champagne in the hands of an inexperienced waiter.

But why did he have to finally come out with those long-expected tears right when she was in the middle of the hell-bent tongue-lashing she'd been wanting to give him for months? Damn his timing. Ten times worse than premature ejaculation. She'd wound herself up, pitched herself into a satisfying tirade, and the boy had to go and cry on her. It wasn't fair. That was supposed to be the woman's trick.

Some men, when you cry and they're in the middle of yelling, it only makes them madder. Others crumble and give you what you want right off. When Balboa started crying, Carmela wanted to be like the first kind of man, get more sarcastic, kick him harder while he was down, yell right into his ear, because he sure as shit deserved it, and she was just getting started on that long, long script about their bad romance, pages and pages of it that she'd written and rewritten in her mind with each passing week until it had become an epic. But, damn it, she responded like the second kind of man. That is, she responded like a woman. When somebody else starts to cry, and you know the tears are real and coming from a place of deep hurt, you want to make it all better. She might as easily have turned away from a lame colt on her farm. It was going to hobble around in the field all day every day, making those eyes at you until you did something about it.

So she took him inside, her still mad, sat him down in the kitchen, and made him a glass of tea. She cracked the ancient metal ice tray in the freezer—the one with the long handle she kept meaning to throw away but kept using—she cracked it as if she were cracking his spine. One swift yank, and the cubes went flying. She overfilled the glass to where the tea spilled on the table, and shoved the glass at him without wiping down the outside. He wasn't getting any sex on this or any subsequent visit, that she meant for real. Her cunt was closed for business. She surely wasn't like those men (she'd dated a couple) who get all horny when a girl cries, God only knows why, and she didn't want to think about why they got horny in a moment of feminine distress; it was too strange. That tumescence was one for the biology textbooks. Maybe there wasn't as much difference between a man and a beast as she had always supposed.

She almost thought about taking back all the stuff she'd said about his friend Clay, hurtful and mean, a vicious swipe, whether it was true or not, but she sensed he'd rather not talk about it anymore. His mind seemed to be moving into some other territory, so apparently jealousy, which she'd been so eager to provoke, was the least of his worries right now. She had a case on her hands. She would have liked to give him a sedative with one of the big syringes she used on the horses, the ones with the wicked-looking needles, and put him out of his misery.

Track condition: fast. That's what the tote board said anyway. Yesterday's gusts had died off, leaving the air still and dead. No plumes of dust rose up on the straightaway. The opening odds on Hellaballoo, in the fourth race, were 5/3.

Lane Quantrell was pouring around nips of good bourbon in his box, trying to make everybody feel at home, as if he were a manservant instead of the track president. Clay let Lane splash some liquor over his cup of ice, then watched the bourbon water down into the melting ice without touching it to his lips. Even though Clay had met Lane in passing at the party with Carmela, Balboa knew Lane even better, as it turned out, and it was through Balboa that the invitation was issued to sit in the president's box, once Lane found out Balboa was in town. This didn't surprise Clay in the least. Who didn't Balboa know?

Carmela declined to attend. Water and wine weren't going to mix that day. Balboa was already deep in conversation with some fellow at the other end of the box, smiling, as if he hadn't mortgaged his life, as if he'd simply blown in for the weekend, nothing wrong, yeah, Viola had started up with the Suzuki method and it looked like maybe she had an ear for music to match her name. Clay had to admire his sheer nerve. How did he go around living by his balls that way? His immediate circumstances would have crushed anyone else. If anyone in the box connected Balboa with Carmela, they had the good sense and decorum not to make mention of that fact. And if anyone came off like the out-of-towner, it was Clay, the native son.

The first race was run, and the racing form's "Win" and "Place" picks both came in as expected, with only the "Show" varying. The figures on the tote board confirmed that plenty of betting was going on, but the crowd seemed subdued, without as much yelling down the home stretch as he'd expected. The first three races were being treated as mere warm-up acts for the fourth. Unlike other days, where he might run two, or even three, races out of ten, Shawn was only on the schedule for the fourth race. He wasn't going to dilute his endeavor.

Among the privileged occupants of Lane's box, there was lots of small talk and gossip about people Clay didn't know or whose names were only vaguely familiar to him. His fellow horseracing aficionados were surprisingly open about certain personal matters, though in a refined, noncommittal, between-the-lines fashion that would be easy to disavow later, if they were called to account on it. In short, expert conversationalists, the kind you'd want to grace your dinner party.

They struck him as more or less on the same keel about everything—easy, casual, yet perfectly aware of what they were perpetrating with their charm. Human suffering might result, down the line, from their almost innocent remarks about other members of their coterie, but they themselves wouldn't be lingering to witness the damage firsthand by the time their innuendo took firm hold on its listeners. They were a crowd you'd want to spend as much time with as possible, if only to ensure that your absence wouldn't give them a chance to make you the topic of conversation. Maybe that's why they socialized so much. If they had anything to say about Balboa and his situation, if they possessed any knowledge of the disastrous particulars, they weren't giving up anything right then. His case could wait until later, when Balboa had split town for whatever his next destination turned out to be.

The ongoing conversation was the predictable delicate sniping about recent divorces or profligate spending on an ostentatious new house. Wealth was supposed to go with discretion. No castles, please. And affairs appeared to be tolerated, though not home wrecking and its subsequent economic dislocations. There were all kinds of social rules to be violated and many ways to go wrong. Deceptively, it took enormous stamina to be part of this set. You had to be able to drink steadily and stay indolent for long periods of time while also keeping your wits sharp and transacting numerous items of important business, sometimes involving large sums of money, without appearing to be doing anything at all.

And if you were going to have a breakdown, please don't do it at the track. Least of all in the president's box.

The women in ribboned hats with pure-gold crosses hanging coyly in their décolletage deliberated over whether to choose a mint or a toffee out of the gift box of sweets being passed around. With their hairdos, accessories, and demure smiles, they could have just recessed from Easter services.

No one seemed to know quite what to make of Clay's presence in the box, except that he'd come in the company of Balboa, which almost made it okay. They must have observed that Lane was also "bringing Clay into the fold" with his all-encompassing hearty manner, his occasional bursts of loud laughter—a luxury of behavior he could afford—and his bad jokes, so they followed suit. ("Clay's a Kentucky boy, but he deserted us for the North.") Clay wasn't part of their circle, but out of good breeding, they fitfully included him in conversations that he wasn't really meant to be a part of. They would have been much more comfortable, though, had he chosen not to show up.

The old woman seated next to Clay, who had gone prematurely blond, turned her surgically sculpted face toward his with the benevolent remnants of a girlish smile. It's said that the face has a disproportionate number of muscles out of all those in the human body, so that humans can be expressive, but this woman had given up her claim on elasticity in order to keep the wrinkles at bay. Now she was left with only a couple of real expressions. It didn't matter that much. Women like her often give up that particular mobility early in life anyway, choosing instead to hold their faces out before themselves like exquisite Egyptian funerary masks. Instead of looking at others, they opt to be looked at, and so their visages, like their bodies, must remain set, ready for public and private inspection at every moment, with an almost military discipline.

He could tell she'd probably once been gorgeous, a drop-dead looker, and had broken a lot of hearts along the way. Even as she aged into her sixties, seventies—who could say just how old she was?—she couldn't let go of that flirtatious manner, that need to be sexy, a doll. Long after menopause, the habit of desire had stayed in her. Now she had only close-fitting Dior dresses and diamond bracelets to console her. The objects she'd bargained her favors for, once upon a time—which at an earlier moment in her life had been merely the tokens of her lovers' willingness to be foolhardy for her sake—those objects had become ends in themselves.

The men who had made gifts to her were doubtless all buried. She was the kind who would outlive them all. Some man had probably shot another on her account, or run his fortune into the ground, or poisoned himself. It had taken a lot of romance and a lot of sacrifice to keep her afloat. He wondered whether the unfinished castle out on Versailles Road had been built for her.

No one was paying much attention to her right now, and as the second and third races came and went, Clay allowed himself to pay her court, as she seemed to desire him to do. The others, family members, friends, enemies, whatever they were, unconsciously or deliberately left her out of their conversations, as if her time had passed. They weren't going to maintain her with their energy anymore, least of all the women, who had their own conquests to make and to whom her tales of romance and betrayal, lurid as they might be, had ceased to be interesting. She didn't have much to contribute to the fresh, intricate, backhanded character assassinations and schemes of infidelity now under way. It was a new generation, with its own scores to settle.

This woman seemed to know that Clay was a sparring partner who hadn't truly competed since he won his Golden Gloves title in his early twenties some years ago. That much information about him had gone around. She thought it was a shame he hadn't remained a competitor; boxing was a virile sport; she still found it quite exciting to watch raw, half-naked men sweating rivers and bashing each other in the face. In her opinion, women were the ideal spectators for that sort of atavistic behavior. Every man, she said with a coquettish frankness, ought to regularly take his girl to a boxing spectacle, let her get excited, then take her home and do what it was that men knew how to do best.

She vividly remembered the names and lives of even some of the obscure boxers from the past, like Purcell Hawkins, a really good fighter from Peytona who had made his name in Louisville, then gone national for a brief season, and just missed being called up to fight Joe Louis. Everybody said he could have become one of the great ones, but his star quickly faded.

He'd become a deacon of the church later and was posthumously awarded a medal for heroism. He'd been standing at the edge of a river dam fishing with his former regular sparring partner. It was illegal to fish there of course, and so they shouldn't have been on top of the dam in the first place. The sparring partner fell off the dam and into the water below. Purcell, who had never been defeated in the ring, still thought he was Superman, that's just the way he was, and he plunged right in to save the friend, not remembering that he himself was wearing waders, which immediately filled with water, making him weigh hundreds of pounds more. He was sucked to the bottom of the pool and drowned.

They'd given him a humanitarian decoration, but it was still a sad funeral; he'd just bought a beautiful house and everything he owned went to that wife of his, who'd been nothing but a gold digger her whole life. But she wasn't going to get into that. The woman was dead now anyway, the hussy, God rest her soul. A bat of eyelashes let Clay know that perhaps Purcell and his seat companion had been acquainted in more than passing.

She used to love boxing, had witnessed many a rivalry, many a grudge match, she'd even inspired one or two herself, but it was a touch too stimulating for her; she was getting on and was supposed to take a more restful approach to things. Today's race with Shawn was about all the masculine excitement she could absorb for a while. But she wished Clay the best of luck on his career. Yes, she was getting on in years.

Clay told her she didn't look a day over fifty.

Oh, you mean I'm "handsome," she said. That's what men start to call us, to flatter, when they can no longer muster themselves to use the word "pretty."

No, Clay insisted, she wasn't "handsome." Whatever beauty had been there to begin with was still there. He wasn't meaning to commit a sophistry. It just slipped out, the way certain phrases will. She patted hair that looked to be the texture of fine steel wool. She seemed to settle down into her accustomed vanity, and they turned their attention back to the track.

The man with the top hat, red tails, and trumpet who had strutted onto the track to announce the fourth race blew his obligatory silver blasts and trotted off, jodphurs flapping, in best Charlie Chaplin style. The horses trotted out onto a dirt straightaway damped down with water to keep them from kicking up too big a cloud of dust. They were in parade formation, snorting and jingling below the president's box. Shawn's colors were purple and gold. His silk jacket rippled lightly with the movement, as if his slender body were emanating a secret strength from within. Hellaballoo, in her cloth mask and flamboyant cuffs, was still acting feisty, like a court jester, turning her head this way and that, goggle-eyed, as if searching for a likely victim to throw a witty barb at.

The drivers and their charges fell into a loose formation and took a slow-motion turn around the track. The semblance of relaxation, as if they were all polite neighbors out for a Sunday drive in their surries. All ten of them. No scratches, a full field of two-year-old trotters. A big, generous purse. The public relations gamble of a preseason race had paid off, because the stands were packed, and the betting on the board was exceptionally heavy. They'd make some money off this little race, an excellent start to the season.

Lane Quantrell looked as self-satisfied as the pope on a balcony in Vatican City giving Easter Mass as he surveyed the churning mob below, plastic cups of beer in one hand and tickets in the other. "Clay, this is the sport of kings," he said, giving his guest's shoulder a fatherly pat.

Clay asked him what the track record was for two-year-olds in a one-mile trotting race. He answered that it was 1:55.1 and had been set by Westgate Crowns. What was the world record for that same event? A big smile spread across Lane's face; Clay had asked the right question. "Clay, son, the Red Mile's track record *is* the world record for that event. Set right here, and I was in this box watching it, just as I am now."

"Well, maybe today will be another one of those days. Glory in the meetinghouse."

"I hope so, Clay, I dearly hope so."

The hunter's bugle sounded, sharp and clear, on key, and the contestants nestled into their places at the starting gates. If there had been hounds, they would have been abarking, leaping at phantom foxes in the air. Hellaballoo stood scrunched in the middle of the pack, position number five, where she was sure to be jostled. On the margin of his program, Clay broke 1:55.1 down into quarter installments. She'd have to run an average of 28.775 per quarter to match the world record.

He realized that he hadn't bet. He didn't stand to make that much anyway, as the odds on Shawn's horse had dropped even further, to 6/5, almost even money. Plenty of spectators were no doubt betting on Hellaballoo just so they could say they'd put money on the winning horse on this historic occasion. Some of them probably wouldn't even cash in their two-dollar tickets, preferring to save them as souvenirs. The bell sounded, the restraining gates dropped, and they were off.

There were indeed bodies bumping, but Hellaballoo somehow made her way out of the pack and took a quick lead, close to a full length. She was going to expend all her energy in the early going, leaving nothing for the final quarter. The other horses scarcely existed, except as a background against which she could be defined. They rounded the first turn, and a couple of seconds later, her quarter time flashed up on the tote board, beside the number 5: 28.8 seconds. There was no digit for hundredths of seconds, so he didn't know whether they had simply rounded her time upward or if she was just a hair off pace to break the standing mark.

On the backstretch, Hellaballoo and the rest of the pack disappeared behind a clump of trees, obstructing his view. The announcer, from his booth above, relayed that one of the horses had stumbled and appeared to have veered off to one side to drop out of the race. A murmur went through the crowd. There was a tense waiting, waiting, waiting, and then they could see the purple and gold colors break into sight. The rest of the pack, minus the stray, came out a second or so behind.

In his concern, Clay had forgotten to glance at the tote board. The halfway-mark time had been posted as 56.7. He checked it against his written calculation and thought he must have made a mistake. By his reckoning, she was now almost a second ahead of the world record. Maybe that's what the murmuring had been about. But he wasn't that deeply into racing. For all he knew, they ran the first half of the race faster, then slowed down some. It made sense. How could you keep that up? From his rounds as a boxer, he knew what a long stretch of time a couple of minutes could be and how it got progressively harder to summon the necessary bursts of energy. Didn't a lot of drivers lie back until the final quarter and then make their moves? At the least, there was no way Hellaballoo could keep on that overheated pace all the way down to the wire.

All the same, her lead over the others was increasing, not narrowing, which either meant she was indeed staying on pace or that the other standardbreds were just getting fagged out from the blistering rhythm she'd set from the beginning. She looked to be a good six or seven lengths ahead of the rest, and there was no question that she would win, unless she had a heart attack.

Everybody had stood up. He didn't even look at the board to see her third-quarter time. Hellaballoo was entering the home stretch. Voices shouted, inflamed with passion, seeming to urge her on. He couldn't hear their exact words, only the name "Hellaballoo." If he'd heard the screaming out of context, the shrieking reiteration of that syllable—hell, hell, hell—he might have thought it was a hate rally. A lynch mob about to swarm onto the track and administer a fatal thrashing.

The sculpted face of the old woman next to him was contorted into a fierce mask. The skin could split at any time. Hoarse and guttural sounds issued from her throat. A preternatural force swelled the veins in her neck. He could imagine her at ringside, getting moist and overworked, yelling at Purcell to beat the living hell out of his opponent. Kill that son of a bitch! Smash his face! Panting, eyes glistening. Spittle at the corners of her mouth. Afterward, she would slide over Purcell's sweat-greased muscles, no shower first. Animal rank, they'd spread wet spots over the hotel sheets.

Hellaballoo sped across the finish. Lane Quantrell was hopping about with joy, and in the midst of his impromptu hornpipe, he spilled bourbon all over Clay. He apologized, but he was laughing about it. He poured a little on his own sleeve, playfully, to even the score, prompting witticisms from others in the box. The announcer said they thought they had a world record but for everybody to hold on to their hats while it was confirmed. A couple of the ladies in the president's box, in a prankish mood, actually reached up and seized the straw brims of their ribboned hats, mugging at one another. They sprinkled the air with the incense of their smoky smiles. Then, as though waiting for the Times Square ball to drop, everyone's eyes watched the tote board until the red letters OFFICIAL blazed alongside a time of 1:54.3. A full eight-tenths of a second beyond the existing record. About the time it took to make the decision to throw a punch and then actually throw it. An ecstatic shout went up. All souls were one for a flickering instant. They belonged to a moment in time.

The attendees in the box kept repeating the words "It's impossible" to each other. Some were crying tears of jubilation. Clay passed the peace with them, grasping one thrust-out hand after another. For a moment, they seemed to forget that he was an outsider. They embraced one another, forgetting their petty rivalries for the nonce, as if an armistice to some larger war had been declared.

"Pardon my sloshing, Clay," said the politic Lane. "Didn't mean to be so oafish in my happiness. Why don't you walk down with me to the winner's circle? Make it up to you. I'll be expected to say a few words. You can stand alongside. I want to give you an experience to remember." Adopt-a-Clay Day. As he stood to take his leave from the box, the old woman next to him did not extend her hand to be shaken or kissed. She had retreated into a fog, her head quivering ever so slightly. "Purcell was going to build me a castle," he heard her muttering.

Lane escorted Clay by the arm through the throngs of people slapping the track president on the back and offering congratulations on the day. Some of the well-wishers patted Clay on the back too, assuming that he must also have something to do with this victory.

When they arrived at the winner's circle, Shawn was unhitching Hellaballoo from her harness so she could be walked around and festooned with garlands. Her sides were streaked with white sweat. Shawn's exultant smile gave his coterie solace. He was a winner, not overly proud but ready to accept his due for a moment he had spent his entire life training for with a singular purpose. Shawn recognized

Clay and gave him a secretive wink, free of malice, full of solidarity. Someone thrust a microphone in front of Lane, then another, and Clay took the opportunity to step a little outside the gathering circle, where he wouldn't be noticed. Not everybody was born to be an agent of history.

He could hear Lane's voice pouring out orotund drafts of wisdom—amiable, confident, caressing the words as they came forth. He couldn't make out all of what the man was saying, just phrases—"legendary future," "one of the all-time greats." The analysis, whatever it was, seemed to satisfy his listeners. Shawn, beaming like a chagrined wedding groom, grinned and nodded his head once in a while at a phrase, chin strap undone and hanging loose, chuckling as if he were listening to a good joke he'd heard many times before but still able to savor the punch line.

On Maxwell Street, diners sat under the umbrella tables of the restaurant patios, enjoying the unseasonal warmth of the evening. Citronella candles in holders of red glass burned on the wrought-iron tables, lending the half-obscured faces a soft light. The occasional scrape of iron chair leg on brick was heard, the quiet clatter of indolent forks, and low-pitched murmurs exchanging casual confidences.

Kelly and me. And Balboa, who had said he way dying to meet my ex. I suggested he stop putting off his call to Janine, he had to talk to her sooner or later, and he told me he would get to that call sooner than I realized. Kelly liked Balboa right away. I wasn't sure how I felt about that. The two of them set up an easy banter, as if they'd known one another for a long time, and quickly fell into telling harmless little "Clay stories," demonstrating that they knew my case, my quirks, better than anybody else in the world. I didn't stand a chance. Having me in common meant they didn't have to go through the awkward business of getting to know each other in a hurry. I provided them with a natural buffer zone, a point of deflection. Before we even reached our destination, they were laughing it up. I hadn't seen Kelly this free and easy out-of-doors for a long time. I kept hoping Balboa would find a natural way to advocate to Kelly my decision to fight Tadeusz and save me the grief. She might accept those words more readily if they came from his mouth. But he knew better than to plead my case. I was the go-between for him, not him for me.

We walked over to Upper, just a few blocks from my pay-by-the-week, cash-only boardinghouse, and passing beneath neon tubes, we entered a narrow bar. On the tiny platform in back that served as a stage, four musicians huddled, as if stranded on a raft. A bassist, guitarist, trumpeter, and drummer. They were in the middle of a song that, after a few bars, I recognized as Miles Davis's "So What?" The trumpeter's rapid succession of sharps and flats cleansed my ears. The passages were left clear for their coolly cerebral noise.

The bassist had a feathery touch. Sometimes a musician bears down on the song so hard you feel like you're staring at an eye chart that you're being forced to read, following a wooden pointer. But this bassist didn't insist on the individual notes; those notes just plain hung out in front of you before they decayed into an open-ended half-life in your mind. You didn't have the sense so much of hearing a "bass solo" as simply being in touch with the melody, one that happened to be played by a bass at that moment in time and could therefore not be played by any other instrument.

Yet the other instruments were all there, hand in glove, following the bassist's restrained improvisation. Without making eye contact, all the musicians understood one another perfectly, much better than if they had been speaking with words. I wondered how Miles Davis had been able to shoot up so much junk for so long and still keep that essential part of his mind so clear.

We chose a table out on the patio, where the music would be distant enough to let us talk but still audible. Kelly ordered chili and a beer, and Balboa, in his sly, gentlemanly way, said he'd have the same. It didn't matter whether he liked it or not; that wasn't the question. Naturally, I followed suit. I wasn't about to risk being left out of the equation by putting forth food preferences of my own. Pints of Harp were brought by the blue-mascaraed waitress, followed by a thick seasoned paste of black beans and ground beef.

smothered in cheese, and bread on a cutting board. The loaf of bread steamed when cut with a serrated knife, making vapor like that from a body sliced open in the snow so you could plunge your hands into the innards and keep from getting frostbite. Everybody agreed it was delicious.

Balboa was in the midst of telling us some relatively mild joke about two monks and a lady of the night when all at once he picked up the cell phone he'd laid on the table. I asked myself how many of these phones he owned. Did he collect them like keychains? He punched a single speed-dial button and held up his finger to us for silence, as if he'd suddenly decided, on a craving, to order us dessert at some rival take-out place, just to watch the delivery boy show up in the no-man's-land of a competing restaurant.

"Hey, sugar. Yeah, it's me. Where am I? Well, I'm sitting at a table outdoors at a restaurant in Lexington, Kentucky, with Clay and his sweet former wife, Kelly. Right. Mhm, right here next to me, both of them. I'm really sorry I cut out with no explanation. I was under a lot of pressure, but I'm feeling together now. No, I don't want to call you back later. These are my friends. Clay is my soul mate. I had to start to make everything right with you this very second; that's why I called."

Kelly and I crossed glances and started to get up, but Balboa emphatically waved to both of us to keep our seats. "And here's a piece of news for you. Clay is going to fight Tadeusz Virkowicz. It's all been settled with his trainer, Smitty. His very lastest fight; they're giving him quite a paycheck for it. He's already opened a mutual fund account for his daughter, just the way you'd want to do for Viola, and he's putting the cashier's check right in the bank for her first thing after the fight, like a good daddy, and that will be the tag end of his boxing career. A fine way to finish. More than I can say for myself right now."

Kelly stared hard at me, saying nothing. She looked as though she'd caught a piece of food in her windpipe and had that stillness about her that people get right before the panic sets in and they jump up from the table, unable to tell you they can't breathe. Sudden-death charades. Then I heard an expulsion of breath, as though somebody had performed the Heimlich maneuver or slapped her hard. She even brought her hand to her cheek, and I had to look down at my own hand to make sure it was still in its rightful place.

All the while, she kept that look trained on me, the one that at first I mistook for fury. Then I recognized it as the kind of terror I'd been able to inspire a couple of times in my opponents. The only other occasion when I'd seen that expression on her face was when she used to wake up from those horrible nightmares she had, the ones she never told me anything about except that she couldn't breathe.

"His wife, I mean his ex-wife, yeah, same difference, she's been real supportive of the whole thing. Watching these two trying to work things out, put aside their differences, it made me come to my own senses. I give them a lot of credit. I been bad, Janine, but I'm getting better. The two of them, they're a team. The way it ought to be. Those are the very words Clay used when he took me out to the woodshed and said I better call you today or else. He wouldn't let me weasel out of it. Stood over me like a warden." Kelly drummed her fingers on the iron table. She started to stand up, but then Balboa took the liberty of gently grasping her arm and smiling at her. Kelly sat back down, rigid, but she wasn't running away.

"Listen, sugar. It hurts my ear when you raise your voice like that. Could I just tell you one—? I can go to work moonlighting at the doc in the box there close to the house. I already talked to them, yesterday. I wanted to come up with a plan before I rang you. They're dying for emergency room docs, begging, been after me for months, and you remember that's the kind of place where I started my career, right after I was an intern. Busted heads, knife wounds, heart attacks, overdoses. My kind of town. The gruesome shit. I know all that. Low prestige but good money. With my pedigree, I'm a bargain for them. Even if I leave that other practice, I can do double shifts in emergency, you know me. I got the stamina of a bull. Six days a week, for six or eight months. We'll do it. We're in the rodeo. It'll be like back when we were both residents, and we'd meet at three in the morning at El Famous Burrito on North Clark to see each other. Remember? Over an orange Formica table, in the white neon light. Everybody chattering Spanish and us not understanding a word of it. Wouldn't that be romantic? Yeah, the kids, I know, but kids are kids. They'll handle it. Viola is a natural-born stoic, exactly like you. And Chance, hardheaded like his daddy. Can't make him understand shit but got a cement head, impossible to break. What? Slow down, honey, I can't make out what you're saying. Face-to-face, sure, I'll be home in a couple days. I got to make sure Clay don't get his head knocked off in this Chicago fight anyway. Hey, I been wanting you to meet Kelly; you and her would hit it off, I just know it. The two of you are so alike. Matter of fact, here she is. I'll call you again tomorrow."

With that, he handed the phone to Kelly. She was stunned, but she took the phone. I knew her abilities well. Me and her could be in the middle of the biggest argument you ever saw, her raving, me saying nothing, and if the phone rang, for some reason, she'd never let the machine pick up. I don't know who she was expecting. Anybody but me. She'd walk over to the phone, blessing me out, and as soon as the receiver came off the cradle, she'd switch right into the telephone voice, soothing, reasonable, in control. The girl could turn on a dime.

"Hi, Janine. Right; the weather has been so warm and breezy, Clay and I decided to take your husband out for local cuisine, because he only just dropped into town. I've heard so much about you. All good, of course. If you're ever down, we'd love to take you out to Shakertown. Such a pretty drive, and a historical foundation bought back all that farmland. They actually till the fields. And there's an old Negro cemetery in Lexington, big, but hardly anybody knows about it."

As Kelly performed the work of the Chamber of Commerce, Balboa leaned over to me and said in a quiet voice, "I want you to drive back out to Wildbrake as soon as you can, and tell Carmela I can't go back there anymore. I don't care what happened between you two."

"Nothing happened."

"Like I said, I don't care what happened. I need you to be my emissary. If I go myself, the attraction is still too strong, on both sides, and I have an idea where we'll end up. It will be the death of me."

"And what about me? Did you think about how this might affect me?"

"You'll survive—Smokehouse."

"Don't call me Smokehouse. That isn't my nickname."

"If you say so, Smokehouse."

When Kelly finished trading pleasantries with Janine, she started to hand the phone back to Balboa. But he indicated with a wave of his hand that he wanted her to just sign off. She did as he asked. If I'd pulled that stunt on Kelly, she would have been all over me, for days. The silent treatment would have followed. But from Balboa, she took it as nothing more than a good-natured prank. She even smiled and waved her finger at him, as if to indicate he'd gotten away with something.

"So, Kelly," he said. "What exactly do you do?"

"I'm an accountant."

"I could use one of those right now."

"And I also write."

"You write?" I asked. "Since when?"

"Let the girl talk."

"Hey, I've known her most of my adult life. And she never said a word about writing."

"Only shows that you don't know everything about her. It's good when a woman can surprise you."

"Easy for you to say."

"Okay, since when do you write? Your husband wants to know."

"Ex-husband."

"All right. Your ex-husband wants to know."

"Since, oh, not that long ago. I've always scribbled, stuff for myself that I keep in the drawer and don't show to anybody. But it's starting to come together."

"And what's it about? Your dreams?"

"I'm not daring enough to put my dreams down on paper. These are stories about people's experiences. Or experiences that they might have had."

"Yours?"

"No, I don't believe in autobiography. I'm too shy to write about myself. Really all I do is make things up."

"What kind of things?"

"Improbable ones."

"Can't you give us a hint? I know my boy is very curious. He's afraid it might be about him. You know how people hate to see their names in the paper, unless it's for all the right reasons."

"Okay. Well, it's similar to working in the emergency room."

"You've got my full attention as a medical man. How so?"

"Have you ever had somebody die on you? Right in front of your eyes? And you were the one in charge of keeping him alive?"

"Yes, that's happened to me a couple of times."

"But he was too far gone. You did what you could to keep him alive. You knew you had. In the end, all you could do was watch him die."

"I know that feeling."

"And even then, you wished that you could take time to mourn him. Observe a moment of silence. But he was already being wheeled out, and someone else was being put before you, who had an equal claim on being alive. Therefore, you couldn't afford the time to grieve him. You had to simply let him slip off into darkness and say to yourself that was the amount of life he had. And you turned your attention to the next case."

"Are we going to stay for dessert?" I said. "Or should we go ahead and ask for the check?"

Superstition. Premonition. Intimation. Call it what you want. Kelly knew he would die in the ring. She had dreamed it many times, for years. Almost since the beginning of their relationship. Only she'd never worked up the courage to tell him about her dreams. He would have laughed, made light of it at her expense. So she tried to pass off her objections to boxing as philosophical, as a moral stance. In truth, morality had nothing whatsoever to do with her objections. It was just a feeling. And a feeling is like God, only worse. You can't explain it, you can't justify it, you can't defend it, and you can't prove it. You can only experience it. She'd woken up crying, many nights. He even knew she had bad dreams, back during the few months they lived as a married couple, and he had comforted her in the bed, only he never connected those dreams with himself. An image so strong it choked her. During all those months when he'd stayed out of touch, she'd convinced herself that he was dead, that he'd gone into a coma after some stupid, inconsequential sparring match. Only she hadn't been able to bring herself to call his number, in spite of holding the telephone receiver in her hand many times. When at last he showed up at her apartment, it was like having him come back from the dead.

Deathtrap roadside carnival. Clay didn't know these places still existed. The combination of squeaky-clean megatheme parks and consumer-protection laws, by rights, should have blotted these rickety recreational afterthoughts from the face of the earth. When he was a child, carnivals set up, without fear of consequences, in any shopping-center parking lot. And here is one now, in a seeming state of semipermanence, sprawling in one of Lexington's outskirts. City of Joy, it's called.

Layabouts on parole with pomaded hair, manning the controls of the rides. Deists, every last one of them. The analogy of the clockmaker doesn't mean shit to them. Coarse mentholated voices barking, barking. They'll give you a second whirl on the eggbeater for free, the one with a secret metal screw starting to loosen, to watch the bottom drop out of your stomach when the cage turns upside down. Guess your age, weight, metabolism, horoscope, IQ, gear ratio, love business. Press an angel into a copper penny. Open a beer bottle with their teeth. They're going to lose those teeth in a fight anyway; what's the diff?

The bandstand, once magnificent, flies its tattered flags over an artificial lake with a mechanical spout. Endless cycle of water, cost efficient, constant stench of fish and loam, pesticide runoff. Rental canoes you paddle with your feet among the isles of algae. Five bucks an hour, can't complain, though they're always one vest short. Raffish, laggard Dixieland sextet hooting on the bandstand in the midday sun. Not a clean collar among them. The law of averages makes some of their notes coincide. They seem as pleasantly surprised as anyone.

Here they are, not just Clay and Kelly, but Chandra and Balboa, too, at Kelly's insistence. Chandra is playing hooky, over Clay's objections. So unlike Kelly to engineer this kind of spontaneous outing. Clay stopped by her apartment, with Balboa, to take her to school in the yellow car, as he'd promised, and Kelly at the threshold of the door, dressed to the nines to receive them, said, "Let's go do something today." She'd made herself all pretty, wearing red lipstick at seven-thirty in the morning. She who disparaged mascara and rouge as the harlot's tools. So, next thing they were cruising the backroads, with no specific plan in mind, when they came upon huckster heaven, and Balboa, overcome by an impetuous fit, wanted to stop, so they did. He was missing his own kids, he said, in an unexpected surge of paternal feeling, and Clay bit his tongue, because he wanted to reply, If you're missing them so much, go on home and see them, instead of farting around in Lexington. You know where they live.

Clay knew if he'd proposed stopping at such a seedy place, he'd get a certain answer from his ex-wife, all about safety and how this was the reason mothers didn't always feel comfortable leaving their daughters in the care of the fathers, because he'd hatch some foolhardy idea not preapproved by the World Association of Vigilant Mothers, such as having the child ride in the back of an open pickup truck along with vicious, salivating hunting dogs and loose croquet balls and open fifty-pound containers of toxic chemical fertilizer. But now, without warning, they were under the new dispensation, where you could stop somewhere questionable just because. And besides, Kelly continued sulking about his decision to go ahead with the exhibition fight. If you gonna fight, her retracted presence said, we gonna fight. The big girl and the little girl each had Balboa by the hand, flanking him on either side, with Clay trailing a few steps behind like a deferential nanny who'd been brought along just in case somebody's diaper needed to be changed.

Already Chandra was calling the newcomer Uncle Balboa, with Kelly's encouragement. Chandra wanted to ride the roller coaster, which looked like it might be made of toothpicks. The world's largest scale model replica of a roller coaster, created from toothpicks on a 1/1 scale by Boy Scout Troop 563 and sold to Deathtrap

Carnival for a hundred dollars cash money at a fund-raiser. Clay waited for the usual objection from Kelly about coffins on wheels, and when none came, Clay offered to take Chandra on the roller coaster himself, even though it always made him nauseous.

"You'll get sick, Daddy. Maybe Uncle Balboa will ride with me."

"I love a roller coaster," said Uncle Balboa. "Always did. Makes me feel like I'm flying."

"It would mean so much to her. Chandra has never been on one," Kelly added, in a subtle rebuke, as if Clay had been derelict these past several years by moving to Chicago specifically so he wouldn't have to take his daughter on any carnival rides, and now it was the day of reckoning.

Balboa turned back to Clay. "You don't mind?"

"No, of course not. I'll stay on the ground and eat a soft pretzel."

"Daddy throws up when his stomach gets too excited."

"Well, then we better not take him along. We surely don't want him puking on us."

When they handed their tickets to the felonious ticket taker, the ruffian gave Chandra a wink with one bloodshot eye, this Rasputin of the rails, this Cycloptic seer, this narcoleptic Nostradamus at the controls. "You and your daddy have a good time."

"We will," said Chandra, taking Balboa more tightly by the hand.

"Her first time?" the ticket taker asked Kelly in a half whisper, as if he were inquiring about Chandra's virginity.

"Yes," Kelly replied with bright expectancy. "She's never done it before."

"She's gonna love it. They all do."

The metal wagons screeched off, and every thirty seconds the duo would undulate past, making the tracks groan, metal against metal, Chandra shrieking with laughter and waving and hugging her vulnerable little body to Balboa's big, safe, solid one.

Kelly beamed and look maternal, her eyes moist with recognition of Chandra's budding courage. "Look at her."

"I'm looking."

"Balboa has got a way with kids. You can see he's a natural."

"Mm."

"Don't you think so?"

"Yeah, he's got kids. His own kids."

"I thought he must. He looks so comfortable with Chandra."

"Mm."

Kelly turned and looked at Clay through her eyelashes. "You're in a mood today."

"No, actually, it's a mood and a half."

"If anybody ought to be in a mood, it's me." She started to say more, then turned and walked over to the makeshift exit barricades to wait for Balboa and Chandra to disembark.

They came staggering off, finding their legs, as if after a long sea voyage, drunk with happiness to be on terra firma at last, in a brave new land, surrounded by pax americana. Clay half expected Balboa Trafalgar to fall on his knees and kiss the ground.

"Homey, you just flat out got to try that sometime. Though Chandra about busted my eardrum with all her hollering."

"Too bad. Now you won't be able to hear her girlish endearments," Clay replied, and felt the acid scorching his own tongue.

Balboa looked a little taken aback. "Hey, did you buy yourself a soft pretzel?"

"No, I guess I forgot."

"Okay, then, let's go get four of them right now, on me, with plenty of packets of mustard besides. Now Chandra, don't go stomping those mustard packets on the ground with your heel," he said with a wicked smile.

"Oh, Uncle Balboa, you're so funny. Isn't he funny, Daddy?"

"He's funny all right."

"While we were on that roller coaster, you wouldn't think we had time to do anything except clutch the iron bar and scream. But Chandra and I discussed her social studies homework, this project she's got to do for Presidents' Day. And I know your daddy is all tied up in knots about you missing a day of school. So when we're done here, we'll swing back by Kelly's apartment, the girls can grab their bathing suits, then we're all going over to my hotel. We'll help Chandra write a skit, we can all act it out—you like to act, don't you, Clay?—then the girls can swim while the boys have a smoke. What do you say?"

"I'd already told Chandra she and I would work on it together tonight."

"Yeah, but if two heads are better than one, four heads gotta be better than two. That's just math."

"Come on, Daddy, don't be a spoilsport."

"I'll tell you what," said Balboa, with Solomonic wisdom. "Let's take a vote on it. Let's observe the principles of Jeffersonian democracy."

Final vote tally: 3 to 0, with one abstention.

Chandra's skit in celebration of Presidents' Day and Thomas Jefferson. With minor contributions by Clay (as a beau) and Balboa (in whiteface, as a descendant of Jefferson). Periwigs optional. Setting: The Campbell House Inn. Music: "John Brown Swung from a Sourwood Tree." Chandra cavorts in the heated pool (squirt gun optional), and Kelly takes a Jacuzzi dip nearby, while the gents retire to the snooker room for a smoke and a talk. Waistcoats, white gloves, Autoharp, hat-check girl, pocket watches to be palmed, livery scrape and bow, etc.

BALBOA: Have a Cuban? I picked these up in South Beach. Sumbitch hand-rolls them right before your eyes.

CLAY: Don't mind if I do. [*Balboa produces a long wooden fireplace match from his trousers pocket, ignites the matchhead on the sole of his shoe, and lights the tip of his friend's cigar. Clay coughs profusely as smoke billows around his head.*]

BALBOA: Don't inhale, dumbass.

CLAY: Cough! Cough! Cough!

BALBOA: Didn't I teach you salon manners, you ruffian?

CLAY: I thought you said saloon manners. Hack! Hack! Hack!

BALBOA: Kelly is comely indeed. Your description of her did not do justice to her charms. A worthy match for yourself, not to be disparaged. [*He blows out the flame, which has burned down perilously close to his thumb, in the nick of time.*] Have a seat in one of the ripped-vinyl, fake-English-leather wingback chairs, my adoptive brother. More port?

CLAY: Thank you, your Lordship. [*He bolts the port to kill the tobacco-ash flame in his throat, and harrumphs, producing phlegm.*] Don't they keep a brass spittoon in here?

BALBOA: Draws too much riffraff. This used to be a private club, but the winds of democracy blew out all the frosted-glass panes.

CLAY: It has been a long road, this courtship. Vexing. My life as a soldier does not please Kelly. Yet I have begun to flatter myself that she might accede to my suit, my poor vocation notwithstanding.

BALBOA: Having interceded on your behalf, Leftenant, I conclude that victory is within reach. Despite your modest bloodline, you prevailed at the Battle of the Variable Toll at Clay's Ferry Crossing, and you shall prevail no less on the field of love. [*He blows a heavy smoke ring in the shape of a heart, then skewers it with another blast from his mouth.*] You a gotdam warrior. Thanks to your bravery, the Shaker farmers can now ship their seed up the Kentucky River to the Ohio and on to Cincinnati, without fear of price gouging. Which is a good thing, because it's the only seed those boys are ever gonna spread. Their experiments in agricultural improvement through seed hybrids may continue unabashed and unabated. That is, until sexual abstinence blots their tribe from the face of the earth. Strange paradox, that. Poor self-abnegating bastards. Never understood that cult chastity shit. Vishnu may be blue in the face, but his balls ain't blue noway.

CLAY: Many thanks for your confidence, brother. It may be said, a beau who has figured in a great many flirtations approaches his lady love with that air of easy confidence and assurance, which betokens victory. Does not the hero of a hundred fights do the same? Both have lost that fear and trepidation that they have felt when they first smelt powder.

BALBOA: The concussive blasts of cannonade have not dulled your rapier wit. You seem apt for the next skirmish.

CLAY: Shall we toast, then, to my nuptials?

BALBOA: Not so fast, homeboy. As you know, my career as a physician, and the subsequent investments I made in land, because of my insider knowledge of the annexation of Puerto Rico and information about where various interstate exits are going to be placed, have served me well. I am prepared to use last night's casino winnings from the tables at the Phoenix Hotel, mere pocket change for me, to set up you and your betrothed in housekeeping, quite comfortably. I skunked Garvis Kincaid out of half a year's insurance earnings with my magic dice. Amortize this, sirrah! Those were my parting words to Garvis.

CLAY: No one can deny that you're a rakehell and a rapscallion.

BALBOA: Or I may just put your housekeeping expenses on my credit card. Either way, noblesse oblige. Yet there is one small matter outstanding before I can display my largesse as is fitten.

CLAY: Namely?

BALBOA: In the course of yourself and Kelly applying for the marriage license, you may remember blood tests, a prenup contract, frozen sperm, DNA tests—

CLAY: Frozen? DNA? Prenup? All I remember is some kind of scratch-n-sniff card they gave us. Mine said PLEASE TRY AGAIN.

BALBOA: Mayhap you're shell-shocked after all from your stint at Clay's Ferry or from the bachelor party at Cowboys. Those lap dancers can get a little crazy. The marriage license requirements are strict in Fayette County. I think it has something to do with the DAR. Be that as it may, irregularities have surfaced to challenge your and Kelly's application. It seems Chandra has been spreading stories at school about her paternity that have either to be substantiated or disproven. I've consulted my attorney.

CLAY: What stories? I'm her father. I'm willing to sign documents to that effect.

BALBOA: Chandra claims to be a direct descendant of Thomas

Jefferson, this whim gotten by way of a fellow who works at the car dealership out on New Circle Road, right there near Winchester Pike. I believe you leased the new canary-yellow coupe you're driving from him.

CLAY: Yes, his name's Antoine. He's currently salesman of the month, for the fourth month in a row. They put a picture of him up on the cork bulletin board.

BALBOA: Yeah, well, while you was at the dealership getting a stuck windshield wiper fixed, being as it was still under warranty, Chandra struck up a conversation with Antoine; I don't know, he gave her a lollipop or something, when you strolled over to check out the stickers on the showroom sports cars. Chandra was sitting in a straight-backed chair by the coffee pot with the TV on, ignoring the prattle of Montel, doing this homework assignment she brought along for social studies. Antoine sat down to help her with the homework so you could peruse the new floor models in peace. Somehow, Antoine placed the notion in Chandra's head that she herself might be a descendant of Thomas Jefferson, and she's been circulating that rumor at school.

CLAY: What are you talking about? I just accompanied her to a PTSA meeting this week. I introduced myself to her teacher. Everybody there knows who her father is.

BALBOA: But you haven't been around in a long time. Not at all to speak of since she began grade school. Looks like it's creating waves in the classroom for Chandra to just turn up, all of a sudden, at seven years old, with a white daddy who's been off the scene. You know how uptight these little redneck kids and their progenitors can get about mixed parentage, and they've been teasing her something fierce, the more so when she tries to explain what you do for a living. So, naturally, she up and created the whole descended-from-Jefferson business.

CLAY: I'll discuss the matter with her. Maybe she needs to see a counselor, to get used to the prospect of me being back in her life full-time. I've been trying not to oversell it. She was assigned to do a book report on one of the American presidents for class, and her hyperactive imagination took hold. She's always making up stories about me, and I used to tell her a lot of tall tales at bedtime myself. Feathered bats, and God knows what else.

BALBOA: Stay thy parental hand, adoptive brother. Bead not thy brow. The DNA tests have proven conclusively that Chandra is indeed a direct descendant of Mustang Sally. It isn't just her fancy. According to the preliminary results, she is the great-great-great-great-great-great-great-great-great-great-great-great-great-grandspawn of one of our greatest American presidents!

CLAY: How can this be so? Me, not her pappy?

BALBOA: This development creates obvious problems for those of us who are trying to preserve the integrity of our forebear's name from spurious mudslinging. Gossip that the Jeffersons kept dusky mistresses and suchlike. Tongues will wag. This claim of Chandra's, if substantiated in a court of law, could create an impediment to your remarriage to Kelly, from a benefactor's point of view. I can hardly give my assent, much less financial support, unless this damaging claim is withdrawn. I'm willing to give y'all money if everybody says pretty please, but not if I'm coerced into doing so because some pint-sized agitator been tying the family fortune up in probate.

CLAY: The DNA test you refer to couldn't interest me less. At this point, I don't care if Chandra says her father is Crispus Attucks or the Cisco Kid. Just invite her to next year's picnic. It's a phase, and she'll get through it.

BALBOA: That little pickaninny's imagination is wild and extravagant, escapes incessantly from every restraint of reason and taste, and, in the course of its vagaries, leaves a tract of thought as incoherent and eccentric as is the course of a meteor through the sky.

CLAY: Kids are weird. She used to think the blinking red light on the answering machine was a vampire eye, and we had to keep a dishtowel thrown over it. She'll get over this fixation too.

BALBOA: Yes, but consider her inherent limitations, my dismissive pseudosibling. Whether the black of the Negro resides in the reticular membrane between the skin and the scarfskin, or in the scarfskin itself, whether it proceeds from the color of the blood, the color of the bile, or from that of some other secretion, the difference is fixed in nature and is as real as if its seat and cause were better known to us.

CLAY: Your makeup is dripping.

BALBOA: Dammit, that's what I get for wearing this water-based ecocrap, just to get the animal-rights activists off my back. Goop not fit for a clown, much less a patrician like myself. If it isn't the Tories busting my chops for owning tobacco plantations in Virginia and Haiti, it's some Green Party maniac trying to protect the endocrine glands of weasels. I already had to resign from the boards of Revlon and R. J. Reynolds because of perceived conflict of interest, just to be able to wear a little foundation, smoke a decent cigar, and file the occasional friend-of-the-court brief, without having to hold a press conference about it. I made a speech before the Senate advising against an invasion of Haiti. What more do they want? I'm a moderate. I try to be enlightened. You know they don't put Condoleezza Rice through this kind of shit.

CLAY: Here, use my monogrammed handkerchief to mop your brow.

BALBOA: There's no disgrace in my credo, nor in my desire to call a spade a spade. Are not the fine mixtures of rouge and white, the expressions of every passion by greater or lesser suffusions of color in the one, preferable to that eternal monotony, which reigns in the countenances, that immovable veil of black that covers all the emotions of the other race? They secrete less by the kidneys and more by the glands of the skin.

CLAY: What in Sam Hill are you talking about?

BALBOA: The unnerving difference between them and me. They seem to require less sleep. A black, after hard labor throughout the day, will be induced by the slightest amusements to sit up until midnight, or later, though knowing he must be out with the first dawn of morning.

CLAY: It's true that Kelly has bad insomnia. She'll stay up half the night reading romance novels even when she has an early appointment. But her daddy's a white college professor. How does that figure into your scheme? And all those pale old geezers at the boardinghouse where I'm living are knocking around on the stairwells at every hour. You saw for yourself when you woke me up in the middle of the night. By the way, what were you yourself doing up unspeakably late when you should have been sleeping?

BALBOA: Well, so much for that theory. I read these treatises and pamphlets in the can, put out by various scientific and philosophical societies, and they start to excite my brain. [*Balboa downs an entire glass of port, and another, and yet another, to fortify himself.*] The real reason I'm upset about this disclosure— oh, my adoptive brother, the words I am about to speak are so hard for me to say—the real reason is that . . . the DNA test I referred to that tested positive for Jeffersonian chromosomes was not Kelly's but yours! You and I truly are related by blood. You aren't simply a failed boxer with a police record for shoplifting, aggravated battery, urinating in public while drunk, and other embarrassing peccadilloes that might shame an offspring. You're not just a woulda-been whose only claim to decency is that he didn't default on his child-support payments. You aren't merely a red-dirt cracker peasant spawned in a shotgun house on the North Side that has now been condemned on account of excessive termite activity. No, you are the miscegenated product of a concubinal relationship between the legendary Monticello mezzo-philosopher and an overachieving house servant. It's you, Clay! You coulda been a contender. I knew the secret of your provenance long before these DNA tests were conducted. I'm sorry about always making you enter my house through the rear door and having you sleep in the carriage house. You're a male octoroon who's been passing. The chromosomal evidence only put the scientific stamp on the secret our clan has long known and kept under wraps. As a physician, a Jeffersonian, and a man of science, living this lie has rent my soul asunder. My parents adopted you to keep our dark deception under wraps within the bosom of the family, to try to contain it. If it hadn't been for our shame, you would have long since achieved the noble destiny that is your birthright. And Chandra wouldn't have to make up a bunch of crazy-ass bullshit to squelch the wicked second-guessing second-grade urchins. I'm going to rectify this mistake at your daughter's very next PTSA meeting, over the public address system, with you and Chandra and Kelly sitting right up onstage in the places of honor. I want her to be proud of her daddy.

Chandra received a B minus on her composition, along with the reminder that "There's a difference between research and make-believe" and the encouraging comment "Good improvement in spelling."

The saddle creaked beneath me as I swung my leg over the horse's back and adjusted myself into the seat. The morning was mellow—bluebells sprouting among the clover, their stems curling like calligraphy, the surrounding woods thickening where branch-bud fingers grew into leaves. Sunlight, buttery buckets of it, poured over my shoulders, the kind that makes you want to close your eyes and nap on a knoll, drowsing as you let the half-eaten apple drop from your relaxed hand and roll away.

My horse, Big Boy, was much too spirited for any lapses in attention. He wheeled away from the barn at the slightest pressure of my hand on the reins, then waited for my next command. He appeared to be expertly broken. Keen-eyed and never at rest but under control. Little dancing steps let me know he was ready to run at the barest hint of consent, but he stayed obediently in place.

Carmela hadn't seemed the least bit surprised to see me again. Her eyes gave me a companionable twinkle as she untied her horse, Minaret, and sprang into her own saddle. In skintight, butter-soft leather riding pants and a bolero jacket sporting Guatemalan designs, she looked damn good.

"You're sure you're not making a mistake? You want to go with me?"

"I'm sure."

Our horses felt their way down the rise of a hollow with their shod but path-sensitive hooves. Storm debris still lay scattered about her property. A cosmic gnashing of teeth, leaving splintered wood in its wake, like so many dropped and shivered balsa toothpicks.

We had to keep making detours off the path, around fallen tree trunks with roots like the nerve endings of massive extracted molars and balls of branches in the shape of giant tumbleweeds. Our mounts splattered through impromptu rivulets, muddy as a delta marsh, and cany, brittle stands of still-dry, wild winter grass. The horses came out of these low thickets with burrs stuck to their undersides, shivering as if they'd touched the ghost of a tick.

"Did you ever hear of a book called Death North of Patagonia?*"* Carmela asked me.

"It's one of my favorites. I didn't think anyone else knew about it. I bought it in a secondhand bookstore. The Black Swan. By—ah, I can't remember the author's name. He wrote the one book and was forgotten, I guess. I lost it somewhere along the way, in one of my moves. I've tried reordering it through the used-book services. But nobody seems to have ever heard of it except me. Until now. Do you have a copy?"

"No. I must have lent it to somebody. And they never gave it back. People are so terrible about returning books. They think it's unethical to steal from a store, but they don't mind stealing from their friends. Don't you think it's just as bad as shoplifting?"

"Uh—yeah. Shoplifting can get you in trouble. What made you mention that book?"

"No reason. I like adventure stories."

I was quiet for a time, as the ground leveled off and we passed underneath an arcade of flexible green branches that grazed our hair. In the scattered, dappled light, we seemed no more than two bright, irregular fragments in a kaleidoscope that, with the turn of a child's hand, could send us and all the other wildlife hidden in these thickets sprawling into a different arrangement, she and I flung far from one another in a senseless, random pattern that only the child's petulant eye could make out as meaningful. That child was our God. Not malevolent, really, but liable to do anything on an impulse, finding us fascinating one instant and tossing us aside the next.

"Balboa doesn't want to see me anymore," she said.

"He wants to. But he doesn't think it's a good idea."

"That's why he sent his proxy. Tell me, do you have full power to represent him? In all things?"

"I think he meant for me to be a messenger, that's all."

"He didn't have the courage to come back to say good-bye to me himself."

"He was afraid how you and he might end up."

"Like you and me, you mean?"

"You're seductive, persuasive, and overpowering. He knew he wouldn't be able to say no to whatever you proposed."

Our horses picked up the pace into a trot, jostling me in the saddle, and began to sigh with their first exertions. Carmela burst into a loud laugh that still managed to sound ladylike. One of her many talents. "Do you really mean that, Clay, or is Big Boy shaking those words out of you with his trot?"

"A little of both," I replied.

"Well, that's why I put you on him. Not only because he's the right size for you. But so you'd have to do my bidding." Water splashed up into sparkling small arcs as we forded a narrow stream. "This creek wasn't here before. Nature made it a couple of weeks ago, just because she felt like it."

"The whim of a woman," I said. Carmela smiled as if I had paid her a compliment.

The horses had turned on to what looked to be the remnants of an old flagstone road. It was flanked on either side by long, low fieldstone walls, made out of close-stacked shelves of limestone and granite. The work of artisans, labor intensive, the kind of rock fence few people could afford now, even if they could find someone willing and with the technical knowledge to repair one, much less make one. Parts of these walls had moldered, though stretches were still in good repair, having held their shape through storm, flood, seismic movement, and the natural weathering of time.

We parked the horses, dismounted, and sat atop one of the walls. "This road is remarkable. Must have been traveled a lot in its day," I ventured.

"Yes. A toll road. Dates back to 1788. The owner of this farm at that time charged horseback travelers, like us, a toll to pass through his property. He built the road, the walls, everything."

"Enterprising. He must have been a slave owner. Nobody would have lugged all these heavy rocks into place unless they had to."

"You'd be surprised at what people will do."

"I thought only pharaohs and Incas could pull that kind of forced labor off. Did he make his blacks do this?"

Carmela got a gleam in her eye. "You're partly right."

"Partly?"

"I guess you could say they were slaves. Or coolies, anyway. According to the records, these rock fences were constructed by poor Irish laborers. Your people, Clay. Not mine. Some of your ancestors may have worked on this very wall."

"I got you."

"Come on; let's ride together." We remounted the horses, and broke through a curtain of green into an open field. Carmela took off galloping at once and looked back at me playfully, daring me to keep pace with her.

It took the barest flick of my heels on Big Boy's flanks to send him careering into speed. He'd seen Minaret break loose anyway, and it was all he could do to contain himself for the couple of seconds' lag until my command. In no time, Big Boy built up to a blur. I crouched as low and horizontal on his back as I could, clinging, observing the riot of field-stubble and loosened clods rocketing beneath me, swiftly being eaten up by the horse's hooves. I forced my head up to look straight through his ears at the windy expanse opening up before me. Big Boy pulled alongside Minaret. We were racing. That is, the horses were racing, and I was along as a mere mounted witness. Carmela's face was set into an unsmiling clench. She wanted to win. A whoosh surged in my ears, the sound of my own churning blood, surging, plunging.

But Big Boy had veered off at a diagonal, and now we ripped alongside a white fence, inches away from its endlessly repeating boards. I looked ahead again and became aware of a thick, solid, stout, nasty tree branch hanging in my path at precisely the height of my head. The oldest trick in the book for a horse that turns mean. Big Boy was on course to knock me right out of my saddle. My skull prepared to strike the branch.

Thank God I had been well trained into head feints. I ducked with split-second timing. A crevice in the bark must have snagged a tuft of my hair, because I felt it yank from the roots as we went under, my cranium clearing by the barest of fractions, feeling the friction.

The backward motion pitched me off Big Boy, and I fell hard, straight onto that perpetually aggravated, woebegone shoulder of mine. And oh, Christ, how it hurt. I let fly a childish moan, like the tyke who tumbles from the monkey bars. I couldn't move the shoulder. It was tingling, stiff, contracted into its socket.

Carmela was out of her saddle in an instant, solicitous, cooing over my injury, making all the right eye gestures. Scolding Big Boy with an outstretched finger, she then lamented that she shouldn't have put me on her most rambunctious horse. It was just that I made such a competent and confident impression, and Shawn had gone on to her all about what a natural horseman I was. I'd made a reputation. She herself would ride Big Boy back to the stable. Something must have spooked him. Maybe a copperhead. All this marshy water had attracted more snakes than usual, could be that he'd trodden on one on the path. She examined his forelegs for any marks, checked to see if he was limping. No, he seemed fine. Whatever it was, he'd shaken it off. It wasn't like him at all to spook; she'd broken him herself.

Carmlea helped me into Minaret's stirrup, and before long, she and I were in her house, where she eased me down onto a comforter as billowy as a featherbed. "How about a glass of bourbon?" Yes, I told her, that would be all right. She poured some, on the rocks, in a water glass and watched me sip, nodding in satisfaction.

"That would have been one hell of an end," I said.

"Comic, not cosmic."

"But maybe slapstick is right for a second-stringer like me."

"Who says you're a second-stringer?"

"Certain people."

"And do you say that as well?"

"Sometimes. It depends what mood I'm in."

"What kind of mood are you in right now?"

I thought of Tadeusz. "Punchy. Edgy. Ready to take a risk."

"Why put yourself through a slugfest? You've got nothing to prove."

"Strange words coming from somebody who is obviously addicted to competition."

"Oh, sometimes. Depends on what I'm competing for." Carmela removed my shirt, careful not to jostle my shoulder socket. She tossed the shirt aside, onto the floor. "Nice chest," she said. "I'd forgotten how broad it was. A lot like Balboa's. Except more curls of hair."

"Forgotten?"

"Sure. I ran my fingers through that thicket once upon a time."

"Seems like I would have remembered."

"You were wasted, messenger boy. Gone, gone, gone. But all the things worked that had to work. Not the most artful night of my life, but sometimes art is overrated. Someday I'll tell you what a good time we had, so you can enjoy it too."

"We were together? You're sure?"

"Thrown together. Pressed together."

"That makes me a traitor and a liar. I've been swearing to everybody who asked about the night of the ball that nothing happened. I've already gotten beat up once on account of it."

"I'm sure you meant to be innocent, in your own mind. But yes, you're a damn dirty dog."

"Don't say that."

"Why not? Haven't you been fantasizing about me? Tell the truth."

"Yes, I have. But I want those thoughts to stay where they belong. In my head."

"Too late. Here we are." She stroked my chest hair. "I'm going to level with you. You said Balboa sent you out here. Well, I'm not operating entirely on my own initiative. So that makes us even. I'm also an emissary."

"For who?"

"We have a patron in common."

"Balboa?"

"Doesn't he wish."

"Janine?"

"Don't even mention that slutty name in this house."

"Sorry. I'm running out of guesses. Lisa?"

"Who?"

"Never mind. I just know that no woman I ever dated went completely out of my life. They keep cropping up at the most inopportune moments. God knows I'll probably run across Lisa again when I least expect it. I half expect her to be hiding in the chifforobe."

"You're missing the most obvious person of all."

"You can't mean Kelly."

"That's right."

"Why would Kelly make you her emissary? Her rival, maybe. So, what did she ask you to do? Kill me?"

"Hmm. No. That's putting it too strongly. Set you free."

"Let me guess. Get me thrown from a horse so that I'd injure my shoulder and wouldn't be able to fight Tadeusz."

"Very astute."

"No, more like me having a firm grasp of the obvious, like Kelly always says. Is there anybody not beholden to her? I had no idea she was so well connected. Those thugs already whomped on me and made it hell for me to train in the gym this week. I'm sore. Thank God for Balboa's capable hands and the fact that only cartoon characters regenerate cells faster than me. I just don't get it. By rights, you and Kelly should be at each other's throats."

"You have quite a high opinion of yourself for a second-stringer."

"I don't. I just know she's jealous of you. Be reasonable. Why would she pick you, of all people?"

"Because the motto of a woman in love, once she sets her goal, is 'By any means necessary.'"

"I see. Is this an international sisterhood?"

"Let me think. No, right now it's just Kelly and me. These alliances happen on an ad hoc basis."

"I've been around, off and on, for the past seven years, and she didn't even show an inkling of interest in me."

"She wasn't in love with you then."

"And now she is?"

"Apparently so. Did you ever notice how men will throw in devastating little phrases, like 'off and on,' that completely change the nature of what's being discussed?"

"You strike me as pretty much your own woman. How did she recruit you?"

"The only real battle, Clay, the only one that counts, is the battle of the sexes. You've squandered yourself fighting other men and forgotten to cover your rear."

"I feel like all of a sudden I'm living in some bizarre romance novel, where I don't really understand the rules. Am I the hero or the villain?"

"It's hard to explain. All I can say is, today, I'm at her beck and call."

"If she loves me, why does she keep hurting me?"

"Oh, that one doesn't need any explanation. You always hurt the one you love. But Clay, if I was you, I'd go with things as they're unfolding. Kelly can pamper or punish, either one, according to what she decides. Luckily for you, Kelly is in a generous mood today, in spite of your sulky behavior at the carnival. She's prepared to make a more than reasonable offer. She knows you've got a thing for me. If you'll renounce the fight right this second, and sign a letter to that effect, you can stay here with me while you convalesce, we can have a little fling, and you can get me all out of your system. We say good-bye. Then Kelly takes over. No questions asked."

"That doesn't sound like the Kelly I know."

"Believe it."

"Sexual healing?"

"That would be one way of looking at it. But even Marvin couldn't take his own advice. He died of a gunshot wound. Oh, how Balboa loved to put Marvin Gaye on the CD player when we made love. 'Got to Give It Up.' That should be your mantra, Clay."

"I can't—where's my shirt?" I tried to sit up, but Carmela pushed me on my back again.

"Can't what? Give it up? It isn't that hard, really."

"I appreciate your offer; it sounds like any man's fantasy come true, but I'm not giving up my fight with Tadeusz. That matter has already been decided. What I want is to get to Chicago, as soon as possible."

"Okay. Nobody can say I didn't try. We'll get you there, if that's truly your wish. There is, however, one other way out."

"Way out? What in God's name are you talking about? You're starting to sound like my fairy godmother."

"I'm talking about the world to come. Though I'm not really sure what waits next for you. First thugs, then a seduction, and then—third time's the charm. Like a fable. But you're still in shock. You need to take it easy. You're in a more delicate condition than you realize."

"Damn it, this socket is killing me. I need to get hold of some painkiller. Acupuncture, drugs, anything. Could I borrow your phone to talk to Balboa?"

"It's all right. I'll take care of it."

She removed a vial from her case and brandished a lethal-looking needle that was definitely not my size. No, it was horse sized, the kind of needle that would serve well for administering tranquilizers to unruly beasts.

She stuck the tip of the needle into the opening of a glass tube and started to draw fluid into it. "Now I know why they call it vile," I said, to try to keep my mind off that needle. She smiled complaisantly at my lame joke. I made myself breathe.

"What are you going to do with that?"

"Inject you, silly."

"I don't think so."

"Are you afraid of needles?"

"I didn't say that. But I changed my mind. I don't think my shoulder needs anything besides rest."

"A lot of men are afraid of needles. You won't feel a thing. This is cortisone," she said, using the objective, reasonable voice one employs to soothe a freaking child. "Not a brand I'd normally use on you, but as far as smooth muscles are concerned, there's no big difference between a man and a beast. Both need to be soothed, and the needle can't tell the difference between one and the other."

"You're not angry at me, are you?"

"Why would I be angry at you? Because you rejected me?"

Before I could protest, she had the needle in the flesh of my shoulder, and most of the medicine had slid in. "If we do this now, you'll get the full effect. This is what you said you wanted, isn't it? I'm sorry we won't get to make love. It would have been so, so nice."

All I felt was an internal gush, and the task was done. She swabbed me with iodine.

"What, no alcohol?"

"It doesn't kill infection very well. I don't even know why they use it. I've got Beta-Dyne."

"I meant booze."

She brought the bottle over and poured me another liberal shot. I gulped it. "Any more last requests?"

"No."

"Then lie down and seek some peace for that poor abused shoulder."

I did as she said, and closed my eyes. The room drifted in the absence *of my vision. But I grew weary of holding its dimensions steady by sheer force of will.*

My needle's in you, baby, and you seem to feel all right. When the medicine go to coming down, baby, I want you to hug me tight.

Nebucchim, Nebucchim.

Cheap, homegrown blues club philosophy.

Let's dance, let's shout, gettin' funky's what it's all about.

The intense aroma of honeysuckle washed over Clay as he climbed out of the gully on foot. A single cricket chirped in the grass nearby, underfoot, out of sight.

He looked up, and met the stream of the Milky Way where it flowed through the middle of the sky. A cosmic flume, ceaseless. He was inside it and apart from it at the same time.

He climbed over a pasture fence and padded across a field in the dark, skirting a drinking pond. Ducks moved in the water, honking softly and cutting a silent swath. He'd worn tennis shoes, and could feel night dew soaking through the mesh into his socks. There was a wary movement of big silhouettes, probably cows, taking stock of the trespasser. Besides that, only the puffing of Clay's breath, as he climbed a fence on the other side. He made his way up an incline, to the top of a hillock. Off in the distance, he could make out the triple gables of a stable, a pinpoint beacon shining in each of them.

The night chill seeped into his bones. He'd forgotten how cold it could get in the open country at night in a high spot, where you aren't protected from the breeze. The cloud cover had blown off as vapor to parts unknown, leaving a clear, deep sky in which the stars stood out like bits of ore on the surface of a rock. There appeared to be nothing between him and heaven, no atmosphere of any kind. On that modest hilltop, he was in outer space, just at the spot where a jet engine starts to fail, as the last wisp of oxygen gives out, and a man goes whirling off into naked and infinite expanses.

Something starts out as a joke and becomes the rest of your life. Knock, knock. Who's there? It's me, only me. No need to give my name. I'm the designated one. Only I can walk through that door reserved for me. Usually, it says MEN'S ROOM, in block letters painted on cinderblock. But someone has been kind enough to tape over it a cardboard sign that says CLAY JUSTIN. The cardboard isn't quite long enough to cover the block letters, however, so the letters ME stick out at the beginning. Me. Clay Justin.

"That's him," a voice remarked as I walked by on my way to the dressing room. Exhibit A. The sucker. The fall guy. The human punching bag.

I'd decided I wasn't going to get psychological. I had worked out several mornings at Ford's Gym in Lexington, over in Cardinal Valley, but I was undertrained. I couldn't afford to play any games. Besides, Tadeusz didn't have an ounce of psychology in his whole being. He only had one mood, and all you needed to do was snap your fingers to unleash it. Any sort of delicacy or subtlety of behavior would have been entirely squandered on him. He lived his life in a comic strip, one without humor, so I was obliged to do the same for tonight. That's called making a mental adjustment.

Smitty came in, looking even more wizened and full of knots than he'd been before I left Chicago. Something was squeezing him down into the density of a plank. The neuralgia he got on the left side of his face when a situation made him tense was working overtime. Somebody had shot him in the face with a BB gun when he was a kid, and twitched the nerve. But he tried to sound hearty. "Ready, sport?"

"Ready as I'm going to get."

"We got a couple minutes. I'll give you a quick rubdown." He uncapped a glass jar of some liniment he swore by, a foul-smelling goop that, if you listened to his story, possessed nearly magical powers. When he brought it out, it was the equivalent of a Lake Shore millionaire having you to dinner and producing his pet vintage out of the wine cellar, the bottle he'd been saving all his life just for you. "I usually do this afterward, but it will warm up those muscles a little." He pasted me with liniment, using his thick, stubby fingers to work it in.

"I don't think they'll let me in the ring greased down like this. His gloves will slip off me."

"I'm gonna wipe off what don't soak in. Quit your bitching."

"Well, the aroma alone ought to knock Tadeusz out, if he gets anywhere close to me."

"Funny, Clay. You got that gallows humor still functioning at the stroke of midnight."

"You know me. The worse things get, the more I joke."

"Jokes won't save you today."

"You think he's going to slaughter me?"

He swiped at my back with a towel. "Enough talking out of you. Do I look like an oddsmaker? And by the way, don't get mouthy on him. Just pisses him off the more. You remember how your ex-wife told you that tongue of yours was gonna get you in trouble. It's your worst enemy. You're a smart aleck. You make a joke about something that's supposed to be serious. Then you get all serious and uptight about stuff that you should be able to laugh at. You let him talk all the trash he wants. Fight your fight. Don't get suckered into his mind games."

"Don't you need a mind to play mind games?"

"This is exactly what I mean. You underestimate the man's intelligence. He's not broad-minded, I grant you, but he's got the kind of smarts he needs for the work he does."

"All right, Smitty. I'll try not to give him any lip."

"*Ecco.* You concentrate on wrecking his face. All it takes is a few solid licks to win. You can win. We got a good referee. Tadeusz starts hitting below the belt, we're going to stop the fight. Pronto. We already talked all that over."

"You really are worried about me, aren't you, Smitty? You do think he's going to take me apart."

"Hey, enough of that." His voice quavered a little. He capped his precious liniment and rose to leave. "By the way, watch your step in the ring. The ropes are loose today." He gave me a significant wink, or was it just a neuralgic spasm?

"Sure. Whatever."

"Okay, Clay, now you talk to whoever you have seances with during these times. Say a prayer, and be sincere. No smarting off to the Higher Power. God wants sincerity. He's not an ironist. We'll see you out there when you're ready." Smitty stepped away with a nod of adieu, leaving me to my own devices and the questionable mercy of the Creator.

Tadeusz was already waiting for me in the ring, as he had been since time immemorial. Lithic and wet. His whole body glistened. Maybe he'd had a rubdown too, only his must have been with baby oil. Smitty was acting as my corner today. "Hey, could we be sure Tadeusz gets wiped off too?" I complained. "He looks like a greased pig."

"That's not fatback. Just sweat. The doors are closed."

"What for?"

"Because they are."

"Christ, can't we get any ventilation in here?" I asked for the squeeze bottle right away, to combat the dry sensation growing in my mouth. There was a lot of chatter going on in the seats. All that lacked was for our audience to be eating cold box lunches while we fought, tearing at gristle with their bared teeth. As a matter of fact, somebody was noshing a plastic-wrapped sandwich. I swear I could hear the rustling of the Saran Wrap from where I stood removing my sweatsuit. I felt mummified in unbreathable Saran Wrap myself. No silk robe for me. No monogram. I wasn't in that category.

In the front row of seats, Balboa held something small and black in his lap. Was it his cell phone? I wanted him to be holding one of those big country doctor bags, the kind you haul along when you have to birth a baby or a foal in the middle of a winter storm. It looked like it could be a pouch. What could he be carrying for me, in such a small space? Chiclets to chew between rounds? Tic-Tacs? Maybe a cyanide pill, in case I went MIA.

The referee was explaining the rules to us, the same bullshit I'd heard many times before in my semiprofessional life, and I paid about as much attention to it as I do to the in-flight attendant when she goes through that business about the exit rows and the luggage in the overhead compartment. If you're not willing to serve in an emergency, please ask someone to trade seats with you. As if they would. Who was going to trade places with me now? I also knew that what the referee was saying would have no bearing whatsoever on how Tadeusz would behave. He'd do whatever he could get away with.

I wasn't going to venture my tender left arm on the first shot. I wanted to get warmed up before I started jabbing with it, so I wouldn't pull the tendons around the socket again. It didn't feel too bad. Tadeusz looked as huge as a bull does when he starts puffing up the hump behind his neck. He was carrying twenty pounds on me, officially, though it looked more like forty to me; the differential had doubled overnight, all of it rock-solid muscle, and, of course, he had about three inches in height on me as well. He was damned well put together, I had to give him that. He'd probably spent the last week downing corn dogs, and through some trick of physiognomy, or alchemy, the cholesterol he ate turned straight into protein and added itself to his muscle fiber.

He also had that streak of white running through his hair, that skunk streak. He probably thought of it as lightning in a night sky, illuminating his manly features. I half suspected that he dyed it that color for effect, though the news stories spread by his PR said it was a "trait" inherited from some distant duke he was descended from in Poland. And I, of course, was descended from the *Dukes of Hazzard*. I imagined him and me as championship wrestlers, the phoniest of phonies, both of us, him sporting a flowing black cape and white gloves, removed by a nubile blond assistant, and me in overalls, no shirt, with my front tooth blacked out. A dreadlock wig. A Rastafarian redneck, descended from the miscegenation of Daisy Mae with a prince from Port-au-Prince. The Double Dukes Duke It Out! One Night Only!

But phony headlocks and whanging one another against the ropes was not to be. This was the real deal, and he was unquestionably ready, sets of muscles rippling no matter which way he turned. I wasn't going to kid myself. There was no way I could stay even six or seven rounds with that mass of supple cement. I'd have to go for a quick knockout. Nobody in this congregation besides me, and maybe Smitty, would like that much, but it was better than getting slowly beaten to a pulp. I would use my right cross. That was my sole hope. I don't think Tadeusz had ever even seen it, really. The cross was an occasional surprise maneuver I'd throw in against someone. Back in my early days, I'd knocked someone out of the ring with it.

We returned to our corners. The bell rang, we came out quick, and as soon as we touched gloves I unleashed with my right cross.

And almost got him. He was expecting my left hook, the tactic I'm most known for. But he caught sight of my flying fist out of the corner of his eye and made a slight adjustment, so I ended up instead smacking him hard upside the head.

I could feel that if I'd connected straight on, it would have brought him down hard. There had been a lot of power in that first punch, more than anyone would give me credit for on their cards, a punch right from my bowels and mineral hard, like the bowels of the earth, but now he knew, and I wouldn't be able to get off another free right cross. It had been a gambit, and I had come up with nothing. As Smitty would say, I'd just hit him hard enough to piss him off.

Then he moved in and went to work on me. Two uppercuts, a jab, a roundhouse, a couple of hooks. Almost all of them connected. What's more, he was pushing me around with his body, bulling me at will. His response time was unbelievably fast. He was bigger, stronger, more enraged than me. I wondered if he'd been doped for the match. I'd never seen this brawler in a more murderous mood than he was in right now. But what freaked me out the most was when I managed to get in another jab at his face and opened a good-sized gash over his lip, he barely bled from the cut. Was his face made of papier-mâché, filled with stuffing? The crowning moment of my career, my one chance to prove I had the skills, and I was going head to head with a human piñata. He gave his upper lip a swat, as if he felt a bead of sweat. That's all. The bell rang, thank God, and I did a seafaring strut to my corner and sat down hard.

"Did you see any newspaper shreds fly out of his face when I raked him?"

"Don't get kooky on me."

"I'm tired already, Smitty. I can't stay with this pace. I didn't train properly."

"When do you ever? You're looking all right. I liked that right cross."

"Yeah, well that penny's already spent." I took in the spectators' faces nearest to me. They had the gleeful look boys get when a schoolyard fight breaks out unexpectedly, just as they're going numb in the skull from boredom. They had to be certain in their minds, from the outset, that I was going to get annihilated—that's the scenario their money was tied up in—but they wanted me to show a little fight, a little spirit, a grasshopper compliantly writhing in the kerosene conflagration before turning to cinders, so that they could be reassured, in another way, that they'd gotten their money's worth.

"Wake up. Rest time is over."

It seemed I barely had time to towel off and get a mouthful of water before the second-round bell rang. Tadeusz and I moved directly toward each other, both of us on sets of good legs. As he got within earshot, I couldn't help myself. The image of his head filled with newspaper shreds, strips of the Sunday comics, wouldn't turn loose of me. I started barking out "Piñata, piñata, piñata."

Tadeusz lunged at me and grabbed me into an unexpected clinch. He brought his mouth close to my ear. "You will not make mirth at my expense. No clown. Or I'm beating the stuffing from you." That was exactly the worst thing he could have said. I burst into giddy peals of laughter. The referee broke us apart, snapping at Tadeusz to keep his hands to himself, and looking at me as if I'd lost my sanity. Both Tadeusz and I were remembering the day I met Balboa and knocked Tadeusz to the canvas. That day was in his consciousness too, right up front. But his smirking eyes told me the same knockdown wasn't going to happen again.

If he'd had a couple of points deducted, he couldn't care less. This one wasn't going to be decided on points. Both of us were aware of that. I wasted my energy on a series of combinations that barely grazed his skin, wearing myself down for nothing. He came back into me and laid down a blistering volley, knocking me this way and that. I simply didn't have the force to hold him back. It was only a matter of time, and short time at that, before he weakened me to the point where he could take my head off, like Brutus beheading Popeye once and for all. My face would explode, that's all, and the walls of the Mid-Town Gym would be papered with a lifetime of desiccated spinach.

The bell announced the end of the second round. "Give him some space," Smitty advised, as I simply lay back on my stool pouring sweat, crying a river through my pores. I was already too exhausted to drink, and Smitty poured liquid into my open mouth.

It poured right back out, most of it, and collected around my ear-lobes and neck.

At last I could speak. "I can't backpedal that fast. I'm like Ginger Rogers, dancing backward and in high heels."

"Save your wit, Clay. You're the only guy I know who can't fucking swallow water but he can sure as hell talk. Don't deplete yourself."

"There's not enough room in that ring," I said nervously. I could feel myself already getting punchy. "Are those the right dimensions? The ring seems small."

Smitty looked around as if fearing he might be heard. "I done told you; it's plenty big today," he whispered. "Think about it. Bigger than ever."

The third-round bell summoned me, and on woozy legs, I struggled to my feet like Peg-Leg Pete. I felt like I'd already fought six or seven rounds. Taduesz, on the other hand, wasn't diminished at all. If anything, he seemed to be gathering strength as he went, sucking mine out like the marrow of an overly soft chicken bone that you pry apart with your bare teeth. Right away he resumed his relentless onslaught, as if the time between rounds had only been a freeze-frame he'd placed on a VCR fight video he was watching at home while he went to take a leak and fix himself another plate of nachos.

The crowd was starting to shout and make impolite remarks. They didn't want this fight to go beyond three rounds. The one visible chink I did notice was a slight vexation on Tadeusz's face. He was probably expected to take me out at a designated time, after showing his prowess to the crowd, showing how he could push me around like a toy, establishing his general superiority and repertoire of moves. It was a complicated exhibition. If he'd knocked me out only fifteen or twenty seconds from the fight's start, that would have been anticlimactic. It might even have come off looking fluky. The prearranged time must be getting close, or maybe had even passed, and now Tadeusz's impatience was growing. I was supposed to throw the fight, in a sense, except none of his people had given me any chance of winning anyway, so I wasn't consulted about the matter. I would simply take a fall when Tadeusz got good and ready for me to do so.

He was definitely coming in for the kill. I could smell that fact more than see it. And I could certainly feel it. I was barely dodging bashing blows to my cranium. My forearms had swelled up like lumps of yeast dough where I had to use them so much as a shield. Usually I could protect my head better than this. More of his blows started finding their mark, and I was getting groggier. There was nowhere to go. The ring had narrowed to the couple of inches between us.

Then I remembered what Smitty had told me in the locker room, what he'd been hinting at during the last break: the ropes were a little loose today. The ring really was bigger. Smitty had no doubt come out a couple of hours before the fight and hand loosened the ropes, in case things came to the pass they were at right now. I fell back against the ropes, letting my torso sprawl, and sure enough, they were as elastic as taffy. So the taffy pull was about to begin. And I was Gumby. I gave Smitty silent thanks.

I laid myself back in the ropes like a babe in a cradle, forcing Tadeusz off balance as he tried to reach me. He looked aggravated, and I smiled to egg him on. In that unnatural position, he really couldn't punch with much force, even when he could reach me. Mostly I was absorbing body blows, hoping to tire his legs out as much as mine.

I moved around the ring's perimeter, always keeping the ropes at my back, throwing myself into them like a clown in a hammock. The crowd started to boo me. Tadeusz was more enraged than ever. I was degrading his performance and postponing the inevitable knockout. I heard his corner complaining to the referee about the ropes, and the referee rejoindering that there was nothing he could do about it now, unless they wanted him to stop the fight. Tadeusz's corner gave a grunt of disgust and shut his mouth.

In his frustration, Tadeusz popped me hard below the belt, dead into my groin. It almost buckled me forward to where I would have served him my head on a platter. But I held back, grimacing, hoping the ball-busting pain would die off. Smitty was screaming like a maniac from my corner about the low blow, insisting that they stop the fight, the way they'd promised. The referee gave Tadeusz a warning, and hollered that there would be a resulting point deduction. Tadeusz didn't seem to give a damn.

In the meantime, I saved my strength, waiting for an opening to unleash the only weapon I still possessed, my left hook. I didn't have that much confidence in it, to be honest, but I reminded myself that I had knocked Tadeusz down before. I didn't have to knock him out, or even win the match, just send him sprawling onto the canvas. That is, if he didn't kill me first. Whatever prior agreements he'd made about showing restraint, not hitting below the belt, fighting cleanly, going for a specific goal, not impugning his good name so that he could take the title from Nazir Salaam, those agreements had gotten tossed out of his mind as soon as I started using the rope-a-dope. No one had ever been able to manage Tadeusz effectively. He cared nothing about living to fight another day. Each bout was treated as his first and last, and in the end, he was going to do what he wanted, no matter what it cost him.

Right now, the only career goal in his mind was to destroy me, utterly and completely. I read that plainly in his depthless eyes. The corner was shouting instructions to him, but Tadeusz simply let them wash over him, so much blather. He had me backed down, shouting that he was going to put my ass in a sling and throw me into space. He blacked my eye, and it swelled up at once. He cracked my jaw.

Every insult about my mediocrity that had ever been hurled at me—every lie, epithet, slur—swirled in the tight cyclonic space in which I was buffeted. This tornado had no eye. There was nowhere to move, nowhere to crouch or surrender, unless I was willing to die. I wasn't that far from death, and it didn't seem that bad a place. Not welcoming, but neutral, blank, unfathomable, the ultimate knock-out. Consciousness was the one thing I'd never been able to lose for long.

I had one good punch left in me, only one, maybe one, if I could get my arms uncrossed from their protective crisscross. I just wanted all two hundred and forty pounds of him off me. If the bell came in the meantime, I would crawl to my corner and quit the match. Humiliated or not, but alive. In the meantime, I had to fight, because time passed so slowly. But there must have been only a few seconds left, in reality, because Tadeusz's corner had started shouting desperate words, ones he finally seemed to hear and attend to. They sounded like "Put him out! Put him out!"

It was time to snuff the candle and lick his blackened thumbs. Carbon on his tongue. For one second, as he angled to land the definitive punch, Tadeusz got a little too free-swinging in his haste, leaving himself open. That's all it took. Not even a whole second, just a fraction of a second. Less time than the margin of Hellaballoo's world record.

I lashed and connected with my hard left hook, opening an ugly gash over his right eye. This time there was blood. He reeled backward and fell to the canvas. At the same instant, I felt the tearing in my arm. I started dry-heaving.

Chills shook me. I groped my way backward toward my corner, not finding it, blubbering, spewing spit and snot out my nose and lips, seeing only blurs through the wash of tears in the one eye that wasn't swollen shut. I was afraid Tadeusz was going to rise up and come after me again. I had nothing left. Maybe the bell had sounded, but if it had, I hadn't heard it.

The referee knelt over Tadeusz, who continued to lie faceup, unmoving. His doctor was climbing into the ring, moving with a peculiar lack of haste. He knelt, examined the body with all due care, and in the preternatural silence, all the static cleared off and I could see and hear his lips speak the words "He's dead." Men from the audience were on their feet, shouting out for him to speak up. He stood, straightened his coat, and repeated, in a half shout that sounded tiny in the cavernous, humid expanse around him, the words he had uttered over the body.

Several uniformed cops jumped into the ring, as if they expected there to be trouble. Everyone there was clearly stunned. I was, too. Tadeusz had been beaten and slain by a second-rate sparring partner whose only claim to fame had been his ability to take limitless punishment.

Someone found his voice, then another, then another. A lot of shouting was going on. I heard someone vehemently insist to a policeman that I had committed murder and should be detained. What surprised me was that the policeman appeared to be listening to the man's argument. Sure enough, the policeman started to climb into the ring. Smitty was all over him in a second, waving his arms histrionically, as if protesting an especially bad call. The cop, a guy with a boyish face, kept Smitty at arm's length, ignoring him like a pro, not answering any of Smitty's increasingly colorful string of accusations. With a seasoned sense of protocol, he announced that he was going to have me booked for the crime of manslaughter. In truth, he probably had no idea what might become of me. Eager to hand me off to someone farther up the line, he handcuffed me for the benefit of his livid observers, quietly handed me my sweat pants to put on, and led me out.

As my police escort and I were making our way to the exit door, a pang of my sympathy went out to Tadeusz, as he lay without motion in the ring, his corpse guarded but still untouched. They'd carry him out, in due time, but there wasn't any big hurry about it.

I awoke in a dark room. I'd slept more soundly than I would have thought possible under the circumstances. The air was stale and close. It had left my throat dry and choky and my sinuses raw. Muffled voices mouthing indistinct words came from somewhere below. I expected my eyes to adjust to the dark, but they didn't. Finding my feet, I stumbled around as if in the hatch of a boat, trying to find a wall at least, to begin to locate myself and steady my legs, but the room appeared to be much larger than the initial echoes would have indicated. Litter rustled at my feet with every step, and I was assaulted by a turpentine reek that was probably piss. Maybe I was still in the holding pen with other criminals who'd been booked, though I recalled my captors moving me quickly to an isolated cell, probably because they thought my now-notorious presence would provoke a disturbance or that I'd get into another fight with somebody.

Everything remained cloudy. I had a hard time shaking off the groggy feeling that had taken possession of the inside of my head. Groping for the wall, I ended up with something in my hand that felt like a wooden handle. An old-fashioned vertical-tank toilet flush, maybe? The dimensions of the room didn't make any sense, though in the dark, you never know for sure how large or small anything is. "How the hell big is this place?" I said aloud, to myself, and listened to my words echo back in the empty, contained space.

A door opened, and light shone around two silhouettes. "The master suite is eighteen by twenty four," said a voice. "But this first bedroom is, let's see what it says on the sheet—I should know this—okay, nine by twelve, that's what I thought, which would be fine for a child, and you can certainly fit bookshelves in here. Did you notice the play structure out back? All treated wood. Property taxes are criminally low in this county, and that's a plus. Let me find the switch."

Artificial light glared me into existence. I stood in the center of a half-white, half-yellow bedroom holding a painter's roller in my hand, facing Janine and Lisa. I had been lucky not to step in the full trough of paint beneath my feet. Lisa wore a business suit with flared pants and carried a clipboard. She had cut her hair really short—"woe-is-me short," she used to call it. I hadn't seen it that short since near the beginning of our relationship, right after she'd broken off with that married professor. Janine had opted for a blue-jeaned skirt and a close-fitting windbreaker.

I closed my eyes, opened them, closed them, opened. It didn't seem to make that much difference either way. As if I had no lids, and I couldn't feel myself blinking when I tried to concentrate on the space below my forehead. Then again, it was hard to tell what was working up there, with my head so numb.

Lisa gave me a characteristic wave where she uses only the tips of her fingers, as if she'd been looking for me in a crowd, and was now summoning me over to introduce me to some old friend she'd stumbled across. A small gem glinted on her index finger. "Hi, Clay. The paint is going to drip if you keep the lights off. Probably easier if you can see what you're doing." Her nose wrinkled. "Oh, my God. What happened to your face? It looks horrible."

I touched a scab on my cheek. "You didn't hear? I killed Tadeusz Virkowicz." She looked fantastic, trim, and hadn't put on any discernible weight since our breakup. If anything, she'd gone in the other direction. The haircut suited her, accentuating her pretty cheekbones and smoldering, playful eyes. She was even wearing an engagement ring. What had it been, three or four weeks at most since we'd broken up? Lisa looked as though she'd spent every day since our breakup at a spa. Her skin glowed as if she'd recently lounged in a steam room. Of course I would run into her under these circumstances.

"Oh, yeah, that's right. I read in yesterday's paper that you'd killed that Polish fighter two days ago. Tough break." I looked down at the mess of newspapers spread on the floor to avoid her offhandedly piercing gaze. Studying the particular sheet of newspaper from the sports section that was stuck to the bottom of my left foot, I could make out my name in a headline. I ripped the sheet from my sole, to see how the incident had been reported and perhaps get some clue as to what lay in store for me, from a judicial point of view. But globs of paint had spilled over most of the article, covering its words. The only phrase I could make out was "had been living in obscurity until."

Lisa sighed. "I wish you'd gotten away from fighting, but I knew I wasn't going to be able to talk you out of it. So I gave up." Janine stood patiently by, listening to our conversation but not intervening. Lisa scribbled something on the edge of her clipboard, as if a thought had suddenly occurred to her. "I hope you're not upset about me finally breaking off with you. I just couldn't take the uncertainty anymore. You were never going to marry me. I was starting to worry that you were only in it for the sex."

"No, I'm not mad or anything. You did what you had to do."

"Thanks for letting me use your garage while I got situated. By the way, do you have my car keys?"

"Not on me. They emptied my pants pockets when they booked me for manslaughter."

"Okay. Well, I had an extra set, so I went by and took my car out of the garage, with you being out of town indefinitely and all. I noticed that dent on the left side, by the way. The least you could have done was tell me."

"Sorry. I had a few other things on my mind. I drove it to a blues club."

"Maybe you could drop the keys in the mail when you get a chance. If you get a chance."

"Sure. Are you—engaged?"

She looked down at the elegant single-carat diamond on her finger, as if surprised herself to see it winking there. "Kind of. I went to a high-school friend's wedding last week, on a lark, and it turned out a guy I used to date casually in high school lives in Chicago now; we didn't even know we were in the same town. Isn't that the most? So, I don't know, one thing led to another. He went crazy over me. I was feeling foxy and confident, so I put on a little black dress and lorded it over all my old classmates that night. I was determined to break every heart in the ballroom, especially those of the guys who never noticed me. Most of all, though, I was trying to get past you once and for all. I cried a river over you. I know it seems kind of kooky and sudden and on the rebound, but the engagement just happened. He proposed like a couple of days after we reconnected."

"I see. Well, congratulations on the upcoming marriage. I know you'll both be."

"I'm not sure we'll actually get married, but it's fun to be engaged for a while. I'm not going to rush. It simply feels nice to be wanted in that way."

"You look great."

"Thanks. You flatterer. I wish I could say the same for you. You're in a terrible fix, and you look it."

"How did you get into real estate?"

"Don't you remember I was studying to take the test? I must have told you that two dozen times. See, you weren't paying attention. Don't you remember that big encyclopedia of a book I was always carrying around?"

"I thought that was to help you see over the windshield."

"Very funny. I passed, and a friend of mine helped get me on with an agency. Right now I'm moonlighting. Not quite ready for the Million Dollar Club. But I'll get there."

"Am I—how exactly did I get here? Does Kelly have something to do with this?"

"Who? Oh, you mean your ex-wife. Gee, I don't think so. You were given this painting detail while your trial is pending. I guess the real-estate lobby came up with some kind of work-release arrangement with the Cook County Jail."

"Isn't that unconstitutional? Shouldn't I have been released on bail for a second-degree charge?"

"Hmm. Yeah, probably, now that you mention it. Maybe you posed an imminent threat to society. Or could be that people outside want to kill you, so they put you here temporarily for your own protection. Still, somebody with influence must have intervened for you to get such a cushy assignment. This doesn't even look like a jail. More like a safe house."

"This arrangement has got to violate all kinds of laws about due process. Me painting houses for Realtors, for free, when I haven't even been convicted of anything yet? They might as well have me out digging sewer ditches. Or at the least picking up trash beside the highway in an orange jumpsuit."

"Oh Clay, you're always so melodramatic. You wouldn't be satisfied unless they stuck you on a chain gang in Mississippi. You read too much literature. You should be happy for this assignment. Anyway, I wouldn't rock the boat if I were you. It beats lying around on an iron cot all day."

"Thanks for the pep talk."

"Well, I've got to run. I have another appointment in fifteen. I hope the lockbox works. I can never get those things open. I'll leave you two here. Janine says she knows you, and she's got her own set of wheels." Lisa fished her keys out of a petite handbag and already had the cell phone to her ear, the one I'd deposited in her glove box, once upon a time. "It was nice seeing you, Clay. We could have been wonderful together, but now I see that splitting up was for the best. I hope you beat the rap."

"If I do, I'll come to your wedding."

Lisa ducked out of the room, and I listened to the rapid tap of her heels as she hurried downstairs, then the once-familiar whoosh of her engine starting and the SUV pulling away, leaving a thick silence in its wake.

Janine and I sized each other up.

"Alone at last," I said.

"Don't get any ideas. This isn't *Last Tango in Paris.*"

"You don't have to worry. The most strenuous activity I'm up to is taking a couple of extra-strength ibuprofen."

Janine rooted in her purse and handed me a packet of foil. "Here. One of the pharmaceutical reps gave me samples."

"This isn't going to send me off into another world, is it?"

She raised her eyebrows. "I don't think so. It has a touch of codeine in it, but all it should do is dull the pain."

"Okay. It's just that I've had recent trouble with women giving me medication." I swallowed the pills without water, and they went down with surprising ease. "Am I dead?"

"I don't think so. You look about half dead. But if you're in discomfort, that's a pretty sure sign that you're alive."

"Well then, I'm definitely alive. But you look a little translucent. Do you mind if I touch you, just to corroborate what my eyes are seeing?"

"I'd prefer that you didn't."

Picking up the roller again, I decided to give the still-yellow wall a few swipes of cream paint with my good, noninflamed arm. Swatches of latex glistened on the wall as I worked my way across. It was some consolation to have a useful task to do that wasn't open to interpretation. Maybe Lisa had been right, in a way. I'd landed in a good place for the moment, fumes or no fumes. I only wished for a window so that I could see the outside world. "So, you're shopping for a new place? Does this mean that you and Balboa are splitting up?"

"I can't really talk about that right now. I am looking at real estate. But the main reason I'm here is to thank you for turning up my husband, and turning his head around a little bit. He's been in touch, and we've started talking. That's as much as I care to say. I know you've been through a lot on my account, and I don't take it for granted. I'm willing to admit I judged you too harshly in the past, lumping you in with all of Balboa's partying friends."

"No, I wouldn't say my life has been much of a party recently."

"Is there anything I can do for you in return for services rendered?"

"You could get me out of this house. I'm starting to get the littlest bit claustrophobic. And the smell of paint is only making my headache worse. I can't shake off this groggy, numb thing in my head. Didn't Lisa say you had a car outside?"

"I'd whisk you away right now if I could. To wherever you want to go. But it appears that right now you're under some sort of—"

"Open house arrest?"

"Yes. Whatever this arrangement can be called. You did kill a man. But I can stay with you for a while. I brought along food for you to eat. I thought you might be hungry." Janine removed from a plastic bag a grease-spotted sack, one with a logo I recognized, and a fragrance emanated from it that made me salivate. All at once I realized how famished I was. It felt good to have another sensation besides pain inhabit my being.

I sighed with the pleasure of anticipation. "Tropic Island."

"Jerk chicken. I don't usually like to venture into that part of town, because it's so disreputable. But I remembered that you and Balboa had bopped down there together late at night several times, so I guessed that this might be one of your favorite meals."

"It is," I agreed, with my mouth already full. My manners were atrocious, but I didn't care.

"Also, you shouldn't be taking medication on an empty stomach."

The jerk chicken was pure heaven. The pungent juice of it spread through my mouth. So many sensations came flooding back to me at the same time, I began to weep, making it hard to swallow. Every place, inside and out, was full of hurting now. For the first time, I let enter into me the enormity of what had happened. I might never see Kelly or Chandra again. This was my way station, to where I didn't know. Sobbing, I found myself also rifling through the bottom of the sack, staining my hands with grease. "Did you bring the sauce?"

"Two kinds," she answered, handing me a tissue. "Mild and extra hot. I didn't know which way you'd want to go." She held out the packets to me.

"Both ways," I said. We looked at each other and burst out laughing together. It was the first time either of us had laughed in the other's presence.

Janine slipped a Tupperware container out of a plastic grocery bag. "I don't know whether you're up for this. But when you arrived at the Valentine's party, I noticed when you first came in the kitchen that the smell of plantains bathed in caramelized sugar really got you going. Your eyes followed my maid upstairs as if she was about to lead you through the gates of paradise." She gave me a sly look and popped the top off the container. "So I had our cook prepare a batch of sweet fried plantains for you."

"Bless you. I didn't know you were watching me that night."

"I notice things when I want to. I just don't let on that I do. And I have something to confess to you, Clay. I wanted you to fall for Carmela Wade. The glance that passed between the two of you in the kitchen, when you wound up in the same room together by chance, was so strong, so full of unexpected lust, it occurred to me that if you crossed paths again, true lightning might strike. I thought it was the only way Balboa might get over her. By having to hand her over to you. The morning after the party, while I was helping to clean trash and discarded brassieres out of the ballroom, I performed my *veve* to the *loas* Papa Legba and Ayida-Weddo."

"Who?"

"Oh, a couple of voodoo gods. I made a pentagram for them out of a few incense sticks."

"Aren't you Presbyterian?"

"Without a doubt. I also lit a candle to the Holy Ghost. However, when it comes to some things—"

"All religions are one at the root?"

"No, I wouldn't go that far. I was only going to say that Presbyterians aren't too good on revenge. They're always preaching against hardness of the heart. Anyway, my grandparents on my mother's side are Haitian, and they schooled me a little in the old gods behind my mother's back, when I was a child."

"You used black magic to try to make me fall in love with your husband's mistress?"

"Please don't use that word. It makes my temples throb."

"Black magic?"

"No, the other one. I know; I shouldn't have involved you in any of this love medicine in the first place. You looked like such a sad sack that night; I thought you might actually enjoy being given this role to play. You said you and Lisa had broken up. I didn't know, though, that you were trying to get back together with your ex-wife. I didn't mean to interfere."

I had no idea what to say. The easy camaraderie that had sprung up between us unbidden started to stiffen.

I wiped my hands on my pants, since she hadn't brought enough napkins (nobody ever does), and I went back to rolling paint on the wall. Beneath the old paint, I could discern faint figures, as if wallpaper hadn't been stripped and was trying to bleed through. Soon I'd be done applying a new coat, and then what would I do with myself? I rolled with a grim efficiency, not bothering whether the thickness of the coat stayed uniform. I probably should have asked Janine for news of Kelly, Chandra, Balboa, or anyone else she might have gotten word of, but it seemed like too much trouble.

"Oh, there is one more thing." She handed me a Priority Mail envelope. "This came to my address, but the note is addressed to you." Inside was a book with a pink Post-it attached. The note said, "I found it. I hadn't loaned it out after all. C.W." The book was *Death North of Patagonia*. The only copy still in existence, for all I knew. "I guess I'd better go." Janine gathered up the picked-over remains of the jerk chicken and carefully dropped them in the grease-spotted sack, leaving me the rest of the half-eaten plantains. She ripped open a lanolin-perfumed towelette packet and wiped her hands clean. Everything I'd eaten had turned to a nauseating ball of cement in my stomach.

"By the way, I'll do what I can to get you out of this."

"This what? This room?"

"The whole situation. Prison, all of it."

"How?" I asked, halfheartedly.

"I have a few ideas. I'd prefer not to discuss them until I see what can be done."

"Yeah, okay. Sure." She left, quietly closing the door behind her with a soft click, as if she were slipping out of the nursery of a newborn she didn't want to jostle awake. And in fact, no sooner had she left than a drowsy stupor began to steal over me, the way it does over a baby. I wanted to read, but my eyelids were too heavy. I couldn't even make it back to the bed. I lay down on the floor and pulled the nearest sheets of newspaper over my body.

Nebucchim stirred. He found himself sprawled in the dirt, face-down. The hard, bare ground was covered with a lacework pattern of hoarfrost, like freshly sprouted bread mold. The summer solstice had passed, kicking straight into Patagonian winter, bypassing slow season-al adjustments. A patch of the frost had left an impression on his cheek. Nebucchim traced its inverted filigree across his facial skin with the tips of his half-numb fingers. For some reason, both hands felt greasy. He was disappointed not to be dead. Consciousness was the one thing he'd never been able to escape for long. The spigot in the yard belched hisses of air mixed with rusty water. With a handful of water, he washed the taste of blood from his mouth, exchanging one iron flavor for another.

Instead of slaying him by bullet, the Duarte Brothers had insisted on challenging him to a bare-knuckles fight, only giving themselves the advantage of two against one. No firearms. After they had dragged him out of the house by his shirt, they flung their gnarly fists at him. As the brothers invited Nebucchim through taunts to retaliate, they seemed in positively high spirits about the escapade, as if it were simply a hazing ritual among blood brothers. They weren't even very good fighters. Their limbs flailed sidewise, so that they hit him as often as not with the open flat of their palms, in a ludicrous exhibition of pseudopugilism.

Eventually, one of them must have gotten fed up with the incon-clusive nature of the combat, after the initial burst of bright enthusi-asm, for he hit Nebucchim in the head from behind with a plank. A clot of dried blood matted the hair around his crown. Their horses were nowhere in sight, so the brothers had probably gone off catting and drinking again, to show off their wounds and thereby elicit enough sym-pathy to be treated to a few rounds of free drinks.

With casual insolence, they had given him back his unheroic exis-tence. There was even a chance he might outlive them. Nebucchim stooped and began to gather deadwood for tinder, to make a fire in the fireplace and shake off the chill he'd picked up from lying inert on the cold ground for God knows how long. Once he got a good blaze going, the first thing he intended to burn was the leather book containing his ancestors' names and his own. There would be that initial unpleasant stench like human flesh as the leather binder curdled from the heat, but that would pass soon enough if he opened the windows and aired the room.

I was released into the custody of Balboa. He showed up at the Cook County Jail wearing V. I. Lenin prescription sunglasses and a glossy leather bomber jacket, with Tweety Bird covering most of the back. And a fez, naturally. We drove in the Audi to a microbrewery, and he asked for a table outside, even though the wind was stiff and icy. We sat there with our noses running, him scarfing down pistachios and Corn Nuts until the negligent waiter came to take our order. The waiter hadn't wanted to open up the patio just for us, but Balboa insisted. It was the strangest sensation to go from a jail cell straight to eating grilled swordfish and drinking a pint of Oktoberfest out of season. No one seemed to have changed his daily habits on account of my incarceration.

"Your hair is starting to look more salt and pepper since last I saw you."

"That's what Chandra always tells me."

"From stress? Almost looks like you got flecks of paint in your hair. They make you paint the warden's office while you was in there? I wouldn't put it past them."

"No comment. Why was I released?"

"All kind of reasons, homey. I know Bobby Rush didn't get depressed about this recent turn of events. Lots of people were happy to see Tadeusz go down."

"Well, I'm not among them."

"Me neither. I mean, I'm not going to pretend I'm crying in my Oktoberfest, but a life is a life. Still, the mainest reason you're sitting here is because of my cousin the alderman. You remember me talking about him?"

"Yes, you ran his campaign and you've got nothing against enlightened nepotism. You mentioned that fact the night we drove around your boyhood projects with you at the wheel of the Audi in Pepe LePew underwear."

"Damn, that seems like about five years ago. Doesn't it? B.K. Before Kentucky. I knew as soon as he hit the canvas that something was not right about Tadeusz. I don't want to take anything away from that sharp left hook of yours, slugger, or your tragic sense of life, but Clay Justin's left hook ain't bringing down no mastodon like him, not all by itself."

"Why not?"

"You sound disappointed. Were you anxious to compile a more impressive prison record?"

"No, not disappointed. I just want to know what really happened."

"And I'ma tell you, if you'll suck on your amber and let me finish. My cousin got an anonymous tip from some woman in the medical profession who had done a little digging around. This person didn't disclose her name, but she seemed to have it on good authority that Tadeusz had a suspect medical record. That being the case, you can believe his manager wanted to hurry the hell out of the autopsy on him. But once we got the tip, I made sure I was there for the inquest. Because me and you, we just got to pull each other's ass out of the fire every so often. Somebody cares enough to come looking for me when I'm higher than a Katmandu kite, I remember that. You want to know what they found?"

"Steroids?"

"Nah, that wouldn't get us anywhere. Better. Cocaine runnin' round his brain. Traces in the bloodstream."

"So what? All that finding would do is disqualify a dead man from an exhibition bout that doesn't count in any record books anyway."

"You're right that by itself, the finding doesn't exonerate you from the involuntary manslaughter charge. I was afraid that even with the drug thing, we were in for a long battle. And expensive. Not that I wouldn't have scared up the money if necessary. But the alderman and me between us, under the circumstances, had enough clout to dig deep into that boy's medical records. His handlers had long kept one little problem under wraps, because they didn't want Tadeusz to lose a shot at the heavyweight title. Tadeusz has had heart problems for quite a long time. Irregular heartbeat. Atrial fib. Sudden speedup. Not enough to knock him out of contention completely but enough to raise serious questions. I have a feeling the most damning medical records had been expunged or cloaked in euphemism, but all I had to do was get my hands on one single serious report to substantiate his medical history, and the rest came flowing out like water from a tap. The cause of death, according to the autopsy, was a massive heart attack. So unless you plain old scared the shit out of him, which I doubt, the combination of coke and cardiac problems took him down. He should never have been in the ring in the first place. Some people just don't know when to get out of fighting. Or am I right?"

"As always, you're right. Thanks for springing me."

"Don't start hugging on me or get me into one of those boxer's clinches. I didn't spring you, nor nothing like. I simply let justice prevail, as it does once in a great while." Balboa removed two cigars from his bomber jacket. "It's time for a celebratory smoke. Doctor's orders." He took several sheets of stapled paper from the breast pocket of his bomber jacket and reached for the brew pub's insignia matchbook. "One thing I learned from the experience. If you want your past to be gone, it has to be completely gone. I been carrying this dog-eared psychiatric report around with me for the last two years like it's some kind of traffic ticket I keep meaning to pay." He ignited the sheaf of papers with a match, dropped it in the ashtray, and together we watched the flames flare up in the buffeting wind.

"Don't I get to read it first?"

"Hell no. I ain't letting you get anything more over me than what you already got. Last remaining copy. Good-bye, BPI." Balboa lit our cigars with his impromptu torch. "Remember, don't inhale, dumbass. This ain't weed."

We smoked in companionable silence for a while, enjoying the mellow taste of the South Beach Cubans. The gusts of wind made the ash-tips grow with unusual speed.

"Hey, and speaking of money." Balboa took out a thin, business-sized manila envelope and kited it across the table to me. I opened the flap. Inside was a cashier's check. "In case I forgot to mention it, this lunch is on you, slugger."

"How did you get them to come through on payment for the fight?"

"Fear, Clay. Most everybody is walking around full of fear. Once they show it, you've got to hit them hard and immediately. You, as a boxer, ought to know that better than anyone." The laggard waiter wandered out to clear our plates. "Lunch is on my buddy there. Therefore, I'll be having some of your tiramisu. Give me a real big slice and a double cappuccino."

The waiter looked noncommittal, but in a surprise move, he came back at once with a slab of dessert and two forks. If I knew Balboa, like as not he wouldn't even touch it. It was part of his natural extravagance that sometimes he liked to order a high-toned dessert just to look at it. What he really wanted to roll around on his tongue was not the confection, but the word "tiramisu."

"Have you been to see Janine?"

Balboa chuckled, the cigar still in his mouth, as if about to tell a joke at the poker table. "Funniest thing. I went back, and it was about as warm a welcome as stepping into an ice cave. All the same, I had my resolve. Ready to declare bankruptcy, just eat my pride in great big gobbets, sell off the house, move into an apartment on the fringe of town. Not that I wanted to, but I been poor so much of my life, I knew it wasn't going to kill me. Make payments to the creditors. As long as you give them something and work steady, they don't want to see you in jail. Chance and Viola would have a big adjustment, and I felt bad about that, but hell, there's worse things than that kind of street education. It didn't cripple me too much. You might even say it made me what I am. And I'd done talked to myself that if Janine asked for a divorce, custody, whatever, I'd sign whatever papers she put in front of me, to start the process of atonement."

"Don't concede automatic custody. I made that mistake. You'll regret it down the road."

"I appreciate the vote of confidence in my mediocre paternal powers. But as it turns out, Janine has no such thing in mind. Ain't no need for the bachelor apartment, and you want to know why?"

"Do tell."

"You remember the auto accident she had on Valentine's Day?"

"The air bag malfunctioned and damaged her hand."

"That's the one. She worked fast, and her attorneys, as I predicted, got right down on the case of the automaker's insurance company, with her being a top dog at the children's hospital, those high-priced hands, and her livelihood endangered and all. The automaker took one look, sized up Janine, figured her to be worth at least twenty million dollars in bad publicity and damages and court costs, and agreed to a two million dollar out-of-court settlement. They tithed. They probably saved themselves a lot of money, if you want to know the truth."

"So you're not in dire financial straits anymore."

"Janine has got a payment schedule worked out."

"Just like that? All is forgiven?"

"No, I wouldn't put it that strongly. I'll be hung in the emotional meat locker for a while, from a big stout hook. Then we got to see if we can make ourselves a marriage. It's possible. We did have one, somewhere back there. And there are certain conditions she's imposed, in exchange for acting as my benefactress."

"Such as?"

"Selling the mansion, to get rid of the megamortgage, and buying a little place in Wheaton."

"Wheaton? You mean where Billy Graham went to school?"

"You got it. Girl already has a house scoped out. Small, by our standards. Only five bedrooms. No ballroom. She doesn't want to be within immediate reach of the Hyde Park ladies in case our misadventures leak out, which they always have a way of doing. So, we'll have very long commutes into town on the Metra until we find ourselves a clinic or a community hospital out that way. Also, me being in Wheaton, I won't run amok down on South Seventieth, she figures. I'm to be kept on a short leash for a time. No more junkets to South Beach. No more taking off in the middle of the night to play golf at sunrise overlooking Las Vegas. No sugar plantations. No booty in Botswana. No Carmela."

"And you agreed to all that."

"Yes, I did. I only hope I can stick to the bargain. Because if I can't, Clay, what comes next is no happy ending."

I deposited the cashier's check and opened a savings account in Chandra's name, with a little maroon passbook to go with it. The check turned out to be six thousand four hundred thirty-two dollars, rather than ten thousand, since they had deducted the self-employment tax before issuing it to me. You'd think a boxer would just be handed a thick sheaf of twenties under the table, but not so. Kelly, the accountant, can tell you that everybody ends up paying taxes, one way or another. So you might as well estimate what you owe and try to pay ahead of time, otherwise you'll end up paying more later.

Two monks were walking through a forest on the way to Gethsemani Abbey, near Bardstown, that nether region where whiskey distilleries abound. Two Trappists traipsing through the woods, trying to make it back in time for vespers without picking up a case of poison ivy, because a monk with a rash, that's not a good combination, having to focus your mind on the Lord when you keep shifting around in your seat, while the vow of silence is on, and you can't even say, "Damn, I got the bad itch." It was that season of excess ground foliage, and poison ivy doesn't know the difference between saints and sinners.

So the two monks stepped lightly, verily, warily, not conversing much, even though this was their last chance to pass words between them before vespers and the beginning of the retreat, where nary a word would be spoken for several days. Already they were settling into a purity of mind.

At the same time, it must be said that the two monks, brothers though they were, men of God, had a little competitive streak ongoing between them and were sometimes given to talking trash, monk style. One might say, "Your latest batch of beeswax extracted from the hive was all comb and not much honey." The other would reply, "No matter, for your soda bread came from the oven unleavened."

Before long, the sojourners reached a rushing stream, and the log they normally used as a footbridge had washed out, so there was no obvious way to cross. Still and all, the two surefooted country monks would find a path, once they removed their shoes. Both were more inclined to catch a chill than to admit defeat. The first monk, quickly unshod, skipped trippingly across a few stones, as if he were playing hopscotch, and landed on the other side with a triumphant thump.

Impatiently, he waited for the second monk to follow. "Come along, Smokehouse," he called out across the rushing waterway. "Forthwith, Scrofulous Brother," replied the second. This second monk, about to cross, just then noticed a well-known harlot who had a reputation for cruising the streets of Bardstown, encouraging the nocturnal naughtiness of unsuspecting shopkeepers. He couldn't figure what she might be doing all the way out in the middle of the woods, red-eyed, seated wistfully, legs apart, on a soggy toadstool-encrusted stump, smoking a cig.

In truth, she wasn't a harlot. That's just the parlance of monks, who don't possess the most subtle vocabulary when it comes to women, because of their limited experience with females besides the one who bore them. This woman, Carmela, had simply made some bad choices in men, as they say on the talk shows, and what's more, she had a hard time getting over them, even when they didn't treat her right. Which only prolonged her sadness. In her heart, she believed the women who let themselves love wholly and foolishly, even when they got hurt in the end, were the lucky ones. She'd say, "A man I love, to me, is like a pack of cigarettes, and I'm addicted to smoking. When I try to give the cigarettes up, I've got to do it slow, with patches and nicotine gum. I can't withdraw cold turkey." So there she sat smoking, taking long, pensive drags, as she studied the currents of the stream with one eye cocked and the thumb splayed on her left hand. There is an art to smoking a cigarette, and that she had mastered.

The second monk couldn't help but gaze on her in wonder as the first monk shot him hectoring glances from the opposite bank. It looked like the woman wanted to cross as well and couldn't quite get up her gumption to plunge into the fast-moving water. She was one or two sheets to the wind, judging by the manner in which she tottered on the stump. The woman didn't appear to have much confidence in her natural-born balance.

Without a word, the second monk scooped her up in his arms and carried her across the stream. Setting her down on a dry patch of ground, he wrung out the hem of his robe. "We're going to miss vespers," the first monk scolded, and without taking their leave of the woman, the two continued on their way as night began to fall. The monks trekked back to Gethsemani in the deepening gloom, without exchanging a syllable, only the crackle of the dry brush underfoot communicating their haste. Otherwise, all remained profound silence, as each monk prepared his separate inner being for the retreat. The second monk, usually the more prone of the two to an outburst, kept a beatific smile on his face, sockless, walking clogs in hand, and in spite of the thick ground cover swishing and slapping and snapping around his bare ankles, his step remained light and quick.

As they approached the monastery, the first monk finally turned to the second. "Brother," he said. "I don't mean to rebuke you, on this of all days, when we won't have a chance to speak to one another again for an entire week, but it is against our creed to defile ourselves by coming into contact with unclean women. I'm horrified that you let your hands touch her wanton body."

"Brother," the second monk replied gently to the first, squeezing the other's shoulder with his hand. "I left that woman back on the creek bank. You have been carrying her with you ever since."

You could say the second monk won the trash-talking contest by virtue of his soft yet witty, perspicacious, and philosophical retort. Nonetheless, during the solitary days in his cell observing the vow of silence, he broke out in an awful case of poison ivy. He was about as allergic to it as you can get. No way could he turn his thoughts to God for more than a minute or two at a time during that retreat. His skin became a welter of blisters and blotches befitting a leper. The only thing that brought him solace as he suffered in his cell, without even calamine lotion to salve his wounds, was to think on that woman and how delightful her flesh had felt cupped in his samaritan's hands.

"Are you pacified?" Kelly asked it the way a preacher might ask "Are you sanctified?" The bruises on his face had turned yellow-green, the most garish hue in the process of convalescence. He'd thought about waiting until he looked better before returning to Lexington to see Kelly but simply couldn't contain himself.

"I'm done fighting. That was the last one, I promise. I have nothing left to give in the ring."

"That isn't what I asked. I want to know whether you got what you went after. I really am curious."

"Well, if you mean am I free from resentments, I won't swear that I am, but I think I've come a long way toward that mark."

She touched one of the bruises on his face, tracing its outline with her fingertips. "Yeah, but I'm not free. I punished you and tried to kill you off all manner of ways. I didn't quite succeed, though. In the killing part. I left you half alive, which is not merciful. I recognize that. If I could get in a boxing ring, the way you did, and beat on somebody real hard—it would need to be you, I suppose—I might could just let it all go afterward, the way some men seem able to do, let bygones be bygones. Knock them to the ground, then pick them up and wish them well."

"Unless they happen to die first."

"Yeah. Unless they happen to die."

"You can hit me if you want. I wish you would. The one thing I know how to do is take a punch."

She gave him a rueful smile. "Yeah, but I could never bring myself to throw one. Even if I knew how."

When he bent down to kiss her, she slapped him hard. Hardass hard. He hadn't committed any transgression—in fact, she wanted him to kiss her, but she was putting him on notice, paying him back in advance for a betrayal she knew he would commit later. It was better that way. Catch him off guard. "That's for nothing." Go ahead and mete out the punishment, so you could get on with the loving part. As his hand, the one that was about to encircle her waist, recoiled to his cheek in surprise, she stood on tiptoe and met his lips, those lips about to utter an exclamation or oath, and silenced them with her own mouth. The way she had to strive to reach his mouth pleased her. Already she could see a welt starting to form beside it. Unlike him, she kissed with her eyes open, and enjoyed the sensation of possessing him. He didn't quite know what to do with her tongue, that sharp tongue, that loving tongue, but he would learn. He was slow, but teachable.

I turned to go. I didn't want to get into another conversation that led nowhere. "Wait," Kelly said. "There is a way." She walked to the refrigerator and removed a whole fish on a platter, a brook trout, with its head still on and its eye staring. Like the eyes in certain oil portraits, its gaze followed you no matter which way you stepped. Opening the drawer where she kept potholders, a flashlight, a yo-yo, and other items that didn't quite go together, she removed a good-sized knife in a sheath. The one section of steel you could see, peeking from the sheath like a woman's bare midriff, gleamed as if it hadn't been used yet.

She spread a couple of sheets of newspaper on the kitchen table, laid the fish across with care, as if it might get hurt by being manhandled, and set the knife down next to it. With a gesture of her arm, Kelly invited me to sit at the table. "Fillet it," she said.

"What?"

"If you can fillet this fish properly, without mauling the meat, I'll give our relationship another chance."

"Excuse me, but what does this brook trout have to do with you and me?"

"By rights, nothing. But according to my rules, everything. I simply want you to perform one, unambiguous act properly. Something I ask you to do. Without making excuses. In a sense, it doesn't matter what I choose."

"This is absurd."

"I agree. But it's what I finally settled on. I gave the matter a lot of thought, and I couldn't come up with anything that wouldn't take weeks or months to accomplish. You know, messy emotional tasks, ways of pleasing me that I had no means of qualifying as right or wrong. They were just too subjective. I wanted to be fair. So, I was in the fish market over on Winchester Road, trying to take my mind off my frustration, and shopping for decent scallops, when this brook trout caught my eye."

"Did it wink at you? Was this some kind of Shroud of Turin experience?"

Ignoring my witticisms, Kelly unsnapped the leather band around the haft and removed the knife with the swift, decisive motion of a samurai. "I appreciate what you did for Chandra, with the six thousand dollars. At bottom, you're a good man. But you expressly went against my wishes. I didn't want you to fight again, and I made that damn clear. You didn't care. You had to have your way, as usual, and follow out your own prerogatives, without taking my wishes into account. I was terrified. My bad dreams started up again. I've barely slept these last couple of weeks. You don't even know what it means to sleep poorly. No matter what happens to you, you go right out."

"I'm sorry," I said. "Sorry for fighting. Sorry for sleeping well." Flipping the knife around so the blade pointed to her, she handed it to me. I took the handle and inspected it. "You got this all ready in advance. How did you know I was going to show up?"

"Balboa's wife called me a couple of days ago to say she expected you to be released and the manslaughter charges against you to be dropped. Her guess was that you'd be coming my way at once. And anyway, I didn't need her to tell me that. I knew you'd show up. Because you can't help yourself, Clay."

I stared at the brook trout and it stared back, defying me to anatomize it with anything approaching precision. "I haven't filleted a fish since I was a teenager. I'm not sure I'll remember how."

"Try hard. Stay close to the bone and don't lift up the knife until the filleting is complete. I had the butcher sharpen the blade for you, to be sure you had every chance."

I turned the blade in my hand, examining its finely serrated sides. "I don't think this type of blade is supposed to be whetted. It's self-sharpening. You may have ruined it. You've got to give me a handicap," I insisted, and I myself heard a whiny note creeping into my voice.

She looked at me through her eyelashes. "You're making excuses."

"Okay. I'll do what you ask. Enough chitchat." I drew in a couple of slow breaths. My hand was shaking. I slipped the knife point in at the gills, heard the clean puncturing sound, like a dying man's final exhalation, and made a sharp turn. The flesh gave way, and the blade sank straight to the sheaf of delicate bones. So far, so good. The subtle curve of my motion started to insinuate itself as I slid the blade downward. Without warning, my hand jerked, gouging a big chunk of fish flesh, which leapt across the table, popping loose from the torn skin, and landing clear off the newspaper. I laid the knife down and, without thinking, wiped my hands on my pants.

"I guess that's that."

"I guess so." Kelly stared morosely at the brook trout, as if it had done her a personal wrong. "I was rooting for you," she said, a sob stuck in her throat.

"Thanks for the mental cruelty."

Her eyes flashed. "You wanna hear about mental cruelty? What the hell you think you been doing to me forever? Did you ever take stock of my suffering?"

I could see her winding up into one of her bona-fide, full-scale tongue-lashings, the kind she hadn't given me since we were married, back when she felt she had complete license to do so. I felt my ears flatten against my skull. Yet Kelly was always one for observing proprieties and knowing where the limits of things lay. The limits of cruelty, the limits of love. Little by little, her face changed as she struggled to master herself. She audibly huffed and puffed, trying to get a hold on her ire. She leaned against the counter, as if having a dizzy spell. "Never mind," she finally said. "I'll leave it at that."

"So we're done?"

"No, we're not done. I want you to take Chandra on a fishing trip."

"Enough with the fish. We already played that game."

"I mean it. Okay, so you've forgotten how to fillet. I'll spot you that one. Get her to catch one fish, then come back and genuinely tell me she likes fishing, and I'll agree to work on seeing whether you and I have any future between us. Is that so much to ask?"

I sighed, my pants already starting to reek of stale fish juice. "Am I in a fairy tale?"

"You might be. But my request isn't as absurd as it sounds. One of the details that has kept me going on you this long, in spite of your stubborn and amateurish attempts at self-destruction, is the rapport I sometimes see between you and that girl. She needs her daddy. My momma always been telling me so, about every other day of my life. And I know that one circumstance by itself ain't gonna change how you and me relate, not necessarily, but it's a start. I set a lot of store by that stubborn, ornery little bitch, God help me, because I love her so much. And I know she loves you, but whether she can tolerate you from day to day is another story. I go through the same changes about you myself, and I keep asking myself whether she and me and you could ever live in the same house without degenerating into flat-out pandemonium. I can tell you for a fact she's mad at you right now."

"About what?"

"Don't ask me. This and that. Every damned thing in the world. So you take her to the lake or river or stream of your choice, get her to straighten up and act right and like what you dish out for her recreation and edification, whether she likes it or not, then come back and talk to me. If you can handle her, maybe you can handle me."

"I haven't fished in more than a decade."

"Too bad. You shoulda practiced more, in case this moment ever came up. I'm sure you can remember how to bait a hook."

"I know how to bait you, but a hook—yeah, I guess I can do that much. I'll have to run over to Sears and buy a rod and reel, hooks, sinkers, tackle box, all that stuff."

"I'll have her ready tomorrow by six A.M. I'm not much of a fisherwoman, but I do know that once the sun comes out good and strong, the fish will be taking a long nap. So set your alarm clock."

"Could you at least tell her that getting up this early was your idea? I don't want her to start off the day in a bad mood on my account. That's one strike against me before we even begin this little trial."

"Ain't gonna tell her nothing. I'll just say you and Daddy are going fishing, honey. After that, it's all you."

Chandra sat in the front passenger seat with her arms folded as she and Clay cruised the byways beyond Nicholasville. She wore overalls, a mauve stretch top with embroidery gracing the ends of the short sleeves, and a matching hair bow. Clay couldn't see her socks, but he was sure they matched too. Everything about her looked unbearably cute, except her rigid body posture and the scowl on her face.

"This is so lame."

"Aren't you a little young for that argot?"

"As if."

"As if what?"

"As if I knew what 'argot' could mean. Lame."

"If I drive faster, and get us there sooner, it will be express lame." He smiled, hoping to soften her by engaging in verbal play, and accelerated on the gas pedal along the winding country road.

She rolled her eyes. "Corny."

"I remember a spot along the palisades I used to go to with my buddies when I was a teenager."

"Daddy!" Her outburst made him hit the brakes hard. It was the panic voice she'd used that time she tripped on a garden hose, during one of his visits, and sliced her knee open. The emergency-room voice. The car fishtailed and skidded to a halt. The smell of smoking rubber filled his sinuses.

On the road in front of them lay a large snapping turtle with a hard arched shell. Not one to mess with. They got out to inspect it. Clay warned Chandra back, but she, on her haunches, craned her neck nearer. The turtle remained motionless.

Clay scoured the roadside for a fallen limb and broke off a stick. He thrust the stick close to the snapping turtle's mouth. It clamped on. Carrying the turtle to the roadside, Clay set it down inside a ditch. Chandra's scowl disappeared. But only until she squatted again and noticed that the turtle's extremities and neck were covered with sticky brown gobs. Her face registered instant distress, mixed with an innate scientific curiosity that kept her leaning over and peering at the turtle, in much the same way she had kept taking sidelong glances at Clay's boxing wounds. "Are those maggots, Clay?" she said, as dispassionately as possible. "Is it sick?"

He couldn't say for sure but had a hunch they might be eggs the turtle herself had spawned. He decided to go ahead and commit to this position and pronounced the blobs to be eggs. Chandra looked doubtful but finally decided she was better off, for the moment, accepting his provisional explanation.

Before long, they were standing on the palisades, atop the slow-moving Kentucky River as it bore downstream its intermittent load of flotsam and trash from the recent floods. If Clay squinted, the river looked as beautiful as he remembered. Otherwise, on the skanky side. He hadn't anticipated how they'd get down to the water from the high bluff. There was an estuary on the other side, he recalled. The slope leading to it, though soupy, made for less steep a descent. Together they scrambled, now on rock, now on muck. Instantly, their clothes, including that beautiful, mauve matching outfit, bespeaking girlish glee, got splotched with natural filth. Paradoxically, as the clothes got darker, Chandra displayed some relative glee. A half smile broke out on her face as she panted and sweated and picked up fine white scratches on her lithe bare forearms while helping her father hoist down the rods and tackle.

"Don't tell your mom we did this."

"I'm not an idiot, Daddy."

At the bottom, on a limestone shelf they settled on as the designated spot, the two arranged their gear around them and turned to size each other up.

Chandra laughed. "Clay, you look so stupid. There's a big wet sloppy streak all across your bottom. It looks like you peed your pants."

"Yeah, well I'm not even going to say what that mud on your pants looks like." An instant of sophomoric happiness welled up between them, the like of which he couldn't have hoped for. Soon, they got down to the business of fishing. Clay did a few awkward casts to remind himself how to throw a line out.

"Brilliant," she said, rolling her eyes. When did this preternatural seven-year-old turn into a smart-alecky teenager? In the past two hours?

He started to say, "We'll see how you do," teasing her back just as hard, but he sensed that she was watching him rediscover the hang of casting, that in fact she wanted him to do it well, and was anxious not to cast wrong herself, when her turn came. So he swallowed his words, and a sober mood settled over them again.

"Not bad," she remarked, in her grudging, subdued little voice, keeping an eye on the fly. He'd brought minnows, but she made it clear, through a single mouish glance into the plastic container holding them, that she was not ready yet to see them pierced and watch the blood trickle from their sides. When the time came to use the live minnows, he'd have to quietly turn his back to her, as if he were changing clothes at a campsite with no privacy, and slip the hook into the minnow's silver side himself.

"There ought to be bream here." Not that he knew too much about varieties of fish, but he happened to remember that he'd caught a bream on this stretch of river once himself, as a boy, or so he was told that's what it was. He sported a vague confidence that the descendants of that bream's extended family ought to be residing in this same spot. "Bream, crappie, maybe catfish," he recited, tentative and authoritative. "You ready to cast?"

"Okay. Let me try." He handed the rod to her and slid his arms around her torso from behind, moving her elbow to and fro in a mock cast to give her the feel of the necessary action. For an instant, she relaxed into that embrace, then shrugged him off, easing back into her earnest scowl. "I can do it, Clay. I can do it by myself."

"Sure." He stepped back to watch the arc she made as she whipped the rod behind her and let fly. The line unspooled, hesitated, and collapsed into itself, scrawling indecipherable words in the air and then dropping into the water right at her feet. Clay started to speak, but her body had become tense. Instead, he leaned over, wordless, clicked a lever on the spool, and nodded with his head for her to reel the line back in. She did.

Only then did he venture to say, "Try again, honey." The second cast, still weak, at least put the hook out into the river. "Okay, let it lie. We'll see if there are any fish stirring."

All at once Chandra tugged. "I think I've got something."

"You probably snagged it on deadwood or a rock. Let me see."

As soon as the rod made contact with his hands, he knew it was live. "Jesus, you got something, baby. Here." He tried to hand the rod back to her, but she backed away, eyes widening.

"No, you go ahead."

Clay reeled in, and the fish fought decently hard, putting up enough of a struggle for him to have to walk up and down the shelf of rock. He thought sure the line would break, at every instant, but unaccountably, before too long, the fish crested the surface, spotted and ugly and much bigger than it had any right to be. A bream or a catfish, or possibly a crappie. Or something else. For Clay, it had always seemed a miracle that you could simply throw a line into the water and a fish would come out. Before he had time to form an opinion about this miracle, he was bringing aground a thrashing lump of live matter.

He thrust the rod into her hands, this time insisting. Picking up the Styrofoam cooler he'd brought along on the extreme off chance that they caught anything, Clay stepped into the shallows, filling his shoes with water, and dipped the cooler down to fill it with a rush of river, because he'd neglected to bring any ice. No sooner had the current burst inside than the cooler shattered into flimsy Styrofoam fragments.

"Damn."

"He's flipping around, Daddy! He's flipping around!" Chandra cried. "I think he's hurt!"

"Okay. Let me think." She had started to wail and was hopping about the fish. He got on his knees to tend to the oxygen-starved catch. "Calm down, baby. Daddy will figure something out. I'll throw him back in the water."

"Don't!" she said in horror. "Don't rip the hook from his mouth! You'll make him suffer!"

"God, if I only had some pliers. Chandra, please listen to me," he told her, in a tone like a hostage trying not to set off a volatile terrorist. "Stay calm, honey, and hear what I'm saying. I will run up the hill as fast as I can. There is a big plastic bucket in the trunk. All I need to do is get the bucket and come back down the hill. Okay? It will take me less than five minutes, I promise." She nodded, speechless, half believing. "Then I will fill the bucket with water and place the fish in it. Then I will lug the bucket, fish, and water all together up the hill."

"Can we buy an aquarium later?"

A child's riddle tried to come into his mind, about a farmer trying to cross the river with a fox, a duck, and a sack of feed corn when he only has room for two of them at a time. He tried to recollect how the farmer figured out how to get them all across, without carnage, as if that might provide him with an answer to his own dilemma.

Chandra was trying hard not to hyperventilate as she contemplated a fellow creature. "What if he dies while you're gone? He's alive."

"He's not gonna die. I promise. I'll make it quick."

"Okay." Her voice had died down to a whimper. "Come back soon."

"I will."

Up the hill he tore, sliding impossibly in the late-winter slop, two steps forward, one step back. Serious erosion occurred with every hop, compounding the ecological crime he had already committed by landing the fish in the first place. Below, in the peculiar acoustic sphere afforded by the hillside, he could hear Chandra's murmur, a hysteria pitched at a low volume, like a late-night television drama of drastic proportions taking place almost mutely as someone drowsed off.

With throbbing quadriceps, Clay crested the hill. The car appeared in the distance, growing, looming as he approached it, ever larger, like the fish he had landed, gargantuan, elephantine, his Moby. He fit the key into the luggage compartment and it popped open, disgorging the plastic bucket. He ran back, picking up speed, and it was a long step-slide down the palisades, land-surfing among roots and rocks and other lurking vegetable outgrowths that threatened to snag his boot and twist cartilage mercilessly before catapulting him into the river.

But no, somehow his feet slid home on the shelf of rock below, where Chandra sat on the bare ground, cross-legged, radiating solicitude toward the listless carp, the catatonic catfish.

"Daddy, I don't think Patches is doing too well."

"Patches? You named the fish?"

"I named him Patches."

"Oh, Chandra. No, this isn't good. We can't keep a fish you've given a name to. This is not a fish we'll be frying. Not that we would have fried it in any case. I don't even want to think about all the noxious pestilence this bottom dweller has consumed in its lifetime."

"Fry it! You said an aquarium. What are you talking about?"

"No, I said we *won't* fry it. I'm agreeing with you. Except it's too big for an aquarium. We'll have to let it go."

"Him."

Clay didn't know how she could possibly have discerned the gender of the fish; he had no idea himself where to look on the fish for confirmation; he didn't even want to think about the gender, social status, tastes, metaphysics, or dashed dreams of the wall-eyed, landlocked, unfortunate fish flesh that lay unprotesting while its gills shrank.

"Are you going to take the hook out of his mouth?"

"I'll try. Just don't make any sudden noises, please." Clay's hand, the same hand that had failed to fillet the refrigerated brook trout properly after the hand went into an involuntary spasm, gingerly approached the bream's mucous membranes. As long as the fish didn't utter actual words, he thought he could go through with it. Who would have thought that after quasi-murdering a man he could be so squeamish? Closing his eyes, Clay palpated the sharp scales and cartilage around its mouth like an aged, blind surgeon being asked late in life to perform one last operation strictly by touch.

"Be kind to Patches, Daddy!"

Locating the protruding barb of the hook, he tried to push on the prong, but it wouldn't slide back through. It was too embedded. Moving his fingers inside the mouth, he made a judgment call. With a merciless but swift yank, he used the other hand to pull the hook free. Opening his eyes, he saw minor mutilation, a small hole, but it could have been much worse.

"His mouth is bleeding just a bit," Chandra whispered, as if she didn't want to bring the fish out of its anesthetic dream state.

"He's going to be all right. I'll put him right back in the water. See?" Clay's hands had stopped shaking and he was also getting a firmer grasp on pronouns. Laying the fish down in the water on its side, Clay released it. The bream, crappie, catfish, carp, swam away with a sudden, unexpected burst of consciousness and movement, cutting a fluid swath all the way out to the middle of the river, putting on a spectacular final performance of false, adrenaline-stoked vitality for Chandra's sake before disappearing beneath an underwater grotto to die among sunken steel radial tires.

To himself, Clay sent up a silent prayer of thanks for the pantomime of the generous fish. He remembered Balboa telling him once about a scene he'd witnessed in one of his travels, a group of pilgrims at dawn carrying hatboxes tied with ribbons, and from the hatboxes removing turtles that they released into the river. With the turtle, you relinquished your sorrows into the water and they dissolved.

On the drive back, Chandra sighed with quiet exhalations, minute expulsions of breath, minor fits of tears, her heels scrunched beneath her bottom in the passenger seat. Clay didn't have the heart to tell her to put her seat belt on. Even under such extreme emotional circumstances, Kelly would not appreciate this, yet another dereliction of duty on his part. What if they went down an embankment? Then what? Would his lax attitude about seat belts, his lackadaisical sense of what was required by the occasion, be a favor to his daughter, in the long run? Well, would it? He had failed the second test too.

Now that he thought about it, driving the car down an embankment didn't seem like that bad of an idea, if he could first ask Chandra to step out of the car, though not before going over 911 and making sure she knew her home phone number and address by memory and giving her correct change and pointing her in the direction of a likely looking female police officer with a clean record of service and no demerits within the past three years.

He and Chandra both looked like hell, covered with mud and spontaneous organic matter, stains and ignominious unidentified blotches, and a few adhering flakes or scales on their fingers that probably belonged to the late Patches. As they pulled onto her street, a few hundred yards from the parking lot and the apartment complex, the end of the line, Clay noticed that Chandra had stopped crying and had flipped down the passenger-side sun visor containing the makeup mirror. She had no makeup to apply, but she studied her face intently.

The condition of her clothes didn't appear to concern her. Rather, she cleaned her face with a couple of tissues and examined the skin around her eyes, blinking in a focused rhythm. Meanwhile, Clay found a parking spot and stopped the car. Chandra tilted her head, moving it left and right before the makeup mirror as if trying to catch herself by surprise. He remembered how, during his visits home, he used to come upon Chandra practicing the expressions of crying before her reflection once in a while. He knew the tears today had been all too real, but something else was asserting itself in her. Chandra looked more than ever like her mother, the spitting image. He'd never realized how wholly her features, gestures, body language, were descended from Kelly.

"Do my eyes look puffy?"

"Not too bad."

"Not red?"

"With all those dirt streaks, there's no way to tell."

"Good." She blew her nose hard, then again, more softly. Swiveling her knees in his direction, she gave him a serious look. "Daddy, please, when we get inside, let me do all the talking. You have no idea what to say."

"I don't have—?"

"And Daddy." Chandra took one of his oversized hands in both her smaller ones. "I had a very nice time today. Okay?" She said this slowly, as if rehearsing the sound of her words for proper phrasing and elocution.

"Sure, pumpkin."

Upstairs, Kelly was at work over a pot of potato soup. The water had begun to simmer. "Lord, Lord," she said, looking us two recent immigrants over from head to foot. Then she went back to peeling, her head bowed over the colander.

I removed my shoes and, not knowing where to set them, let them hang from my hand, grasping them together by the tongues, in my sock feet. "Sorry about the mess."

"Well, I hope you had a good time anyway."

"Oh, we did, Mom. The place was hard to get to. That's why we're so muddy. But it was a whole lot of fun. Wow, what an adventure."

"Indeed. Then I expect you got something for your trouble. We can serve potato soup as a side dish. Did you bring back a couple of catfish for me to fry? That is, as long as Clay will fillet them. That's my rule. I'll cook 'em, but I won't gut 'em or fillet 'em."

"No, Mommy. We caught one but we decided to throw him back. He was really cute. By the way, I've decided to become a vegetarian." Chandra kissed her mother on the cheek, a quick peck. "I'm going to go take a shower before we eat. Thanks again for the date, Daddy." She skipped off down the hall.

"Take off those shoes, young lady! This isn't a shed. My, she's chipper. You sure turned that vinegar to apple cider in a hurry."

"Okay, let's cut the crap. I'm too wrung out for verbal fencing."

"What? What's gotten into you? I can't pay you a compliment? She hasn't kissed me for a week, and all of a sudden she's one hundred percent sugar."

"The test. I failed the test. She doesn't like to fish."

"You could have fooled me. Anyway, what test?"

"The test you gave me to accomplish."

"I gave you a test? Honestly, Clay, I have no idea what you're talking about."

"Don't you remember that you sent me out in search of the Golden Fleece? Okay, so I didn't retrieve it, in spite of covering myself from head to toe in slime and gore."

"To tell you the truth, honey—you'll have to forgive me, but my memory must be slipping. I got two calls this afternoon, people wanting to get started on their income taxes early. Wouldn't you know? Usually I don't get inquiries until March. Then one of them insisted on sending documents over, had to be right this minute, of course, and my fax machine jammed. I may get you to take a look at that later, if you don't mind. I got all mad at the machine and popped loose some indispensable piece of plastic. All this happened right when I was trying to get dinner together. So I completely forgot where you all said you were going today, right until you showed up on the doorstep." All this time, she looked intently into the pot.

I decided not to contradict her version directly. "Well, it was Chandra's first fishing trip and, I believe, her last. It's a good thing you happened to cook vegetarian today."

"Hungry?"

"As a matter of fact, I am. Potato soup is just the ticket. But I'd better run out to the car and get clean clothes. I don't think any of mine are here."

Kelly smiled. "No, I haven't seen any of your clothes hanging in the closet lately. Before you get cleaned up, would you mind starting a fire? There's tinder next to the hearth, in a copper pail, and a couple of seasoned oak logs I've kept on hand exactly for a chilly, last-gasp-of-winter afternoon like this one. I thought you'd better build the fire before you change, so you won't have to eat supper with dirty cuffs."

As I hunkered to sweep the hearth with a whisk before laying the fire, I noticed an awful lot of papery black ash, no longer burning but still warm to the touch. Now that I paid close attention, the room had a sooty smell. "Have you been burning old newspapers?" I called out. "You know Lexington does have curbside recycling now. I've seen the bins."

Kelly came out of the kitchen and leaned against the doorframe. "No, it wasn't newspaper. I got rid of a bunch of old pages this morning. I didn't need them any longer."

"Pages? What kind of pages?"

"Oh, nothing. A story I was working on. It never amounted to anything. Amateurish."

"Your book? The one you mentioned to Balboa? I hope that wasn't your only copy." This information alarmed me, bringing me to a standing position. As if someone had accidentally burned my birth certificate, mistaking it for an inconsequential scrap.

"Yes, it was my only copy. So what?"

"There's no electronic version?"

"Deleted."

"No backup?"

"Killed with a keystroke."

"Kelly, you can't destroy months of your own work. What were you thinking?"

"Settle down, Professor. It's my damn book, and I'll burn it if I take a mind. You know how it is. Sometimes you labor at a thing, you labor and labor in a certain way, a frame of mind you get locked into, and it just isn't coming out the way you thought it would. So, as painful as it might be, you've simply got to trash that rough version and start over. Your characters ain't getting it right the first time around. That's when you got to give them a second chance. Another version of the story, and maybe that second time through, they'll get it right. We'll see. Now, could you lay that fire please, sir?"

Kelly asked me whether I wanted to stay overnight and sleep on the hide-a-bed in the living room. I replied yes, that would be nice, because I'd given up my room in Hooftown when I went back to Chicago for the match. She hoped I didn't mind that she didn't invite me into her room for the night. She didn't mean anything by it except there was a lot to think about, she had insomnia and would probably end up keeping me awake anyway, because she doubtless would end up reading half the night, one of those tawdry romance novels I detested, and she didn't want to put me through all her toss-ings and turnings after the day I'd had. Nor did she want to hear my griping about her tastes. We would talk about things tomorrow, all kinds of things, after she packed Chandra off to school.

Naturally, I liked better the idea of ending the day in Kelly's bed, even though I would lose consciousness right away, sinking into one of my famous dead man's slumbers. Yet once I got settled on the hide-a-bed by myself, covered with a blanket I vaguely recognized, washed so many times over that it had become appeal-ingly soft, I felt all right. Chandra stole into the living room in her nightshirt to say good night, holding what looked to be a child's fantasy paperback. She sat down on the edge of the mattress, as if she were putting me to bed.

For a moment I thought she planned to read to me out loud, a gruesome and implausible tale out of a parallel universe, perhaps a cybernetic doppelgänger who plagues the life of a being he's never met, a man who isn't even aware of the double's existence. Cheap thrills. Instead, she leaned over, coming close, and flicked my face with the whip-ends of her hair. What she used to call an octopus kiss. Then she scampered off to her bedroom and closed the door. With three small beeps, I set the alarm on my wristwatch for 6:45 A.M., so I'd be sure not to miss saying good-bye to Chandra before Kelly walked her down to the bus stop. The watch was a piece of junk, but something in its precise tone annoyed me, making it a reliable jolt, so I kept it close at hand.

The bare embers of the fire I'd made earlier illuminated the living room. In the corner, a minute amber light indicated that the paper jam in the fax still needed to be attended to. I'd have to get to it tomorrow. The door to Kelly's bedroom remained slightly ajar at the far end of the hall, and from it suffused the soft light of her reading lamp. I figured I might as well get some reading done myself, because everybody else in the household was recumbent yet still wakeful, engrossed in pages of their own. But I didn't have a book going, and Kelly's usual fare, the titles of which I couldn't quite make out on the shelves across the living room, were sure not to satisfy my tastes.

Yes, I'm a picky reader, I admit it, hypercritical, hard to satisfy. I was in the mood to reread something I knew by heart, a tale that would deliver to me the pleasure of remembrance rather than the thrill of discovery. Or at the least expose me to the demons I knew rather than new ones who lay in wait. I'd already made enough discoveries to last me for a week or two. It came into my mind that Janine had given to me a book the day she visited on the house-painting detail. When I stretched my left arm to the floor and groped along the textured carpet, I encountered the suitcase I had brought upstairs from the car for a change of clothes. In one of the zippered pouches the book lay tucked, and I slid it out. The volume was dense but small, easy to hold in one hand as I lay back on the pillow—a perfect nightcap.

Nebucchim Jacinto felt the filigree of the pocket watch with his fingers as he lay supine on an iron cot in a room in a hovel in the pampas.

About the Author

Johnny Payne is an associate professor in the English department at Florida Atlantic University and the director of Florida Atlantic's creative writing program. His works include *Conquest of the New Word: Experimental Fiction and Translation in the Americas* and the novels *Chalk Lake, Baja,* and *Kentuckiana,* published by TriQuarterly Books/Northwestern University Press. He is the editor and translator of *She-Calf and Other Quechua Folk Tales.*